THE DEAD SPEAK DOOM

Sparhawk and his companions reached the burial mound of King Sarak, and Tynian began his necromancy. He took the coil of rope and laid a peculiar pattern on the ground as he made his incantation.

The ghost of the long-dead King Sarak rose slowly from the cold earth. His chain-mail armor was archaic and showed huge rents. He was enormous—but he wore no crown.

He stared sternly from his hollow eyes. "This is unseemly. Return me at once, lest I grow wroth."

"Forgive me, your Majesty," Tynian apologized. "We would not have disturbed thy rest but for a matter of desperate urgency. The Queen of Elenia is gravely ill, and only Bhelliom can heal her. We will return the jewel to thy grave when we have completed our task."

"Return or keep it," the ghost said indifferently. "Thou shalt not find it in my grave, however. I do not have it."

By David Eddings
Published by Ballantine Books:

THE BELGARIAD

THE MALLOREON

THE ELENIUM

HIGH HUNT

*Forthcoming

Book Two
of The Elenium

THE
RUBY
KNIGHT

David
Eddings

DEL REY

A Del Rey Book
BALLANTINE BOOKS
NEW YORK

For young Mike
"Put it in the car"
And for Peggy
"What happened to my balloons?"

PROLOGUE

A History of the House of Sparhawk
—From the Chronicles of the Pandion Brotherhood

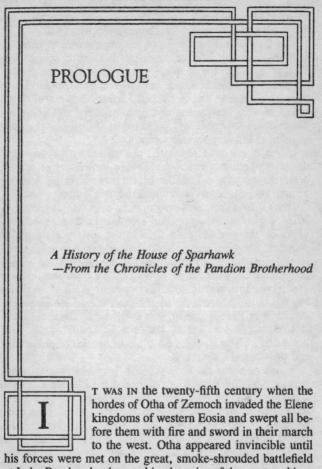

I T WAS IN the twenty-fifth century when the hordes of Otha of Zemoch invaded the Elene kingdoms of western Eosia and swept all before them with fire and sword in their march to the west. Otha appeared invincible until his forces were met on the great, smoke-shrouded battlefield at Lake Randera by the combined armies of the western kingdoms and the concerted might of the Knights of the Church. The battle there in central Lamorkand is said to have raged for weeks before the invading Zemochs were finally pushed back and turned to flee for their own borders.

The victory of the Elenes was thus complete, but fully half of the Church Knights lay slain upon the battlefield, and the armies of the Elene kings numbered their dead by the scores of thousands. When the victorious but exhausted survivors returned to their homes, they faced an even grimmer foe—the famine that is one of the common results of war.

The famine in Eosia endured for generations, threatening at times to depopulate the continent. Inevitably, social organization began to break down, and political chaos reigned in the Elene kingdoms. Rogue barons paid only lip service to their oaths of fealty to their kings. Private disputes often resulted in ugly little wars, and open banditry was common. These conditions generally prevailed until well into the early years of the twenty-seventh century.

It was in this time of turmoil that an accolyte appeared at the gates of our motherhouse at Demos, expressing an earnest desire to become a member of our order. As his training began, our preceptor soon realized this young postulant, Sparhawk by name, was no ordinary man. He quickly outstripped his fellow novices and even mastered seasoned Pandions on the practice field. It was not merely his physical prowess, however, that so distinguished him, since his intellectual gifts were also towering. His aptitude for the secrets of Styricum was the delight of his tutor in those arts, and the aged Styric instructor guided his pupil into areas of magic far beyond those customarily taught the Pandion Knights. The Patriarch of Demos was no less enthusiastic about the intellect of this novice, and by the time Sir Sparhawk had won his spurs, he was also skilled in the intricacies of philosophy and theological disputation.

It was at about the time that Sir Sparhawk was knighted that the youthful King Antor ascended the Elenian throne in Cimmura, and the lives of the two young men soon became intricately intertwined. King Antor was a rash, even foolhardy youth, and an outbreak of banditry along his northern border enraged him to the point where he threw caution to the winds and mounted a punitive expedition into that portion of his kingdom with a woefully inadequate force. When word of this reached Demos, the Preceptor of the Pandion Knights dispatched a relief column to rush north to the king's aid, and among the knights in that column was Sir Sparhawk.

King Antor was soon far out of his depth. Although no one could dispute his personal bravery, his lack of experience often led him into serious tactical and strategic blunders. Since he was oblivious to the alliances between the various bandit barons of the northern marches, he ofttimes led his men against one of them without giving thought to the fact that another was very likely to come to the aid of his ally. Thus, King Antor's already seriously outnumbered force was steadily whittled down by surprise attacks directed at the rear of his army. The barons of the north gleefully outflanked him again and again as he charged blindly forward, and they steadily decimated his reserves.

And so it stood when Sparhawk and the other Pandion Knights arrived in the war zone. The armies that had been so sorely pressing the young king were largely untrained, a rabble recruited from local robber bands. The barons who led them fell back to take stock of the situation. Although their numbers were still overwhelming, the reputed skill of the Pandions on the battlefield was something to be taken into account. A few of their number, made rash by their previous successes, urged their allies to press the attack, but older and wiser men advised caution. It seems relatively certain that a fair number of the barons, young and old alike, saw the way to the throne of Elenia opening before them. Should King Antor fall in battle, his crown might easily become the property of any man strong enough to wrest it from his companions.

The barons' first attacks on the combined forces of the Pandions and King Antor's troops were tentative, more in the nature of tests of the strength and resolve of the Church Knights and their allies. When it became evident that the response was in large measure defensive, these assaults grew more serious, and ultimately there was a pitched battle not far from the Pelosian border. As soon as it became evident that the barons were committing their full forces to the struggle, the Pandions reacted with their customary savagery. The defensive posture they had adopted during the first probing attacks had been clearly a ruse designed to lure the barons into an all-out confrontation.

The battle raged for the better part of a spring day. Late in the afternoon, when bright sunlight flooded the field, King Antor became separated from the troops of his household guard. He found himself horseless and hard-pressed and he resolved to sell his life as dearly as possible. It was at this point that Sir Sparhawk entered the fray. He quickly cut his way through to the king's side, and, in the fashion as old as the history of warfare, the two stood back to back, holding off their foes. The combination of Antor's headstrong bravery and Sparhawk's skill was convincing enough to hold their enemies at bay until by mischance, Sparhawk's sword was broken. With triumphant shouts the force encircling the two rushed in for the kill. This proved to be a fatal error.

Snatching a short, broad-bladed battle spear from one of the fallen, Sparhawk decimated the ranks of the charging troops. The culmination of the struggle came when the swarthy-faced baron who had been leading the attack rushed in to slay the sorely wounded Antor and died with Sparhawk's spear in his vitals. The baron's fall demoralized his men. They fell back and ultimately fled the scene.

Antor's wounds were grave, and Sparhawk's only slightly less so. Exhausted, the two sank side by side to the ground as evening settled over the field. It is impossible to reconstruct the conversation of the two wounded men there on that bloody field during the early hours of the night, since in later years neither would reveal what had passed between them. What is known, however, is that at some point during their discussions, they traded weapons. Antor bestowed the royal sword of Elenia upon Sir Sparhawk and took in exchange the battle spear with which Sir Sparhawk had saved his life. The king was to cherish that rude weapon to the end of his days.

It was nearly midnight when the two injured men saw a torch approaching through the darkness, and, not knowing if the torchbearer was friend or foe, they struggled to their feet and wearily prepared to defend themselves. The one who approached, however, was not an Elene, but was rather a white-robed and hooded Styric woman. Wordlessly, she tended their wounds. Then she spoke to them briefly in a lilting voice and gave them the pair of rings that came to symbolize their life-long friendship. Tradition has it that the oval stones set in the rings were as pale as diamond when the two received them, but that their mingled blood permanently stained the stones, and they appear to this day to be deep red rubies. Once she had done this, the mysterious Styric woman turned without a further word and walked off into the night, her white robe glowing in the moonlight.

As misty dawn lightened the field, the troops of Antor's household guard and a number of Sparhawk's fellow Pandions found the two wounded men at last, and they were borne on litters to our motherhouse here at Demos. Their recovery consumed months; by the time they were well enough to travel, they were fast friends. They went by easy stages to Antor's capital at Cimmura, and there the king made a startling announcement. He declared that henceforth the Pandion Sparhawk would be his champion and that, so long as both their families survived, the descendants of Sparhawk would serve the rulers of Elenia in that capacity.

As inevitably happens, the king's court at Cimmura was filled with intrigues. The various factions, however, were taken aback somewhat by the appearance at court of the grim-faced Sir Sparhawk. After a few tentative attempts to enlist his support for this or that faction had been sternly rebuffed, the couriers uncomfortably concluded that the King's Champion was incorruptible. Moreover, the friendship between the king and Sparhawk made the Pandion Knight the king's confidant and closest adviser. Since Sparhawk, as has been pointed out, had a towering intellect, he easily saw through the ofttimes petty scheming of the various officials at court and brought them to the attention of his less-gifted friend. Within a year, the court of King Antor had become remarkably free of corruption as Sparhawk imposed his own rigid morality upon those around him.

Of even greater concern to the various political factions in Elenia was the growing influence of the Pandion order in the kingdom. King Antor was profoundly grateful, not only to Sir Sparhawk, but also to his champion's brother knights. The king and his friend journeyed often to Demos to confer with the preceptor of our order, and major policy decisions were more often made in the motherhouse than in the chambers of the royal council where courtiers had customarily dictated royal policy with an eye more to their own advantage than to the good of the kingdom.

Sir Sparhawk married in middle life, and his wife soon bore him a son. At Antor's request, the child was also named Sparhawk, a tradition which, once established, has continued unbroken in the family to this very day. When he had reached a suitable age, the younger Sparhawk entered the Pandion motherhouse to begin the training for the position he would one day fill. To their fathers' delight, young Sparhawk and Antor's son, the crown prince, had become close friends during their boyhood, and the relationship between king and champion was thus ensured to continue unbroken.

When Antor, filled with years and honors, lay on his deathbed, his last act was to bestow his ruby ring and the short, broad-bladed spear upon his son; at the same time, the elder Sparhawk passed his ring and the royal sword on to *his* son. This tradition has also persisted down to this very day.

It is widely believed among the common people of Elenia that for so long as the friendship between the royal family and the house of Sparhawk shall persist, the kingdom will prosper and that no evil can befall it. Like many superstitions, this one is to some degree based in fact. The descendants of Sparhawk have always been gifted men and, in addition to their Pandion training, they have also received special instruction in statecraft and diplomacy, the better to prepare them for their hereditary task.

Of late, however, there has been a rift between the royal family and the house of Sparhawk. The weak King Aldreas, dominated by his ambitious sister and the Primate of Cimmura, rather coldly relegated the current Sparhawk to the lesser, even demeaning position as caretaker of the person of Princess Ehlana—possibly in the hope that the champion would be so offended that he would renounce his hereditary position. Sir Sparhawk, however, took his duties seriously and educated the child who would one day be Queen of Elenia in those areas that would prepare her to rule.

When it became obvious that Sparhawk would not willingly give up his post, Aldreas, at the instigation of his sister and Primate Annias, sent the Knight Sparhawk into exile in the Kingdom of Rendor.

Upon the death of King Aldreas, his daughter Ehlana ascended the throne as Queen. Hearing this news, Sparhawk returned to Cimmura only to find that his young Queen was gravely ill and that her life was being sustained only by a spell cast by the Styric sorceress Sephrenia—a spell, however, which could keep Ehlana alive for no more than a year.

In consultation, the preceptors of the four militant orders of Church Knights decided that the four orders must work in concert to discover a cure for the Queen's illness and to restore her to health and power, lest the corrupt Primate Annias achieve his goal, the throne of the Archprelacy in the basilica of Chyrellos. To that end, the preceptors of the Cyrinics, the Alciones, and the Genidians dispatched their own champions to join with the Pandion Sparhawk and his boyhood friend

Kalten to seek out the cure that would not only restore Queen Ehlana, but also her kingdom, which suffered in her absence from a grave malaise.

Thus it stands. The restoration of the Queen's health is vital not only to the Kingdom of Elenia, but to the other Elene kingdoms as well, for should the venal Primate Annias gain the Archprelate's throne, we may be sure that the Elene kingdoms will be wracked by turmoil, and our ancient foe, Otha of Zemoch, stands poised on our eastern frontier, ready to exploit any division or chaos. The cure of the Queen who is so near to death, however, may daunt even her champion and his stalwart companions. Pray for their success, my brothers, for should they fail, the whole of the Eosian continent will inevitably fall into general warfare, and civilization as we know it will cease to exist.

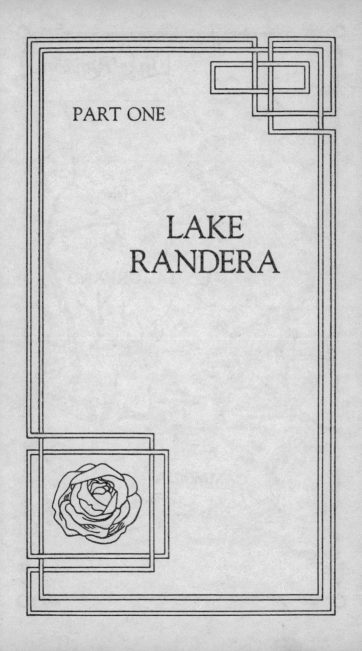

PART ONE

LAKE
RANDERA

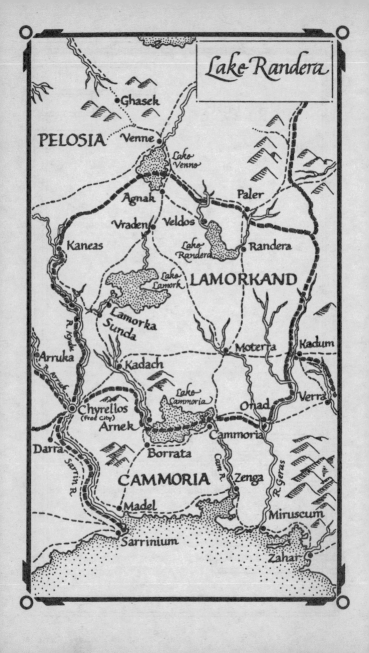

CHAPTER ONE

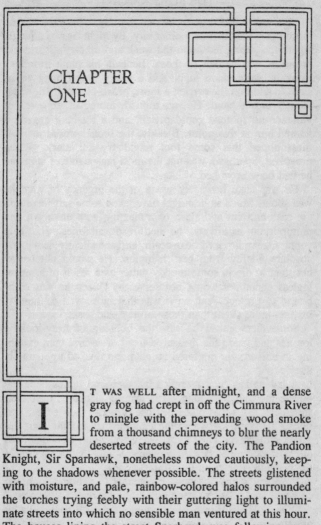

IT WAS WELL after midnight, and a dense gray fog had crept in off the Cimmura River to mingle with the pervading wood smoke from a thousand chimneys to blur the nearly deserted streets of the city. The Pandion Knight, Sir Sparhawk, nonetheless moved cautiously, keeping to the shadows whenever possible. The streets glistened with moisture, and pale, rainbow-colored halos surrounded the torches trying feebly with their guttering light to illuminate streets into which no sensible man ventured at this hour. The houses lining the street Sparhawk was following were hardly more than looming black shadows. Sparhawk moved on, his ears even more than his eyes wary, for in this murky night sound was far more important than sight to warn of approaching danger.

11

This was a bad time to be out. By day, Cimmura was no more dangerous than any other city. By night, it was a jungle where the strong fed upon the weak and unwary. Sparhawk, however, was neither of those. Beneath his plain traveller's cloak he wore chain mail, and a heavy sword hung at his side. In addition, he carried a short, broad-bladed battle spear loosely in one hand. He was trained, moreover, in levels of violence no footpad could match, and a seething anger inflamed him at this point. Bleakly, the broken-nosed man almost hoped that some fool might try an attack. When provoked, Sparhawk was not the most reasonable of men and he had been provoked of late.

He was also, however, aware of the urgency of what he was about. Much as he might have taken some satisfaction in the rush and cut and slash of a meeting with unknown and unimportant assailants, he had responsibilities. His pale young Queen hovered near death, and she silently demanded absolute fidelity from her champion. He would not betray her, and to die in some muddy gutter as a result of a meaningless encounter would not serve the Queen he was oath-bound to protect. And so it was that he moved cautiously, his feet more silent than those of any paid assassin.

Somewhere ahead he saw the bobbing of hazy-looking torches and heard the measured tread of several men marching in unison. He muttered an oath and ducked up a smelly alley.

A half-dozen men marched by, their red tunics bedewed by the fog and with long pikes leaning slantwise over their shoulders. "It's that place in Rose Street," their officer was saying arrogantly, "where the Pandions try to hide their ungodly subterfuge. They know we're watching, of course, but our presence restricts their movements and leaves his Grace, the primate, free from their interference."

"We know the reasons, Lieutenant," a bored-sounding corporal said. "We've been doing this for over a year now."

"Oh." The self-important young lieutenant sounded a bit crestfallen. "I just want to be sure that we all understood, is all."

"Yes, sir," the corporal said tonelessly.

"Wait here, men," the lieutenant said, trying to make his boyish voice sound gruff. "I'll look on ahead." He marched on up the street, his heels smashing noisily on the fog-wet cobblestones.

"What a jackass," the corporal muttered to his companions.

"Grow up, Corporal," an old, gray-haired veteran said. "We take the pay, so we obey their orders and keep our opinions to ourselves. Just do your job and leave opinions to the officers."

The corporal grunted sourly. "I was at court yesterday," he said. "Primate Annias had summoned that young puppy up there, and the fool absolutely *had* to have an escort. Would you believe the lieutenant was actually fawning all over the bastard Lycheas?"

"That's what lieutenants do best." The veteran shrugged. "They're born boot-lickers, and the bastard *is* the Prince Regent, after all. I'm not sure if that makes his boots taste any better, but the lieutenant's probably got calluses on his tongue by now."

The corporal laughed. "That's God's truth, but wouldn't he be surprised if the Queen recovered and he found out that he'd eaten all that boot polish for nothing?"

"You'd better hope she doesn't, Corporal," one of the other men said. "If she wakes up and takes control of her own treasury again, Annias won't have the money to pay us next month."

"He can always dip into the church coffers."

"Not without giving an accounting, he can't. The Hierocracy in Chyrellos squeezes every penny of church money until it squeaks."

"All right, you men," the young officer called out of the fog, "the Pandion inn is just up ahead. I've relieved the soldiers who were on watch, so we'd better go there and take up our positions."

"You heard him," the corporal said. "Move out." The church soldiers marched off into the fog.

Sparhawk smiled briefly in the darkness. It was seldom that he had the opportunity to hear the casual conversations of the enemy. He had long suspected that the soldiers of the Primate of Cimmura were motivated more by greed than from any sense of loyalty or piety. He stepped out of the alley and then jumped soundlessly back as he heard other footsteps coming up the street. For some reason the usually empty nighttime streets of Cimmura were awash with people. The footsteps were loud, so whoever it was out there was not trying to sneak up on anybody. Sparhawk shifted the short-handled spear in his hands. Then he saw the fellow looming out of the fog. The man wore a dark-colored smock, and he had a large basket balanced on one shoulder. He appeared to be a workman of some kind, but there was no way to be sure of that. Sparhawk remained silent and let him pass. He waited until the sound of the footsteps was gone, then he stepped into the street again. He walked carefully, his soft boots making little sound on the wet cobblestones, and he kept his gray cloak wrapped tightly about him to muffle any clinking of his chain mail.

He crossed an empty street to avoid the flickering yellow lamplight coming through the open door of a tavern where voices were raised in bawdy song. He shifted the spear to his left hand and pulled the hood of his cloak even farther forward to shadow his face as he passed through the mist-shrouded light.

He stopped, his eyes and ears carefully searching the foggy street ahead of him. His general direction was toward the east gate, but he had no particular fanaticism about that. People who walk in straight lines are predictable, and predictable people get caught. It was absolutely vital that he leave the city unrecognized and unseen by any of Annias' men, even if it took him all night. When he was satisfied that the street was empty, he moved on, keeping to the deepest shadows. At a corner beneath a misty orange torch, a ragged beggar sat against a wall. He had a bandage across his eyes and a number of authentic-looking sores on his arms and legs. Sparhawk knew that this was not a profitable time for begging, so the fellow was probably up to something else. Then a slate from a rooftop crashed into the street not far from where Sparhawk stood.

"Charity!" the beggar called in a despairing voice, although Sparhawk's soft-shod feet had made no sound.

"Good evening, neighbor," the big knight said softly, crossing the street. He dropped a couple of coins into the begging bowl.

"Thank you, my Lord. God bless you."

"You're not supposed to be able to see me, neighbor,"

Sparhawk reminded him. "You don't know if I'm a lord or a commoner."

"It's late," the beggar apologized, "and I'm a little sleepy. Sometimes I forget."

"Very sloppy," Sparhawk chided. "Pay attention to business. Oh, by the way, give my best to Platime." Platime was an enormously fat man who ruled the underside of Cimmura with an iron fist.

The beggar lifted the bandage from his eyes and stared at Sparhawk, his eyes widening in recognition.

"And tell your friend up on that roof not to get excited," Sparhawk added. "You might tell him, though, to watch where he puts his feet. That last slate he kicked loose almost brained me."

"He's a new man." The beggar sniffed. "He still has a lot to learn about burglary."

"That he does," Sparhawk agreed. "Maybe you can help me, neighbor. Talen was telling me about a tavern up against the east wall of the city. It's supposed to have a garret that the tavern keeper rents out from time to time. Do you happen to know where it's located?"

"It's in Goat Lane, Sir Sparhawk. It's got a sign that's supposed to look like a bunch of grapes. You can't miss it." The beggar squinted. "Where's Talen been lately? I haven't seen him for quite a while."

"His father's sort of taken him in hand."

"I didn't know Talen even *had* a father. That boy will go far if he doesn't get himself hanged. He's just about the best thief in Cimmura."

"I know," Sparhawk said. "He's picked my pocket a few times." He dropped a couple more coins in the begging bowl. "I'd appreciate it if you'd keep the fact that you saw me tonight more or less to yourself, neighbor."

"I never saw you, Sir Sparhawk." The beggar grinned.

"And I never saw you and your friend on the roof, either."

"Something for everybody then."

"My feelings exactly. Good luck in your enterprise."

"And the same to you in yours."

Sparhawk smiled and moved off down the street. His brief exposure to the seamier side of Cimmuran society had paid off again. Though not exactly a friend, Platime and the shadowy world he controlled could be very helpful. Sparhawk cut over one street to make sure that should the clumsy burglar on the roof be surprised in the course of his activities, the inevitable hue and cry would not bring the watch running down the same street he was traversing.

As they always did when he was alone, Sparhawk's thoughts reverted to his Queen. He had known Ehlana since she had been a little girl, though he had not seen her during the ten years he had been in exile in Rendor. The memory of her seated on her throne, encased in diamond-hard crystal, wrenched at his heart. He began to regret the fact that he had not taken advantage of the opportunity to kill the Primate Annias earlier tonight. A poisoner is always contemptible, but the man who had poisoned Sparhawk's Queen had placed himself in mortal danger, since Sparhawk was not one to let old scores simmer too long.

Then he heard furtive footsteps behind him in the fog, and he stepped into a recessed doorway and stood very still.

There were two of them, and they wore nondescript clothing. "Can you still see him?" one of them whispered to the other.

"No. This fog's getting thicker. He's just ahead of us, though."

"Are you sure he's a Pandion?"

"When you've been in this business as long as I have, you'll learn to recognize them. It's the way they walk and the way they hold their shoulders. He's a Pandion all right."

"What's he doing out in the street at this time of night?"

"That's what we're here to find out. The primate wants reports on all their movements."

"The notion of trying to sneak up behind a Pandion on a foggy night makes me just a little nervous. They all use magic, and they can feel you coming. I'd rather not get his sword in my guts. Did you ever see his face?"

"No. He had his hood up, so his face was in shadow."

The two of them crept on up the street, unaware of the fact that their lives had hung in the balance for a moment. Had either of them seen Sparhawk's face, they would have died on the spot. Sparhawk was a very pragmatic man about things like that. He waited until he could no longer hear their footfalls. Then he retraced his steps to an intersection and went up a side street.

The tavern was empty except for the owner, who dozed

with his feet up on a table and with his hands clasped over his paunch. He was a stout, unshaven man wearing a dirty smock.

"Good evening, neighbor," Sparhawk said quietly as he entered.

The tavern keeper opened one eye. "Morning is more like it," he grunted.

Sparhawk looked around. The tavern was a fairly typical workingman's place with a low, beamed ceiling smudged with smoke and with a utilitarian counter across the back. The chairs and benches were scarred, and the sawdust on the floor had not been swept up and replaced for months. "It seems to be a slow night," he noted in his quiet voice.

"It's always slow this late, friend. What's your pleasure?"

"Arcian red—if you've got any."

"Arcium's hip deep in red grapes. Nobody ever runs out of Arcian red." With a weary sigh the tavern keeper heaved himself to his feet and poured Sparhawk a goblet of red wine. The goblet, Sparhawk saw, was none too clean. "You're out late, friend," the fellow observed, handing the big knight the sticky goblet.

"Business." Sparhawk shrugged. "A friend of mine said you have a garret on the top floor of the house."

The tavern keeper's eyes narrowed suspiciously. "You don't look like the sort of fellow who'd have a burning interest in garrets," he said. "Does this friend of yours have a name?"

"Not one he cares to have generally known," Sparhawk replied, taking a sip of his wine. It was a distinctly inferior vintage.

"Friend, I don't know you, and you have a sort of official look about you. Why don't you just finish your wine and leave? That's unless you can come up with a name I can recognize."

"This friend of mine works for a man named Platime. You may have heard the name."

The tavern keeper's eyes widened slightly. "Platime must be branching out. I didn't know that he had anything to do with the gentry—except to steal from them."

Sparhawk shrugged. "He owed me a favor."

The unshaven man still looked dubious. "Anybody could throw Platime's name around," he said.

"Neighbor," Sparhawk said flatly, setting his wineglass

down, "this is starting to get tedious. Either we go up to your garret or I go out looking for the watch. I'm sure they'll be very interested in your little enterprise."

The tavern keeper's face grew sullen. "It'll cost you a silver half crown."

"All right."

"You're not even going to argue?"

"I'm in a bit of a hurry. We can haggle about the price next time."

"You seem to be in quite a rush to get out of town, friend. You haven't killed anybody with that spear tonight, have you?"

"Not yet." Sparhawk's voice was flat.

The tavern keeper swallowed hard. "Let me see your money."

"Of course, neighbor. And then let's go upstairs and have a look at this garret."

"We'll have to be careful. With this fog, you won't be able to see the guards coming along the parapet."

"I can take care of that."

"No killing. I've got a nice little sideline here. If somebody kills one of the guards, I'll have to close it down."

"Don't worry, neighbor. I don't think I'll have to kill anybody tonight."

The garret was dusty and appeared unused. The tavern keeper carefully opened the gabled window and peered out into the fog. Behind him, Sparhawk whispered in Styric and released the spell. He could feel the fellow out there. "Careful," he said quietly. "There's a guard coming along the parapet."

"I don't see anybody."

"I heard him," Sparhawk replied. There was no point in going into extended explanations.

"You've got sharp ears, friend."

The two of them waited in the darkness as the sleepy guard strolled along the parapet and disappeared in the fog.

"Give me a hand with this," the tavern keeper said, stooping to lift one end of a heavy timber up onto the windowsill. "We slide it across to the parapet, and then you go on over. When you get there, I'll throw you the end of this rope. It's anchored here, so you'll be able to slide down the outside of the wall."

"Right," Sparhawk said. They slid the timber across the intervening space. "Thanks, neighbor," Sparhawk said. He straddled the timber and inched his way across to the parapet. He stood up and caught the coil of rope that came out of the misty darkness. He dropped it over the wall and swung out on it. A few moments later, he was on the ground. The rope slithered up into the fog, and then he heard the sound of the timber sliding back into the garret. "Very neat," Sparhawk muttered, walking carefully away from the city wall. "I'll have to remember that place."

The fog made it a bit difficult to get his bearings, but, by keeping the looming shadow of the city wall to his left, he could more or less determine his location. He set his feet down carefully. The night was quiet, and the sound of a stick breaking would be very loud.

Then he stopped. Sparhawk's instincts were very good, and he knew that he was being watched. He drew his sword slowly to avoid the telltale sound it made as it slid out of its sheath. With the sword in one hand and the battle spear in the other, he stood peering out into the fog.

And then he saw it. It was only a faint glow in the darkness, so faint that most people would not have noticed it. The glow drew closer, and he saw that it had a slight greenish cast to it. Sparhawk stood perfectly still and waited.

There was a figure out there in the fog, indistinct perhaps, but a figure nonetheless. It appeared to be robed and hooded in black, and that faint glow seemed to be coming out from under the hood. The figure was quite tall and appeared to be impossibly thin, almost skeletal. For some reason it chilled Sparhawk. He muttered in Styric, moving his fingers on the hilt of the sword and the shaft of the spear. Then he raised the spear and released the spell with its point. The spell was a relatively simple one, its purpose being only to identify the emaciated figure out in the fog. Sparhawk almost gasped when he felt the waves of pure evil emanating from the shadowy form. Whatever it was, it was certainly not human.

After a moment, a ghostly metallic chuckle came out of the night. The figure turned and moved away. Its walk was jerky as if its knees were put together backward. Sparhawk stayed where he was until that sense of evil faded away. Whatever the thing was, it was gone now. "I wonder if that was another of Martel's little surprises," Sparhawk muttered under his breath. Martel was a renegade Pandion Knight who had been expelled from the order. He and Sparhawk had once been friends, but no more. Martel now worked for Primate Annias, and it had been he who had provided the poison with which Annias had very nearly killed the Queen.

Sparhawk continued slowly and silently now, his sword and the spear still in his hands. Finally he saw the torches that marked the closed east gate of the city, and he took his bearings from them.

Then he heard a faint snuffling sound behind him, much like the sound a tracking dog would make. He turned, his weapons ready. Again he heard that metallic chuckle. He amended that in his mind. It was not so much a chuckle as it was a sort of stridulation, a chittering sound. Again he felt that sense of overpowering evil, which once again faded away.

Sparhawk angled slightly out from the city wall and the filmy light of those two torches at the gate. After about a quarter of an hour, he saw the square, looming shape of the Pandion chapterhouse just ahead.

He dropped into a prone position on the fog-wet turf and cast the searching spell again. He released it and waited.

Nothing.

He rose, sheathed his sword, and moved cautiously across the intervening field. The castlelike chapterhouse was, as always, being watched. Church soldiers, dressed as workmen, were encamped not far from the front gate with piles of the cobblestones they were ostensibly laying heaped around their tents. Sparhawk, however, went around to the back wall and carefully picked his way through the deep, stake-studded fosse surrounding the structure.

The rope down which he had clambered when he had left the house was still dangling behind a concealing bush. He shook it a few times to be certain the grappling hook at its upper end was still firmly attached. Then he tucked the war spear under his sword belt. He grasped the rope and pulled down hard.

Above him, he could hear the points of the hook grating into the stones of the battlement. He started to climb up, hand over hand.

"Who's there?" The voice came sharply out of the fog overhead. It was a youthful voice and familiar.

Sparhawk swore under his breath. Then he felt a tugging

on the rope he was climbing. "Leave it alone, Berit," he grated, straining to pull himself up.

"Sir Sparhawk?" the novice said in a startled voice.

"Don't jerk on the rope," Sparhawk ordered. "Those stakes in the ditch are very sharp."

"Let me help you up."

"I can manage. Just don't displace that hook." He grunted as he heaved himself up over the battlement, and Berit caught his arm to help him. Sparhawk was sweating from his exertions. Climbing a rope when one is wearing chain mail can be very strenuous.

Berit was a novice Pandion who showed much promise. He was a tall, rawboned young man who was wearing a mail shirt and a plain, utilitarian cloak. He carried a heavy-bladed battle-ax in one hand. He was a polite young fellow, so he did not ask any questions, although his face was filled with curiosity. Sparhawk looked down into the courtyard of the chapterhouse. By the light of a flickering torch, he saw Kurik and Kalten. Both of them were armed, and sounds from the stable indicated that someone was saddling horses for them. "Don't go away," he called down to them.

"What are you doing up there, Sparhawk?" Kalten sounded surprised.

"I thought I'd take up burglary as a sideline," Sparhawk replied dryly. "Stay there. I'll be right down. Come along, Berit."

"I'm supposed to be on watch, Sir Sparhawk."

"We'll send somebody up to replace you. This is important." Sparhawk led the way along the parapet to the steep stone stairs that led down into the courtyard.

"Where have you been, Sparhawk?" Kurik demanded angrily when the two had descended. Sparhawk's squire wore his usual black leather vest, and his heavily muscled arms and shoulders gleamed in the orange torchlight that illuminated the courtyard. He spoke in the hushed voice men use when talking at night.

"I had to go to the cathedral," Sparhawk replied quietly.

"Are you having religious experiences?" Kalten asked, sounding amused. The big blond knight, Sparhawk's boyhood friend, was dressed in chain and had a heavy broadsword belted at his waist.

"Not exactly," Sparhawk told him. "Tanis is dead. His ghost came to me about midnight."

"Tanis?" Kalten's voice was shocked.

"He was one of the twelve knights who were with Sephrenia when she encased Ehlana in crystal. His ghost told me to go to the crypt under the cathedral before it went to give up its sword to Sephrenia."

"And you went? At night?"

"The matter was of a certain urgency."

"What did you do there? Violate a few tombs? Is that how you got the spear?"

"Hardly," Sparhawk replied. "King Aldreas gave it to me."

"Aldreas!"

"His ghost anyway. His missing ring is hidden in the socket." Sparhawk looked curiously at his two friends. "Where were you going just now?"

"Out to look for you." Kurik shrugged.

"How did you know I'd left the chapterhouse?"

"I checked in on you a few times," Kurik said. "I thought you knew I usually did that."

"Every night?"

"Three times at least," Kurik confirmed. "I've been doing that every night since you were a boy—except for the year you were in Rendor. The first time tonight, you were talking in your sleep. The second time—just after midnight—you were gone. I looked around, and when I couldn't find you, I woke up Kalten."

"I think we'd better go wake the others," Sparhawk said bleakly. "Aldreas told me some things, and we've got some decisions to make."

"Bad news?" Kalten asked.

"It's hard to say. Berit, tell those novices in the stable to go replace you on the parapet. This might take awhile."

They gathered in Preceptor Vanion's brown-carpeted study in the south tower. Sparhawk, Berit, Kalten, and Kurik were there, of course. Sir Bevier, a Cyrinic Knight, was there as well, as were Sir Tynian, an Alcione Knight, and Sir Ulath, a huge Genidian Knight. The three were the champions of their orders, and they had joined with Sparhawk and Kalten when the preceptors of the four orders had decided that the restoration of Queen Ehlana was a matter that concerned them all. Sephrenia, the small, dark-haired Styric woman who instructed the Pandions in the secrets of Styricum, sat by the fire with the little girl they called Flute at her side. The boy, Talen, sat by the window, rubbing at his eyes with his fists. Talen was a sound sleeper, and he did not like being awakened. Vanion, the preceptor of the Pandion Knights, sat at the table he used for a writing desk. His study was a pleasant room, low, dark beamed, and with a deep fireplace that Sparhawk had never seen unlighted. As always, Sephrenia's simmering teakettle stood on the hob.

Vanion did not look well. Roused from his bed in the middle of the night, the Preceptor of the Pandion Order, a grim, careworn knight who was probably even older than he looked, wore an uncharacteristic Styric robe of plain white homespun cloth. Sparhawk had watched this peculiar change in Vanion over the years. Caught at times unawares, the preceptor, one of the stalwarts of the Church, sometimes seemed almost half Styric. As an Elene and a Knight of the Church, it was Sparhawk's duty to reveal his observations to the Church authorities. He chose, however, not to. His loyalty to the Church was one thing—a commandment from God. His loyalty to Vanion, however, was deeper, more personal.

The preceptor was gray faced, and his hands trembled slightly. The burden of the swords of the three dead knights he had compelled Sephrenia to relinquish to him was obviously weighing him down more than he would have admitted. The spell Sephrenia had cast in the throne room and which sustained the Queen had involved the concerted assistance of twelve Pandion Knights. One by one those knights would die, and their ghosts would deliver their swords to Sephrenia. When the last had died, she would follow them into the House of the Dead. Earlier that evening, Vanion had compelled her to give those swords to him. It was not the weight of the swords alone that made them such a burden. There were other things that went with them, things about which Sparhawk could not even begin to guess. Vanion had been adamant about taking the swords. He had given a few vague reasons for his action, but Sparhawk privately suspected that the preceptor's main reason had been to spare Sephrenia as much as possible. Despite all the strictures forbidding such things, Sparhawk believed that Vanion loved the dear, small woman who had instructed all Pandions for generations in the secrets of Styricum. All Pandion Knights loved and revered Sephrenia. In Vanion's case, however, Sparhawk surmised that love and reverence went perhaps a step further. Sephrenia also, he had noticed, seemed to have a special affection for the preceptor that went somehow beyond the love of a teacher for her pupil. This was also something that a Church Knight should reveal to the Hierocracy in Chyrellos. Again, Sparhawk chose not to.

"Why are we gathering at this unseemly hour?" Vanion asked wearily.

"Do you want to tell him?" Sparhawk asked Sephrenia.

The white-robed woman sighed and unwrapped the long, cloth-bound object she held to reveal another ceremonial Pandion sword. "Sir Tanis has gone into the House of the Dead," she told Vanion sadly.

"Tanis?" Vanion's voice was stricken. "When did this happen?"

"Just recently, I gather," she replied.

"Is that why we're here tonight?" Vanion asked Sparhawk.

"Not entirely. Before he went to deliver his sword to Sephrenia, Tanis visited me—or at least his ghost did. He told me that someone in the royal crypt wanted to see me. I went to the cathedral and I was confronted by the ghost of Aldreas. He told me a number of things and then gave me this." He twisted the shaft of the spear out of its socket and shook the ruby ring from its place of concealment.

"So *that's* where Aldreas hid it," Vanion said. "Maybe he was wiser than we thought. You said he told you some things. Such as what?"

"That he had been poisoned," Sparhawk replied. "Probably the same poison they gave Ehlana."

"Was it Annias?" Kalten asked grimly.

Sparhawk shook his head. "No. It was Princess Arissa."

"His own *sister*?" Bevier exclaimed. "That's monstrous!" Bevier was an Arcian, and he had deep moral convictions.

"Arissa's fairly monstrous," Kalten agreed. "She's not the sort to let little things stand in her way. How did she get out of the cloister in Demos to dispose of Aldreas, though?"

"Annias arranged it," Sparhawk told him. "She entertained Aldreas in her usual fashion, and when he was exhausted, she gave him the poisoned wine.''

"I don't quite understand." Bevier frowned.

"The relationship between Arissa and Aldreas went somewhat beyond what is customary for a brother and sister," Vanion told him delicately.

Bevier's eyes widened and the blood drained from his olive-skinned face as he slowly gathered Vanion's meaning.

"Why did she kill him?" Kalten asked. "Revenge for locking her up in that cloister?"

"No, I don't think so," Sparhawk told him. "I think it was a part of the overall scheme she and Annias had hatched. First they poisoned Aldreas and then Ehlana."

"So the way to the throne would be clear for Arissa's bastard son?" Kalten surmised.

"It's sort of logical," Sparhawk agreed. "It fits together even tighter when you know that Lycheas the bastard is Annias' son, too."

"A Primate of the Church?" Tynian said, looking a bit startled. "Do you people here in Elenia have different rules from the rest of us?"

"Not really, no," Vanion replied. "Annias seems to feel that he's above the rules, and Arissa goes out of her way to break them."

"Arissa's always been just a little indiscriminate," Kalten added. "Rumor has it that she was on very friendly terms with just about every man in Cimmura."

"That might be a slight exaggeration," Vanion said. He stood up and went to the window. "I'll pass this information on to Patriarch Dolmant," he said, looking out at the foggy night. "He may be able to make some use of it when the time comes to elect a new Archprelate."

"And perhaps the Earl of Lenda might be able to use it as well," Sephrenia suggested. "The royal council is corrupt, but even they might balk if they find that Annias is trying to put his own bastard son on the throne." She looked at Sparhawk. "What else did Aldreas tell you?" she asked.

"Just one other thing. We know we need some magic object to cure Ehlana. He told me what it is. It's Bhelliom. It's the only thing in the world with enough power."

Sephrenia's face blanched. "No!" she gasped. "Not Bhelliom!"

"That's what he told me."

"It presents a big problem," Ulath declared. "Bhelliom's been lost since the Zemoch war, and even if we're lucky enough to find it, it won't respond unless we have the rings."

"Rings?" Kalten asked.

"The Troll-Dwarf Ghwerig made Bhelliom," Ulath explained. "Then he made a pair of rings to unlock its power. Without the rings, Bhelliom's useless."

"We already have the rings," Sephrenia told him absently, her face still troubled.

"We do?" Sparhawk was startled.

"You're wearing one of them," she told him, "and Aldreas gave you the other this very night."

Sparhawk stared at the ruby ring on his left hand, then back at his teacher. "How's that possible?" he demanded. "How did my ancestor and King Antor come by these particular rings?"

"I gave them to them," she replied.

He blinked. "Sephrenia, that was three hundred years ago."

"Yes," she agreed, "approximately."

Sparhawk stared at her, then swallowed hard. *"Three hundred years?"* he demanded incredulously. "Sephrenia, just how old *are* you?"

"You know I'm not going to answer that question, Sparhawk. I've told you that before."

"How did *you* get the rings?"

"My Goddess Aphrael gave them to me—along with certain instructions. She told me where I'd find your ancestor and King Antor, and she told me to deliver the rings to them."

"Little mother," Sparhawk began, and then broke off as he saw her bleak expression.

"Hush, dear one," she commanded. "I will say this only once, Sir Knights," she told them all. "What we do puts us in conflict with the Elder Gods, and that is not lightly undertaken. Your Elene God forgives; the Younger Gods of Styricum can be persuaded to relent. The Elder Gods, however, demand absolute compliance with their whims. To counter the commands of an Elder God is to court worse than death. They obliterate those who defy them—in ways you cannot imagine. Do we *really* want to bring Bhelliom back into the light again?"

"Sephrenia! We have to!" Sparhawk exclaimed. "It's the only way we can save Ehlana—and you and Vanion for that matter."

"Annias will not live forever, Sparhawk, and Lycheas is hardly more than an inconvenience. Vanion and I are temporary, and so, for that matter—regardless of how you feel personally—is Ehlana. The world won't miss any of us all that much." Sephrenia's tone was almost clinical. "Bhelliom, however, is another matter—and so is Azash. If we fail and put the stone into that foul God's hands, we will doom the world forever. Is it worth the risk?"

"I'm the Queen's Champion," Sparhawk reminded her. "I have to do whatever I possibly can to save her life." He rose and strode across the room to her. "So help me God, Sephrenia," he declared, "I'll break open Hell itself to save that girl."

Sephrenia sighed. "He's such a child sometimes," she said to Vanion. "Can't you think of some way to make him grow up?"

"I was sort of considering going along," the preceptor replied, smiling. "Sparhawk might let me hold his cloak while he kicks in the gate. I don't think anybody's assaulted Hell lately."

"You too?" She covered her face with her hands. "Oh, dear. All right then, gentlemen," she said, giving up, "if you're all so bent on this, we'll try it—but only on one condition. If we do find Bhelliom, and it restores Ehlana, we must destroy it immediately after the task is done."

"Destroy it?" Ulath exploded. "Sephrenia, it's the most precious thing in the world."

"And also the most dangerous. If Azash ever comes to possess it, the world will be lost, and all mankind will be plunged into the most hideous slavery imaginable. I must insist on this, gentlemen. Otherwise, I'll do everything in my power to prevent your finding that accursed stone."

"I don't see that we've got much choice here," Ulath said gravely to the others. "Without her help, we don't have much hope of unearthing Bhelliom."

"Oh, somebody's going to find it all right," Sparhawk told him firmly. "One of the things Aldreas told me was that the time has come for Bhelliom to see the light of day again, and no force on earth can prevent it. The only thing that concerns me right now is whether it's going to be one of us who finds it or some Zemoch, who'll carry it back to Otha.''

"Or if it rises from the earth all on its own," Tynian added moodily. "Could it do that, Sephrenia?"

"Probably, yes."

"How did you get out of the chapterhouse without being seen by the primate's spies?" Kalten asked Sparhawk curiously.

"I threw a rope over the back wall and climbed down."

"How about getting in and out of the city after the gates were all closed?"

"By pure luck, the gate was still open when I was on my way to the cathedral. I used another way to get out."

"That garret I told you about?" Talen asked.

Sparhawk nodded.

"How much did he charge you?"

"A silver half crown."

Talen looked shocked at that. "And they call *me* a thief. He gulled you, Sparhawk."

Sparhawk shrugged. "I needed to get out of the city."

"I'll tell Platime about it," the boy said. "He'll get your money back. A half crown? That's outrageous." The boy was actually spluttering.

Sparhawk remembered something. "Sephrenia, when I was on my way back here, something was out in the fog watching me. I don't think it was human."

"The Damork?"

"I couldn't say for sure, but it didn't feel the same. The Damork's not the only creature subject to Azash, is it?"

"No. The Damork is the most powerful, but it's stupid. The other creatures don't have its power, but they're more clever. In many ways, they can be even more dangerous."

"All right, Sephrenia," Vanion said then. "I think you'd better give me Tanis' sword now."

"My dear one—" she began to protest, her face anguished.

"We've had this argument once already tonight," he told her. "Let's not go through it again."

She sighed. Then the two of them began to chant in unison in the Styric tongue. Vanion's face turned a little grayer at the end when Sephrenia handed him the sword and their hands touched.

"All right," Sparhawk said to Ulath after the transfer had been completed. "Where do we start? Where was King Sarak when his crown was lost?"

"No one really knows," the big Genidian Knight replied. "He left Emsat when Otha invaded Lamorkand. He took a few retainers and left orders for the rest of his army to follow him to the battlefield at Lake Randera."

"Did anyone report having seen him there?" Kalten asked.

"Not that I've ever heard. The Thalesian army was seriously decimated, though. It's possible that Sarak did get there before the battle started, but that none of the few survivors ever saw him."

"I expect that's the place to start then," Sparhawk said.

"Sparhawk," Ulath objected, "that battlefield is immense. All the Knights of the Church could spend the rest of their lives digging there and still not find the crown."

"There's an alternative," Tynian said, scratching his chin.

"And what is that, friend Tynian?" Bevier asked him.

"I have some skill at necromancy," Tynian told him. "I don't like it much, but I know how it's done. If we can find out where the Thalesians are buried, I can ask them if any of them saw King Sarak on the field and if any know where he might be buried. It's exhausting, but the cause is worth it."

"I'll be able to aid you, Tynian," Sephrenia told him. "I don't practice necromancy myself, but I know the proper spells."

Kurik rose to his feet. "I'd better get the things we'll need together," he said. "Come along, Berit. You too, Talen."

"There'll be ten of us," Sephrenia told him.

"Ten?"

"We'll be taking Talen and Flute along with us."

"Is that really necessary?" Sparhawk objected, "or even wise?"

"Yes, it is. We'll be seeking the aid of some of the Younger Gods of Styricum, and they like symmetry. We were ten when we began this search, so now we have to be the same ten every step of the way. Sudden changes disturb the Younger Gods."

"Anything you say." He shrugged.

Vanion rose and began to pace up and down. "We'd better get started with this," he said. "It might be safer if you left the chapterhouse before daylight and before this fog lifts. Let's not make it too easy for the spies who watch the house.''

"I'll agree with that," Kalten approved. "I'd rather not have to race Annias' soldiers all the way to Lake Randera.''

"All right, then," Sparhawk said, "Let's get at it. Time's running a little short on us.''

"Stay a moment, Sparhawk," Vanion said as they began to file out.

Sparhawk waited until the others had left, and then he closed the door.

"I received a communication from the Earl of Lenda this evening," the preceptor told his friend.

"Oh?"

"He asked me to reassure you. Annias and Lycheas are taking no further action against the Queen. Apparently the failure of their plot down in Arcium embarrassed Annias a great deal. He's not going to take the chance of making a fool of himself again.''

"That's a relief."

"Lenda added something I don't quite understand, though. He asked me to tell you that the candles are still burning. Do you have any idea what he meant by that?''

"Good old Lenda," Sparhawk said warmly. "I asked him not to leave Ehlana sitting in the throne room in the dark.''

"I don't think it makes much difference to her, Sparhawk.''

"It does to me," Sparhawk replied.

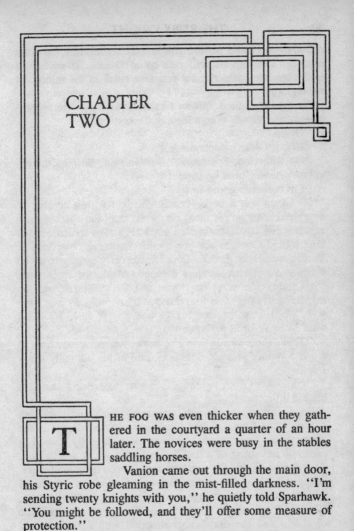

CHAPTER TWO

T HE FOG WAS even thicker when they gathered in the courtyard a quarter of an hour later. The novices were busy in the stables saddling horses.

Vanion came out through the main door, his Styric robe gleaming in the mist-filled darkness. "I'm sending twenty knights with you," he quietly told Sparhawk. "You might be followed, and they'll offer some measure of protection."

"We sort of need to hurry, Vanion," Sparhawk objected. "If we take others with us, we won't be able to move any faster than the pace of the slowest horse."

"I know that, Sparhawk," Vanion replied patiently. "You won't need to stay with them for very long. Wait until you're out in open country and the sun comes up. Make sure

31

nobody's too close behind you and then slip away from the column. The knights will ride on to Demos. If anybody's following, they won't know you aren't still in the middle of the column.''

Sparhawk grinned. ''Now I know how you got to be preceptor, my friend. Who's leading the column?''

''Olven.''

''Good. Olven's dependable.''

''Go with God, Sparhawk,'' Vanion said, clasping the big knight's hand, ''and be careful.''

''I'm certainly going to try.''

Sir Olven was a bulky Pandion Knight with a number of angry red scars on his face. He came out of the chapterhouse wearing full armor enamelled black. His men trailed out behind him. ''Good to see you again, Sparhawk,'' he said as Vanion went back inside. Olven spoke very quietly to avoid alerting the church soldiers camped outside the front gate. ''All right,'' he went on, ''you and the others ride in the middle of us. With this fog, those soldiers probably won't see you. We'll drop the drawbridge and go out fast. We don't want to be in sight for more than a minute or two.''

''That's more words than I've heard you use at one time in the last twenty years,'' Sparhawk said to his normally silent friend.

''I know,'' Olven agreed. ''I'll have to see if I can't cut back a little.''

Sparhawk and his friends wore mail shirts and traveller's cloaks, since formal armor would attract attention out in the countryside. Their armor, however, was carefully stowed in packs on the string of a half-dozen horses Kurik would lead. They mounted, and the armored men formed up around them. Olven made a signal to the men at the windlass that raised and lowered the drawbridge, and the men slipped the rachets, allowing the windlass to run freely. There was a noisy rattle of chain, and the drawbridge dropped with a huge boom. Olven was galloping across it almost before it hit the far side of the fosse.

The dense fog helped enormously. As soon as he had galloped across the bridge, Olven cut sharply to the left, leading the column across the open field toward the Demos road. Behind them, Sparhawk could hear startled shouts as the church soldiers ran out of their tents to stare after the column in chagrin.

"Slick," Kalten said gaily. "Across the drawbridge and into the fog in under a minute."

"Olven knows what he's doing," Sparhawk said, "and what's even better is that it's going to be at least an hour before the soldiers can mount any kind of pursuit."

"Give me an hour's head start, and they'll never catch me." Kalten laughed delightedly. "This is starting out very well, Sparhawk."

"Enjoy it while you can. Things will probably start to go wrong later on."

"You're a pessimist, do you know that?"

"No. I'm just used to little disappointments."

They slowed to a canter when they reached the Demos road. Olven was a veteran, and he always tried to conserve his horses. Speed might be necessary later, and Sir Olven took very few chances.

A full moon hung above the fog, and it made the thick mist deceptively luminous. The glowing white fog around them confused the eye and concealed far more than it illuminated. There was a chill dampness in the fog, and Sparhawk pulled his cloak about him as he rode.

The Demos road swung north toward the city of Lenda before turning southeasterly again to Demos, where the Pandion motherhouse was located. Although he could not see it, Sparhawk knew that the countryside along the road was gently rolling and that there were large patches of trees out there. He was counting on those trees for concealment once he and his friends left the column.

They rode on. The fog had dampened the dirt surface of the road, and the sound of their horses' hooves was muffled.

Every now and then the black shadows of trees loomed suddenly out of the fog at the sides of the road as they rode by. Talen shied nervously each time it happened.

"What's the problem?" Kurik asked him.

"I hate this," the boy replied. "I absolutely hate it. Anything could be hiding beside the road—wolves, bears—or even worse."

"You're in the middle of a party of armed men, Talen."

"That's easy for you to say, but I'm the smallest one here—except for Flute, maybe. I've heard that wolves and things like that always drag down the smallest when they attack. I really don't want to be eaten, Father."

"That keeps cropping up," Tynian noted curiously to Sparhawk. "You never did explain why the boy keeps calling your squire by that term."

"Kurik was indiscreet when he was younger."

"Doesn't anybody in Elenia sleep in his own bed?"

"It's a cultural peculiarity. It's not really as widespread as it might seem, though."

Tynian rose slightly in his stirrups and looked ahead to where Bevier and Kalten rode side by side deep in conversation. "A word of advice, Sparhawk," he said confidentially. "You're an Elenian, so you don't seem to have any problem with this sort of thing, and in Deira we're fairly broad-minded about such things, but I don't know that I'd let Bevier in on this. The Cyrinic Knights are a pious lot—just like all Arcians—and they disapprove of these little irregularities very strongly. Bevier's a good man in a fight, but he's a little narrow-minded. If he gets offended, it might cause problems later on."

"You're probably right," Sparhawk agreed. "I'll talk with Talen and ask him to keep his relationship with Kurik to himself."

"Do you think he'll listen?" the broad-faced Deiran asked skeptically.

"It's worth a try."

They occasionally passed a farmhouse standing beside the foggy road with hazy golden lamplight streaming from its windows, a sure sign that, even though the sky had not yet started to lighten, day had already begun for the country folk.

"How long are we going to stay with this column?" Tynian asked. "Going to Lake Randera by way of Demos is a very long way around."

"We can probably slip away later this morning," Sparhawk replied, "once we're sure that nobody's following us. That's what Vanion suggested."

"Have you got somebody watching to the rear?"

Sparhawk nodded. "Berit's riding about a half mile back."

"Do you think any of the primate's spies saw us leave your chapterhouse?"

"They didn't really have very much time for it," Sparhawk

said. "We'd already gone past them before they came out of their tents."

Tynian grunted. "Which road do you plan to take when we leave this one?"

"I think we'll go across country. Roads tend to be watched. I'm sure that Annias has guessed that we're up to something by now."

They rode on through the tag end of a foggy night. Sparhawk was pensive. He privately admitted to himself that their hastily conceived plan had little chance of success. Even if Tynian could raise the ghosts of the Thalesian dead, there was no guarantee that any of the spirits would know the location of King Sarak's final resting place. This entire journey could well be futile and serve only to use up what time Ehlana had left. Then a thought came to him. He rode on forward to speak with Sephrenia. "Something just occurred to me," he said to her.

"Oh?"

"How well known is the spell you used to encase Ehlana?"

"It's almost never practiced because it's so very dangerous," she replied. "A few Styrics might know of it, but I doubt that any would dare to perform it. Why do you ask?"

"I think I'm right on the edge of an idea. If no one but you is really willing to use the spell, then it's rather unlikely that anybody else would know about the time limitation."

"That's true. They wouldn't."

"Then nobody could tell Annias about it."

"Obviously."

"So Annias doesn't know that we only have so much time left. For all he knows, the crystal could keep Ehlana alive indefinitely."

"I'm not certain that gives us any particular advantage, Sparhawk."

"I'm not either, but it's something to keep in mind. We might be able to use it someday."

The eastern sky was growing gradually lighter as they rode, and the fog was swirling and thinning. It was about a half hour before sunrise when Berit came galloping up from the rear. He was wearing his mail shirt and plain blue cloak, and his war ax was in a sling at the side of his saddle. The young novice, Sparhawk decided almost idly, was going to need some instruction in swordsmanship soon, before he grew too attached to that ax.

"Sir Sparhawk," he said, reining in, "there's a column of church soldiers coming up behind us." His hard-run horse was steaming in the chill fog.

"How many?" Sparhawk asked him.

"Fifty or so, and they're galloping hard. There was a break in the fog, and I saw them coming."

"How far back?"

"A mile or so. They're in that valley we just came through."

Sparhawk considered it. "I think a little change of plans might be in order," he said. He looked around and saw a dark blur back in the swirling fog off to the left. "Tynian," he said, "I think that's a grove of trees over there. Why don't you take the others and ride across this field and get into the grove before the soldiers catch up? I'll be right along." He shook Faran's reins. "I want to talk with Sir Olven," he told the big roan.

Faran flicked his ears irritably, then moved alongside the column at a gallop.

"We'll be leaving you here, Olven," Sparhawk told the scar-faced knight. "There's a half-hundred church soldiers coming up from the rear. I want to be out of sight before they come by."

"Good idea," Olven approved. Olven was not one to waste words.

"Why don't you give them a bit of a run?" Sparhawk suggested. "They won't be able to tell that we're not still in the column until they catch up with you."

Olven grinned crookedly. "Even so far as Demos?" he asked.

"That would be helpful. Cut across country before you reach Lenda and pick up the road again south of town. I'm sure Annias has spies in Lenda too."

"Good luck, Sparhawk," Olven said.

"Thanks," Sparhawk said, shaking the scar-faced knight's hand. "We might need it." He backed Faran off the road, and the column thundered past him at a gallop.

"Let's see how fast you can get to that grove of trees over there," Sparhawk said to his bad-tempered mount.

Faran snorted derisively, then leaped forward at a dead run.

Kalten waited at the edge of the trees, his gray cloak blending into the shadows and fog. "The others are back in the woods a ways," he reported, "Why's Olven galloping like that?"

"I asked him to," Sparhawk replied, swinging down from his saddle. "The soldiers won't know that we've left the column if Olven stays a mile or two ahead of them."

"You're smarter than you look, Sparhawk," Kalten said, also dismounting. "I'll get the horses back out of sight. The steam coming off them might be visible." He squinted at Faran. "Tell this ugly brute of yours not to bite me."

"You heard him, Faran," Sparhawk told his war-horse.

Faran laid his ears back.

As Kalten led their horses back among the trees, Sparhawk sank down onto his stomach behind a low bush. The grove of trees lay no more than fifty yards from the road; as the fog began to dissipate with the onset of morning, he could clearly see that the whole stretch of road they had just left was empty. Then a single red-tunicked soldier galloped along, coming from the south. The man rode stiffly, and his face seemed strangely wooden.

"A scout?" Kalten whispered, crawling up beside Sparhawk.

"More than likely," Sparhawk whispered back.

"Why are we whispering?" Kalten asked. "He can't hear us over the noise of his horse's hooves."

"You started it."

"Force of habit, I guess. I always whisper when I'm skulking."

The scout reined in his mount at the top of the hill, then wheeled and rode back along the road at a dead run. His face was still blank.

"He's going to wear out that horse if he keeps doing that," Kalten said.

"It's his horse."

"That's true, and he's the one who gets to walk when the horse plays out on him."

"Walking is good for church soldiers. It teaches them humility."

About five minutes later, the church soldiers galloped by,

their red tunics dark in the dawn light. Accompanying the leader of the column was a tall, emaciated figure in a black robe and hood. It might have been a trick of the misty morning light, but a faint greenish glow seemed to emanate from under the hood, and the figure's back appeared to be grossly deformed.

"They're definitely trying to keep an eye on that column," Kalten said.

"I hope they enjoy Demos," Sparhawk replied. "Olven's going to stay ahead of them every step of the way. I need to talk with Sephrenia. Let's go back to the others. We'll sit tight for an hour or so until we're sure the soldiers are out of the area and then move on."

"Good idea. I'm about ready for some breakfast anyway."

They led their horses back through the damp woods to a small basin surrounding a trickling spring that emerged from a fern-covered bank.

"Did they go by?" Tynian asked.

"At a gallop." Kalten grinned. "And they didn't look around very much. Does anybody have anything to eat? I'm starving."

"I've got a slab of cold bacon," Kurik offered.

"Cold?"

"Fire makes smoke, Kalten. Do you really want these woods full of soldiers?"

Kalten sighed.

Sparhawk looked at Sephrenia. "There's somebody—or something—riding with those soldiers," he said. "It gave me a very uneasy feeling, and I think it was the same thing I caught a glimpse of last night."

"Can you describe it?"

"It's quite tall and very very thin. Its back seems to be deformed, and it's wearing a black hooded robe, so I couldn't see any details." He frowned. "Those church soldiers in the column seemed to be half-asleep. They usually pay closer attention to what they're doing."

"This thing you saw," she said seriously. "Was there anything else unusual about it?"

"I can't say for sure, but it seemed to have a sort of greenish light coming from its face. I noticed the same thing last night."

Her face grew bleak. "I think we'd better leave immediately, Sparhawk."

"The soldiers don't know we're here," he objected.

"They will before long. You've just described a Seeker. In Zemoch they're used to hunt down runaway slaves. The lump on its back is caused by its wings."

"Wings?" Kalten said skeptically. "Sephrenia, no animal has wings—except maybe a bat."

"This isn't a mammal, Kalten," she replied. "It more closely resembles an insect—although neither term is very exact when you're talking about the creatures Azash summons."

"I hardly think we need to worry about a bug," he said.

"We do with this particular creature. It has very little in the way of a brain, but that doesn't matter, because the spirit of Azash infuses it and provides its thoughts for it. It can see a long ways in the dark or fog. Its ears are very sharp, and it has a very keen sense of smell. As soon as those soldiers come in sight of Olven's column, it's going to know that we're not riding with the knights. The soldiers will come back at that point."

"Are you saying that church soldiers will take orders from an insect?" Bevier asked incredulously.

"They have no choice. They have no will of their own anymore. The Seeker controls them utterly."

"How long does that last?" he asked her.

"For as long as they live—which usually isn't very long. As soon as it has no further need of them, it consumes them. Sparhawk, we're in very great danger. Let's leave here at once."

"You heard her," Sparhawk said grimly. "Let's get out of here."

They rode out of the grove of trees at a canter and crossed a wide green meadow where brown and white spotted cows grazed in knee-deep grass. Sir Ulath pulled in beside Sparhawk. "It's really none of my business," the shaggy-browned Genidian Knight said, "but you had twenty Pandions with you back there. Why didn't you just turn around and eliminate those soldiers and their bug?"

"Fifty dead soldiers scattered along a road would attract attention," Sparhawk explained, "and new graves are almost as obvious."

"Makes sense, I guess." Ulath grunted. "Living in an overpopulated kingdom has its own special problems, doesn't it? Up in Thalesia, the Trolls and Ogres usually clean up that sort of thing before anybody chances by."

Sparhawk shuddered. "Will they really eat carrion?" he asked, looking back over his shoulder for any sign of pursuit.

"Trolls and Ogres? Oh, yes—as long as the carrion's not too ripe. A nice fat church soldier will feed a family of Trolls for a week or so. That's one of the reasons there aren't very many church soldiers or their graveyards in Thalesia. The point, though, is that I don't like leaving live enemies behind me. Those church soldiers might come back to haunt us, and, if that thing they've got with them is as dangerous as Sephrenia says, we probably should have gotten it out of the way while we had the chance."

"Maybe you're right," Sparhawk admitted, "but it's too late now, I'm afraid. Olven's far out of reach. About all we can do is make a run for it and hope the soldiers' horses play out before ours do. When we get a chance, I'll want to talk with Sephrenia some more about that Seeker. I've got a feeling there were some things about it she wasn't telling me."

They rode hard for the rest of the day and saw no signs that the soldiers were anywhere behind them.

"There's a roadside inn just ahead," Kalten said as evening settled over the rolling countryside. "Do you want to chance it?"

Sparhawk looked at Sephrenia. "What do you think?"

"Only for a few hours," she said, "just long enough to feed the horses and give them some rest. The Seeker knows that we're not with that column by now, and it's certain to be following our trail. We have to move on."

"We could at least get some supper," Kalten added, "and maybe a couple hours of sleep. I've been up for a long time. Besides, we might be able to pick up some information if we ask the right questions."

The inn was run by a thin, good-humored fellow and his plump, jolly wife. It was a comfortable place and meticulously clean. The broad fireplace at one end of the common room did not smoke, and there were fresh rushes on the floor.

"We don't see many city folk this far out in the country," the innkeeper noted as he brought a platter of roast beef to the table, "and very seldom any knights—at least I judge from your garb that you're knights. What brings you this way, my Lords?''

"We're on our way to Pelosia," Kelten lied easily. "Church business. We're in a hurry, so we decided to cut across country.''

"There's a road that runs on up into Pelosia about three leagues to the south," the innkeeper advised helpfully.

"Roads wander around a lot," Kalten said, "and, as I told you, we're in a hurry.''

"Anything interesting happening hereabouts?'' Tynian asked as if only mildly curious.

The innkeeper laughed wryly. "What can possibly happen in a place like this? The local farmers spend all their time talking about a cow that died six months ago.'' He drew up a chair and sat down uninvited. He sighed. "I used to live in Cimmura when I was younger. Now, there's a place where things really happen. I miss all the excitement.''

"What made you decide to move out here?'' Kalten asked, spearing another slice of beef with his dagger.

"My father left me this place when he died. Nobody wanted to buy it, so I didn't have any choice.'' He frowned slightly. "Now that you mention it, though," he said, returning to the previous topic, "there has been something a little unusual happening around here for the last few months.''

"Oh?'' Tynian said carefully.

"We've been seeing bands of roving Styrics. The countryside's crawling with them. They don't usually move around that much, do they?''

"Not really," Sephrenia replied. "We're not a nomadic people.''

"I thought you might be Styric, lady—judging from your looks and your clothes. We've got a Styric village not far from here. They're nice enough people, I suppose, but they keep pretty much to themselves.'' He leaned back in his chair. "I do think you Styrics could avoid a lot of the trouble that breaks out from time to time if you'd just mingle with your neighbors a little more.''

"It's not our way,'' Sephrenia murmured. "I don't believe Elenes and Styrics are supposed to mingle.''

"There could be something to what you say,'' he agreed.

"Are these Styrics doing anything in particular?'' Sparhawk asked, keeping his voice neutral.

"Asking questions is about all. They seem to be very curious about the Zemoch war for some reason." He rose to his feet. "Enjoy your supper," he said and went back to the kitchen.

"We have a problem," Sephrenia said gravely. "Western Styrics do not wander about the countryside. Our Gods prefer to have us stay close to their altars."

"Zemochs then?" Bevier surmised.

"Almost certainly."

"When I was in Lamorkand, there were reports of Zemochs infiltrating the country east of Motera," Kalten remembered. "They were doing the same thing—wandering about the country asking questions, mostly having to do with folklore."

"Azash seems to have a plan that closely resembles ours," Sephrenia said. "He's trying to gather information that will lead him to Bhelliom."

"It's a race then," Kalten said.

"I'm afraid so, and he's got Zemochs out there ahead of us."

"And church soldiers behind," Ulath added. "You've gone and got us surrounded, Sparhawk. Could that Seeker be controlling those wandering Zemochs the same way it's controlling the soldiers?" the big Thalesian asked Sephrenia. "We could be riding into an ambush if it is, you know."

"I'm not entirely certain," she replied. "I've heard a great deal about Otha's Seekers, but I've never actually seen one in action."

"You didn't have time to be very specific this morning," Sparhawk said. "Exactly how is that thing controlling Annias' soldiers?"

"It's venomous," she said. "Its bite paralyzes the will of its victims—or of those it wants to dominate."

"I'll make a point of not letting it bite me then," Kalten said.

"You may not be able to stop it," she told him. "That green glow is hypnotic. That makes it easier for it to get close enough to inject the venom."

"How fast can it fly?" Tynian asked.

"It doesn't fly at this stage of its development," she replied. "Its wings don't mature until it becomes an adult. Besides, it has to be on the ground to follow the scent of the one it's trying to catch. Normally, it travels on horseback, and since the horse is controlled in the same way people are, the Seeker simply rides the horse to death and then finds another. It can cover a great deal of ground that way.''

"What does it eat?'' Kurik asked. "Maybe we can set a trap for it.''

"It feeds primarily on humans,'' she told him.

"That would make baiting a trap a little difficult,'' he admitted.

They all went to bed directly after supper, but it seemed to Sparhawk that his head had no sooner touched the pillow when Kurik shook him awake.

"It's about midnight,'' the squire said.

"All right,'' Sparhawk said wearily, sitting up in bed.

"I'll wake the others,'' Kurik said, "and then Berit and I'll go saddle the horses.''

After he had dressed, Sparhawk went downstairs to have a word with the sleepy innkeeper. "Tell me, neighbor,'' he said, "is there by any chance a monastery hereabouts?''

The innkeeper scratched his head. "I think there's one near the village of Verine,'' he replied. "That's about five leagues east of here.''

"Thanks, neighbor,'' Sparhawk said. He looked around. "You've got a nice, comfortable inn here,'' he said, "and your wife keeps clean beds and sets a very fine table. I'll mention your place to my friends.''

"Why, that's very kind of you, Sir Knight.''

Sparhawk nodded to him and went outside to join the others.

"What's the plan?'' Kalten asked.

"The innkeeper thinks there's a monastery near a village about five leagues away. We should reach it by morning. I want to get word of all this to Dolmant in Chyrellos.''

"I could take the message to him for you, Sir Sparhawk,'' Berit offered eagerly.

Sparhawk shook his head. "The Seeker probably has your scent by now, Berit. I don't want you getting ambushed on the road to Chyrellos. Let's send some anonymous monk instead. That monastery's on our way anyhow, so we won't be losing any time. Let's mount up.''

The moon was full and the night sky was clear as they rode away from the inn. "That way,'' Kurik said, pointing.

"How do you know that?" Talen asked him.

"The stars," Kurik replied.

"Do you mean you can actually tell direction by the stars?" Talen sounded impressed.

"Of course you can. Sailors have been doing that for thousands of years."

"I didn't know that."

"You should have stayed in school."

"I don't plan to be a sailor, Kurik. Stealing fish sounds a little too much like work to me."

They rode on through the moon-drenched night, moving almost due east. By morning they had come perhaps five leagues, and Sparhawk rode to a hilltop to look around. "There's a village just ahead," he told the others when he returned. "Let's hope it's the one we're looking for."

The village lay in a shallow valley. It was a small place, perhaps a dozen stone houses with a church at one end of its single cobbled street and a tavern at the other. A large, walled building stood atop a hill just outside of town. "Excuse me, neighbor," Sparhawk asked a passerby as they clattered into town. "Is this Verine?"

"It is."

"And is that the monastery up on that hill there?"

"It is," the man replied again, his voice a bit sullen.

"Is there some problem?"

"The monks up there own all the land hereabouts," the fellow replied. "Their rents are cruel."

"Isn't that always the way? All landlords are greedy."

"The monks insist on tithes as well as the rent. That's going a bit far, wouldn't you say?"

"You've got a point there."

"Why do you call everybody 'neighbor'?" Tynian asked as they rode on.

"Habit, I suppose." Sparhawk shrugged. "I got it from my father, and it sort of puts people at their ease."

"Why not call them 'friend'?"

"Because I never know that for sure. Let's go talk to the abbot of that monastery."

The monastery was a severe-looking building surrounded by a wall made of yellow sandstone. The fields around it were well tended, and monks wearing conical hats woven from local straw worked patiently under the morning sun in long, straight rows of vegetables. The gates of the monastery stood open, and Sparhawk and the others rode into the central courtyard. A thin, haggard-looking brother came out to meet them, his face a bit fearful looking.

"Good day, brother," Sparhawk said to him. He opened his cloak to reveal the heavy silver amulet hanging on a chain about his neck that identified him as a Pandion Knight. "If it's not too much trouble, we'd like to have a word with your abbot."

"I'll bring him immediately, my Lord." The brother scurried back inside the building.

The abbot was a jolly little fat man with a well-shaved tonsure and a bright red, sweaty face. His was a small, remote monastery and had little contact with Chyrellos. He was almost embarrassingly obsequious at the sudden unexpected appearance of Church Knights on his doorstep. "My Lords." He almost grovelled. "How may I serve you?"

"It's a small thing, my Lord Abbot," Sparhawk told him gently. "Are you acquainted with the Patriarch of Demos?"

The abbot swallowed hard. "Patriarch Dolmant?" he said in an awed voice.

"Tall fellow," Sparhawk agreed. "Sort of lean and underfed-looking. Anyway, we need to get a message to him. Have you a young monk who's got some stamina and a good horse who could carry a message to the Patriarch for us? It's in the service of the Church."

"O-of course, Sir Knight."

"I'd hoped you'd feel that way about it. Do you have a quill pen and ink handy, my Lord Abbot? I'll compose the message, and then we won't bother you anymore."

"One other thing, my Lord Abbot," Kalten added. "Might we trouble you for a bit of food? We've been some time on the road, and our supplies are getting low. Nothing too exotic, mind—a few roast chickens, perhaps, maybe a ham or two, a side of bacon, a hindquarter of beef, maybe?"

"Of course, Sir Knight," the abbot agreed quickly.

Sparhawk composed the note to Dolmant while Kurik and Kalten loaded the supplies on a pack horse.

"Did you have to do that?" Sparhawk asked Kalten as they rode away.

"Charity is a cardinal virtue, Sparhawk," Kalten replied loftily. "I like to encourage it whenever I can."

The countryside through which they galloped grew increasingly desolate. The soil was thin and poor, fit only for thornbushes and weeds. Here and there were pools of stagnant water, and the few trees standing near them were stunted and sick-looking. The weather had turned cloudy, and they rode through the tag end of a dreary afternoon.

Kurik pulled his gelding in beside Sparhawk. "Doesn't look too promising, does it?" he noted.

"Dismal," Sparhawk agreed.

"I think we're going to have to make camp somewhere tonight. The horses are almost played out."

"I'm not feeling too spry myself," Sparhawk admitted. His eyes felt gritty, and he had a dull headache.

"The only trouble is that I haven't seen any clean water for the last league or so. Why don't I take Berit and see if we can find a spring or stream?"

"Keep your eyes open," Sparhawk cautioned.

Kurik turned in his saddle. "Berit," he called, "I need you."

Sparhawk and the others rode on at a trot while the squire and the novice ranged out in search of clean water.

"We could just ride on, you know," Kalten said.

"Not unless you feel like walking before morning," Sparhawk replied. "Kurik's right. The horses don't have very much left in them."

"That's true, I suppose."

Then Kurik and Berit came pounding down a nearby hill at a gallop. "Get ready!" Kurik shouted, shaking loose his chain mace. "We've got company!"

"Sephrenia!" Sparhawk barked, "take Flute and get back behind those rocks. Talen, get the pack horses." He drew his sword and moved to the front, even as the others armed themselves.

There were fifteen or so of them, and they drove their horses over the hilltop at a run. It was an oddly assorted group, church soldiers in their red tunics, Styrics in homespun smocks, and a few peasants. Their faces were all blank, and their eyes dull. They charged on mindlessly, even though the heavily armed Church Knights were rushing to meet them.

Sparhawk and the others spread out, preparing to meet the charge. "For God and the Church!" Bevier shouted, brandishing his Lochaber ax. Then he spurred his horse forward, crashing into the middle of the oncoming attackers. Sparhawk was taken off guard by the young Cyrinic's rash move, but he quickly recovered and charged in to his companion's aid. Bevier, however, appeared to need little in the way of help. He warded off the clumsy-appearing sword strokes of the mindlessly charging ambushers with his shield, and his long-handled Lochaber whistled through the air to sink deep into the bodies of his enemies. Though the wounds he inflicted were hideous, the men he struck down made no outcry as they fell from their saddles. They fought and died in an eerie silence. Sparhawk rode behind Bevier, cutting down any of the numb-faced men who tried to attack the Cyrinic from behind. His sword sheared a church soldier almost in half, but the man in the red tunic did not even flinch. He raised his sword to strike at Bevier's back, but Sparhawk split his head open with a vast overhand stroke. The soldier toppled out of his saddle and lay twitching on the bloodstained grass.

Kalten and Tynian had flanked the attackers on either side and were chopping their way into the mêlée, while Ulath, Kurik, and Berit intercepted the few survivors who managed to make their way through the concerted counterattack.

The ground was soon littered with bodies in red tunics and bloody white Styric smocks. Riderless horses plunged away from the fight, squealing in panic. In normal circumstances, Sparhawk knew the attackers bringing up the rear would falter and then flee when they saw what had befallen their comrades. These expressionless men, however, continued their attack, and it was necessary to kill them to the last man.

"Sparhawk!" Sephrenia shouted. "Up there!" She was pointing toward the hilltop over which the attack had come. It was the tall, skeletal figure in the black hooded robe that Sparhawk had seen twice before. It sat its horse atop the hill with that faint green glow emanating from its concealed face.

"That thing's starting to bore me," Kalten said. "The best way to get rid of a bug is to step on it." He raised his shield and thumped his heels to his horse's flanks. He started to gallop up the hill, his blade held menacingly aloft.

"Kalten! No!" Sephrenia's shout was shrill with fright. But Kalten paid no attention to her warning. Sparhawk swore and started after his friend.

But then Kalten was suddenly hurled from his saddle by some unseen force as the figure atop the hill gestured almost contemptuously. With revulsion Sparhawk saw that what emerged from the sleeve of the black robe was not a hand, but more closely resembled the front claw of a scorpion.

And then, even as he swung down from Faran's back to run to Kalten's aid, Sparhawk gaped in astonishment. Somehow Flute had escaped from Sephrenia's watchful eye and had advanced to the foot of the hill. She stamped one grass-stained little foot imperiously and lifted her rude pipes to her lips. Her melody was stern, even slightly discordant; for some peculiar reason, it seemed to be accompanied by a vast, unseen choir of human voices. The hooded figure on the hilltop reeled back in its saddle as if it had been struck a massive blow. Flute's song rose, and that unseen choir swelled its song in a mighty crescendo. The sound was so overpowering that Sparhawk was forced to cover his ears. The song had reached the level of physical pain.

The figure shrieked, a dreadfully inhuman sound, and it also clapped its claws to the sides of its hooded head. Then it wheeled its horse and fled down the far side of the hill.

There was no time to pursue the monstrosity. Kalten lay gasping on the ground, his face pale and his hands clutching at his stomach.

"Are you all right?" Sparhawk demanded, kneeling beside his friend.

"Leave me alone," Kalten wheezed.

"Don't be stupid. Are you hurt?"

"No. I'm lying here for fun." The blond man drew in a shuddering breath. "What did it hit me with? I've never been hit that hard before."

"You'd better let me have a look at you."

"I'm all right, Sparhawk. It just knocked the breath out of me, that's all."

"You idiot. You know what that thing is. What were you thinking of?" Sparhawk was suddenly, irrationally angry.

"It seemed like a good idea at the time." Kalten grinned weakly. "Maybe I should have thought my way through it a little more."

"Is he hurt?" Bevier asked, dismounting and coming toward them, his face showing his concern.

"I think he'll be all right." Then Sparhawk rose, controlling his temper with some effort. "Sir Bevier," he said rather formally, "you've had training in this sort of thing. You know what you're supposed to do when you're under attack. What possessed you to dash into the middle of them like that?''

"I didn't think there were all that many of them, Sparhawk," Bevier replied defensively.

"There were enough. It only takes one to kill you."

"You're vexed with me, aren't you, Sparhawk?" Bevier's voice was mournful.

Sparhawk looked at the young knight's earnest face for a moment. Then he sighed. "No, Bevier, I guess not. You just startled me, that's all. Please, for the sake of my nerves, don't do unexpected things any more. I'm not getting any younger, and surprises age me."

"Perhaps I didn't consider the feelings of my comrades," Bevier admitted contritely. "I promise it will not happen again."

"I appreciate that, Bevier. Let's help Kalten back down the hill. I want Sephrenia to take a look at him, and I'm sure she'll want to have a talk with him—a nice long one."

Kalten winced. "I don't suppose I could talk you into leaving me here? This is nice soft dirt."

"Not a chance, Kalten," Sparhawk replied ruthlessly. "Don't worry, though. She likes you, so she probably won't do anything to you—nothing permanent, anyway."

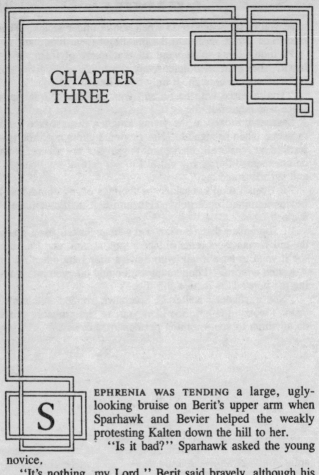

CHAPTER
THREE

SEPHRENIA WAS TENDING a large, ugly-looking bruise on Berit's upper arm when Sparhawk and Bevier helped the weakly protesting Kalten down the hill to her.

"Is it bad?" Sparhawk asked the young novice.

"It's nothing, my Lord," Berit said bravely, although his face was pale.

"Is that the very first thing they teach you Pandions?" Sephrenia asked acidly. "To make light of your injuries? Berit's mail shirt stopped most of the blow, but in about an hour his arm's going to be purple from elbow to shoulder. He'll barely be able to use it."

"You're in a cheerful humor this afternoon, little mother," Kalten said to her.

She pointed a threatening finger at him. "Kalten," she said, "sit. I'll deal with you after I've tended Berit's arm."

Kalten sighed and slumped down onto the ground.

Sparhawk looked around. "Where are Ulath, Tynian, and Kurik?" he asked.

"They're scouting around to make sure there aren't any more ambushes laid for us, Sir Sparhawk," Berit replied.

"Good idea."

"That creature didn't look so very dangerous to me," Bevier said. "A little mysterious perhaps, but not all that dangerous."

"It didn't hit *you*," Kalten told him. "It's dangerous, all right. Take my word for it."

"It's more dangerous than you could possibly imagine," Sephrenia said. "It can send whole armies after us."

"If it's got the kind of power that knocked me off my horse, it doesn't *need* armies."

"You keep forgetting, Kalten. Its mind is the mind of Azash. The Gods prefer to have humans do their work for them."

"The men who came down that hill were like sleepwalkers," Bevier said, shuddering. "We cut them to pieces, and they didn't make a sound." He paused, frowning. "I didn't think Styrics were so aggressive," he added. "I've never seen one with a sword in his hand before."

"Those weren't western Styrics," Sephrenia said, tying off the padded bandage around Berit's upper arm. "Try not to use that too much," she instructed. "Give it time to heal."

"Yes, ma'am," Berit replied. "Now that you mention it, though, it *is* getting a little sore."

She smiled and put an affectionate hand on his shoulder. "This one may be all right, Sparhawk. His head isn't *quite* solid bone—like some I could name." She glanced meaningfully at Kalten.

"Sephrenia," the blond knight protested.

"Get out of the mail shirt," she told him crisply. "I want to see if you've broken anything."

"You said the Styrics in that group weren't western Styrics," Bevier said to her.

"No. They were Zemochs. It's more or less what we guessed at back at that inn. The Seeker will use anybody, but a western Styric is incapable of using weapons made of steel.

If they'd been local people, their swords would have been bronze or copper.'' She looked critically at Kalten, who had just removed his mail shirt. She shuddered. "You look like a blond rug," she told him.

"It's not my fault, little mother," he said, suddenly blushing. "All the men in my family have been hairy."

Bevier looked puzzled. "What finally drove that creature off?" he asked.

"Flute," Sparhawk replied. "She's done it before. She even ran off the Damork once with her pipes."

"This tiny child?" Bevier's tone was incredulous.

"There's more to Flute than meets the eye," Sparhawk told him. He looked out across the slope of the hill. "Talen," he shouted, "stop that."

Talen, who had been busily pillaging the dead, looked up with some consternation. "But Sparhawk—" he began.

"Just come away from there. That's disgusting."

"But—"

"Do as he says!" Berit roared.

Talen sighed and came back down the hill.

"Let's go round up the horses, Bevier," Sparhawk said. "As soon as Kurik and the others get back, I think we'll want to move on. That Seeker is still out there, and it can come at us with a whole new group of people at any time."

"It can do that at night as well as in the daylight, Sparhawk," Bevier said dubiously, "and it can follow our scent."

"I know. At this point I think speed is our only defense. We're going to have to try to outrun that thing again."

Kurik, Ulath, and Tynian returned as dusk was settling over the desolate landscape. "There doesn't seem to be anybody else out there," the squire reported, swinging down from his gelding.

"We're going to have to keep going," Sparhawk told him.

"The horses are right on the verge of exhaustion, Sparhawk," the squire protested. He looked at the others. "And the people aren't in much better shape. None of us has had very much sleep in the past two days."

"I'll take care of it," Sephrenia said calmly, looking up from her examination of Kalten's hairy torso.

"How?" Kalten sounded just a bit grumpy.

She smiled at him and wiggled her fingers under his nose. "How else?"

"If there's a spell that counteracts the way we're all feeling right now, why didn't you teach it to us before?" Sparhawk was also feeling somewhat surly, since his headache had returned.

"Because it's dangerous, Sparhawk," she replied. "I know you Pandions. Given certain circumstances, you'd try to go on for weeks."

"So? If the spell really works, what difference does it make?"

"The spell only makes you *feel* as if you've rested, but you have not, in fact. If you push it too far, you'll die."

"Oh. That stands to reason, I guess."

"I'm glad you understand."

"How's Berit?" Tynian asked.

"He'll be sore for a while, but he's all right," she replied.

"The young fellow shows some promise," Ulath said. "When his arm heals, I'll give him some instruction with that ax of his. He's got the right spirit, but his technique's a little shaky."

"Bring the horses over here," Sephrenia told them. She began to speak in Styric, uttering some of the words under her breath and concealing her moving fingers from them. Try though he might, Sparhawk could not catch all of the incantation nor even guess at the gestures that enhanced the spell. Then he suddenly felt enormously refreshed. The dull headache was gone, and his mind was clear. One of the pack horses, whose head had been drooping and whose legs had been trembling violently, actually began to prance around like a colt.

"Good spell," Ulath said laconically. "Shall we get started?"

They helped Berit into his saddle and rode out in the luminous twilight. The full moon rose an hour or so later, and it gave them sufficient light to risk a canter.

"There's a road just over that hill up ahead," Kurik told Sparhawk. "We saw it when we were looking around. It goes more or less in the right direction, and we could make better time if we follow it instead of stumbling over broken ground in the dark."

"I expect you're right," Sparhawk agreed, "and we want to get out of this area as quickly as possible."

When they reached the road, they pushed on to the east at

a gallop. It was well past midnight when clouds moved in from the west, obscuring the night sky. Sparhawk muttered an oath and slowed their pace.

Just before dawn they came to a river, and the road turned north. They followed it, searching for a bridge or a ford. The dawn was gloomy under the heavy cloud cover. They rode upriver a few more miles, and then the road bent east again and ran down into the river to emerge on the far side.

Beside the ford stood a small hut. The man who owned the hut was a sharp-eyed fellow in a green tunic who demanded a toll to cross. Rather than argue with him, Sparhawk paid what he asked. "Tell me, neighbor," he said when the transaction was completed, "how far is the Pelosian border?"

"About five leagues," the sharp-eyed fellow replied. "If you move along, you should reach it by afternoon."

"Thanks, neighbor. You've been most helpful."

They splashed on across the ford. When they reached the other side, Talen rode up beside Sparhawk. "Here's your money back," the young thief said, handing over several coins.

Sparhawk gave him a startled look.

"I don't object to paying a toll to cross a bridge," Talen sniffed. "After all, somebody had to go to the expense of building it. That fellow was just taking advantage of a natural shallow place in the river, though. It didn't cost him anything, so why should he make a profit from it?"

"You cut his purse, then?"

"Naturally."

"And there was more in it than just my coins?"

"A bit. Let's call it my fee for recovering your money. After all, I deserve a profit too, don't I?"

"You're incorrigible."

"I needed the practice."

From the other side of the river there came a howl of anguish.

"I'd say he just discovered his loss," Sparhawk observed.

"It does sort of sound that way, doesn't it?"

The soil on the far side of the river was not a great deal better than the scrubby wasteland through which they had just passed. Occasionally they saw poor farmsteads where shabby-looking peasants in muddy brown smocks labored long and hard to wrest scanty crops from the unyielding earth. Kurik sniffed disdainfully. "Amateurs," he grunted. Kurik took farming very seriously.

About midmorning, the narrow track they were following joined a well-travelled road that ran due east. "A suggestion, Sparhawk," Tynian said, shifting his blue-blazoned shield.

"Suggest away."

"It might be better if we took this road to the border rather than cutting across country again. Pelosians tend to be sensitive about people who avoid the manned border crossings. They're obsessively concerned about smugglers. I don't think we'd accomplish very much in a skirmish with one of their patrols."

"All right," Sparhawk agreed. "Let's stay out of trouble if we can."

Not very long after a dreary, sunless noon, they reached the border and passed without incident into the southern end of Pelosia. The farmsteads here were even more run-down than they had been in northeastern Elenia. The houses and outbuildings were universally roofed with sod, and agile goats grazed on the roofs. Kurik looked about disapprovingly, but said nothing.

As evening settled over the landscape, they crested a hill and saw the twinkling lights of a village in the valley below. "An inn perhaps?" Kalten suggested. "I think Sephrenia's spell is starting to wear off. My horse is staggering, and I'm not in much better shape."

"You won't sleep alone in a Pelosian inn," Tynian warned. "Their beds are usually occupied by all sorts of unpleasant little creatures."

"Fleas?" Kalten asked.

"And lice and bedbugs the size of mice."

"I guess we'll have to risk it," Sparhawk decided. "The horses won't be able to go much farther, and I don't think the Seeker would attack us inside a building. It seems to prefer open country." He led the way down the hill to the village.

The streets of the town were unpaved, and they were ankledeep in mud. They reached the town's only inn, and Sparhawk carried Sephrenia to the porch while Kurik followed with Flute. The steps leading up to the door were caked with mud, and the boot scraper beside the door showed little signs of use. Pelosians, it appeared, were indifferent to mud. The interior of the inn was dim and smoky, and it smelled strongly of stale sweat and spoiled food. The floor had at one time been covered with rushes, but, except in the corners, the rushes were buried in dried mud.

"Are you sure you don't want to reconsider this?" Tynian asked Kalten as they entered.

"My stomach's fairly strong," Kalten replied, "and I caught a whiff of beer when we came in."

The supper the innkeeper provided was at least marginally edible, although a bit overgarnished with boiled cabbage, and the beds, mere straw pallets, were not nearly so bug-infested as Tynian had predicted.

They rose early the next morning and rode out of the muddy village in a murky dawn.

"Doesn't the sun ever shine in this part of the world?" Talen asked sourly.

"It's spring," Kurik told him. "It's always cloudy and rainy in the spring. It's good for the crops."

"I'm not a radish, Kurik," the boy replied. "I don't need to be watered."

"Talk to God about it." Kurik shrugged. "I don't make the weather."

"God and I aren't on the best of terms," Talen said glibly. "He's busy, and so am I. We try not to interfere with each other."

"The boy is pert," Bevier observed disapprovingly. "Young man," he said, "it is not proper to speak so of the Lord of the Universe."

"You are an honored Knight of the Church, Sir Bevier," Talen pointed out. "I am but a thief of the street. Different rules apply to us. God's great flower garden needs a few weeds to offset the splendor of the roses. I'm a weed. I'm sure God forgives me for that, since I'm a part of his grand design."

Bevier looked at him helplessly, and then began to laugh.

They rode warily across southeastern Pelosia for the next several days, taking turns scouting on ahead and riding to hilltops to survey the surrounding countryside. The sky remained dreary as they pushed on to the east. They saw peasants—serfs actually—laboring in the fields with the crudest of implements. There were birds nesting in the hedges, and occasionally they saw deer grazing among herds of scrubby cattle.

While there were people about, Sparhawk and his friends saw no more church soldiers or Zemochs. They remained cautious, however, avoiding people when possible, and continuing their scouting, since they all knew the black-robed Seeker could enlist even normally timid serfs to do its bidding.

As they came closer to the border of Lamorkand, they received increasingly disturbing reports concerning turmoil in that kingdom. Lamorks were not the most stable people in the world. The King of Lamorkand ruled only at the sufferance of the largely independent barons, who retreated in times of trouble to positions behind the walls of massive castles. Blood feuds dating back a hundred years or more were common, and rogue barons looted and pillaged at will. For the most part, Lamorkand existed in a state of perpetual civil war.

They made camp one night perhaps three leagues from the border of that most troubled of western kingdoms, and Sparhawk stood up directly after a supper of the last of Kalten's hindquarter of beef. "All right," he said, "what are we walking into? What's stirring things up in Lamorkand? Any ideas?"

"I spent the last eight or nine years in Lamorkand," Kalten said seriously. "They're strange people. A Lamork will sacrifice anything he owns for the sake of revenge—and the women are even worse than the men. A good Lamork girl will spend her whole life—and all her father's wealth—for the chance to sink a spear into somebody who refused her invitation to the dance at some midwinter party. I spent all those years there, and in all that time, I never heard anyone laugh or saw anyone smile. It's the bleakest place on earth. The sun is forbidden to shine in Lamorkand."

"Is this universal warfare we've been hearing about from the Pelosians a common thing?" Sparhawk asked.

"Pelosians are not the best judges of Lamork peculiarities," Tynian replied thoughtfully. "It's only the influence of the Church—and the presence of the Church Knights—that's kept Pelosia and Lamorkand from blithely embarking on a war of mutual extinction. They despise each other with a passion that's almost holy in its mindless ferocity."

Sephrenia sighed. "Elenes," she said.

"We have our faults, little mother," Sparhawk conceded. "We're going to run into trouble when we cross the border then, aren't we?"

"Not entirely," Tynian said, rubbing his chin. "Are you open to another suggestion, maybe?"

"I'm always open to suggestions."

"Why don't we put on our formal armor? Not even the most wild-eyed Lamork baron will willingly cross the Church, and the Church Knights could grind western Lamorkand into powder if they felt like it."

"What if somebody calls our bluff?" Kalten asked. "There are only five of us, after all."

"I don't think they'd have any reason to," Tynian said. "The neutrality of the Church Knights in these local disputes is legendary. Formal armor might be just the thing to avoid misunderstandings. Our purpose is to get to Lake Randera, not to engage in random disputes with hotheads."

"It might work, Sparhawk," Ulath said. "It's worth a try, anyway."

"All right, let's do it then," Sparhawk decided.

When they arose the following morning, the five knights unpacked their formal armor and began to put it on with the help of Kurik and Berit. Sparhawk and Kalten wore Pandion black with silver surcoats and formal black capes. Bevier's armor was burnished to a silvery sheen, and his surcoat and cape were pristine white. Tynian's armor was simply massive steel, but his surcoat and cape were a brilliant sky blue. Ulath put aside the utilitarian mail shirt he had worn on the trail and replaced it with chain-mail trousers and a mail coat that reached to midthigh. He stowed away his simple conical helmet and green traveller's cloak and put on instead a green surcoat and a very impressive-looking helmet surmounted by a pair of the curled and twisted horns he had identified as having come from an Ogre.

"Well?" Sparhawk said to Sephrenia when they had finished putting on their finery, "how do we look?"

"Very impressive," she complimented them.

Talen, however, eyed them critically. "They look sort of like an ironworks that sprouted legs, don't they?" he observed to Berit.

"Be polite," Berit said, concealing a smile behind one hand.

"That's depressing," Kalten said to Sparhawk. "Do you think we really look that ridiculous to the common people?"

"Probably."

Kurik and Berit cut lances from a nearby yew grove and affixed steel points to them.

"Pennons?" Kurik asked.

"What do you think?" Sparhawk asked Tynian.

"It couldn't hurt. Let's try to look as impressive as we can, I suppose."

They mounted with some difficulty, adjusted their shields and moved their pennon-flagged lances into positions where they were prominently displayed, and rode out. Faran immediately began to prance. "Oh, stop that," Sparhawk told him disgustedly.

They crossed into Lamorkand not much past noon. The border guards looked suspicious, but automatically gave way to the Knights of the Church dressed in their formal armor and wearing expressions of inexorable resolve.

The Lamork city of Kadach stood on the far side of a river. There was a bridge, but Sparhawk decided against going through that bleak, ugly place. Instead, he checked his map and turned north. "The river branches upstream," he told the others. "We'll be able to ford it up there. We're going more or less in that direction anyway, and towns are filled with people who just might want to talk to alien strangers asking questions about us."

They rode on north to the series of small streams that fed into the main channel. It was when they were crossing one of those shallow streams that afternoon that they saw a large body of Lamork warriors on the far bank.

"Spread out," Sparhawk commanded tersely. "Sephrenia, take Talen and Flute to the rear."

"You think they might belong to the Seeker?" Kalten asked, moving his hand up the shaft of his lance.

"We'll find out in a minute. Don't do anything rash, but be ready for trouble."

The leader of the group of warriors was a burly fellow wearing a chain coat, a steel helmet with a protruding, pig-faced visor, and stout leather boots. He advanced into the stream alone and raised his visor to show that he had no hostile intentions.

"I think he's all right, Sparhawk," Bevier said quietly. "He doesn't have that blank look on his face that the men we killed back in Elenia had."

"Well met, Sir Knights," the Lamork said.

Sparhawk nudged Faran forward a bit through the swirling current. "Well met indeed, my Lord," he replied.

"This is a fortunate encounter," the Lamork continued. "It seemed me that we might have ridden even so far as Elenia ere we had encountered Church Knights."

"And what is your business with the Knights of the Church, my Lord?" Sparhawk asked politely.

"We require a service of you, Sir Knight—a service that bears directly on the well-being of the Church."

"We live but to serve her," Sparhawk said, struggling to conceal his irritation. "Speak further concerning this necessary service."

"As all the world knows, the Patriarch of Kadash is the paramount choice for the Archprelate's throne in Chyrellos," the helmeted Lamork stated.

"I hadn't heard that," Kalten said quietly from behind.

"Hush," Sparhawk muttered over his shoulder. "Say on, my Lord," he said to the Lamork.

"Misfortunately, civil turmoil mars western Lamorkand presently," the Lamork continued.

"I like 'misfortunately,'" Tynian murmured to Kalten. "It's got a nice ring to it."

"*Will* you two be quiet?" Sparhawk snapped. Then he looked back at the man in the chain coat. "Rumor has advised us of this discord, my Lord," he replied. "But surely this is a local matter, and does not involve the Church."

"I will speak to the point, Sir Knight. The Patriarch Ortzel of Kadach has been forced by the turmoil I but recently mentioned to seek shelter in the stronghold of his brother, the Baron Alstrom, whom I have the honor to serve. Rude civil discord rears its head here in Lamorkand, and we anticipate with some certainty that the foes of my Lord Alstrom will shortly besiege his fortress."

"We are but five, my Lord," Sparhawk pointed out. "Surely our aid would be of little use in a protracted siege."

"Ah, no, Sir Knight," the Lamork said with a disdainful

smile. "We can sustain ourselves and my Lord Alstrom's castle without the aid of the invincible Knights of the Church. My Lord Alstrom's castle is impregnable, and his foes may freely dash themselves to bits against its walls for a generation or more without causing us alarm. As I have said, however, the Patriarch Ortzel is the paramount choice for the Archprelacy—in the event of the demise of the revered Cluvonus, which, please God, may be delayed for a time. Thus I charge you and your noble companions, Sir Knight, to convey his Grace safe and whole to the sacred city of Chyrellos so that he may stand for election, should that mournful necessity come to pass. With that end in view, I will forthwith convey you and your knightly companions to the stronghold of my Lord of Alstrom so that you may undertake this noble task. Let us then proceed."

CHAPTER
FOUR

HE CASTLE OF Baron Alstrom was situated on a rocky promontory on the east bank of the river. The promontory jutted out into the main channel a few leagues above the town of Kadach. It was a bleak, ugly fortress, squatting toadlike under a cheerless sky. Its walls were thick and high, seeming to reflect the stiff, unyielding arrogance of its owner.

"Impregnable?" Bevier murmured derisively to Sparhawk as the knight in the chain coat preceded them along the short causeway that led out to the castle gate. "I could reduce these walls within the space of two years. No Arcian noble would feel secure within such flimsy fortifications."

"Arcians have more time to build their castles," Sparhawk pointed out to the white-caped knight. "It takes longer to start a war in Arcium than it does here in Lamorkand. You can start a war here in about five minutes, and it's likely to go on for generations.''

"Truly," Bevier agreed. He smiled faintly. "In my youth I gave some time to the study of military history. When I turned to the volumes dealing with Lamorkand, I threw up my hands in despair. No rational man could sort out all the alliances, betrayals, and blood feuds that seethe just below the surface of this unhappy kingdom.''

The drawbridge boomed down, and they clattered on across it into the castle's main court. "And it please you, Sir Knights," the Lamork knight said, dismounting, "I will convey you directly into the presence of the Baron Alstrom and his Grace, the Patriarch Ortzel. Time is pressing, and we must see his Grace safely out of the castle ere the forces of Count Gerrich mount their siege.''

"Lead on, Sir Knight," Sparhawk said, clanking down from Faran's back. He leaned his lance against the wall of the stable, hung his silver-embossed black shield on his saddle, and handed his reins to a waiting groom.

They went up a broad stone staircase and through the pair of massive doors at its top. The hallway beyond was torchlit, and the stones of its walls were massive. "Did you warn that groom?" Kalten asked, falling in beside Sparhawk, his long black cape swirling about his ankles.

"About what?"

"Your horse's disposition."

"I forgot," Sparhawk confessed. "He'll find out on his own, I imagine.''

"He probably already has."

The room to which the Lamork knight led them was bleak. In many respects it was more like an armory than living quarters. Swords and axes hung on the walls, and pikes in clusters of a dozen or so leaned in the corners. A fire burned in a huge, vaulted fireplace, and the few chairs were heavy and unpadded. There was no carpeting on the floor, and a number of huge wolfhounds dozed here and there.

Baron Alstrom was a grim-faced, melancholy-looking man. His black hair and beard were shot with gray. He wore a mail coat and had a broadsword at his waist. His surcoat was black and elaborately embroidered in red, and like the knight in the pig-faced helmet, he wore boots.

Their escort bowed stiffly. "By good fortune, my Lord, I encountered these Knights of the Church no more than a league from your walls. They were gracious enough to accompany me here."

"Did we have any choice?" Kalten muttered.

The Baron rose from his chair with a movement made clumsy by the encumbrance of armor and sword. "Greetings, Sir Knights," he said in a voice without much warmth. "It was indeed fortuitous that Sir Enmann encountered you so near this stronghold. The forces of mine enemy will presently besiege me here, and my brother must be safely away before they come."

"Yes, my Lord," Sparhawk replied, removing his black helmet and looking after the departing Lamork in the chain coat. "Sir Enmann advised us of the circumstances. Might it not have been more prudent, however, to have sent your brother on his way with an escort of your own troops? It was only a chance meeting that brought us to your gate before your enemies come."

Alstrom shook his head. "The warriors of County Gerrich would certainly attack my men on sight. Only under escort of the Knights of the Church will my brother be safe, Sir—?"

"Sparhawk."

Alstrom looked briefly surprised. "The name is not unknown to us," he said. He looked inquiringly at the others, and Sparhawk made the introductions.

"An oddly assorted party, Sir Sparhawk," Alstrom observed after he had bowed perfunctorily to Sephrenia. "But is it wise to take the lady and the two children on a journey that might involve danger?"

"The lady is essential to our purpose," Sparhawk replied. "The little girl is under her care, and the boy is her page. She would not leave them behind."

"Page?" he heard Talen whisper to Berit. "I've been called a lot of things, but that's a new one."

"Hush," Berit whispered back.

"What astonishes me even more, however," Alstrom continued, "is the fact that all four of the militant orders are represented here. Relations between the orders have not been cordial of late, I've been told."

"We are embarked upon a quest which directly involves

the Church," Sparhawk explained, taking off his gauntlets. "It is of such pressing urgency that our preceptors brought us together that we might by our unity prevail."

"The unity of the Church Knights, like that of the Church herself, is long overdue," a harsh voice said from the far side of the room. A churchman stepped out of the shadows. His black cassock was plain, even severe, and his hollow-cheeked face was bleakly ascetic. His hair was pale blond, streaked with gray, and it fell straight to his shoulders, appearing to have been hacked off at that point with the blade of a knife.

"My brother," Alstrom introduced him, "the Patriarch Ortzel of Kadach."

Sparhawk bowed, his armor creaking slightly. "Your Grace," he said.

"This Church matter you mentioned interests me," Ortzel said, coming forward into the light. "What can it be that is of such urgency that it impels the preceptors of the four orders to set aside old enmities and to send their champions forth as one?"

Sparhawk thought only a moment, then gambled. "Is your Grace perhaps acquainted with Annias, Primate of Cimmura?" he asked, depositing his gauntlets in his helmet.

Ortzel's face hardened. "We've met," he said flatly.

"We've also had that pleasure," Kalten said dryly, "often enough more than to satisfy me, at least."

Ortzel smiled briefly. "I gather that our opinions of the good primate more or less coincide," he suggested.

"Your Grace is perceptive," Sparhawk noted smoothly. "The Primate of Cimmura aspires to a position in the Church for which our preceptors feel he is unqualified."

"I have heard of his aspirations in that direction."

"This is the main thrust of our quest, your Grace," Sparhawk explained. "The Primate of Cimmura is deeply involved in the politics of Elenia. The lawful Queen of that realm is Ehlana, daughter to the late King Aldreas. She is, however, gravely ill, and Primate Annias controls the royal council—which means, of course, that he also controls the royal treasury. It is his access to that treasury that fuels his hopes to ascend the throne of the Archprelacy. He has more or less unlimited funds at his disposal, and certain members of the Hierocracy have proved to be susceptible to his blandishments. It is our mission to restore the Queen to health so that she might once again take the rulership of her kingdom into her own hands.''

"An unseemly state of affairs," Baron Alstrom observed disapprovingly. "No kingdom should be ruled by a woman."

"I have the honor to be the Queen's Champion, my Lord," Sparhawk declared, "and, I hope, her friend as well. I have known her since she was a child and I assure you that Ehlana is no ordinary woman. She has more steel in her than almost any other monarch in all of Eosia. Once she is restored to health, she will be more than a match for the Primate of Cimmura. She will cut off his access to the treasury as easily as she would snip off a stray lock of hair, and without that money, the Primate's hopes die."

"Then your quest is a noble one, Sir Sparhawk," Patriarch Ortzel approved, "but why has it brought you to Lamorkand?"

"May I speak frankly, your Grace?"

"Of course."

"We have recently discovered that Queen Ehlana's illness is not of natural origin, and to cure her we must resort to extreme measures."

"You're speaking too delicately, Sparhawk," Ulath growled, removing his Ogre-horned helmet. "What my Pandion brother is trying to say, your Grace, is that Queen Ehlana has been poisoned, and that we'll have to use magic to bring her back to health."

"Poisoned?" Ortzel paled. "Surely you do not suspect Primate Annias?"

"Everything points that way, your Grace," Tynian said, pushing back his blue cape. "The details are tedious, but we have strong evidence that Annias was behind it all."

"You must bring these charges before the Hierocracy!" Ortzel exclaimed. "If they are true, this is monstrous."

"The matter is already in the hands of the Patriarch of Demos, your Grace," Sparhawk assured him. "I think we can trust him to lay it before the Hierocracy at the proper time."

"Dolmant is a good man," Ortzel agreed. "I'll abide by his decision in the matter—for the time being, at least."

"Please be seated, Sir Knights," the baron said. "The urgency of this present situation has made me remiss in matters of courtesy. Might I offer you some refreshment?"

Kalten's eyes brightened.

"Never mind," Sparhawk muttered to him, holding a chair for Sephrenia. She sat, and Flute came over and climbed up into her lap.

"Your daughter, Madame?" Ortzel surmised.

"No, your Grace. She's a foundling—of sorts. I'm fond of her, however."

"Berit," Kurik said, "we're just in the way here. Let's go to the stables. I want to check over the horses." And the two of them left the room.

"Tell me, my Lord," Bevier said to Baron Alstrom, "what is it that has brought you to the brink of war? Some ancient dispute, perhaps?"

"No, Sir Bevier," the baron replied, his face hardening, "this is an affair of more recent origin. Perhaps a year ago my only son became friendly with a knight who said he was from Cammoria. I have since discovered that the man is a villain. He encouraged my young and foolish son in a vain hope of obtaining the hand of the daughter of my neighbor, Count Gerrich. The girl seemed amenable, though her father and I have never been friends. Not long after, however, Gerrich announced that he had promised his daughter's hand to another. My son was enraged. His so-called friend goaded him on in this and proposed a desperate plan. They could abduct the girl, find a priest willing to marry her to my son, and present Gerrich with a number of grandchildren to still his wrath. They scaled the walls of the count's castle and crept into the girl's bedchamber. I have since discovered that my son's supposed friend had alerted the count, and Gerrich and his sister's seven sons sprang from hiding as the two entered. My son, believing that it had been the count's daughter who had betrayed him, plunged his dagger into her breast before the count's nephews fell upon him with their swords." Alstrom paused, his teeth clenched and his eyes brimming.

"My son was obviously in the wrong," he admitted, continuing his story, "and I would not have pursued the matter, grieved though I was. It was what happened after my son's death that has set eternal enmity between Gerrich and myself. Not content with merely killing my son, the count and his sister's savage brood mutilated his body and contemptuously deposited it at my castle gate. I was outraged, but the Cammorian knight, whom I still trusted, advised guile. He pled matters of pressing urgency in Cammorian, but promised me the aid of two of his trusted retainers. It was but last week when the two arrived at my door to tell me that the time for my revenge had come. They led my soldiers to the house of the count's sister, and there they slaughtered the count's seven nephews. I have since discovered that these two underlings inflamed my soldiers, and they took certain liberties with the person of Gerrich's sister.''

"That's a delicate way to put it," Kalten whispered to Sparhawk.

"Be still," Sparhawk whispered back.

"The lady was dispatched—naked, I'm afraid—to her brother's castle. Reconciliation is now quite impossible. Gerrich has many allies, as do I, and western Lamorkand now hovers on the brink of general war.''

"A melancholy tale, my Lord," Sparhawk said sadly.

"The impending war is *my* concern. What is important now is to remove my brother from this house and to convey him safely to Chyrellos. Should he also fall during Gerrich's attack, the Church will have no choice but to send in her Knights. The murder of a patriarch—particularly one who is a strong candidate for elevation to the Archprelacy—would be a crime she could not ignore. Thus it is that I implore you to safeguard him on his way to the Holy City.''

"One question, my Lord," Sparhawk said. "The activities of this Cammorian knight have a familiar ring to them. Can you describe him and his underlings to us?''

"The knight himself is a tall man with an arrogant bearing. One of his companions is a huge brute, scarcely human. The other is a rabbity fellow with an excessive fondness for strong drink.''

"Sounds a bit like some old friends, doesn't it?" Kalten said to Sparhawk. "Was there anything unusual about this knight?''

"His hair was absolutely white," Alstrom replied, "and he was not that old.''

"Martel certainly moves around, doesn't he?" Kalten observed.

"You know this man, Sir Kalten?" the baron asked.

"The white-haired man is named Martel," Sparhawk explained. "His two hirelings are Adus and Krager. Martel's a renegade Pandion Knight who hires out his services in various parts of the world. Most recently, he's been working for the Primate of Cimmura.''

"But what would be the primate's purpose in fomenting discord between Gerrich and me?''

"You've already touched on that, my Lord,'' Sparhawk replied. "The preceptors of the four militant orders are firmly opposed to the notion of Annias sitting on the Archprelate's throne. They will be present—and voting—during the election in the Basilica of Chyrellos, and their opinion carries great weight with the Hierocracy. Moreover, the Knights of the Church would respond immediately to the first hint of any irregularities in the election. If Annias is to succeed, he must get the Church Knights out of Chyrellos before the election. We were recently able to thwart a plot that Martel was hatching in Rendor that would have pulled the Knights out of the Holy City. It's my guess that this unhappy affair you told us about is yet another. Martel, acting on orders from Annias, is roaming the world building bonfires in the hope that sooner or later the Knights of the Church will be forced to move out of Chyrellos to extinguish them.''

"Is Annias truly so depraved?'' Ortzel asked.

"Your Grace, Annias will do *anything* to ascend that throne. I'm positive that he'd order the massacre of half of Eosia to get what he wants.''

"How is it possible for a churchman to stoop so low?''

"Ambition, your Grace,'' Bevier said sadly. "Once it sinks its claws into a man's heart, the man becomes blind to all else.''

"This is all the more reason to get my brother safely to Chyrellos,'' Alstrom said gravely. "He is much respected by the other members of the Hierocracy, and his voice will carry great weight in their deliberations.''

"I must advise you and your brother, my Lord Alstrom, that there is a certain risk involved in your plan,'' Sparhawk warned them. "We are being pursued. There are those bent on thwarting us in our quest. Since your brother's safety is your first concern, I should tell you that I cannot guarantee it. The ones who are pursuing us are determined and very dangerous.'' He spoke obliquely, since neither Alstrom nor Ortzel would give him much credence if he told them the bald truth about the nature of the Seeker.

"I'm afraid I have no real choice in the matter, Sir Sparhawk. With this anticipated siege hanging over my head, I have to get my brother out of the castle, no matter what the risk."

"As long as you understand, my Lord." Sparhawk sighed. "Our mission is of the gravest urgency, but this matter over-shadows even that."

"Sparhawk!" Sephrenia gasped.

"We have no choice, little mother," he told her. "We absolutely *must* get his Grace safely out of Lamorkand and to Chyrellos. The baron is right. If anything happens to his brother, the Church Knights will ride out of Chyrellos to retaliate. Nothing could prevent it. We'll have to take his Grace to the Holy City and then try to make up for lost time."

"What precisely is the object of your search, Sir Sparhawk?" the Patriarch of Kadach asked.

"As Sir Ulath explained, we are forced to resort to magic to restore the Queen of Elenia to health, and there's only one thing in the world with that much power. We're on our way to the great battlefield at Lake Randera to seek out the jewel which once surmounted the royal crown of Thalesia."

"The Bhelliom?" Ortzel was shocked. "Surely you would not bring that accursed thing to light again?"

"We have no choice, your Grace. Only Bhelliom can re-store my Queen."

"But Bhelliom is tainted. All the wickedness of the Troll-Gods infects it."

"The Troll-Gods aren't all that bad, your Grace," Ulath said. "They're capricious, I'll grant you, but they're not truly evil."

"The Elene God forbids consorting with them."

"The Elene God is wise, your Grace," Sephrenia told him. "He has also forbidden contact with the Gods of Styricum. He made an exception to his prohibition, however, when the time came to form the militant orders. The Younger Gods of Styricum agreed to assist Him in His design. One wonders if He might not also be able to enlist the aid of the Troll-Gods. He is, I understand, most persuasive."

"Blasphemy!" Ortzel gasped.

"No, your Grace, not really. I am Styric and therefore not subject to Elene theology."

"Hadn't we better get going?" Ulath suggested. "It's a

long ride to Chyrellos, and we need to get his Grace out of this castle before the fighting starts.''

"Well put, my laconic friend," Tynian approved.

"I shall make ready at once," Ortzel said, going to the door. "We will be able to depart within the hour." And he went out.

"How long do you think it's likely to be before the count's forces reach here, my Lord?" Tynian asked the baron.

"No more than a day, Sir Tynian. I have friends who are impeding his march northward from his keep, but he has a sizeable army, and I'm certain he will soon break his way through."

"Talen," Sparhawk said sharply, "put it back."

The boy made a wry face and laid a small dagger with a jeweled hilt back on the table from which he had taken it. "I didn't think you were watching," he said.

"Don't ever make that mistake," Sparhawk said. "I always watch you."

The baron looked puzzled.

"The boy has not yet learned to grasp some of the finer points of property ownership, my Lord," Kalten said lightly. "We've been trying to teach him, but he's a slow learner."

Talen sighed and took up his sketch pad and pencil. Then he sat at a table on the far side of the room and began to draw. He was, Sparhawk remembered, very talented.

"I am most grateful to you all, gentlemen," the baron was saying. "The safety of my brother has been my only concern. Now I shall be able to concentrate on the business at hand." He looked at Sparhawk. "Do you think you might possibly encounter this Martel person during the course of your quest?"

"I most certainly *hope* so," Sparhawk said fervently.

"And is it your intention to kill him?"

"That's been Sparhawk's intention for the last dozen years or so," Kalten said. "Martel sleeps very lightly when Sparhawk's in the same kingdom with him."

"May God aid your arm then, Sir Sparhawk," the baron said. "My son will rest more peacefully once his betrayer joins him in the House of the Dead."

The door burst open, and Sir Enmann hurried into the room. "My Lord!" he said to Alstrom in urgent tones, "come quickly!"

Alstrom came to his feet. "What is it, Sir Enmann?"

"Count Gerrich has deceived us. He has a fleet of ships on the river, and even now his forces are landing on both sides of this promontory."

"Sound the alarm!" the baron commanded, "and raise the drawbridge!"

"At once, my Lord." Enmann hurried from the room.

Alstrom sighed bleakly. "I'm afraid it's too late, Sir Sparhawk," he said. "Both your quest and the task I set you are doomed now. We are under siege, and we will all be trapped within these walls for a number of years, I fear."

CHAPTER
FIVE

T HE BOOMING CRASH of boulders slamming against the walls of Alstrom's castle came with monotonous regularity as the siege engines of Count Gerrich moved into place and began pounding the fortress.

Sparhawk and the others had remained in the cheerless, weapons-cluttered room at Alstrom's request, and they sat awaiting his return.

"I've never been under siege before," Talen said, looking up from his drawings. "How long do they usually last?"

"If we can't come up with a way to get out of here, you'll be shaving by the time it's over," Kurik told him.

"Do something, Sparhawk," the boy said urgently.

"I'm open to suggestions."

Talen looked at him helplessly.

Baron Alstrom came back into the room. His face was bleak. "I'm afraid we're completely encircled," he said.

"A truce, perhaps?" Bevier suggested. "It's customary in Arcium to grant safe passage to women and churchmen before pressing a siege."

"Unfortunately, Sir Bevier," Alstrom replied, "this is not Arcium. This is Lamorkand, and there's no such thing as a truce here."

"Any ideas?" Sparhawk asked Sephrenia.

"A few, perhaps," she said. "Let me have a try at your excellent Elene logic. First, the use of main force to break out of the castle is quite out of the question, wouldn't you say?"

"Absolutely."

"And, as you pointed out, a truce would probably not be honored?"

"I certainly wouldn't want to gamble his Grace's life or yours on a truce."

"Then there's the possibility of stealth. I don't think that would work either, do you?"

"Too risky," Kalten agreed. "The castle is surrounded, and the soldiers will be on the alert for people trying to sneak out."

"Subterfuge of some kind?" she asked.

"Not under these circumstances," Ulath said. "The troops surrounding the castle are armed with crossbows. We'd never get close enough to tell them stories."

"That leaves only the arts of Styricum, doesn't it?"

Ortzel's face stiffened. "I will not be a party to the use of heathen sorcery," he declared.

"I was afraid he might look at it that way," Kalten murmured to Sparhawk.

"I'll try to reason with him in the morning," Sparhawk replied under his breath. He looked at Baron Alstrom. "It's late, my Lord," he said, "and we're all tired. Some sleep might clear our heads and hint at other solutions."

"Well said, Sir Sparhawk," Alstrom agreed. "My servants will convey you and your companions to safe quarters, and we shall consider this matter further on the morrow."

They were led through the bleak halls of Alstrom's castle to a wing that, while comfortable, showed little signs of use. Supper was brought to them in their rooms, and Sparhawk and Kalten removed their armor. After they had eaten they sat talking quietly in the chamber they shared.

"I could have told you that Ortzel would feel the way he does about magic. The churchmen here in Lamorkand feel almost as strongly about it as Rendors."

"If it'd been Dolmant, we might have talked our way around him," Sparhawk agreed glumly.

"Dolmant's more cosmopolitan," Kalten said. "He grew up next door to the Pandion motherhouse, and he knows a great deal more about the secrets than he lets on."

There was a light rap on the door. Sparhawk rose and answered it. It was Talen. "Sephrenia wants to see you," he told the big knight.

"All right. Go to bed, Kalten. You're still looking a bit worse for wear. Lead the way, Talen."

The boy took Sparhawk to the end of the corridor and tapped on the door.

"Come in, Talen," Sephrenia replied.

"How did you know it was me?" Talen asked curiously as he opened the door.

"There are ways," she said mysteriously. The small Styric woman was gently brushing Flute's long black hair. The child had a dreamy look on her small face, and she was humming to herself contentedly. Sparhawk was startled. It was the first vocal sound he had ever heard her utter. "If she can hum, why is it she can't talk?" he asked.

"Whatever gave you the idea she can't talk?" Sephrenia continued her brushing.

"She never has done so."

"What does that have to do with it?"

"What did you want to see me about?"

"It's going to take something rather spectacular to get us out of here," she replied, "and I may need your help and that of the others to manage it."

"All you have to do is ask. Have you got any ideas at all?"

"A few. Our first problem is Ortzel, though. If he bows his neck on this, we'll never get him out of the castle."

"Suppose I just hit him on the head before we leave and tie him across his saddle until we're safely away?"

"Sparhawk," she chided him.

"It was a thought." He shrugged. "What about Flute here?"

"What about her?"

"She made those soldiers on the docks at Vardenais and the spies outside the chapterhouse ignore us. Couldn't she do that here too?"

"Do you realize how large that army outside the gate is, Sparhawk? She's just a little girl, after all."

"Oh. I didn't know that would make a difference."

"Of course it does."

"Couldn't you put Ortzel to sleep?" Talen asked her. "You know, sort of wiggle your fingers at him until he drops off?"

"It's possible, I suppose."

"Then he won't know you used magic to get us out of here until he wakes up."

"Interesting notion," she conceded. "How did you come up with it?"

"I'm a thief, Sephrenia." He grinned impudently. "I wouldn't be very good at it if I couldn't think faster than the other fellow."

"However we manage Ortzel is beside the point," Sparhawk said. "Our main concern is getting Alstrom's co-operation. He might be a little reluctant to risk his brother's life on something he doesn't understand. I'll talk with him in the morning."

"Be *very* persuasive, Sparhawk," Sephrenia said.

"I'll try. Come along, Talen. Let the ladies get some sleep. Kalten and I have a spare bed in our room. You can sleep there. Sephrenia, don't be afraid to call on me and the others if you need help with any spells."

"I'm never afraid, Sparhawk—not when I have you to protect me."

"Stop that," he told her. Then he smiled. "Sleep well, Sephrenia."

"You too, dear one."

"Good night, Flute," he added.

She blew him a little trill on her pipes.

The following morning, Sparhawk rose early and went back into the main part of the castle. As chance had it, he encountered Sir Enmann in the long, torchlit corridor. "How do things stand?" he asked the Lamork knight.

Enmann's face was gray with fatigue. He had obviously been up all night. "We've had some success, Sir Sparhawk," he replied. "We repelled a fairly serious assault on the castle's main gate about midnight, and we're moving our own engines into place. We should be able to begin destroying Gerrich's siege machines—and his ships—before noon."

"Will he pull back at that point?"

Enmann shook his head. "More likely, he'll begin digging earthwork fortifications. It's probable that the siege will be protracted."

Sparhawk nodded. "I thought that might be the case," he agreed. "Have you any idea where I might find Baron Alstrom? I need to talk with him—out of the hearing of his brother."

"My Lord Alstrom is atop the battlements at the front of the castle, Sir Sparhawk. He wants Gerrich to be able to see him. That may goad the count into some rash move. He's alone there. His brother is customarily in chapel at this hour."

"Good. I'll go talk with the baron then."

It was windy atop the battlements. Sparhawk had drawn his cloak about his armor to conceal it, and the wind whipped it around his legs.

"Ah, good morning, Sir Sparhawk," Baron Alstrom said. His voice was weary. He wore a full suit of armor, and the visor of his helmet had that peculiar pointed construction common in Lamorkand.

"Good morning, my Lord," Sparhawk replied, staying back from the battlements. "Is there someplace back out of sight where we can talk? I'm not sure it's a good idea to let Gerrich know that there are Church Knights inside your walls just yet, and I'm sure he has a number of sharp-eyed men watching you."

"The tower there above the gate," Alstrom suggested. "Come along, Sir Sparhawk." He led the way along the parapet.

The room inside the tower was grimly functional. A dozen crossbowmen stood at the narrow embrasures along its front unloosing their bolts at the troops below.

"You men," Alstrom commanded, "I have need of this room. Go shoot from the battlements for a while."

The soldiers filed out, their metal-shod feet clinking on the stone floor.

"We have a problem, my Lord," Sparhawk said when the two of them were alone.

"I noticed that," Alstrom said dryly, glancing out one of the embrasures at the troops massed before his walls.

Sparhawk grinned at this rare flash of humor in a usually dour race. "That particular problem is yours, my Lord," he said. "Our mutual one is what we're going to do about your brother. Sephrenia got directly to the point last night. No purely natural effort is going to effect his escape from the siege. We have no choice. We have to use magic—and his Grace appears to be unalterably opposed."

"I would not presume to instruct Ortzel in theology," Alstrom said.

"Nor would I, my Lord. Might I point out, however, that should his Grace ascend to the Archprelacy, he's going to have to modify his position—or at least learn to look the other way when this sort of thing happens. The four orders are the military arm of the Church, and we routinely utilize the secrets of Styricum in completing our tasks."

"I'm aware of that, Sir Sparhawk. My brother, however, is a rigid man and unlikely to change his views."

Sparhawk began to pace up and down, thinking fast. "Very well, then," he said carefully. "What we'll have to do to get your brother out of the castle will seem unnatural to you, but I assure you that it will be very effective. Sephrenia is highly skilled in the secrets. I've seen her do things that verge on the miraculous. You have my guarantee that she will in no way endanger your brother."

"I understand, Sir Sparhawk."

"Good. I was afraid that you might object. Most people are reluctant to rely on things they don't understand. Now, then, his Grace will in no way participate in what we may have to do. To put it bluntly, he'd just be in the way. All he's going to do is take advantage of it. He will in no way be personally involved in what he considers a sin."

"Understand me, Sir Sparhawk, I am not opposed to you in this. I will try reason with my brother. Sometimes he listens to me."

"Let's hope this is one of those times." Sparhawk glanced out the window and swore.

"What is it, Sir Sparhawk?"

"Is that Gerrich standing on top of that knoll at the rear of his troops?"

The baron looked out the embrasure. "It is."

"You might recognize the man standing beside him. That's Adus, Martel's underling. It seems that Martel's been playing both sides in this affair. The one that concerns me, though, is that figure standing off to one side—the tall one in the black robe."

"I don't think it poses much of a threat, Sir Sparhawk. It seems to be hardly more than a skeleton."

"You notice how its face seems to glow?"

"Now that you mention it, yes, I do. Isn't that odd?"

"It's more than odd, Baron Alstrom. I think I'd better go talk with Sephrenia. She needs to know about this immediately."

Sephrenia sat beside the fire in her room with her ever-present teacup in her hands. Flute sat cross-legged on the bed, weaving a cat's cradle of such complexity that Sparhawk pulled his eyes away from it, lest his entire mind become lost in trying to trace out the individual strands. "We've got trouble," he told his tutor.

"I noticed that," she replied.

"It's a little more serious than we'd thought. Adus is out there with Count Gerrich, and Krager's probably lurking around somewhere in the background."

"Martel's beginning to make me very tired."

"Adus and Krager don't add much to the problems we've already got, but that thing, the Seeker, is out there too."

"Are you sure?" She came quickly to her feet.

"It's the right size and shape, and that same glow is coming out from under its hood. How many humans can it take over at any one time?"

"I don't think there are any limits, Sparhawk, not when Azash is controlling it."

"Do you remember those ambushers back near the Pelosian border? How they just kept coming even though we were cutting them to pieces?"

"Yes."

"If the Seeker can gain control of Gerrich's whole army, they'll mount an assault that Baron Alstrom's forces won't be able to withstand. We'd better get out of here in a hurry, Sephrenia. Have you come up with anything yet?"

"There are a few possibilities," she replied. "The presence of the Seeker complicates things a bit, but I think I know a way to get around it."

"I hope so. Let's go talk with the others."

It was perhaps a half hour later when they all gathered again in the room where they had first met the previous day. "Very well, gentlemen," Sephrenia said to them. "We are in great danger."

"The castle is quite secure, Madame," Alstrom assured her. "In five hundred years it has never once fallen to be-siegers."

"I'm afraid things are different this time. A besieging army usually assaults the walls, doesn't it?"

"It's the common practice, once the siege engines have weakened the fortifications."

"After the assaulting force has taken heavy casualties, they normally fall back, don't they?"

"That's been my experience."

"Gerrich's men will *not* fall back. They will continue their attack until they overwhelm the castle."

"How can you be so sure?"

"You remember the figure in the black robe I pointed out to you, my Lord?" Sparhawk said.

"Yes. It seemed to cause you some concern."

"With good reason, my Lord. That's the creature that's been pursuing us. It's called a Seeker. It's not human, and it's subject to Azash."

"Beware of what you say, Sir Sparhawk," Patriarch Ortzel said ominously. "The Church does not recognize the exis-tence of the Styric Gods. You are treading very close to the brink of heresy."

"Just for the purposes of this discussion, let's assume that I know what I'm talking about," Sparhawk replied. "Putting Azash aside for the moment, it's important for you and your brother to understand just how dangerous that thing out there really is. It will be able to control Gerrich's troops com-pletely, and it will hurl them against this castle until they succeed in taking it."

"Not only that," Bevier added bleakly, "they will pay no attention to wounds that would incapacitate a normal man. The only way to stop them is to kill them. We've met men under the Seeker's control before and we had to kill every last one of them."

"Sir Sparhawk," Alstrom said, "Count Gerrich is my mortal enemy, but he's still an honorable man and a faithful son of the Church. He would not consort with a creature of darkness.''

"It's entirely possible that the count doesn't even know it's there," Sephrenia said. "The whole point here, however, is that we're all in deadly peril.''

"Why would that creature join forces with Gerrich?" Alstrom asked.

"As Sparhawk said, it's been pursuing us. For some reason, Azash looks upon Sparhawk as a threat. The Elder Gods have some ability to see into the future, and it's possible that Azash has caught a glimpse of something He wants to prevent. He's already made several attempts on Sparhawk's life. It's my belief that the Seeker is here for the express purpose of killing Sparhawk—or at the very least preventing his recovering Bhelliom. We must leave, my Lord, and quickly.'' She turned to Ortzel. "I'm afraid, your Grace, that we have no choice. We're compelled to resort to the arts of Styricum.''

"I will not be a party to that," he said stiffly. "I know that you are Styric, Madame, and therefore ignorant of the dictates of the true faith, but how dare you propose to practice your black arts in my presence? I am a churchman, after all.''

"I think that in time you may be obliged to modify your views, your Grace," Ulath said calmly. "The militant orders are the arms of the Church. We receive instruction in the secrets so that we may better serve her. This practice has been approved by every Archprelate for nine hundred years.''

"Indeed," Sephrenia added, "no Styric will consent to teach the Knights until approval is given by each new Archprelate.''

"Should it come to pass that I ascend the throne in Chyrellos, that practice shall cease.''

"Then the West will surely be doomed," she predicted, "for without these arts, the Church Knights will be helpless against Azash, and without the Knights, the West will fall before the hordes of Otha.''

"We have no evidence that Otha is coming.''

"We have no evidence that summer is coming either," she said dryly. She looked at Alstrom. "I believe I have a plan that may effect our escape, my Lord, but first I'll need to go to your kitchen and talk with your cook.''

He looked puzzled.

"The plan involves certain ingredients normally found in kitchens. I need to be certain they're available."

"There's a guard at the door, Madame," he said. "He will escort you to the kitchen."

"Thank you my Lord. Come along, Flute." And she went out.

"What's she up to?" Tynian asked.

"Sephrenia almost never explains things in advance," Kalten told him.

"Or afterward either, I've noticed," Talen added, looking up from his drawing.

"Speak when you're spoken to," Berit told him.

"If I did that, I'd forget how to talk."

"Surely you're not going to permit this, Alstrom," Ortzel said angrily.

"I don't have much choice," Alstrom replied. "We absolutely must get you to safety, and this seems to be the only way."

"Did you see Krager out there too?" Kalten asked Sparhawk.

"No, but I imagine he's around somewhere. Somebody's got to keep an eye on Adus."

"Is this Adus so very dangerous?" Alstrom asked.

"He's an animal, my Lord," Kalten replied, "and a very stupid one. Sparhawk's promised that I get to kill Adus if I don't interfere when he goes after Martel. Adus can barely talk, and he kills for the sheer pleasure of it."

"He's dirty and he smells bad too," Talen added. "He chased me down a street once in Cammoria, and the odor almost knocked me off my feet."

"You think Martel might be with them?" Tynian asked hopefully.

"I doubt it," Sparhawk said. "I think I nailed his foot to the floor down in Rendor. It's my guess that he set things up here in Lamorkand and then went to Rendor to hatch things there. Then he sent Krager and Adus back here to set things in motion."

"I think the world would be better off without this Martel of yours," Alstrom said.

"We're going to do what we can to arrange that, my Lord," Ulath rumbled.

A few moments later, Sephrenia and Flute returned.

"Did you find the things you need?" Sparhawk asked.

"Most of them," she replied. "I can make the others."
She looked at Ortzel. "You might wish to retire, your Grace,"
she suggested. "I don't want to offend your sensibilities."

"I will remain, Madame," he said coldly. "Perhaps my
presence will prevent this abomination from coming to pass."

"Perhaps, but I rather doubt it." She pursed her lips and
looked critically at the small earthen jar she had carried from
the kitchen. "Sparhawk," she said, "I'm going to need an
empty barrel."

He went to the door and spoke with the guard.

Sephrenia walked to the table and picked up a crystal goblet. She spoke at some length in Styric, and with a soft rustling sound, the goblet was suddenly filled with a powder that
looked much like lavender sand.

"Outrageous," Ortzel muttered.

Sephrenia ignored him. "Tell me, my Lord," she said to
Alstrom, "you have pitch and naphtha, I assume."

"Of course. They're a part of the castle's defenses."

"Good. If this is to work, we're going to need them."

The soldier entered, rolling a barrel.

"Right here, please," she instructed, pointing to a spot
away from the fire.

He set the barrel upright, saluted the baron, and left.

Sephrenia spoke briefly to Flute. The little girl nodded and
lifted her pipes. Her melody was strange, hypnotic, and almost languorous.

The Styric woman stood over the barrel, speaking in Styric
and holding the jar in one hand and the goblet in the other.
Then she began to pour their contents into the barrel. The
pungent spices in the jar and the lavender sand in the goblet
came spilling out, but neither vessel emptied. The two
streams, mixing as they fell, began to glow, and the room
was suddenly filled with starlike glitterings that soared, fire-
flylike, and sparkled on the walls and ceiling. Sephrenia
poured on and on. Minute after minute the small woman
continued to pour from the two seemingly inexhaustible containers.

It took nearly half an hour to fill the barrel. "There,"
Sephrenia said at last, "that should be enough." She looked
down into the glowing barrel.

Ortzel was making strangling sounds.

She put the two containers far apart on the table. "I wouldn't let these two get mixed together, my Lord," she cautioned Alstrom, "and keep them away from any kind of fire."

"What are we doing here?" Tynian asked her.

"We must drive the Seeker away, Tynian. We'll mix what's in this barrel with naphtha and pitch and load the baron's siege engines with the mixture. Then we'll ignite it and throw it in among Count Gerrich's troops. The fumes will force them to withdraw, temporarily at least. That's not the main reason we're doing it, however. The Seeker has a much different breathing apparatus than humans do. The fumes are noxious to humans. To the seeker, they're lethal. It will either flee or die."

"That sounds encouraging," he said.

"Was it really all so very terrible, your Grace?" she asked Ortzel. "It's going to save your life, you know."

His face was troubled. "I had always thought that Styric sorcery was mere trickery, but there was no way you could have done what I just saw by charlatanism. I will pray on this matter. I will seek guidance from God."

"I wouldn't take too long, your Grace," Kalten advised. "If you do, it could be that you'll arrive in Chyrellos just in time to kiss the ring of the Archprelate Annias."

"That must never happen," Alstrom declared sternly. "The siege at the gates is *my* concern, Ortzel, not yours. Therefore I must regretfully withdraw my hospitality. You will leave my castle just as soon as it's convenient."

"Alstrom!" Ortzel gasped. "This is my home. I was born here."

"But our father left it to *me*. *Your* proper home is in the Basilica of Chyrellos. I advise you to go there at once."

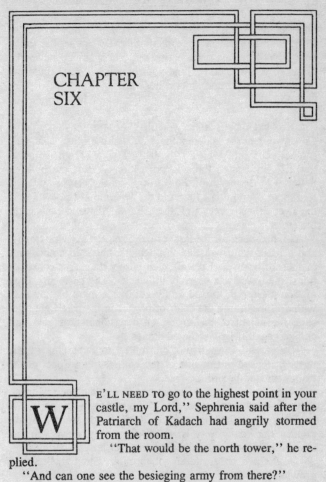

CHAPTER
SIX

W E'LL NEED TO go to the highest point in your castle, my Lord," Sephrenia said after the Patriarch of Kadach had angrily stormed from the room.

"That would be the north tower," he replied.

"And can one see the besieging army from there?"

"Yes."

"Good. First, however, we must give your soldiers instructions on how to proceed with this." She pointed at the barrel. "All right, gentlemen," she said crisply, "don't just stand there. Pick the barrel up and bring it along, and whatever you do, don't drop it or get it near any fire."

Her instructions to the soldiers manning the catapults were fairly simple, explaining the proper mixture of the powder, naphtha, and pitch. "Now," she went on, "listen very carefully. Your own safety depends on this. Do not set fire to the naptha until the last possible instant, and if any of the smoke blows in your direction, hold your breath and run. Under no circumstances breathe any of those fumes."

"Will they kill us?" one soldier asked in a frightened voice.

"No, but they'll make you ill and confuse your minds. Cover your noses and mouths with damp cloths. That may protect you a bit. Wait for the baron's signal from the north tower." She tested the wind direction. "Hurl the burning material to the north of those troops on the causeway," she told them, "and don't forget to throw some at those ships in the river as well. Very well then, Baron Alstrom. Let's go to the tower."

As it had been for the last several days, the sky was cloudy, and a brisk wind whistled through the unpaned embrasures of the north tower. Like all such purely defensive constructions, the tower was severely utilitarian. The besieging army of Count Gerrich looked oddly antlike, a mass of tiny men with armor glinting the color of pewter in the pale light. Despite the height of the tower, an occasional crossbow bolt chinked against its weathered stones.

"Be careful," Sparhawk murmured to Sephrenia as she thrust her head out of one of the embrasures to peer at the troops massed before the gate.

"There's no danger," she assured him as the wind whipped at her hooded white robe. "My Goddess protects me."

"You can believe in your Goddess all you want," he replied, "but your safety is *my* responsibility. Have you any idea of what Vanion would do to me if I let you get hurt?"

"And that's only after *I* got through with him," Kalten growled.

She stepped back from the embrasure and stood tapping one finger thoughtfully against her pursed lips.

"Forgive me, Madame," Alstrom said. "I recognize the necessity of chasing off that creature out there, but a purely temporary withdrawal of Gerrich's troops won't really do us all that much good. They'll return as soon as the smoke dissipates, and we still won't be any closer to getting my brother safely away from here."

"If we do this right, they won't return for several days, my Lord."

"Are the fumes that powerful?"

"No. They'll clear off in an hour or so."

"That's hardly time enough for you to make good your escape," he pointed out. "What's to prevent Gerrich from coming back and continuing the siege?"

"He's going to be very busy."

"Busy? With what?"

"He's going to be chasing some people."

"And who is that?"

"You, me, Sparhawk, and the others, your brother, and a fair number of men from your garrison."

"I don't think that's wise, Madame," Alstrom said critically. "We have secure fortifications here. I don't propose to abandon them and risk all our lives in flight."

"We're not going anywhere just yet."

"But you just said—"

"Gerrich and his men will think they're pursuing us. What they'll actually be chasing, however, will be an illusion." She smiled briefly. "Some of the best magic is illusion," she said. "You trick the mind and the eye into believing wholly in something that's not really there. Gerrich will be absolutely convinced that we're trying to take advantage of the confusion to bolt. He'll follow with his army, and that should give us plenty of time to slip your brother away to safety. Is that forest on the horizon fairly extensive?"

"It goes on for several leagues."

"Very good. We'll lead Gerrich in there with our illusion and let him wander around among the trees for the next few days."

"I think there's a flaw here, Sephrenia," Sparhawk said. "Won't the Seeker come back just as soon as the smoke clears? I don't think an illusion would deceive it, would it?"

"The Seeker won't come back for at least a week," she assured him. "It will be very, very ill."

"Should I signal the troops manning the catapults?" Alstrom asked.

"Not yet, my Lord. We have other things to do first. Timing is very important in this. Berit, I'll need a basin of water."

"Yes, ma'am." The novice went toward the stairs.

"Very well, then," she continued. "Let's get started."
She began patiently to instruct the Church Knights in the
spell. There were Styric words Sparhawk had not learned
before, and Sephrenia adamantly insisted that each of them
repeat them over and over until pronunciation and intonation
were absolutely perfect. "Stop that!" she commanded at one
point when Kalten tried to join in.

"I thought I could help," he protested.

"I know just how inept you are at this, Kalten. Just stay
out of it. All right, gentlemen, let's try it again."

Once she was satisfied with their pronunciation, she instructed Sparhawk to weave the spell. He began to repeat the
Styric words and to gesture with his fingers. The figure that
appeared in the center of the room was vaguely amorphous,
but it did appear to be wearing Pandion black armor.

"You didn't put a face on it, Sparhawk," Kalten
pointed out.

"I'll take care of that," Sephrenia said. She spoke two
words and gestured sharply.

Sparhawk stared at the shape before him. It was much like
looking into a mirror.

Sephrenia was frowning.

"Something wrong?" Kalten asked her.

"It's not too hard to duplicate familiar faces," she replied,
"or those of people who are actually present, but if I have to
go look at the face of everybody in the castle, this could take
days."

"Would these help?" Talen asked, handing her his
sketch pad.

She leafed through the pages, her eyes widening as she
turned each page. "The boy's a genius!" she exclaimed.
"Kurik, when we get back to Cimmura, apprentice him to
an artist. That might keep him out of trouble."

"It's only a hobby, Sephrenia," Talen said, blushing modestly.

"You do know that you could make far more as a painter
than as a thief, don't you?" she said pointedly.

He blinked, and then his eyes narrowed speculatively.

"All right. Now it's your turn, Tynian," Sephrenia told
the Dieran.

After each had created a mirror image of himself, she led
them to an embrasure overlooking the courtyard. "We'll build

the large illusion down there," she told them. "It might get
a little crowded if we tried to do it up here."

It took them an hour to complete the illusion of a mass
of armed and mounted men down in the courtyard. Then
Sephrenia went through Talen's sketch pad again and put
a face on each figure. Then she made a broad sweep of
her arm, and the images of the Church Knights joined the
illusion below.

"They aren't moving," Kurik said.

"Flute and I will take care of that," Sephrenia told him.
"The rest of you will need to concentrate to keep the images
from breaking up. You'll have to hold them together until they
reach that forest over there."

Sparhawk was already sweating. Building a spell and then
releasing it was one thing. Holding one in place was quite
something else. He suddenly realized how much strain Sephrenia was bearing.

It was early afternoon by now. Sephrenia looked out the
embrasure at Count Gerrich's troops. "All right," she said.
"I guess we're ready. Signal the catapults, my Lord," she
said to Alstrom.

The baron took a piece of red cloth out from under his
sword belt and waved it out of the embrasure. Below, the
catapults began to thud, hurling their burning missiles over
the wall and into the midst of the besieging army while other
engines showered the ships in the river. Even from this distance, Sparhawk could hear the soldiers coughing and chok-
ing on the dense cloud of lavender smoke coming from the
burning balls of pitch, naphtha, and Sephrenia's powder. The
smoke rolled across the field in front of the castle, sparkling
with that firefly glitter. Then it engulfed the knoll where Gerrich, Adus, and the Seeker were standing. Sparhawk heard
an animal-like screech, and then the black-robed Seeker burst
from the smoke, flogging its horse mercilessly. It seemed
unsteady in its saddle, and it was holding the edge of its hood
tightly across its face with one pale claw. The soldiers who
had been blocking the road leading from the castle gate came
reeling out of the smoke, coughing and retching.

"All right, my Lord," Sephrenia said to Alstrom, "lower
the drawbridge."

Alstrom signalled again, this time with a green cloth. A
moment later, the drawbridge boomed down.

"Now, Flute," Sephrenia said, and began to speak rapidly in Styric even as the little girl raised her pipes.

The mass of illusory men in the courtyard, who had until now been rigidly immobile, seemed to come to life all at once. They rode out through the gate at a gallop and plunged directly into the smoke. Sephrenia passed her hand over the basin of water Berit had brought to the tower and peered intently into it. "Hold them, gentlemen," she said. "Keep them intact."

A half-dozen of Gerrich's soldiers who had escaped from the smoke stood coughing, retching, and digging at their eyes on the causeway leading away from the castle. The illusory army rode directly through them. The soldiers fled screaming.

"Now we wait," Sephrenia said. "It's going to take a few minutes for Gerrich to get his wits together and realize what seems to be happening down there."

Sparhawk heard startled shouts coming from below and then bellowed commands.

"A little faster, Flute," Sephrenia said quite calmly. "We don't want Gerrich to catch up with the illusion. He might begin to grow suspicious if his sword goes through the baron here without any effect."

Alstrom was staring at Sephrenia in awe. "I would not have believed this possible, my Lady," he said in a shaking voice.

"It did turn out rather well, didn't it?" she said. "I wasn't entirely positive I could pull it off."

"You mean—"

"I've never done it before, but we can't learn without experimentation, can we?"

On the field below, Gerrich's troops were scrambling into their saddles. Their pursuit was disorganized, a chaos of galloping horses and brandished weapons.

"They didn't even think to charge that open drawbridge," Ulath noted critically. "Very unprofessional."

"They aren't thinking very clearly just now," Sephrenia told him. "The smoke does that to people. Are they all clear of the area yet?"

"There are a few still floundering around down there," Kalten advised. "They seem to be trying to catch their horses."

"Let's give them time to get out of our way. Continue to hold the illusion, gentlemen," she said, looking into her basin of water. "It's still a couple of miles to those woods."

Sparhawk clenched his teeth. "Can't you speed things up a bit?" he asked her. "This isn't easy, you know."

"Nothing worthwhile is ever easy, Sparhawk," she told him. "If the images of those horses start to fly, Gerrich is going to get very, very suspicious—even in his present condition."

"Berit," Kurik said, "you and Talen come with me. Let's go down and get the horses ready. I think we all might want to leave in a hurry."

"I'll go with you," Alstrom said. "I want to talk with my brother before he leaves. I'm sure I've offended him, and I'd rather have us part friends."

The four of them went on down the stairs.

"Just a few minutes longer now," Sephrenia said. "We're almost to the edge of the woods."

"You look as if you just fell into a river," Kalten said, glancing at Sparhawk's sweaty face.

"Oh, shut up," Sparhawk said irritably.

"There," Sephrenia said finally. "Let it go now."

Sparhawk let out an explosive breath of relief and released the spell. Flute lowered her pipes and winked at him.

Sephrenia continued to look into her basin. "Gerrich's about a mile from the edge of the trees," she reported. "I think we should let him get well into the woods before we leave."

"Whatever you say," Sparhawk replied, leaning wearily against a wall.

It was about fifteen minutes later when Sephrenia set her basin on the floor and straightened. "I think we can go down now," she said.

They descended to the courtyard where Kurik, Talen, and Berit had the horses. The Patriarch Ortzel, stiff-lipped and pale with anger, was with them, and his brother was at his elbow. "I shall not forget this, Alstrom," he said, pulling his black ecclesiastical robe tighter about him.

"You may feel differently after you've had time to think about it. Go with God, Ortzel."

"Stay with God, Alstrom," Ortzel replied, more out of

habit, Sparhawk thought, than from any real sense of emotion.

They mounted and rode out through the gate and on across the drawbridge. "Which way?" Kalten asked Sparhawk.

"North," Sparhawk replied. "Let's get clear of this place before Gerrich comes back."

"That's supposed to be a number of days."

"Let's not take any chances."

They rode north at a gallop. It was late afternoon by the time they reached the shallow ford where they had first encountered Sir Enmann. Sparhawk reined in and dismounted. "Let's consider our options," he said.

"What precisely did you do back there, Madame?" Ortzel was saying to Sephrenia. "I was in the chapel, and so I did not see what happened."

"A bit of deception is all, your Grace," she replied. "Count Gerrich thought he saw your brother and the rest of us escaping. He gave chase."

"That's all?" He looked surprised. "You didn't—" He left it hanging.

"Kill anybody? No. I strongly disapprove of killing."

"That's one thing we agree about, anyway. You're a very strange woman, Madame. Your morality seems to coincide rather closely with that laid down by the true faith. I would not have expected that from a heathen. Have you ever given any thought to conversion?"

She laughed. "You too, your Grace? Dolmant's been trying to convert me for years now. No, Ortzel. I'll remain faithful to my Goddess. I'm far too old to change religions at this stage in my life."

"Old, Madame? You?"

"You wouldn't believe it, your Grace," Sparhawk told him.

"You have all given me much to consider," Ortzel said. "I have followed what I perceived to be the letter of Church doctrine. Perhaps I should look beyond that perception and seek guidance from God." He walked a ways upstream, his face lost in thought.

"It's a step," Kalten muttered to Sparhawk.

"A fairly big one, I'd say."

Tynian had been standing at the edge of the shallow ford looking thoughtfully toward the west. "I have a sort of an idea, Sparhawk," he said.

"I'm willing to listen."

"Gerrich and his soldiers are all searching that forest, and, if Sephrenia's right, the Seeker will be unable to give chase for at least a week. There won't be any enemies on the other side of this river."

"That's true, I suppose. We should probably have a look around on the other side before we get overconfident, though."

"All right. That's the safest way, I suppose. What I'm getting at is that, if there aren't any troops over there, it wouldn't take more than a couple of us to escort his Grace safely to Chyrellos while the rest of us go on to Lake Randera. If things are quiet, we don't all have to ride to the Holy City."

"He's got a good point, Sparhawk," Kalten agreed.

"I'll think about it," Sparhawk said. "Let's go on across and have a look around before we make any decisions."

They remounted and splashed on across the shallow ford. There was a thicket on the far side. "It's going to get dark soon, Sparhawk," Kurik said, "and we're going to have to make camp. Why don't we hole up in that thicket for the night? Once it gets completely dark, we can come out and look for campfires. No group of soldiers is going to set up for the night without building fires, and we'll be able to see them. That would be a lot easier and faster than riding up and down the river all day tomorrow trying to flush them out."

"Good idea. Let's do it that way then."

They made camp for the night in the center of the thicket and built only a small cook-fire. By the time they had finished eating, night had fallen over Lamorkand. Sparhawk rose to his feet. "All right," he said, "let's go have a look. Sephrenia, you and the children and his Grace stay here out of sight." He led the way out of the thicket. Once they were clear of the trees, he and his companions fanned out, all of them peering intently into the night. The clouds obscured the moon and stars and made the darkness almost total.

Sparhawk moved around the thicket. On the far side he bumped into Kalten.

"It's darker than the inside of your boots out here," Kalten said.

"Did you see anything?"

"Not a glimmer. There's a hill on the back side of these trees, though. Kurik's going up to the top to look around."

"Good. I'll trust Kurik's eyes any time."

"Me too. Why don't you get him knighted, Sparhawk? When you get right down to it, he's better than any of us."

"Aslade would kill me. She's not set up to be the wife of a knight."

Kalten laughed as they moved on, straining their eyes into the blackness.

"Sparhawk." Kurik's voice came from not far away.

"Over there."

The squire joined them. "That's a fairly high hill," he puffed. "The only light I saw was coming from a village a mile or so to the south."

"You're sure it wasn't a campfire?" Kalten asked him.

"Campfires make a different kind of light from lamps shining through a dozen windows, Kalten."

"That's true, I suppose."

"I guess that's it, then," Sparhawk said. He raised his fingers to his lips and whistled, a signal for the others to return to the camp.

"What do you think?" Kalten asked as they pushed their way through the stiffly rustling brush toward the center of the thicket where the dim light of their banked cook-fire was scarcely more than a faint red glow in the darkness.

"Let's ask his Grace," Sparhawk replied. "It's his neck we'll be risking." They entered the brush-clogged encampment and Sparhawk pushed back the hood of his cloak. "We have a decision to make, your Grace," he told the patriarch. "The area appears to be deserted. Sir Tynian has suggested that two of us could escort you to Chyrellos in as much safety as the whole group. Our search for Bhelliom must not be delayed, if we're to keep Annias off the Archprelate's throne. The choice is up to you, though."

"I can go on to Chyrellos alone, Sir Sparhawk. My brother is overly concerned about my well-being. My cassock alone will protect me."

"I'd rather not gamble on that, your Grace. You'll recall that I mentioned that something was pursuing us?"

"Yes. I believe you called it a Seeker."

"Exactly. The creature is ill now because of the fumes Sephrenia created, but there's no way to be positive of how long its illness will last. It wouldn't look upon you as an enemy, though. If it should attack, run away. It's unlikely that it would follow you. I think that under the circumstances, though, Tynian's right. Two of us will be enough to ensure your safety."

"As you see fit, my son."

The others had entered the camp during the conversation, and Tynian volunteered immediately.

"No," Sephrenia rejected that idea. "You're the one most skilled at necromancy. We're going to need you as soon as we reach Lake Randera."

"I'll go," Bevier said. "I have a fast horse and can catch up with you at the lake."

"I'll go with him," Kurik offered. "If you run into more trouble, Sparhawk, you'll need knights with you."

"There's not that much difference between you and a knight, Kurik."

"I don't wear armor, Sparhawk," the squire pointed out. "The spectacle of Church Knights charging with lances makes people start thinking about their own mortality. It's a good way to avoid serious fighting."

"He's right, Sparhawk," Kalten said, "and if we run into more Zemochs and Church soldiers, you're going to need men wearing steel around you."

"All right," Sparhawk agreed. He turned to Ortzel. "I want to apologize for having offended your Grace," he said. "I don't really see that we had much choice, though. If we'd all been forced to stay penned up in your brother's castle, both of our missions would have failed, and the Church could not afford that."

"I still do not entirely approve, Sir Sparhawk, but your argument is most cogent. No apology is necessary."

"Thank you, your Grace," Sparhawk said. "Try to get some sleep. You'll be a long time in the saddle tomorrow, I think." He stepped away from the fire and rummaged through one of the packs until he found his map. Then he motioned to Bevier and Kurik. "Ride due west tomorrow," he told them. "Try to get back across the border into Pelosia before dark. Then go south to Chyrellos on that side of the line. I don't think even the most rabid Lamork soldier will violate that boundary and risk a confrontation with Pelosian border patrols."

"Sound reasoning," Bevier approved.

"When you get to Chyrellos, drop Ortzel off at the Basilica, then go see Dolmant. Tell him what's been going on here and ask him to pass the word on to Vanion and the other preceptors. Urge them very strongly to resist the idea of sending the Church Knights out here into the hinterlands to put out the brush fires Martel's been starting. We're going to need the four orders in Chyrellos if Archprelate Cluvonus dies, and luring them out of the Holy City's what's been behind all of Martel's scheming."

"We will, Sparhawk," Bevier promised.

"Make the trip as quickly as you can. His Grace appears to be fairly robust, so a little hard riding won't hurt him. The quicker you get across the border into Pelosia, the better. Don't waste any time, but be careful."

"You can count on that, Sparhawk," Kurik assured him.

"We'll rejoin you at Lake Randera as soon as we can," Bevier declared.

"Have you got enough money?" Sparhawk asked his squire.

"I can get by." Then Kurik grinned, his teeth flashing white in the dim light. "Besides, Dolmant and I are old friends. He's always good for a loan."

Sparhawk laughed. "Get to bed, you two," he said. "I want you and Ortzel on your way to Pelosia at first light in the morning."

They arose before dawn and sent Bevier and Kurik off to the west with the Patriarch of Kadach riding between them. Sparhawk consulted his map again by the light of their cookfire. "We'll go back across this ford again," he told the others. "There's a larger channel east of here, so we'll probably need to find a bridge. Let's go north. I'd rather not run across any of Count Gerrich's patrols."

They splashed across the ford after breakfast and angled away from it as a ruddy light to the east indicated that somewhere behind the dreary cloud cover the sun had risen.

Tynian fell in beside Sparhawk. "I don't want to sound disrespectful," he said, "but I rather hope that the election doesn't fall to Ortzel. I think the Church—and the four orders—would be in for a bad time if he ascends the throne."

"He's a good man."

"Granted, but he's very rigid. An Archprelate needs to be

flexible. Times are changing, Sparhawk, and the Church needs to change with them. I don't think the notion of change would appeal to Ortzel very much.''

"That's in the hands of the Hierocracy, though, and I'd definitely prefer Ortzel to Annias.''

"That's God's own truth.''

About midmorning, they overtook the clattering wagon of a shabby-looking itinerant tinker who was also travelling northward. "What cheer, neighbor?'' Sparhawk asked him.

"Scant cheer, Sir Knight,'' the tinker replied glumly. "These wars are bad for business. Nobody worries about a leaky pot when his house is under siege.''

"That's probably very true. Tell me, do you know of a bridge or a ford hereabouts where we can get across that river ahead?''

"There's a toll bridge a couple of leagues north,'' the tinker advised. "Where are you bound, Sir Knight?''

"Lake Randera.''

The tinker's eyes brightened. "To search for the treasure?'' he asked.

"What treasure?''

"Everybody in Lamorkand knows that there's a vast treasure buried somewhere on the old battlefield at the lake. People have been digging there for five hundred years. About all they turn up is rusty swords and skeletons, though.''

"How did people find out about it?'' Sparhawk asked him, sounding casual.

"It was the oddest thing. The way I understand it, not too long after the battle, people started seeing Styrics digging there. Now, that doesn't really make any sense, does it? What I mean is that everybody knows that Styrics don't pay very much attention to money, and Styric menfolk are very reluctant to pick up shovels. That sort of tool doesn't seem to fit their hands, for some reason. At any rate, or so the story goes, people began to wonder just exactly what it was the Styrics were looking for. That's when the rumors started about the treasure. That ground's been plowed and sifted over a hundred times or more. Nobody's sure what they're looking for, but everybody in Lamorkand goes there once or twice in his lifetime.''

"Maybe the Styrics know what's buried there.''

"Maybe so, but no one can talk to them. They run away any time somebody gets near them."

"Peculiar. Well, thank you for the information, neighbor. Have a nice day."

They rode on, leaving the tinker's clanking wagon behind. "That's gloomy," Kalten said. "Somebody got there with a shovel before we did."

"A lot of shovels," Tynian amended.

"He's right about one thing, though," Sparhawk said. "I've never known a Styric to be interested enough in money to go out of his way for it. I think we'd better find a Styric village and ask a few questions. Something's going on at Lake Randera that we don't know about, and I don't like surprises."

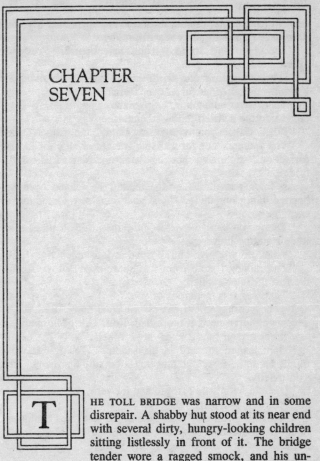

CHAPTER SEVEN

T HE TOLL BRIDGE was narrow and in some disrepair. A shabby hut stood at its near end with several dirty, hungry-looking children sitting listlessly in front of it. The bridge tender wore a ragged smock, and his unshaven face was gaunt and hopeless. His eyes clouded with disappointment when he saw the armor of the knights. "No charge," he sighed.

"You'll never make a living that way, friend," Kalten told him.

"It's a local regulation, my Lord," the bridge tender said unhappily. "No charge is made to Church people."

"Do very many people cross here?" Tynian asked him.

"No more than a few a week," the fellow replied. "Hardly

99

enough to make it possible for me to pay my taxes. My children haven't had a decent meal in months.''

"Are there any Styric villages hereabouts?" Sparhawk asked him.

"I believe there's one on the other side of the river, Sir Knight—in that cedar forest over there."

"Thank you, neighbor," Sparhawk said, pouring some coins into the startled fellow's hand.

"I can't charge you to cross, my Lord," the man objected.

"The money's not for crossing, neighbor. It's for the information." Sparhawk nudged Faran and started across the bridge.

As Talen passed the bridge tender, he leaned over and handed him something. "Get your children something to eat," he said.

"Thank you, young master," the man said, tears of gratitude standing in his eyes.

"What did you give him?" Sparhawk asked.

"The money I stole from that sharp-eyed fellow back at the ford," Talen replied.

"That was very generous of you."

The boy shrugged. "I can always steal more. Besides, he and his children need it more than I do. I've been hungry a few times myself, and I know how it feels."

Kalten leaned forward in his saddle. "You know, there might be some hope for this boy after all, Sparhawk," he said quietly.

"It could be a little early to say for sure."

"At least it's a start."

The damp forest on the far side of the river was composed of mossy old cedars with low-swooping green boughs, and the trail leading into it was poorly marked. "Well?" Sparhawk said to Sephrenia.

"They're here," she told him. "They're watching us."

"They'll hide when we approach their village, won't they?"

"Probably. Styrics have little reason to trust armed Elenes. I should be able to persuade at least some of them to come out, though."

Like all Styric villages, the place was rude. The thatch-roofed huts were scattered haphazardly in a clearing, and there was no street of any kind. As Sephrenia had predicted, there was no one about. The small woman leaned over and spoke briefly to Flute in that Styric dialect Sparhawk did not understand. The little girl nodded, lifted her pipes, and began to play.

At first nothing happened.

"I think I just saw one of them back in the trees," Kalten said after a few moments.

"Timid, aren't they?" Talen said.

"They have reason to be," Sparhawk told him. "Elenes don't treat Styrics very well."

Flute continued to play. After a time, a white-bearded man in a smock made of unbleached homespun emerged hesitantly from the forest. He put his hands together in front of his chest and bowed respectfully to Sephrenia, speaking to her in Styric. Then he looked at Flute, and his eyes widened. He bowed again, and she gave him an impish little smile.

"Aged one," Sephrenia said to him, "do you perchance speak the language of the Elenes?"

"I have a passing familiarity with it, my sister," he replied.

"Good. These knights have a few questions, and then we'll leave your village and trouble you no more."

"I will answer as best I can."

"Some time back," Sparhawk began, "we chanced upon a tinker who told us something a bit disquieting. He said that Styrics have been digging in the battlefield at Lake Randera for centuries, searching for a treasure. That doesn't seem like the sort of thing Styrics would do."

"It is not, my Lord," the old man said flatly. "We have no need of treasure, and we would most certainly not violate the graves of those who sleep there."

"I thought that might be the case. Have you any idea of who those Styrics might be?"

"They are not of our kindred, Sir Knight, and they serve a God whom we despise."

"Azash?" Sparhawk guessed.

The old man blanched slightly. "I will not speak his name aloud, Sir Knight, but you have hit upon my meaning."

"Then the men digging at the lake are Zemochs?"

The old man nodded. "We have known of their presence there for centuries. We do not go near them, for they are unclean."

"I think we'd all agree to that," Tynian said. "Have you got any idea of what they're looking for?"

"Some ancient talisman that Otha craves for his God."

"The tinker we spoke with said that most people around here believe there's a vast treasure there somewhere."

The old man smiled. "Elenes tend to exaggerate things," he said. "They cannot believe that the Zemochs would devote so much effort to the finding of one single thing—although the thing they seek is of greater worth than all the treasure in the world."

"That answers that question, doesn't it?" Kalten noted.

"Elenes have an indiscriminate lust for gold and precious gems," the old Styric went on, "and so it's entirely possible that they don't even know what they're looking for. They expect huge chests of treasure, but there are no such chests to be found on that field. It's not impossible that some one of them might already have found the object and cast it aside, not knowing its worth."

"No, aged master," Sephrenia disagreed. "The talisman of which you speak has not yet been found. Its uncovering would ring like a giant bell through all the world."

"It may be as you say, my sister. Do you and your companions also journey to the lake in search of the talisman?"

"Such is our intent," she replied, "and our quest is of some urgency. If nothing else, we must deny possession of the talisman to Otha's God."

"I shall pray to *my* God for your success then." The old Styric looked back at Sparhawk. "How fares it with the head of the Elene Church?" he asked carefully.

"The Archprelate is very old," Sparhawk told him truthfully, "and his health is failing."

The old man sighed. "It is as I feared," he said. "Although I am sure he would not accept the good wishes of a Styric, I nonetheless also pray to my God that he will live for many more years."

"Amen to that," Ulath said.

The white-bearded Styric hesitated. "Rumor states that the primate of a place called Cimmura is most likely to become the head of your Church," he said cautiously.

"That could be a bit exaggerated," Sparhawk told him. "There are many in the Church who oppose the ambitions of

Primate Annias. A part of *our* purpose is to thwart him as well."

"Then I shall pray for you doubly, Sir Knight. Should Annias reach the throne in Chyrellos, it will be a disaster for Styricum."

"And for just about everybody else as well," Ulath grunted.

"It will be far more deadly for Styrics, Sir Knight. The feelings of Annias of Cimmura about our race are widely known. The authority of the Elene Church has kept the hatred of the Elene commons in check, but should Annias succeed, he will probably remove that restraint, and I fear Styricum will be doomed."

"We will do all we can to prevent his reaching the throne," Sparhawk promised.

The old Styric bowed. "May the hands of the Younger Gods of Styricum protect you, my friends." He bowed again to Sephrenia and then to Flute.

"Let's move on," Sephrenia said. "We're keeping the other villagers away from their homes."

They rode out of the village and back into the forest.

"So the people digging up the battlefield are Zemochs," Tynian mused. "They're creeping all over western Eosia, aren't they?"

"We have known that it's all part of Otha's plan for generations," Sephrenia said. "Most Elenes cannot tell the difference between western Styrics and Zemochs. Otha does not want any kind of alliance or reconciliation between western Styrics and Elenes. A few well-placed atrocities have kept the prejudices of the Elene common people inflamed, and the stories of such incidents grow with every telling. This has been the source of centuries of general oppression and random massacres."

"Why does the possibility of an alliance worry Otha so much?" Kalten sounded puzzled. "There aren't enough Styrics in the west to pose that much of a threat, and since they won't touch steel weapons, they wouldn't be of much use if war breaks out again, would they?"

"The Styrics would fight with magic, not steel, Kalten," Sparhawk told him, "and Styric magicians know a lot more about it than the Church Knights."

"The fact that the Zemochs are at Lake Randera is promising, though," Tynian said.

"How so?" Kalten asked.

"If they're still digging, it means they haven't found Bhelliom yet. It also sort of hints at the fact that we're going to the right place."

"I'm not so sure," Ulath disagreed. "If they've been looking for Bhelliom for the last five hundred years and still haven't found it, maybe Lake Randera's *not* the right place."

"Why haven't the Zemochs tried necromancy the way we're going to?" Kalten asked.

"Thalesian spirits would not respond to a Zemoch necromancer," Ulath replied. "They'll probably talk to me, but not to anybody else."

"It's a good thing you're along then, Ulath," Tynian said. "I'd hate to go to all the trouble of raising ghosts and then find out that they won't talk to me."

"If you raise them, I'll talk with them."

"You didn't ask him about the Seeker," Sparhawk said to Sephrenia.

"There was no need. It would only have frightened him. Besides, if those villagers had known the Seeker was in this part of the world, the village would have been abandoned."

"Maybe we should have warned him."

"No, Sparhawk. Life is hard enough for those people without turning them into vagabonds. The Seeker is looking for *us*. The villagers are in no danger."

It was late afternoon by the time they reached the edge of the woods. They halted there and peered out over seemingly deserted fields. "Let's camp back here among the trees," Sparhawk said. "That's awfully open ground out there. I'd rather not have anyone see our fires if I can avoid it."

They rode back among the trees a ways and set up camp for the night. Kalten walked out to the edge of the wood to keep watch. Shortly after dark, he returned. "You'd better hide that fire a little better," he told Berit. "You can see it from the edge of the trees."

"Right away, Sir Kalten," the young novice replied. He took a spade and banked more earth around their small cookfire.

"We're not the only ones around here, Sparhawk," the big

blond Pandion said seriously. "There are a couple of fires about a mile out there in those fields."

"Let's go have a look," Sparhawk said to Tynian and Ulath. "We'll need to pinpoint the locations so we can slip around them in the morning. Even if the Seeker won't be a problem for several more days, there are still other people trying to keep us away from the lake. Coming, Kalten?"

"Go ahead," his friend said. "I haven't eaten yet."

"We might need you to point the fires out to us."

"You can't miss them," Kalten said, filling his wooden bowl. "Whoever built them wants lots of light."

"He's very attached to his stomach, isn't he?" Tynian said as the three knights walked toward the edge of the wood.

"He eats a great deal," Sparhawk admitted, "but he's a big man, so it takes a lot of food to keep him going."

The fires far out in the open fields were clearly visible. Sparhawk carefully noted the locations. "We'll swing north, I think," he said quietly to the others. "Probably we'll want to stay in the woods until we get well past those camps out there."

"Peculiar," Ulath said.

"What is?" Tynian asked.

"Those camps aren't very far apart. If the men out there know each other, why didn't they make just one camp?"

"Maybe they don't like each other."

"Why did they camp so close together then?"

Tynian shrugged. "Who knows why Lamorks do anything?"

"There's nothing we can do about them tonight," Sparhawk said. "Let's go back."

Sparhawk awoke just before dawn. When he went to rouse the others, he found that Tynian, Berit, and Talen were missing. Tynian's absence was easily explained. He was on watch at the edge of the woods. The novice and the boy, however, had no business being out of their beds. Sparhawk swore and went to wake Sephrenia. "Berit and Talen have gone off somewhere," he told her.

She looked around at the darkness pressing in on their well-hidden camp. "We'll have to wait until it gets light," she said. "If they're not back by then, we'll have to go look for them. Stir up the fire, Sparhawk, and put my teakettle near the flame."

The sky to the east was growing lighter when Berit and Talen returned to camp. They both looked excited, and their eyes were very bright.

"Just where have you two been?" Sparhawk demanded angrily.

"Satisfying a curiosity," Talen replied. "We went to pay a visit on our neighbors."

"Can you translate that for me, Berit?"

"We crept across the fields to have a look at the people around those campfires out there, Sir Sparhawk."

"Without asking me first?"

"You were asleep," Talen explained quickly. "We didn't want to wake you."

"They're Styrics, Sir Sparhawk," Berit said seriously, "at least some of them are. There's a fair scattering of Lamork peasants among them, though. The men around the other fire are all Church soldiers."

"Could you tell if the ones you saw were western Styrics or Zemochs?"

"I can't tell one kind of Styric from another, but the ones out there have swords and spears." Berit frowned. "This might have been my imagination, but all the men out there are sort of numb-looking. Do you remember how blank the faces of that group of ambushers back in Elenia were?"

"Yes."

"The people out there look more or less the same, and they're not talking to each other or even sleeping, and they haven't posted any sentries."

"Well, Sephrenia?" Sparhawk said. "Could the Seeker have recovered more quickly than you thought it would?"

"No," she replied, frowning. "It could have set those men in our path before it went on to Cimmura, however. They'd follow any instructions it might have given them, but they wouldn't be able to respond to any new situations without its presence."

"They'd recognize us though, wouldn't they?"

"Yes. The Seeker would have implanted that in their minds."

"And they'd attack us if they saw us?"

"Inevitably."

"Then I think we'd better move on," he said. "Those people out there are just a little too close to make me feel entirely comfortable. I don't like riding through strange country before it's fully light, but under the circumstances—'' Then he turned sternly to Berit. ''I appreciate the information you've brought us, Berit, but you shouldn't have gone off without telling me first, and you most definitely should not have taken Talen along. You and I are paid to take certain risks, but you had absolutely no right to endanger him.''

''He didn't know I was tagging along behind him, Sparhawk,'' Talen said glibly. ''I saw him get up, and I was curious about what he was doing, so I sneaked after him. He didn't even know I was there until we were almost to those campfires.''

''That's not precisely true, Sir Sparhawk,'' Berit disagreed with a pained look. ''Talen woke me and suggested that the two of us should go have a look at those men out there. It seemed like a very good idea at the time. I'm sorry. I didn't even think of the fact that I was putting him in danger.''

Talen looked at the novice with some disgust. ''Now why did you do that?'' he asked. ''I was telling him a perfectly good lie. I could have kept you out of trouble.''

''I've taken an oath to tell the truth, Talen.''

''Well, I haven't. All you had to do was keep your mouth shut. Sparhawk won't hit *me* because I'm too little. He might decide to thrash you, though.''

''I love these little arguments about comparative morality before breakfast,'' Kalten said. ''Speaking of which—'' He looked meaningfully toward the fire.

''It's your turn,'' Ulath told him.

''What?''

''It's your turn to do the cooking.''

''It surely can't be my turn again already.''

Ulath nodded. ''I've been keeping track.''

Kalten put on a pious expression. ''Sparhawk's probably right, though. We really should move on. We can have something to eat later.''

They broke camp quietly and saddled their horses. Tynian came back from the edge of the woods where he had been keeping watch. ''They're breaking up into small parties,'' he reported. ''I think they're going to scour the countryside.''

''We'll want to keep to the woods then,'' Sparhawk said. ''Let's ride.''

They moved cautiously, staying well back from the edge

of the trees. Tynian rode out to the fringe of the forest from time to time to scout out the movements of the numb-faced men out in the open fields. ''They seem to be ignoring these woods entirely,'' he said after one such foray.

''They're unable to think independently,'' Sephrenia explained.

''No matter,'' Kalten said. ''They're between us and the lake. As long as they're patrolling those fields out there, we can't get through. We're going to run out of woods eventually, and then we'll be at a standstill.''

''Just exactly which ones are patrolling this section?'' Sparhawk asked Tynian.

''Church soldiers. They're riding in groups.''

''How many in each group?''

''About a dozen.''

''Are the groups staying in sight of each other?''

''They're spreading out more and more.''

''Good.'' Sparhawk's face was bleak. ''Go keep an eye on them and let me know when they're far enough apart so they can't see each other.''

''All right.''

Sparhawk dismounted and tied Faran's reins to a sapling.

''What have you got in your mind, Sparhawk?'' Sephrenia asked suspiciously as Berit helped her and Flute down from her white palfrey.

''We know that the Seeker was probably sent by Otha—which means Azash.''

''Yes.''

''Azash knows that Bhelliom's about to emerge again, right?''

''Yes.''

''The Seeker's primary task is to kill us, but if it fails to do that, wouldn't it settle for keeping us away from Lake Randera?''

''Elene logic again,'' she said disgustedly. ''You're transparent, Sparhawk. I can see where you're leading with this.''

''Even though their minds are blank, the church soldiers would still be able to pass information to each other, wouldn't they?''

''Yes.'' She said it grudgingly.

''Then we don't have any choice in the matter. If any of

them see us, we'll have them all right behind us within an hour.''

"I don't quite follow," Talen said, looking puzzled.

"He's going to kill all the men in one of those patrols," Sephrenia said.

"To the last man," Sparhawk said grimly, "and just as soon as the others are all out of sight."

"They can't even run away, you know."

"Good. Then I won't have to chase them."

"You're plotting deliberate murder, Sparhawk."

"That's not precisely accurate, Sephrenia. They'll attack as soon as they see us. What we'll be doing is defending ourselves."

"Sophistry," she snapped, and stalked away, muttering to herself.

"I didn't think she even knew what that word means," Kalten said.

"Do you know how to use a lance?" Sparhawk asked Ulath.

"I've been trained with it," the Thalesian replied. "I much prefer my ax, though."

"With a lance you don't have to get in quite so close. Let's not take too many chances. We should be able to put a fair number of them down with our lances, and then we can finish up with our swords and axes."

"There are only five of us, you know," Kalten said, "counting Berit."

"So?"

"I just thought I'd mention it."

Sephrenia came back, her face pale. "Then you're absolutely set on this?" she demanded of Sparhawk.

"We have to get to the lake. Can you think of any alternatives?"

"No, as a matter of fact, I can't." Her tone was sarcastic. "Your impeccable Elene logic has completely disarmed me."

"I've been meaning to ask you something, little mother," Kalten said, obviously trying to head off an argument by changing the subject. "Exactly what does this Seeker thing look like? It seems to go to a great deal of trouble to keep itself hidden."

"It's hideous." She shuddered. "I've never seen one, but the Styric magician who taught me how to counter it described it to me. Its body is segmented, very pale and very thin. At this stage, its outer skin has not yet completely hardened, and it oozes out a kind of ichor from between its segments to protect the skin from contact with the air. It has crablike claws, and its face is horrible beyond belief."

"Ichor? What's that?"

"Slime," she replied shortly. "It's in its larval stage—sort of like a caterpillar or a worm, although not quite. When it reaches adulthood, its body hardens and darkens and its wings emerge. Not even Azash can control an adult. All they're concerned with at that stage is reproducing. Set a pair of adults loose, and they'd turn the entire world into a hive and feed every living creature on earth to their young. Azash keeps a pair for breeding purposes in a place from which they can't escape. When one of the larvae he uses as Seekers approaches adulthood, he has it killed."

"Working for Azash has its risks, doesn't it? But I've never seen any kind of insect that looks like that."

"Normal rules don't apply to the creatures who serve Azash." She looked at Sparhawk, her expression agonized. "Do we really have to do this?" she asked him.

"I'm afraid we do," he replied. "There's no other way."

They sat on the damp forest loam, waiting for Tynian to return. Kalten went to one of the pack saddles and cut large slabs from a cheese and a loaf of bread with his dagger. "This takes care of my turn at cooking, right?" he said to Ulath.

Ulath grunted. "I'll think about that."

The sky overhead was still cloudy, and birds drowsed among the dark green cedar boughs that filled the wood with their fragrance. Once, a deer approached them, stepping delicately along a forest trail. One of the horses snorted, and the deer bounded away, his white tail flashing and his velvet-covered antlers flaring above his head. It was peaceful here, but Sparhawk pushed that peace from his mind, steeling himself for the task ahead.

Tynian returned. "There's one group of soldiers sort of stationed a few hundred yards north of us," he reported quietly. "All the others are out of sight."

"Good," Sparhawk said, rising to his feet. "We might as well get started. Sephrenia, you stay here with Talen and Flute."

"What's the plan?" Tynian asked.

"No plan," Sparhawk replied. "We're just going to ride out there and eliminate that patrol. Then we'll ride on to Lake Randera."

"It has a certain direct charm," Tynian agreed.

"Remember, all of you," Sparhawk went on, "they won't react to wounds the way normal people would. Make sure of them so they won't come at you from behind when you move on to the next one. Let's go."

The fight was short and brutal. As soon as Sparhawk and the others burst from the wood in a thundering charge, the blank-faced Church soldiers drove their horses across the grassy field toward them, their swords aloft. When the two parties were perhaps fifty paces apart, Sparhawk, Kalten, Tynian, and Ulath lowered their lances and set themselves. The shock of the impact was terrific. The soldier Sparhawk struck was picked out of his saddle by the lance that drove through his chest and emerged from his back. Sparhawk reined Faran in sharply to avoid breaking his lance. He pulled it free of the body and then charged on. His lance broke off in the body of another soldier. He discarded it and drew his sword. He lopped an arm off a third soldier then drove the point of his sword through the man's throat. Ulath had broken his lance on the first soldier he attacked but then had driven the broken end into the body of another. Then the big Genidian had reverted to his ax. He smoothly brained yet another soldier. Tynian had driven his lance through another soldier's belly and had finished him with his sword and moved on to another. Kalten's lance had shattered against a soldier's shield, and he was being hard-pressed by two others until Berit rode in and chopped the top off one of their heads with his ax. Kalten finished the other with a broad stroke. The remaining soldiers were milling around in confusion, their venom-numbed minds unable to react quickly enough to the assault by the Knights of the Church. Sparhawk and his companions crushed them together in a tangle and methodically butchered them.

Kalten swung down from his saddle and walked among the fallen soldiers lying in huddled heaps on the bloody grass. Sparhawk turned his head away as his friend systematically ran his sword into each body. "Just wanted to be sure,"

Kalten said, sheathing his sword and remounting. "None of them are going to do any talking now."

"Berit," Sparhawk said, "go get Sephrenia and the children. We'll keep watch here. Oh, one other thing. You'd better cut us some new lances as well. The ones we had seem to be all used up."

"Yes, Sir Sparhawk," the novice said, and rode back toward the woods.

Sparhawk looked around and saw a brush-choked draw not far away. "Let's hide these," he said, looking at the bodies. "We don't want to make it obvious that we've come this way."

"Did their horses all run off?" Kalten asked, looking around.

"Yes," Ulath replied. "Horses do that when there's fighting."

They dragged the mutilated corpses to the draw and dumped them into the brush. By the time they had finished, Berit was returning with Sephrenia, Talen, and Flute. He carried the new lances across his saddle. Sephrenia kept her eyes averted from the bloodstained grass where the fight had taken place.

It took but a few minutes to affix the steel points to the lances, and then they all remounted.

"Now I'm *really* hungry," Kalten said as they set out at a gallop.

"How *can* you?" Sephrenia demanded in a tone of revulsion.

"What did I say?" Kalten asked Sparhawk.

"Never mind."

The next several days passed without incident, although Sparhawk and the others kept wary eyes to the rear as they galloped on. They took shelter each night in places of concealment and built small, well-shielded fires. And then the cloudy skies finally fulfilled their promise. A steady drizzle began to fall as they pushed on toward the northeast.

"Wonderful," Kalten said sardonically, looking up at the soggy sky.

"Just pray that it rains harder," Sephrenia told him. "The Seeker should be moving about again by now, but it won't be able to follow our scent if it's been washed out by rain."

"I suppose I hadn't thought of that," he admitted.

Sparhawk periodically dismounted to cut a stick from a particular kind of low-lying bush and to lay it carefully on the ground pointing in the direction they were going.

"Why do you keep doing that?" Tynian asked him finally, pulling his dripping blue cloak tighter about him.

"To let Kurik know which way we've gone," Sparhawk replied, remounting.

"Very clever, but how will he know which bush to look behind?"

"It's always the same kind of bush. Kurik and I worked that out a long time ago."

The sky continued to weep. It was a depressing kind of rain that soaked into everything. Campfires were difficult to get started and tended to go out without much advance notice. Occasionally they passed Lamork villages and now and then an isolated farmstead. The people for the most part were staying in out of the rain, and the cattle grazing in the fields were wet and dispirited-looking.

They were not too far from the lake when Bevier and Kurik finally caught up with them on a blustery afternoon when the steady rain was blowing almost horizontally to the ground.

"We delivered Ortzel to the Basilica," Bevier reported, wiping his dripping face. "Then we went to Dolmant's house and told him about what was happening here in Lamorkand. He agrees that the upheaval is probably designed to pull the Church Knights out of Chyrellos. He'll do what he can to block that."

"Good," Sparhawk said. "I like the notion of all Martel's efforts being wasted. Did you have any problems along the way?"

"Nothing serious," Bevier said. "The roads are all being patrolled, though, and Chyrellos is crawling with soldiers."

"And all the soldiers are loyal to Annias, I suppose?" Kalten said sourly.

"There are other candidates for the Archprelacy, Kalten," Tynian pointed out. "If Annias is bringing his troops into Chyrellos, it stands to reason that the others would bring in theirs as well."

"We certainly don't want open fighting in the streets of the Holy City," Sparhawk said. "How's Archprelate Cluvonus?" he asked Bevier.

"He's fading fast, I'm afraid. The Hierocracy can't even hide his condition from the common people any more."

"That makes what we're doing all the more urgent," Kalten said. "If Cluvonus dies, Annias will start to move, and at that point, he won't *need* the Elenian treasury any more."

"Let's press on, then," Sparhawk said. "It's still a day or so to the lake."

"Sparhawk," Kurik said critically, "you've let your armor get rusty."

"Really?" Sparhawk pulled back his sodden black cloak and looked at his red-tinged shoulder plates with some surprise.

"Couldn't you find the oil bottle, my Lord?"

"I had my mind on other things."

"Obviously."

"I'm sorry. I'll deal with it."

"You wouldn't know how. Don't fool with the armor, Sparhawk. I'll tend to it."

Sparhawk looked around at his companions. "If anybody makes an issue of this, there's going to be a fight," he said ominously.

"We would sooner die than offend you, my Lord Sparhawk," Bevier promised with an absolutely straight face.

"I appreciate that," Sparhawk told him, and then rode resolutely off into the driving rain, his rusty armor creaking.

CHAPTER EIGHT

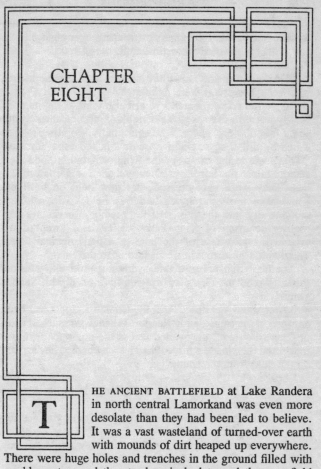

T HE ANCIENT BATTLEFIELD at Lake Randera in north central Lamorkand was even more desolate than they had been led to believe. It was a vast wasteland of turned-over earth with mounds of dirt heaped up everywhere. There were huge holes and trenches in the ground filled with muddy water, and the steady rain had turned the vast field into a quagmire.

Kalten sat his horse beside Sparhawk, looking helplessly out at the muddy field that seemed to stretch off to the horizon. "Where do we start?" he asked, sounding baffled at the enormity of the task before them.

Sparhawk remembered something. "Bevier," he called.

The Arcian rode forward. "Yes, Sparhawk?"

"You said that you'd made a study of military history."

"Yes."

"Since this was the biggest battle that's ever been fought, you probably devoted some time to it, didn't you?"

"Of course."

"Do you think you might be able to locate the general area where the Thalesians were fighting?"

"Give me a few moments to orient myself." Bevier rode slowly out into the soggy field, looking around intently for some landmark. "There," he said finally, pointing toward a nearby hill that was half obscured in the misty drizzle. "That's where the troops of the King of Arcium made their stand against the hordes of Otha and their supernatural allies. They were hard-pressed, but they held on until the Knights of the Church reached this field." He squinted thoughtfully into the rain. "If my memory serves me correctly, the army of King Sarak of Thalesia swept down around the east side of the lake in a flanking maneuver. They would have fought much farther to the east."

"At least that narrows things down a little bit," Kalten said. "Would the Genidian Knights have been with Sarak's army?"

Bevier shook his head. "All the Church Knights had been engaged in the campaign in Rendor. When word reached them of Otha's invasion, they sailed across the inner sea to Cammoria and then made a forced march to get here. They arrived on the field from the south."

"Sparhawk," Talen said quietly, "over there. Some people are trying to hide behind that big mound of dirt—the one with that tree stump halfway up the side."

Sparhawk carefully avoided turning. "Could you get any kind of a look at them?"

"I couldn't tell what kind of people they are," the boy replied. "They're all covered with mud."

"Did they have any kind of weapons?"

"Shovels, mostly. I think a couple of them had crossbows."

"Lamorks, then," Kalten said. "Nobody else uses that weapon."

"Kurik," Sparhawk said to his squire, "what's the effective range of a crossbow?"

"Two hundred paces with any kind of accuracy. After that, you sort of have to rely on luck."

Sparhawk looked around, trying to appear casual. The heaped-up mound of dirt was perhaps fifty yards away. ''We'll want to go on that way,'' he said in a voice loud enough to be heard by the lurking treasure seekers. He raised one steel-gauntleted hand and pointed east. ''How many are there, Talen?'' he asked quietly.

''I saw eight or ten. There could be more.''

''Keep your eyes on them, but don't be too obvious about it. If any of them starts to raise his crossbow, warn us.''

''Right.''

Sparhawk started out at a steady trot. Faran's hooves splashed up the semiliquid mud. ''Don't look back,'' he warned the others.

''Wouldn't a gallop be more appropriate about now?'' Kalten asked in a strained voice.

''Let's not let them know that we've seen them.''

''This is very hard on my nerves, Sparhawk,'' Kalten muttered, shifting his shield. ''I've got this very uneasy feeling right between my shoulder blades.''

''So do I,'' Sparhawk admitted. ''Talen, are they doing anything?''

''Just watching us,'' the boy replied. ''I can see a head pop up every so often.''

They trotted on, splashing through the mud.

''We're almost clear,'' Tynian said tensely.

''The rain's settling down around that hill,'' Talen reported. ''I don't think they can see us now.''

''Good,'' Sparhawk said, letting out an explosive breath of relief. ''Let's slow down. It's obvious that we're not alone out here, and we don't want to blunder into anything.''

''Nervous,'' Ulath commented.

''Wasn't it, though?'' Tynian agreed.

''I don't know why *you* were worried,'' Ulath said, eyeing Tynian's massive Deiran armor, ''considering all the steel you've got wrapped around you.''

''At close range, a crossbow bolt will penetrate even this.'' Tynian rapped his fist on the front of his armor. It made a ringing sound, almost like a bell. ''Sparhawk, the next time you talk to the Hierocracy, why don't you suggest that they outlaw crossbows? I felt positively naked out there.''

''How do you carry all that armor?'' Kalten asked him.

''Painfully, my friend, very painfully. The first time they

strapped it on me, I collapsed. It took me an hour to get back on my feet.''

"Keep your eyes open," Sparhawk cautioned. "A few Lamork treasure hunters are one thing, but men controlled by the Seeker are something else; if it had those men back there near the woods, it's certain to have some here as well.''

They splashed on through the mud, looking about cautiously. Sparhawk consulted his map again, shielding it from the rain with his cloak. "The city of Randera's up on the east shore of the lake," he said. "Bevier, did any of your books say anything about whether the Thalesians occupied it?''

"That portion of the battle is a bit obscure in the chronicles I've read," the white-cloaked knight replied. "About the only accounts of that part of the battle just say that the Zemochs occupied Randera fairly early in their campaign. Whether or not the Thalesians did anything about that, I simply don't know.''

"They wouldn't have," Ulath declared. "Thalesians have never been very good at sieges. We don't have that kind of patience. King Sarak's army probably bypassed it.''

"This might be easier than I thought," Kalten said. "The only area we have to search is what lies between Randera and the south end of the lake.''

"Don't get your hopes up too much, Kalten," Sparhawk told him. "It's still a lot of ground." He looked off into the drizzle toward the lake. "The lake shore seems to be sand, and wet sand is better to ride on than mud." He turned Faran and led the others toward the lake.

The sandy beach that stretched off into the distance along the south shore of the lake did not seem to have been excavated in the same way the rest of the field had. Kalten looked around as they rode out onto the expanse of damp sand. "I wonder why they haven't been digging here," he said.

"High water," Ulath replied cryptically.

"I beg your pardon?''

"The water level rises in the winter, and it washes the sand back into any holes they might have dug.''

"Oh. That makes sense, I suppose.''

They rode cautiously along the edge of the water for the next half hour.

"How far do we have to go?" Kalten asked Sparhawk. "You're the one with the map.''

"Ten leagues, anyway," Sparhawk replied. "This beach seems to be open enough to make a gallop safe." He nudged Faran with his heels and led the way.

The rain continued unabated, and the dimpled surface of the lake was the color of lead. They had ridden some miles along the water's edge when they saw another group of men digging somewhat furtively out in the sodden field.

"Pelosians," Ulath disdainfully identified them.

"How can you tell?" Kalten asked him.

"Those silly pointed hats."

"Oh."

"I think they fit the shape of their heads. They probably heard rumors about the treasure and came down from the north. Do you want us to run them off, Sparhawk?"

"Let them dig. They're not bothering us—at least not as long as they stay where they are. Men who belong to the Seeker wouldn't be interested in treasure."

They rode on along the beach until late afternoon. "What do you say to making camp up there?" Kurik suggested, pointing to a large pile of driftwood just ahead. "I've got some dry wood in one of the packs, and we ought to be able to find more near the bottom of that pile."

Sparhawk looked up at the dripping clouds, gauging the time of day. "It's time to stop anyway," he agreed.

They reined in beside the driftwood, and Kurik built his fire. Berit and Talen began pulling relatively dry sticks out from under the pile, but after a little while, Berit went back to his horse for his battle-ax.

"What are you going to do with that?" Ulath asked him.

"I'm going to chop up some of those larger pieces with it, Sir Ulath."

"No, you're not."

Berit looked a bit startled.

"That's not what it was made for. You'll dull the edge, and you might need that edge before long."

"My ax is in that pack over there, Berit," Kurik told the shamefaced novice. "Use that. I don't plan to hit anybody with it."

"Kurik," Sephrenia said from inside the tent Sparhawk and Kalten had just erected for her and Flute, "put up a cover near the fire, and string a rope under it." She emerged from the tent wearing a Styric smock and carrying her dripping white robe in one hand and Flute's garment in the other. "It's time to dry out some clothes."

After the sun went down, a night breeze began to blow in off the lake, making the tents flap and tossing the flames of their fire. They ate a meager supper and then sought their beds.

About midnight, Kalten came back from where he had been standing watch. He shook Sparhawk awake. "It's your turn," he said quietly to avoid waking the others.

"All right." Sparhawk sat up, yawning. "Did you find a good place?"

"That hill just behind the beach. Watch your step climbing it, though. They've been digging in the sides of it."

Sparhawk began to put on his armor.

"We're not alone here, Sparhawk," Kalten said, removing his helmet and his dripping black cloak. "I saw a half-dozen fires a good ways out in that field."

"More Pelosians and Lamorks?"

"It's a little hard to say. A fire doesn't usually have any kind of identifying marks on it."

"Don't tell Talen and Berit. I don't want them creeping around in the dark any more. Get some sleep, Kalten. Tomorrow might be a long day."

Sparhawk carefully climbed the pitted side of the hill and took up a position on top. He immediately saw the fires Kalten had mentioned, but saw also that they were a long way off and posed little threat.

They had been long on the road now, and a growing sense of impatient urgency gnawed at Sparhawk. Ehlana sat alone in the silent throne room back in Cimmura with her life ticking away. A few more months and her heartbeat would falter and then stop. Sparhawk pulled his mind away from that thought. As he usually did when that apprehension came over him, he deliberately set his mind on other matters and other memories.

The rain was chill and damp and unpleasant, so he turned his thoughts to Rendor, where the blistering sun burned all trace of moisture from the air. He remembered the lines of black-veiled women gracefully going to the well at dawn before the sun made the streets of Jiroch unbearable. He remembered Lillias with a wry smile, and he wondered if the

melodramatic scene in the street near the docks had earned
her the kind of respect she so desperately needed.

And then he remembered Martel. That night in Arasham's
tent in Dabour had been a good one. To see his hated enemy
filled with chagrin and frustration had been almost as satisfying as killing him might have been. "Someday, though,
Martel," he muttered. "You have a lot to pay for, and I think
it's almost time for me to collect." It was a good thought,
and Sparhawk dwelt on it as he stood in the rain. He thought
about it in some detail until it was time to rouse Ulath for his
turn on watch.

They broke camp at daybreak and rode on down the rain-
swept beach.

About midmorning, Sephrenia reined in her white palfrey
with a warning hiss. "Zemochs," she said sharply.

"Where?" Sparhawk asked.

"I can't be sure. They're close, though, and their intentions are unfriendly."

"How many?"

"It's very hard to tell, Sparhawk. At least a dozen, but
probably fewer than a score."

"Take the children and ride back to the edge of the water."
He looked at his companions. "Let's see if we can flush them
out," he said. "I don't want them following us."

The knights advanced across the muddy field at a walk,
their lances lowered. Berit and Kurik flanked them on either
side.

The Zemochs were hiding in a shallow trench less than a
hundred yards from the beach. When they saw the seven
Elenes resolutely bearing down on them, they rose with their
weapons in their hands. There were perhaps fifteen of them,
but the fact that they were on foot put them at a distinct
disadvantage. They made no sound, uttered no war cries, and
their eyes were empty.

"The Seeker sent them," Sparhawk barked. "Be careful."

As the knights approached, the Zemochs shambled forward, and several even blindly hurled themselves on the lance
points. "Drop the lances!" Sparhawk commanded. "They're
too close!" He cast aside his lance and drew his sword. Again
the men controlled by the Seeker charged in eerie silence,
and paid no attention to their fallen comrades. Although they
had the advantage of numbers, they were really no match for

the mounted knights, and their doom was sealed when Kurik and Berit outflanked them and came at them from the rear.

The fight lasted for perhaps ten minutes, and then it was over.

"Is anybody hurt?" Sparhawk asked, looking around quickly.

"Several, I'd say," Kalten replied, looking at the bodies lying in the mud. "This is getting to be a little too easy, Sparhawk. They charge in, almost asking to be killed."

"I'm always glad to oblige," Tynian said, wiping his sword with a Zemoch smock.

"Let's drag them back to that trench they were hiding in," Sparhawk said. "Kurik, go back and get your spade. We'll cover them over."

"Hide the evidence, eh?" Kalten said gaily.

"There may be others around," Sparhawk said. "Let's not announce that we've been here."

"Right, but I want to make sure of them before we start dragging. I'd rather not have one wake up when my hands are occupied with his ankles."

Kalten dismounted and went through the grim business of making sure of them. Then they all fell to work. The slippery mud made dragging the inert bodies easier. Kurik stood at the edge of the trench scooping mud over the corpses with his spade.

"Bevier," Tynian said, "are you really so attached to that Lochaber?"

"It's my weapon of choice," Bevier replied. "Why do you ask?"

"It's a little inconvenient when the time comes to tidy up. When you lop off their heads like that, it means we have to make two trips with each one." Tynian bent over and picked up two severed heads by the hair as if to emphasize his point.

"How droll," Bevier said dryly.

After they had dropped all the bits and pieces of the Zemoch bodies and their weapons in the trench and Kurik had covered them with mud, they rode back to the beach, where Sephrenia sat on her horse, carefully keeping Flute's face covered with the hem of her cloak and trying to keep her own eyes turned away. "Have you finished?" she asked as Sparhawk and the others approached.

"It's all over," he assured her. "You can look now." He

frowned. "Kalten just raised a point. He said that this was getting to be almost too easy. These people just charge in without thinking. It's as if they want to be killed."

"That's not really it, Sparhawk," she replied. "The Seeker has men to spare. It will throw away hundreds just to kill one of us—and hundreds more to kill the next one."

"That's depressing. If it has so many, why is it sending them out in such small groups?"

"They're scouting parties. Ants and bees do exactly the same thing. They send out small groups to find what the colony is looking for. The Seeker is still an insect, after all, and, in spite of Azash, it still thinks like one."

"At least they're not reporting back," Kalten said. "None of the ones we've met so far, anyway."

"They already have," she disagreed. "The Seeker knows when its forces have been diminished. It may not know precisely where we are, but it knows that we've been killing its soldiers. I think we'd better leave here. If there was one group out there, there are probably others as well. We don't want them converging on us."

Ulath was talking seriously to Berit as they rode out at a trot. "Keep your ax under control at all times," he advised. "Don't ever make a swing so wide that you can't recover instantly."

"I think I see," Berit replied seriously.

"An ax can be just as delicate a weapon as a sword—if you know what you're doing," Ulath said. "Pay attention, boy. Your life might depend on this."

"I thought the whole idea was to hit somebody with it as hard as you can."

"There's no real need of that," Ulath replied. "Not if you keep it sharp. When you're cracking a walnut with a hammer, you hit it just hard enough to break the shell. You don't want to smash it into little bits. It's the same with an ax. If you hit somebody too hard with one, there's a fair chance that the blade's going to hang up in the body somewhere, and that leaves you at a definite disadvantage when you have to face your next opponent."

"I didn't know an ax was that complicated a weapon," Kalten said quietly to Sparhawk.

"I think it's a part of the Thalesian religion," Sparhawk replied. He looked at Berit, whose face was rapt as he listened to Ulath's insruction. "I hate to say this, but we've probably lost a good swordsman there. Berit's very fond of that ax, and Ulath's encouraging him."

Late in the day the lake shore began to curve toward the northeast. Bevier looked around, getting his bearings. "I think we'd better stop here, Sparhawk," he advised. "As closely as I can tell, this is approximately where the Thalesians came up against the Zemochs."

"All right," Sparhawk agreed. "I guess the rest is up to you, Tynian."

"First thing in the morning," the Alcione Knight replied.

"Why not now?" Kalten asked him.

"It's going to start getting dark soon," Tynian said, his face bleak. "I don't raise ghosts at night."

"Oh?"

"Just because I know how to do it doesn't mean that I like it. I want lots of daylight around me when they start to appear. These men were killed in battle, so they won't be very pretty to look at. I'd rather not have any of them coming up to me in the dark."

Sparhawk and the other knights scouted the general area while Kurik, Berit, and Talen set up camp. The rain was slacking slightly as they returned.

"Anything?" Kurik asked, looking out from under the sheets of canvas he had erected at an angle over the fire.

"There's some smoke a few miles off to the south," Kalten replied, swinging down from his horse. "We didn't see anybody, though."

"We'll still have to post a watch," Sparhawk said. "If Bevier knows that this is the general area where the Thalesians were fighting, we can be fairly sure the Zemochs will too, and the Seeker probably knows what we're looking for, so it's certain to have people in this area."

They were all unusually quiet that evening as they sat under Kurik's makeshift canvas cover that kept the rain from quenching their fire. This place had been their goal in the weeks since they had left Cimmura, and very soon they would find out if the trip had served any real purpose. Sparhawk in particular was anxious and worried. He definitely wanted to get on with it, but he respected Tynian's feeling in the matter. "Is the process very complicated?" he asked the broad-shouldered Deiran. "Necromancy, I mean?"

"It's not your average spell, if that's what you mean," Tynian replied. "The incantation's fairly long, and you have to draw diagrams on the ground to protect yourself. Sometimes the dead don't want to be awakened, and they can do some fairly nasty things to you if they're really upset."

"How many of them do you plan to raise at a time?" Kalten asked him.

"One," Tynian said very firmly. "I don't want a whole brigade of them coming at me all at once. It might take a little longer, but it's a great deal safer."

"You're the expert, I guess."

The morning dawned wet and dreary. The rain had returned during the night. The sodden earth had already received more water than it could hold, and rain-dimpled puddles stood everywhere.

"A perfect day for raising the dead," Kalten observed sourly. "It just wouldn't seem right if we did it in the sunshine."

"Well," Tynian said, rising to his feet, "I suppose we might as well get started."

"Aren't we going to eat breakfast first?" Kalten objected.

"You really don't want anything in your stomach, Kalten," Tynian replied. "Believe me, you don't."

They walked out into the field.

"They don't seem to have been doing as much digging here," Berit said, looking around. "Maybe the Zemochs don't know where the Thalesians are buried after all."

"We can hope," Tynian said. "I guess this is as good a place to start as any." He picked up a dead stick and prepared to draw a diagram on the sodden ground.

"Use this instead," Sephrenia advised, handing him a coil of rope. "A diagram drawn on dry ground is all right, but there are puddles here, and the ghosts might not see the whole thing."

"We really wouldn't want that to happen," Tynian agreed. He began to lay out the rope on the ground. The design was a strangely compelling one with obscure curves and circles and irregularly shaped stars. "Is that about right?" he asked Sephrenia.

"Move that one slightly to the left," she said, pointing.

He did that.

"Much better," she said. "Repeat the spell out loud. I'll correct you if you do anything wrong."

"Just out of curiosity, why don't *you* do this, Sephrenia?" Kalten asked her. "You seem to know more about it than anybody."

"I'm not strong enough," she admitted. "What you're really doing in this ritual is wrestling with the dead to compel them to rise. I'm a little small for that sort of thing."

Tynian began to speak in Styric, intoning the words sonorously. There was a peculiar cadence to his speech, and the gestures he made had a slow stateliness to them. His voice grew louder and more commanding. Then he raised both his hands and brought them together sharply.

At first nothing seemed to happen. Then the ground inside his diagram seemed to ripple and shudder. Slowly, almost painfully, something rose from the earth.

"God!" Kalten gasped in horror as he stared at the grotesquely mutilated thing.

"Talk to it, Ulath," Tynian said from between clenched teeth. "I can't hold it here very long."

Ulath stepped forward and began to speak in a harshly guttural language.

"Old Thalesian," Sephrenia identified the dialect. "Common soldiers at the time of King Sarak would have spoken it."

The ghastly apparition replied haltingly in a dreadful voice. Then it made a jerky pointing motion with one bony hand.

"Let it go back, Tynian," Ulath said. "I've got what we need."

Tynian's face was gray and his hands were shaking. He spoke two words in Styric, and the apparition sank back into the earth.

"That one didn't really know anything," Ulath told them, "but it pointed out the spot where an earl is buried. The earl was in the household of King Sarak, and if anyone around here knows where the king's buried, he would. It's right over there."

"Let me get my breath first," Tynian said.

"Is it really that difficult?"

"You have no idea, my friend."

They waited while Tynian stood gasping painfully. After a

few moments he coiled up his rope and straightened. "All right. Let's go wake up the earl."

Ulath led them to a small knoll that stood nearby. "Burial mound," he said. "It's customary to raise one when you bury a man of importance."

Tynian laid out his design atop the mound, then stepped back and began the ritual again. He finished it and clapped his hands once more.

The apparition that rose from the mound was not as hideously mutilated as the first had been. It was dressed in traditional Thalesian chain mail and had a horned helmet on its head. "Who art thou who hast disturbed my sleep?" it demanded of Tynian in the archaic speech of five centuries past.

"He hath brought thee once again into the light of day at my urging, my Lord," Ulath replied. "I am of thy race and would speak with thee."

"Speak quickly then. I am discontent that thou hast done this thing."

"We seek the resting place of his Majesty King Sarak," Ulath said. "Knowest thou, my Lord, where we might search?"

"His Majesty doth not lie on this battlefield," the ghost responded.

Sparhawk's heart sank.

"Knowest thou what befell him?" Ulath pressed.

"His Majesty departed from his capital at Emsat when word reached him of the invasion of Otha's hordes," the ghost declared. "He took with him a small party of his household retainers. The rest of us remained behind to marshal the main force. We were to follow when the army was gathered. When we arrived here, his Majesty was nowhere to be found. None here knoweth what befell him. Seek ye, therefore, elswhere."

"One last question, my Lord," Ulath said. "Knowest thou perchance which route it was his Majesty's intention to follow to reach this field?"

"He sailed to the north coast, Sir Knight. No man—alive or dead—knoweth where he made landfall and disembarked. Seek ye therefore in Pelosia or Deira, and return me to my rest."

"Our thanks, my Lord," Ulath said with a formal bow.

"Thy thanks have no meaning for me," the ghost said indifferently.

"Let him go back, Tynian," Ulath said sadly.

Once again, Tynian released the spirit as Sparhawk and the others stood looking at each other, their faces filled with chagrin.

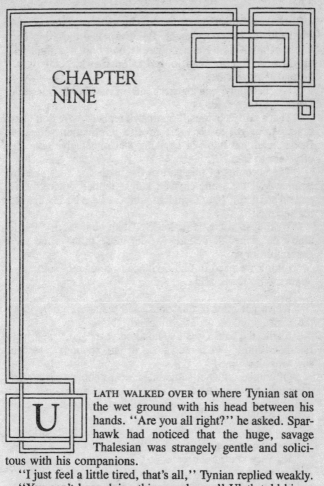

CHAPTER NINE

ULATH WALKED OVER to where Tynian sat on the wet ground with his head between his hands. "Are you all right?" he asked. Sparhawk had noticed that the huge, savage Thalesian was strangely gentle and solicitous with his companions.

"I just feel a little tired, that's all," Tynian replied weakly.

"You can't keep doing this, you know," Ulath told him.

"I can hold out for a little longer."

"Teach me the spell," Ulath urged. "I can wrestle with the best—alive or dead."

Tynian smiled wanly. "I'll wager that you could, my friend. Have you ever been bested?"

"Not since I was about seven," Ulath said modestly. "That was when I crammed my older brother's head into the wooden

129

well-bucket. It took our father two hours to get him out of it. My brother's ears got caught. He always had those big ears. I sort of miss him. He came out second best in a fight with an Ogre.'' The big man looked at Sparhawk. "All right," he said, "now what?"

"We certainly can't search all of northern Pelosia or Deira," Kalten said.

"That's fairly obvious," Sparhawk replied. "We don't have time. We've got to get more precise information somehow. Bevier, can you think of anything that might give us a clue of where to look?"

"The accounts of this part of the battle are very sketchy, Sparhawk," the white-cloaked knight replied dubiously. He smiled at Ulath. "Our Genidian brothers are a bit lax in keeping records."

"Writing in runes is tedious," Ulath confessed. "Particularly on stone. Sometimes we let those things slide for a generation or so."

"I think we need to find a village or a town of some sort, Sparhawk," Kurik said.

"Oh?"

"We've got a lot of questions, and we aren't going to get the answers unless we ask somebody."

"Kurik, the battle was five hundred years ago," Sparhawk reminded him. "We're not going to find anybody alive who saw what happened."

"Of course not, but sometimes local people—particularly commoners—keep track of an area's traditions, and landmarks have names. The name of a mountain or a stream could be just the clue we need."

"It's worth a try, Sparhawk," Sephrenia said seriously. "We're not getting anywhere here."

"It's very slim, Sephrenia."

"What other options do we have?"

"We'll keep going north then, I suppose."

"And probably past all the excavations," she added. "If the ground's been ploughed over, it's a fairly sure sign that Bhelliom's not there."

"That's true, I suppose. All right, we'll go on north, and if something promising turns up, Tynian can raise another ghost."

Ulath looked dubious at that. "I think we'll have to be

careful there," he said. "Just the effort of raising these two almost put him on his back."

"I'll be all right," Tynian protested weakly.

"Of course you will—at least you would be if we had time to let you rest in bed for several days."

They helped Tynian into his saddle, pulled his blue cape around him, and rode north in the continuing drizzle.

The city of Randera stood on the east shore of the lake. It was surrounded by high walls, and there were grim watch-towers at each corner.

"Well?" Kalten said, looking speculatively at the bleak Lamork city.

"Waste of time," Kurik grunted. He pointed at a large mound of dirt slowly melting down in the rain. "We're still coming across diggings. We need to go farther north."

Sparhawk looked critically at Tynian. Some of the color had returned to the Alcione Knight's face, and he seemed to be slowly recovering. Sparhawk nudged Faran into a canter and led his friends through the dreary landscape.

It was midafternoon by the time they passed the last signs of excavations. "There's some kind of a village down there by the lake, Sir Sparhawk," Berit said, pointing.

"It's probably not a bad place to start," Sparhawk agreed. "Let's see if we can find an inn down there. I think it's time for us to have a hot meal, get in out of the rain, and dry out a bit anyway."

"And a tavern, perhaps," Kalten added. "People in taverns usually like to talk, and there are always a few old men around who pride themselves on how well they know local history."

They rode on down to the shore of the lake and into the village. The houses were uniformly run-down, and the cobbled streets were in disrepair. At the lower end of town, a series of docks protruded out into the lake, and there were nets hanging on poles along the shore. The smell of long-dead fish permeated the air in the narrow streets. A suspicious-eyed villager directed them to the only inn the village had, a very old, sprawling stone building with a slate roof.

Sparhawk dismounted in the innyard and went inside. A fat man with a bright red face and raggedly cut hair was rolling a beer barrel across the floor toward a wide door near the back. "Have you any empty rooms, neighbor?" Sparhawk asked him.

"The whole loft is empty, my Lord," the fat man replied respectfully, "but are you sure you want to stop here? My accommodations are good enough for ordinary travellers, but they're hardly suitable for the gentry."

"I'm sure they'd be better than sleeping under a hedge on a rainy night."

"That's surely true, my Lord, and I'll be happy to have guests. I don't get many visitors at this time of year. That taproom back there is about the only thing that keeps me in business."

"Are there any people in there at the moment?"

"A half dozen or so, my Lord. Business picks up when the fishermen come in off the lake."

"There are ten of us," Sparhawk told him, "so we'll need quite a few rooms. Do you have someone who can see to our horses?"

"My son takes care of the stables, Sir Knight."

"Warn him to be careful of the big roan. The horse is playful, and he's very free with his teeth."

"I'll mention it to my son."

"I'll get my friends then, and we'll go upstairs and have a look at your loft. Oh, incidentally, do you happen to have a bathtub? My friends and I have been out in the weather, and we're a little rusty-smelling."

"There's a bathhouse out back, my Lord. Nobody uses it very often, though."

"All right. Have some of your people start heating water, and I'll be right back." He turned and went back outside into the rain.

The rooms, though a bit dusty from lack of use, were surprisingly comfortable-looking. The beds were clean and seemed bug-free, and there was a large common room at one end of the loft.

"Very nice, actually," Sephrenia said, looking around.

"There's a bathhouse as well," Sparhawk told her.

"Oh, that's just lovely." She sighed happily.

"We'll let you use it first."

"No, dear one. I don't like to be rushed when I bathe. You gentlemen go ahead." She sniffed at them critically.

"Don't be afraid to use soap," she added. "Lots and lots of soap—and wash your hair as well."

"After we bathe, I think we'll want to change into plain tunics," Sparhawk advised the others. "We want to ask these people questions, and armor's just a bit intimidating."

The five knights pulled off their armor, took up their tunics, and trooped with Kurik, Berit, and Talen down the back stairs in the padded and rust-splotched undergarments they wore beneath their steel. They bathed in large, barrellike tubs, and emerged feeling refreshed and cleansed.

"This is the first time I've been warm for a week," Kalten said. "I think I'm ready to visit that taproom now."

Talen was pressed into service to carry their padded undergarments back upstairs, and he was a little sullen about it.

"Don't make faces," Kurik told him. "I wasn't going to let you go into the taproom, anyway. I owe that much to your mother. Tell Sephrenia that she and Flute can have the bathhouse now. Come back down with her and guard the door to make sure they're not interrupted."

"But I'm hungry."

Kurik put his hand threateningly on his belt.

"All right, all right, don't get excited." The boy hurried on up the stairs.

The taproom was a bit smoky, and the floor was covered with sawdust and silvery fish scales. The five plain-clad knights, along with Kurik and Berit, entered unobtrusively and seated themselves at a vacant corner table.

"We'll have beer," Kalten called to the serving wench, "lots of beer."

"Don't overdo it," Sparhawk muttered. "You're heavy, and we don't want to have to carry you back upstairs."

"Never fear, my friend," Kalten replied expansively. "I spent a full ten years here in Lamorkand and never once got fuddled. The beer here is weak and watery stuff."

The serving girl was a typical Lamork woman—large-hipped, blond, busty, and none too bright. She wore a peasant blouse, cut very low, and a heavy red skirt. Her wooden shoes clattered across the floor, and she had an inane giggle. She brought them large, copper-bound wooden tankards of foamy beer. "Don't go just yet, lass," Kalten said to her. He lifted his tankard and drained it without once taking it from his lips. "This one seems to have gone empty on me. Be a good girl and fill it again." He patted her familiarly on the bottom. She giggled and scurried away with his tankard.

"Is he always like this?" Tynian asked Sparhawk.

"Every chance he gets."

"As I was saying before we came in," Kalten said loudly enough to be heard in most parts of the room, "I'll wager a silver half crown that the battle never got this far north."

"And I'll wager two that it did," Tynian replied, picking up the ruse immediately.

Bevier looked puzzled for an instant, and then his eyes showed that he understood. "It shouldn't be too hard to find out," he said, looking around. "I'm sure that someone here would know."

Ulath pushed back his bench and stood up. He thumped his huge fist on the table for attention. "Gentlemen," he said loudly to the other men in the taproom. "My two friends here have been arguing for the last four hours, and they've finally got to the point of putting money down on the issue. Frankly, I'm getting a little tired of listening to them. Maybe some of you can settle the matter and give my ears a rest. There was a battle here five hundred years ago or so," He pointed at Kalten. "This one with the beer foam on his chin says that the fighting didn't get this far north. The other one with the round face says that it did. Which one is right?"

There was a long silence, and then an old man with pink cheeks and wispy white hair shambled across the room to their table. He was shabbily dressed, and his head wobbled on his neck. "I b'leeve I kin settle yer dispute, good masters," he said in a squeaky voice. "My old gaffer, he used to tell me stories about that there battle ye was talkin' about."

"Bring this good fellow a tankard, dearie," Kalten said familiarly to the serving girl.

"Kalten," Kurik said disgustedly, "keep your hand off her bottom."

"Just being friendly is all."

"Is that what you call it?"

The serving girl blushed rosily and went back for more beer, rolling her eyes invitingly at Kalten.

"I think you've just made a friend," Ulath said dryly to the blond Pandion, "but try not to take advantage of it here in public.'' He looked at the old man with the wobbly neck. ''Sit down, old fellow,'' he invited.

''Why, thankee, good master. I read by the look of 'ee that ye be from far north Thalesia.'' He sat down shakily on the bench.

''You read well, old man,'' Ulath said. ''What did your gaffer tell you about that ancient battle?''

''Well,'' the wobbly fellow said, scratching at his stubbled cheek, ''as I recall it, he says to me, he says—'' He paused as the busty serving girl slid a tankard of beer to him. ''Why, thankee, Nima,'' he said.

The girl smiled, sidling up to Kalten. ''How's yours?'' she asked, leaning against him.

Kalten flushed slightly. ''Ah—just fine, dearie,'' he faltered. Oddly, her directness seemed to take him off guard.

''You *will* let me know if you want anything, won't you?'' she encouraged. ''*Anything* at all. I'm here to please, you know.''

''At the moment—no,'' Kalten told her. ''Maybe later.''

Tynian and Ulath exchanged a long look, and then they both grinned.

''You northern knights look at the world differently than we do,'' Bevier said, looking slightly embarrassed.

''You want some lessons?'' Ulath asked him.

Bevier suddenly blushed.

''He's a good boy.'' Ulath smiled broadly to the others and patted Bevier on the shoulder. ''We just have to keep him out of Arcium for a while until we have time to corrupt him. Bevier, you're my dear brother, but you're awfully stiff and formal. Try to relax a bit.''

''Am I so very rigid?'' Bevier asked, looking a bit shamefaced.

''We'll fix it for you,'' Ulath assured him.

Sparhawk looked across the table at the toothlessly grinning old Lamork. ''Can you settle this stupid argument for us, grandfather? Did the battle really come this far north?''

''Why, yes indeed it did, young master,'' the old man mumbled, ''and even further, if the truth be known. My old gaffer, he tole me as there was fightin' an' killin' as far north as up into Pelosia. Y'see, the hull army of the Thalesians, they come slippin' around the upper end of the lake an' fell on them Zemochs from behind. Only thing is, was that there was a hull lot more of them there Zemochs than there was Thalesians. Well, sir, the way I understand it was that the Zemochs got over their surprise an' come roarin' back up this way, killin' most ever'thin' in sight. Folks hereabouts hid in their cellars while they was goin' on, let me tell you.'' He paused to take a long drink from his tankard. ''Well, sir,'' he continued, ''the battle *seemed* t' be more or less over, the Zemochs havin' won an' all, but then a hull bunch of them Thalesian lads, what had probably had to wait around for boats up there in the north country, come chargin' in an' done some real awful things to them there Zemochs.'' He glanced at Ulath. ''Yer people are a real bad-tempered sort, if y' don't mind my sayin' so, friend.''

''I think it has to do with the climate,'' Ulath agreed.

The old man looked mournfully into his tankard. ''Could ye maybe see yer way clear to do this again?'' he asked hopefully.

''Of course, grandfather,'' Sparhawk said. ''See to it, Kalten.''

''Why me?''

''Because you're on better speaking terms with the barmaid than I am. Go on with your story, grandfather.''

''Well, sir, I been told there was this awful battle that went on about a couple leagues or so north of here. Them Thalesian fellers was *real* unhappy about what had happened to their friends an' kinfolk down to the south end of the lake, an' they went at the Zemochs with axes an' such. They's graves up there as has got a thousand or more in 'em—an' they hain't all human, I'm told. The Zemochs wasn't none too particular about who they took up with, or so the story goes. Ye kin see the graves up there in the fields—big heaps of dirt all growed over with grass an' bushes an' such like. Local farmers been turnin' up bones an' old swords an' spears an' axheads with their plows fer nigh onto five hunnerd years now.''

''Did your gaffer by any chance tell you who led the Thalesians?'' Ulath asked carefully. ''I had some kin in that battle, and we could never find out what happened to them. Do you think the leader might possibly have been the King of Thalesia?''

''Never heard one way or t'other,'' the old Lamork admitted. ''Course, the folks hereabouts wasn't none too anxious to get right down there in the middle of the killin' an' all. Common folks don't have no business gettin' mixed up in that sort of thing.''

"He wouldn't have been too hard to recognize," Ulath said. "The old legends in Thalesia say that he was near to seven feet tall, and that his crown had a big blue jewel on top of it.''

"Never heard of nobody matchin' that description—but like I said, the common folk was stayin' *real* far back from the fightin'.''

"Do you think there might be somebody else around here who's perhaps heard other stories about the battle?" Bevier asked in a neutral tone.

"It's possible, I s'pose," the old fellow said dubiously, "but my old gaffer, he was one of the best storytellers in these here parts. He got hisself runned over by a wagon when he was fifty or so, an' it broke up his back real cruel. He used to set hisself on a bench out there on the porch of this very inn, him an' his cronies. They'd swap the old stories by the hour, an' he took real pleasure in it—not havin' nothin' else to do, him bein' so crippled up an' all, don't y' know. An' he passed all the old tales down t' me—me bein' his favorite an' all, on accounta I used t' bring him his bucket of beer from this very taproom.'' He looked at Ulath. "No, sir," he said. "None of the old stories I ever heard say nothin' about no king such as you described, but like I say, it was a awful big battle, an' the local folk stayed a long way back from it. It could be that this here king of yers was there, but nobody I ever knew mentioned it.''

"And this battle took place a couple or so leagues north of here, you say?" Sparhawk prompted.

"Maybe as much as seven mile," the old fellow replied, taking a long drink from the fresh tankard the broad-hipped serving wench had brought him. "T' be downright honest with'ee, young master, I been a bit stove up of late, an' I don't walk out so far no more." He squinted at them appraisingly. "If y' don't mind me sayin' it, young masters, y' seem t' have a powerful curiosity about that there long ago King of Thalesia an' what not.''

"It's fairly simple, grandfather," Ulath said easily. "King Sarak of Thalesia was one of our national heroes. If I can track down what really happened to him, I'll get a great deal of credit out of it. King Wargun might even reward me with an earldom—that's if he ever gets sober enough.''

The old man cackled. "I heered of him," he said. "Does he really drink as much as they say?''

"More, probably.''

"Well, now—an earldom, y' say? Now, that's a goal that's worth goin' after. What y' might want to do, yer earlship, is go on up t' that there battlefield an' poke around a bit. Might could be that ye kin turn up somethin' as'll give 'ee a clue. A man seven feet tall—an' a king to boot—well, sir, he'd have some mighty impressive armor an' such. I know a farmer up there—name of Wat. He's fond of the old tales same as me, an' that there battleground is in his back yard, so t'speak. If anybody's turned up anythin' that might lead ye t'what yer lookin' fer, he'd know it.''

"The man's name is Wat, you say?" Sparhawk asked, trying to sound casual.

"Can't miss him, young master. Walleyed feller. Scratches hisself a lot. He's had the seven-year itch fer about thirty year now." He shook his tankard hopefully.

"Ho there, my girl," Ulath called, fishing several coins out of the pouch at his belt. "Why don't you keep your old friend here drinking until he falls under the table?''

"Why, thankee, yer earlship." The old man grinned.

"After all, grandfather," Ulath laughed, "an earldom ought to be spread around, shouldn't it?''

"I couldn't of put it better meself, me Lord.''

They left the taproom and started up the stairs. "That worked out rather well, didn't it?" Kurik said.

"We were lucky," Kalten said. "What if that old fellow hadn't been in the taproom tonight?''

"Then someone would have directed us to him. Common people like to be helpful to the ones buying the beer.''

"I think we'll want to remember the story Ulath told the old fellow," Tynian said. "If we tell people that we want the king's bones to take back to Thalesia, they won't start speculating about our real reason for being so curious about where he's buried.''

"Isn't that the same as lying?" Berit said.

"Not really," Ulath told him. "We *do* plan to rebury him after we get his crown, don't we?''

"Of course.''

"Well, there you are, then."

Berit looked a little dubious about that. "I'll go see about supper," he said, "but I think there's a hole in your logic, Sir Ulath."

"Really?" Ulath said, looking surprised.

It was still raining the following morning. At some time during the night, Kalten had slipped from the room he shared with Sparhawk. Sparhawk had certain suspicions about his friend's absence in which the broad-hipped and very friendly barmaid Nima figured rather prominently. He did not press the issue, however. Sparhawk was, after all, a knight and a gentleman.

They rode north for the better part of two hours until they came to a broad meadow dotted with grass-covered burial mounds. "I wonder which one I should try first," Tynian said as they all dismounted.

"Take your pick," Sparhawk replied. "This Wat we heard about might be able to give you more precise information, but let's try it this way first. It might save some time, and we're starting to get short on that."

"You worry about your Queen all the time, don't you, Sparhawk?" Bevier asked shrewdly.

"Of course. It's what I'm supposed to do."

"I think, my friend, that it might go a bit deeper than that. Your affection for your Queen is more than a duty."

"You're being absurdly romantic, Bevier. She's only a child." Sparhawk felt suddenly offended, and at the same time defensive. "Before we get started, gentlemen," he said brusquely, "let's have a look around. I don't want any stray Zemochs watching us, and I definitely don't want any of the Seeker's empty-headed soldiers creeping up behind us while we're busy."

"We can deal with them," Kalten said confidently.

"Probably, yes, but you're missing the point. Every time we kill one of them, we announce our general location to the Seeker."

"Otha's bug is beginning to irritate me," Kalten said. "All this sneaking and skulking is unnatural."

"Maybe so, but I think you'd better get used to it for a while."

They left Sephrenia and the children in the shelter of a propped-up sheet of canvas and scoured the general vicinity.

They found no sign of anyone. Then they rode back to the burial mound.

"How about that one?" Ulath suggested to Tynian, pointing at a low earthen mound. "It looks sort of Thalesian."

Tynian shrugged. "It looks as good as any of the others."

They dismounted again. "Don't overdo this," Sparhawk told Tynian. "If you start to get too tired, back away from it."

"We need information, Sparhawk. I'll be all right." Tynian removed his heavy helmet, dismounted, took his coil of rope, and began to lay it out on the top of the mound in the same design as he had the previous day. Then he straightened with a slight grimace. "Well," he said, "here goes." He threw back his blue cloak and began to speak sonorously in Styric, weaving the intricate gestures of the spell with his hands as he did. Finally, he clapped his hands sharply together.

The mound shook violently as if it had been seized by an earthquake, and what came up from the ground this time did not rise slowly. It burst from the ground roaring—and it was not human.

"Tynian!" Sephrenia shouted. "Send it back!"

Tynian, however, stood transfixed, his eyes starting from his head in horror.

The hideous creature rushed at them, bowling over the thunderstruck Tynian and falling on Bevier, clawing and biting at his armor.

"Sparhawk!" Sephrenia cried as the big Pandion drew his sword. "Not that! It won't do any good! Use Aldreas' spear instead!"

Sparhawk spun and wrenched the short-handled spear from his saddle skirt.

The monstrous thing that was attacking Bevier lifted the white-cloaked knight's armored body as easily as a man might lift a child and smashed it to the ground with terrible force. Then it leaped at Kalten and began wrenching at his helmet. Ulath, Kurik, and Berit dashed to their friend's aid, hacking at the monster with their weapons. Astonishingly, their heavy axes and Kurik's mace did not sink into the thing's body, but bounced off in great showers of glowing sparks. Sparhawk dashed in, holding the spear low. Kalten was being shaken like a rag doll, and his black helmet was dented and scarred.

Deliberately, Sparhawk drove the spear into the monster's side with all his strength. The thing shrieked and turned on him. Again and again Sparhawk struck, and with each blow he felt a tremendous surge of power flowing through the spear. At last he saw an opening, feinted once, and then sank the spear directly into the monster's chest. The hideous mouth gaped open, but what gushed forth was not blood, but a kind of black slime. Grimly, Sparhawk twisted the spear inside the creature's body, making the wound bigger. It shrieked again and fell back. Sparhawk jerked his spear out of the beast's body, and the creature fled, howling and clutching at the gaping hole in its chest. It staggered up the side of the burial mound to the place whence it had emerged from the earth and plunged back into the depths.

Tynian was on his knees in the mud, clutching at his head and sobbing. Bevier lay motionless on the ground, and Kalten sat moaning.

Sephrenia moved quickly to Tynian and, after a quick glance at his face, began to speak rapidly in Styric, weaving the spell with her fingers. Tynian's sobbing lessened, and after a moment, he toppled over on his side. "I'll have to keep him asleep until he recovers," she said. "*If* he recovers. Sparhawk, you help Kalten. I'll see to Bevier."

Sparhawk went to Kalten. "Where are you hurt?" he asked.

"I think it cracked some of my ribs," Kalten gasped. "What was that thing? My sword just bounced off it."

"We can worry about what it was later," Sparhawk said. "Let's get you out of that armor and wrap those ribs. We don't want one of them jabbing into your lungs."

"I'd agree to that." Kalten winced. "I'm sore all over. I don't need any other problems. How's Bevier?"

"We don't know yet. Sephrenia's looking after him."

Bevier's injuries appeared to be more serious than Kalten's. After Sparhawk had bound a wide linen cloth tightly around his friend's chest and checked him over for any other injuries, he wrapped his cloak about him and then went to check on the Arcian. "How is he?" he asked Sephrenia.

"It's fairly serious, Sparhawk," she replied. "There aren't any cuts or gashes, but I think he may be bleeding inside."

"Kurik, Berit," Sparhawk called. "Set up the tents. We've got to get them in out of the rain." He looked around and saw Talen riding away at a gallop. "Now where's *he* going?" he demanded in exasperation.

"I sent him off to see if he can find a wagon," Kurik told him. "These men need to get to a physician fast, and they're in no condition to sit a saddle."

Ulath was frowning. "How did you manage to get your spear into that thing, Sparhawk?" he asked. "My ax just bounced off."

"I'm not sure," Sparhawk admitted.

"It was the rings," Sephrenia said, not looking up from Bevier's unconscious form.

"I *thought* I felt something happening while I was stabbing at that monster," Sparhawk said. "How is it that they've never seemed to have that sort of power before?"

"Because they were separated," she replied. "But you've got one on your hand and the other is in the socket of the spear. When you put them together like that, they have great power. They're a part of Bhelliom itself."

"All right," Ulath said. "What went wrong? Tynian was trying to raise Thalesian ghosts. How did he wake up that monstrosity?"

"Apparently he opened the wrong grave by mistake," she said. "Necromancy's not the most precise of the arts, I'm afraid. When the Zemochs invaded, Azash sent certain of his creatures with them. Tynian accidentally raised one of them."

"What's the matter with him?"

"The contact with that being has almost destroyed his mind."

"Is he going to be all right?"

"I don't know, Ulath, I really don't."

Berit and Kurik finished erecting the tents, and Sparhawk and Ulath moved their injured friends inside one of them. "We're going to need a fire," Kurik said, "and that's not going to be easy today, I'm afraid. I've got a little dry wood left, but not enough to last for very long. Those men are wet and cold, and we absolutely have to get them dried out and warm."

"Any suggestions?" Sparhawk asked him.

"I'll work on it."

It was sometime after noon when Talen returned, driving a rickety wagon that was hardly more than a cart. "This was the best I could find," he apologized.

"Did you have to steal it?" Kurik asked him.

"No. I didn't want the farmer chasing me. I bought it."

"With what?"

Talen looked slyly at the leather purse hanging from his father's belt. "Don't you feel just a little light on that side, Kurik?"

Kurik swore and looked closely at the purse. The bottom had been neatly slit open.

"Here's what I didn't need, though," Talen said, handing over a small handful of coins.

"You actually stole from *me*?"

"Be reasonable, Kurik. Sparhawk and the others are all wearing armor, and their purses are on the inside. Yours was the only one I could get to."

"What's under that canvas?" Sparhawk asked, looking into the wagon bed.

"Dry firewood," the boy replied. "The farmer had stacks of it in his barn. I picked up a few chickens, too. I didn't steal the wagon," he noted clinically, "but I *did* steal the firewood and the chickens—just to keep in practice. Oh, incidentally, the farmer's name is Wat. He's a walleyed fellow who scratches a lot. It seems to me that when I was outside the taproom door last night somebody was saying that he might be sort of significant for some reason."

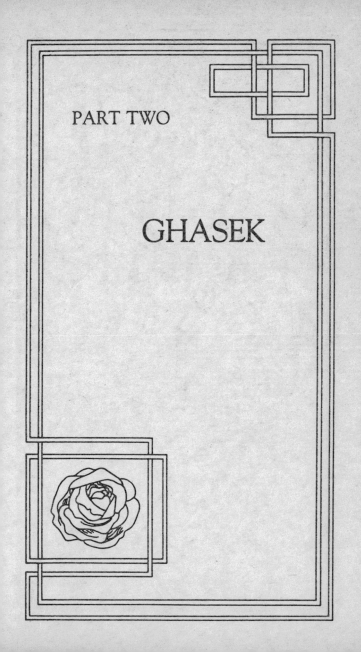

PART TWO

GHASEK

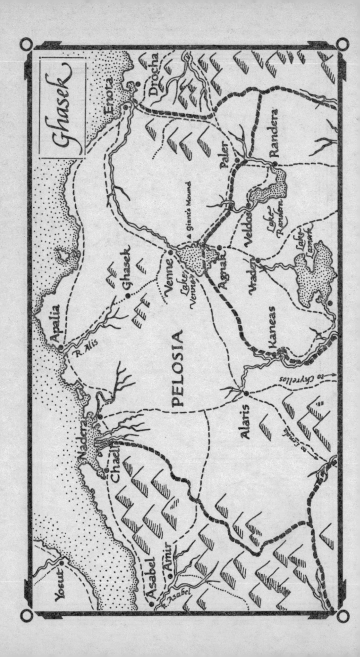

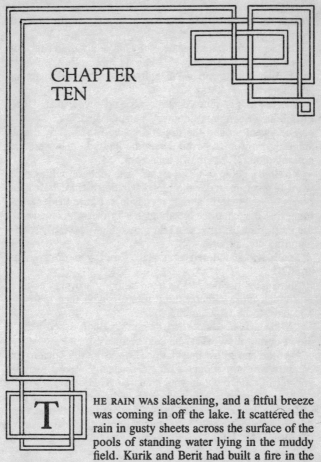

CHAPTER TEN

THE RAIN WAS slackening, and a fitful breeze was coming in off the lake. It scattered the rain in gusty sheets across the surface of the pools of standing water lying in the muddy field. Kurik and Berit had built a fire in the center of their circle of tents and set a canvas sheet on poles to the windward side, in part to protect the blaze from being quenched, but also in part to deflect its heat into the tent where the injured knights lay.

Ulath came out of one of the other tents, wrapping a dry cloak about his huge mailed shoulders. He raised his shaggy-browed face toward the sky. "It seems to be letting up," he said to Sparhawk.

"We can hope," Sparhawk said. "I don't think putting

Tynian and the others in that wagon in a rainstorm would do them much good."

Ulath grunted his agreement. "This really didn't turn out very well, did it, Sparhawk?" he said morosely. "We've got three men down, and we're still not any closer to finding Bhelliom."

There was not much Sparhawk could say to that. "Let's go see how Sephrenia's doing," he suggested.

They went around the fire and entered the tent where the small Styric woman hovered over the injured. "How are they coming along?" Sparhawk asked her.

"Kalten's going to be all right," she replied, pulling a red wool blanket up under the blond Pandion's chin. "He's had bones broken before, and he mends fast. I gave Bevier something that may stop the bleeding. It's Tynian who worries me the most, though. If we can't do something—and fairly soon—his mind will slip away."

Sparhawk shuddered at that. "Can't you do anything at all?"

She pursed her lips. "I've been thinking it over. The mind is a much more difficult thing to work with than the body. You have to be very careful."

"What actually happened to him?" Ulath asked her. "I didn't quite follow what you said before."

"At the end of his incantation, he was totally open to that creature from the mound. The dead usually wake slowly, so you've got time to put up your defenses. That beast isn't really dead, so it came at him before he had time to protect himself." She looked down at Tynian's ashen face. "There's one thing that might work," she mused doubtfully. "It's worth a try, I suppose. I don't think anything else will save his sanity. Flute, come here."

The little girl rose from where she had been sitting cross-legged on the canvas ground sheet of the tent. Her bare feet were grass-stained, Sparhawk noted absently. In spite of all the mud and wet, Flute's feet always seemed to have those greenish stains on them. She softly crossed the tent to Sephrenia, her dark eyes questioning.

Sephrenia spoke to her in that peculiar Styric dialect.

Flute nodded.

"All right, gentlemen," Sephrenia said to Sparhawk and

Ulath, "there's nothing you can do here, and at the moment, you're just underfoot."

"We'll wait outside," Sparhawk said, feeling slightly abashed at the crisp way they had been dismissed.

"I'd appreciate it."

The two knights went out of the tent. "She can be very abrupt, can't she?" Ulath noted.

"When she has something serious on her mind."

"Has she always treated you Pandions this way?"

"Yes."

Then they heard the sound of Flute's pipes coming from inside the tent. The melody was much like the peculiarly drowsy one she had played to lull the attention of the spies outside the chapterhouse and the soldiers on the dock at Vardenais. There were slight differences, however, and Sephrenia was speaking sonorously in Styric as a sort of counterpoint. Suddenly, the tent began to glow with a peculiar golden light.

"I don't believe I've ever heard that spell before," Ulath admitted.

"Our instruction only covers the things we're likely to need to know," Sparhawk replied. "There are whole realms of Styric magic we don't even know exist. Some are too difficult, and some are too dangerous." Then he raised his voice. "Talen," he called.

The young thief poked his head out of one of the other tents. "What?" he said flatly.

"Come here. I want to talk to you."

"Can't you do it inside? It's wet out there."

Sparhawk sighed. "Just come here, Talen," he said. "Please don't argue with me every time I ask you to do something."

Grumbling, the boy came out of the tent. He approached Sparhawk warily. "Well, am I in trouble again?"

"Not that I know of. You said that farmer you bought the wagon from is named Wat?"

"Yes."

"How far is his farm from here?"

"A couple of miles."

"What does he look like?"

"His eyes look off in two different directions, and he

scratches a lot. Isn't he the fellow that old man in the taproom was telling you about?''

"How did you know about that?"

Talen shrugged. "I was listening outside the door."

"Eavesdropping?"

"I don't know if I'd really put it that way. I'm a child, Sparhawk—or at least people think I am. Grownups don't think they have to tell things to children. I've found that if I really need to know anything, I'm going to have to find it out for myself.''

"He's probably got a point, Sparhawk," Ulath said.

"You'd better get your cloak," Sparhawk told the boy. "In just a little bit, you and I are going to pay a visit to this itchy farmer.''

Talen looked out over the rainy field and sighed.

From inside the tent, Flute's pipesong broke off, and Sephrenia ceased her incantation.

"I wonder if that's a good sign or a bad one," Ulath said.

They waited tensely. Then, after a few moments, Sephrenia looked out. "I think he'll be all right now. Come in and talk to him. I'll know better once I hear how he answers.''

Tynian was propped up on a pillow, although his face was still ashy gray and his hands were trembling. His eyes, however, though still haunted, appeared rational.

"How are you feeling?" Sparhawk asked him, trying to sound casual.

Tynian laughed weakly. "If you really want to know the truth, I feel as if I'd been turned inside out and then put together again backward. Did you manage to kill that monstrosity?''

"Sparhawk drove it off with that spear of his," Ulath told him.

A haunted fear came into Tynian's eyes. "It might come back then?" he asked.

"Not very likely," Ulath replied. "It jumped back into the burial mound and pulled the ground in after it."

"Thank God," Tynian said with relief.

"I think you'd better sleep now," Sephrenia told him. "We can all talk more later.''

Tynian nodded and lay back again.

Sephrenia covered him with a blanket, motioned to Sparhawk and Ulath, and led them outside. "I think he's going to be all right," she said. "I felt much better when I heard him laugh. It's going to take some time, but at least he's on the mend."

"I'm going to take Talen and go talk to that farmer," Sparhawk told them. "He seems to be the one the old man at the inn told us about. He might be able to give us some idea of where to go next."

"It's worth a try, I suppose," Ulath said a bit doubtfully. "Kurik and I'll keep an eye on things here."

Sparhawk nodded and went into the tent he normally shared with Kalten. He removed his armor and put on his plain mail shirt and stout woolen leggings instead. He belted on his sword and then pulled his gray, hooded traveller's cloak about his shoulders. He went back out to the fire. "Come along, Talen," he called.

The boy came out of the tent with a look of resignation on his face. His still-damp cloak was wrapped tightly about him. "I don't suppose I could talk you out of this," he said.

"No."

"I hope that farmer hasn't looked into his barn yet, then. He might be a little touchy about the missing firewood."

"I'll pay for it if I have to."

Talen winced. "After I went to all the trouble of stealing it? Sparhawk, that's degrading. It might even be immoral."

Sparhawk looked at him quizzically. "Someday you're going to have to explain the morality of a thief to me."

"It's really very simple, Sparhawk. The first rule is not to pay for anything."

"I thought it might be something like that. Let's go."

The sky to the west was definitely growing lighter as Sparhawk and Talen rode toward the lake, and the rain had become no more than sporadic showers. That in itself lightened Sparhawk's mood. It had been a bleak time. The uncertainty that had dogged his steps from the moment they had left Cimmura had proved to be fully justified, but even now the certainty that they had taken a wrong course provided him with firm ground for a new beginning. Sparhawk accepted his losses stoically and went on toward the lightening sky.

The house and outbuildings of the farmer Wat lay in a little dell. It was a slovenly-looking sort of place, surrounded by a log palisade that leaned dispiritedly away from the prevail-

ing wind. The house, half log and half stone, had a poorly
thatched roof and looked definitely run-down. The barn was
even worse, appearing to continue to stand more out of habit
than from any structural integrity. A broken-down cart sat in
the muddy yard, and rusting tools lay wherever their owner
had discarded them. Wet, dishevelled chickens scratched in
the mud without much hope, and a scrawny black and white
pig rooted near the doorstep of the house.

"Not very neat, is he?" Talen observed as he and Sparhawk rode in.

"I saw the cellar you were living in back in Cimmura,"
Sparhawk replied. "It wasn't exactly what you'd call tidy."

"But at least it was out of sight. This fellow's messy in
public."

A man with eyes that did not track together and unkempt,
dirty hair shambled out of the house. His clothing appeared
to be tied together with bits of twine, and he was absently
scratching at his stomach. "What's yer business here?" he
asked in an unfriendly tone. He levelled a kick at the pig.
"Get outta there, Sophie," he said.

"We were talking with an old man back there in the village," Sparhawk replied, pointing with his thumb back over
his shoulder. "He was a white-haired fellow with a wobbly
neck who seemed to know a lot of old stories."

"You must mean old Farsh," the farmer said.

"Never did catch his name," Sparhawk said easily. "We
met him in the taproom at the inn."

"That's Farsh, all right. He likes to stay close to the beer.
What's this got to do with me?"

"He said you were fond of the old stories, too—the ones
that have to do with the battle that went on here some five
hundred or so years ago."

The walleyed man's face brightened. "Oh, so that's it,"
he said. "Me'n Farsh always used to swap those old tales.
Why don't you an' yer boy come inside, yer worship? I
ha'nt had a chance t' talk about the good ol' days fer a long
time now."

"Why, that's mighty obliging of you, neighbor," Sparhawk said, swinging down from Faran's back. "Come along,
Talen."

"Lemme put yer mounts in the barn," the itchy fellow
offered.

Faran looked at the rickety structure and shuddered.

"Thanks all the same, neighbor," Sparhawk said, "but the rain's letting up, and the breeze ought to dry their coats. We'll just put them out in your meadow, if that's all right."

"Somebody might come along an' try to steal 'em."

"Not this horse," Sparhawk told him. "This is not the sort of horse people want to steal."

"Yer the one as gets to walk if yer wrong." The walleyed man shrugged, turning to open the door to his house.

The interior of the house was if anything more untidy than the yard had been. The remains of several meals sat on the table, and dirty clothes lay in heaps in the corners. "The name's Wat," the walleyed man identified himself. He flopped down in a chair. "Sit yerselves," he invited. Then he squinted at Talen. "Say, you was the young fella as bought my ol' wagon."

"Yes," Talen replied a bit nervously.

"She run all right fer you? I mean, none of the wheels fell off or nothin'?"

"It worked just fine," Talen said with some relief.

"Glad t' hear it. Now, which particular stories was you interested in?"

"What we're really looking for, Wat," Sparhawk began, "is any information you might be able to give us about what happened to the old King of Thalesia during the battle. A friend of ours is distantly related to him, and the family wants his bones brought back to Thalesia for proper burial."

"Never heard nothin' about no Thalesian king," Wat admitted, "but that don't mean all that much. This was a big battle, and there was Thalesians fightin' with the Zemochs from the south end of the lake all the way up into Pelosia. Y'see now, what happened was that when the Thalesians started to land on the north coast up there, Zemoch patrols they seen 'em, an' Otha, he started to send some good-sized forces up there to try to keep 'em from gettin' to the main battlefield. At first, the Thalesians come down in small groups, an' the Zemochs, they had things pretty much their own way. There was a pretty fair number of runnin' fights up there when this group or that of the Thalesians got theirselves waylaid. But then the main body of the Thalesian army landed, an' they turned things around. Say, I got some home-brewed beer back there. Could I interest you in some?"

"I wouldn't mind," Sparhawk said, "but the boy's a bit young."

"Got some milk, if that'd suit you, young feller," Wat offered.

Talen sighed. "Why not?" he said.

Sparhawk thought things over. "The Thalesian King would have been one of the first to land," he said. "He left his capital before his army did, but he never got as far as the battlefield."

"Then most likely he's layin' somewhere up there in Pelosia or maybe someplace in Deira," Wat replied. He rose to fetch beer and milk.

"It's a big stretch of country." Sparhawk winced.

"That it is, friend, that it is, but yer followin' the right trail. There's them in Pelosia an' Deira as takes the same pleasure in the old tales as me 'n' old Farsh does, an' the closer y' get to wherever it is this king yer lookin' fer is buried, the better yer chances are gonna be of findin' somebody as kin tell y' what y' want to know."

"That's true, I suppose." Sparhawk took a sip of beer. It was cloudy, but it was about the best he had ever tasted.

Wat leaned back in his chair, scratching at his chest. "Fact of the matter is, friend, that the battle was just too big fer any one man t' see it all. I pretty much know what went on around here, an' Farsh, he knows what went on down around the village an' on south. We all know in a general sorta way what happened overall, but when y' want to get down to specifics, y' gotta talk with somebody as lives fairly close to where it actual happened."

Sparhawk sighed. "It's just a matter of pure luck, then," he said glumly. "We could ride right past the man who knows the story and never even think to ask him."

"Now, that's not entirely true, friend," Wat disagreed. "Us fellers is like to swap stories, we knows one another. Old Farsh, he sent y' t' me, an' I kin send y' on to another feller I know in Paler up there in Pelosia. He's gonna know a lot more about what went on up there than I do, an' he'll know others as knows even more about what went on close t' where *they* live. That's what I meant when I said y' was followin' the right trail. All y' need t' do is go from feller t' feller until y' git the story y' want. It's a lot faster'n diggin' up all of northern Pelosia or Deira."

"You might be right at that."

The walleyed man grinned crookedly. "Not meanin' no offense, yer worship, but you gentlefolk think that us commoners don't know nothin', but when y' stack us all together, there's not very much in this world we *don't* know."

"I'll remember that," Sparhawk said. "Who's this man in Paler?"

"He's a tanner, name of Berd—silly name, but Pelosians is like that. His tanyard's just outside the north gate of the city. They wouldn't let him set up inside the walls on accounta the smell, y' know. You go see Berd, an' if he don't know the story y' want to hear, he'll probably know somebody as does—or at least somebody as kin tell y' who y' oughta talk to."

Sparhawk rose to his feet. "Wat," he said, "you've been a real help." He handed the fellow a few coins. "The next time you go to the village, have yourself a few tankards of beer, and if you run into Farsh, buy him one too."

"Why, thankee, yer worship," Wat said. "I most surely will. An' good luck in yer search."

"Thank you." Then Sparhawk remembered something. "I'd like to buy some firewood from you, if you can spare any." He handed Wat a few more coins.

"Why, certainly, yer worship. Come along to the barn, an' I'll show you where it's stacked."

"That's all right, Wat," Sparhawk smiled. "We've already got it. Come along, Talen."

The rain had stopped entirely when Sparhawk and Talen came out of the house, and they could see blue sky out over the lake to the west.

"You had to go and do that, didn't you?" Talen said in a disgusted tone of voice.

"He *was* very helpful, Talen," Sparhawk said defensively.

"That has nothing to do with it. Did we really get very far with this?"

"It was a start," Sparhawk replied. "Wat may not look very bright, but he's really very shrewd. The plan of going from storyteller to storyteller is about the best we've come up with so far."

"It's going to take awhile, you know."

"Not as long a while as some of the other notions we've had."

"The trip wasn't wasted then."

"We'll know better after we talk with that tanner in Paler."

Ulath and Berit had strung a rope near the fire and were hanging wet clothes over it when Sparhawk and the boy returned to camp. "Any luck?" Ulath asked.

"Some, I hope," Sparhawk replied. "It's fairly certain that King Sarak didn't get this far south. It seems that there was a lot more fighting up in Pelosia and Deira than Bevier read about."

"What next, then?"

"We go to the town of Paler up in Pelosia and talk to a tanner named Berd. If he hasn't heard about Sarak, he can probably send us on to someone who has. How's Tynian?"

"He's still asleep. Bevier's awake, though, and Sephrenia got him to drink some soup."

"That's a good sign. Let's go inside and talk with her. Now that the weather's clearing, I think it's safe to move on."

They trooped into the tent, and Sparhawk repeated the gist of what Wat had said.

"The plan has merit, Sparhawk," Sephrenia approved. "How far is it to Paler?"

"Talen, go get my map, would you?"

"Why me?"

"Because I asked you to."

"Oh. All right."

"Just the map, Talen," Sparhawk added. "Don't take anything else out of the pack."

The boy returned after a few moments, and Sparhawk unfolded the map. "All right," he said. "Paler's up here at the north end of the lake—just across the Pelosian border. I make it about ten leagues."

"That wagon won't move very fast," Kurik told him, "and we don't want to jolt these men around. It's probably going to take at least two days."

"At least once we get them to Paler we should be able to find a physician for them," Sephrenia said.

"We really don't have to use the wagon," Bevier objected. His face was pale, and he was sweating profusely. "Tynian is much better, and Kalten and I aren't hurt that badly. We can ride."

"Not while I'm giving the orders, you can't," Sparhawk told him. "I'm not going to gamble your lives just to save a few hours." He went to the door of the tent and looked out. "It's coming on to evening," he noted. "We'll all get a good night's sleep and start out first thing in the morning."

Kalten grunted and sat up painfully. "Good," he said. "Now that that's settled, what's for supper?"

After they had eaten, Sparhawk went out and sat by the fire. He was staring morosely into the flames when Sephrenia joined him. "What is it, dear one?" she asked him.

"Now that I've had time to think about it, this is really a farfetched notion, isn't it? We could wander around Pelosia and Deira for the next twenty years listening to old men tell stories."

"I don't really think so, Sparhawk," she disagreed. "Sometimes I get hunches—little flashes of the future. Somehow I feel that we're on the right course."

"Hunches, Sephrenia," he said with some amusement.

"Maybe a little stronger than that, but it's a word that Elenes wouldn't understand."

"Are you trying to to say you can actually see into the future?"

She laughed. "Oh, no," she replied. "Only the Gods can do that, and even they're imperfect at it. About all I can really perceive is when something's right and when it isn't. This somehow *feels* right. There's one other thing, too," she added. "The ghost of Aldreas told you that the time has come for Bhelliom to emerge again. I know what Bhelliom is capable of. It can control things in ways we can't even imagine. If it wants *us* to be the ones who find it, nothing on earth will be able to stop us. I think you might find that the story-tellers up there in Pelosia and Deira will tell us things they've thought they've forgotten, and even things they never knew."

"Isn't that just a little mystic?"

"Styrics *are* mystics, Sparhawk. I thought you knew that."

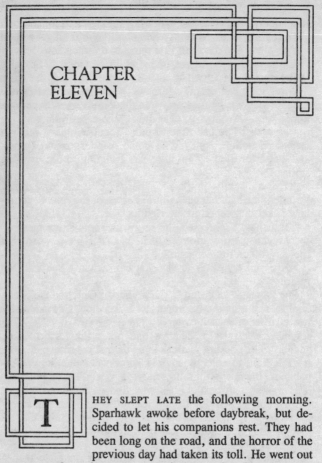

CHAPTER ELEVEN

T HEY SLEPT LATE the following morning. Sparhawk awoke before daybreak, but decided to let his companions rest. They had been long on the road, and the horror of the previous day had taken its toll. He went out some way from the tents to watch the sunrise. The sky overhead was clear, and the stars were still out. Despite Sephrenia's assurances the previous evening, Sparhawk's mood was somber. When they had begun, the sense that their cause was just and noble had led him to believe that somehow they would prevail against almost anything. The events of the previous day, however, had proved to him just how wrong he had been about that. He would venture anything to bring his pale young Queen back to health, even to the point of throw-

158

ing his own life into the crucible, but did he have the right
to risk his friends'?

"What's the problem?" He recognized Kurik's voice without looking around.

"I don't know, Kurik," he admitted. "It all feels as if I'm
trying to hold sand in my fist, and this plan of ours doesn't
really make much sense, does it? Trying to track down five-
hundred-year-old stories is really kind of absurd, don't you
think?"

"No, Sparhawk," Kurik said, "not really. You could run
around northern Pelosia or Deira with a spade for the next
two hundred years and not even come close to Bhelliom. That
farmer was right, you know. Trust the people, my Lord. In
many ways, the people are wiser than the nobility—or even
the Church, for that matter." Kurik coughed uncomfortably.
"You don't necessarily have to tell Patriarch Dolmant I said
that," he amended.

"Your secret is safe, my friend." Sparhawk smiled. "There's
something we're going to have to talk about."

"Oh?"

"Kalten, Bevier, and Tynian are more or less out of action."

"You know, I believe you're right."

"That's a bad habit, Kurik."

"Aslade says the same thing."

"Your wife's a wise woman. All right. Part of our success
in getting around difficulties has been the presence of men in
armor. Most people don't interfere with the Knights of the
Church. The trouble is that now there's only going to be
Ulath and me."

"I can count, Sparhawk. What's your point?"

"Could you fit into Bevier's armor?"

"Probably. It might not be very comfortable, but I could
adjust the straps a bit. The point, though, is that I won't do
it."

"What's the problem? You've worn armor on the practice
field."

"That was on the field. Everybody knew who I was, and
they knew why I was doing it. This is out in the world, and
that's altogether different."

"I really don't see the distinction, Kurik."

"There are laws about that sort of thing, Sparhawk. Only knights are permitted to wear armor, and I'm not a knight."

"The difference is very slight."

"But it's still a difference."

"You're going to make me order you to do this, aren't you?"

"I wish you wouldn't."

"I wish I didn't have to. I'm not trying to offend your sensibilities, Kurik, but this is an unusual situation. It involves our safety. You'll wear Bevier's armor, and I think we can stuff Berit into Kalten's. He's worn mine before, and Kalten and I are about the same size."

"You're going to insist, then?"

"I don't really have any choice. We've got to get through to Paler without any incidents along the way. I've got some injured men, and I don't want to risk them."

"I understand the reasons, Sparhawk. I'm not stupid, after all. I don't like it, but you're probably right."

"I'm glad we agree."

"Don't get too ecstatic about it. I want it clearly understood that I'm doing this under protest."

"If there's ever any trouble about it, I'll swear to that."

"That's assuming you're still alive," Kurik replied sourly. "You want me to wake the others?"

"No. Let them sleep. You were right last night. It's going to take two days to get to Paler. That gives us a little time to play with."

"You're very worried about time, aren't you, Sparhawk?"

"We've only got so much of it left," Sparhawk replied somberly. "This business of running around listening to old men tell stories is likely to chew up a great deal of it. It's coming up to the point where another one of the twelve knights is going to die, and he'll give his sword to Sephrenia. You know how that weakens her."

"She's a lot stronger than she looks. She could probably carry as much as you and I put together." Kurik glanced back toward the tents. "I'll go build up the fire and put her teakettle on to boil. She usually wakes up early." And he went back toward the camp.

Ulath, who had been standing watch nearby, loomed out of the shadows. "That was a very interesting conversation," he rumbled.

"You were listening."

"Obviously. Voices carry a long way at night for some reason."

"You don't approve—about the armor, I mean?"

"It doesn't bother me, Sparhawk. We're a lot less formal in Thalesia than you are down here. A fair number of Genidian Knights are not, strictly speaking, of noble birth." He grinned, his teeth flashing. "We usually wait until King Wargun is roaring drunk and then file them in so he can bestow titles on them. Several of my friends are barons of places that don't even exist." He rubbed at the back of his neck. "Sometimes I think this whole nobility business is a farce, anyway. Men are men—titled or not. I don't think God cares, so why should we?"

"You're going to stir up a revolution talking like that, Ulath."

"Maybe it's time for one. It's starting to get light over there." Ulath pointed toward the eastern horizon.

"Right. It looks as if we might have good weather today."

"Check with me this evening, and I'll let you know."

"Don't people in Thalesia try to predict the weather?"

"Why? You can't do anything about it. Why don't we go have a look at your map? I know a bit about ships and currents and prevailing winds and the like. It could just be that I can make some guesses about where King Sarak made his landfall. We might be able to figure out which route he took. That could narrow things down just a bit."

"Not a bad idea," Sparhawk agreed. "If we can work that out, at least we'll have some idea of where to start asking questions." Sparhawk hesitated. "Ulath," he said seriously, "is Bhelliom really as dangerous as they say it is?"

"Probably even more so. Ghwerig made it, and he's not really very pleasant—even for a Troll."

"You said 'is.' Don't you mean 'was'? He's dead by now, isn't he?"

"Not that I've heard, and I sort of doubt it. There's something you ought to know about Trolls, Sparhawk. They don't die of old age like other creatures. You have to kill them. If somebody had managed to kill Ghwerig, he'd have boasted about it, and I'd have heard the story. There's not much to do in Thalesia in the wintertime except listen to stories. The snow piles up by the foot there, so we usually stay inside. Let's go have a look at that map.''

As they walked back toward the tents, Sparhawk decided that he liked Ulath. The huge Genidian Knight was normally very silent, but once you managed to unlock his friendship, he spoke with a kind of droll understatement that was often even more amusing than Kalten's exaggerated humor. Sparhawk's companions were good men—the best, actually. They were all different, of course, but that was only to be expected. Whatever the outcome of their search might be, he was glad that he had had the opportunity to know them.

Sephrenia stood by the fire drinking tea. ''You're up early,'' she noted as the two knights came into the circle of light. ''Have the plans changed? Are we in some hurry to leave?''

''Not really,'' Sparhawk told her, kissing her palm in greeting.

''Please don't spill my tea,'' she cautioned.

''No, ma'am,'' he agreed. ''We're not going to be able to cover much more than five leagues today, so let the others sleep awhile longer. That wagon's not going to move very fast, and besides, after what's been happening, I don't think wandering around in the dark would be such a good idea. Is Berit awake yet?''

''I think I heard him stirring around.''

''I'm going to put him in Kalten's armor and have Kurik wear Bevier's. Maybe we can intimidate anybody who might be feeling unfriendly.''

''Is that all you Elenes ever think about?''

''A good bluff is sometimes better than a good fight,'' Ulath growled. ''I like deceiving people.''

''You're as bad as Talen is.''

''No, not really. My fingers aren't nimble enough for cutting purses. If I decide I want what's in a man's purse, I'll hit him on the head and take it.''

She laughed. ''I'm surrounded by scoundrels.''

The day dawned bright and sunny. The sky was very blue, and the wet grass that covered the surrounding hills was shiny green.

''Whose turn is it to cook breakfast?'' Sparhawk asked Ulath.

''Yours.''

''Are you sure?''

"Yes."

They roused the others, and Sparhawk got the cooking utensils out of one of the packs.

After they had eaten, Kurik and Berit cut spare lances from a nearby thicket while Sparhawk and Ulath helped their injured friends into Talen's rickety wagon.

"What's wrong with the ones we've got?" Ulath asked when Kurik returned with the lances.

"They tend to break," Kurik said, tying the poles to the side of the wagon, "particularly in view of the way you gentlemen use them. It never hurts to have extra ones along."

"Sparhawk," Talen said quietly, "there are some more of those people in white smocks out there. They're hiding in that brush along the edge of the field."

"Could you tell what kind they were?"

"They had swords," the boy replied.

"Zemochs then. How many of them are there?"

"I saw four."

Sparhawk went over to Sephrenia. "There's a small group of Zemochs hiding at the edge of the field. Would the Seeker's people try to hide?"

"No. They'd attack immediately."

"That's what I thought."

"What are you going to do?" Kalten asked.

"Run them off. I don't want any of Otha's men trailing along behind us. Ulath, let's mount up and chase those people for a while."

Ulath grinned and hauled himself into his saddle.

"You want your lances?" Kurik asked.

Ulath grunted, drawing his ax. "Not for a job this small."

Sparhawk climbed up onto Faran's back, strapped on his shield, and drew his sword. He and Ulath set out at a menacing walk. After a few moments, the hidden Zemochs broke from their cover and fled, crying out in alarm. "Let's run them for a bit," Sparhawk suggested. "I want them to be too winded to turn around and come back."

"Right," Ulath agreed, pushing his horse into a canter.

The two mounted knights crashed through the bushes at the edge of the field and pursued the fleeing Zemochs across a broad stretch of ploughed ground.

"Why not just kill them?" Ulath shouted to Sparhawk.

"It's probably not really necessary," Sparhawk shouted

back. "There are only four of them, and they don't pose much of a threat."

"You're getting soft, Sparhawk."

"Not really."

They pursued the Zemochs for perhaps twenty minutes, then reined in.

"They run very well, don't they?" Ulath chuckled. "Why don't we go on back now? I'm getting tired of looking at this place."

They rejoined the others, and they all set out, going north along the lake. They saw peasants in the fields, but no signs of any other Zemochs. They rode at a walk with Ulath and Kurik in the lead.

"Any guesses about what those people were up to?" Kalten asked Sparhawk. The blond knight was driving the wagon, the reins held negligently in one hand and the other pressed against his injured ribs.

"I'd imagine that Otha's having his men keep an eye on anybody poking around the battlefield," Sparhawk replied. "If somebody happens to stumble across Bhelliom, he'd definitely want to know about it."

"There may be more, then. It might not hurt to keep our eyes open."

The sun grew warmer as the day progressed, and Sparhawk began almost to wish for a return of the clouds and rain of the past week or more. Grimly he rode on, sweltering in his black-enamelled armor.

They camped that night in a grove of stately oaks not far from the Pelosian border and rose early the following morning. The guards posted at the boundary stood aside for them respectfully, and by midafternoon they crested a hill and looked down on the Pelosian city of Paler.

"We made better time than I thought we would," Kurik noted as they rode down the long slope toward the city. "Are you sure that map of yours is accurate, Sparhawk?"

"No map is entirely accurate. About the best you can hope for is an approximation."

"Knew a map maker in Thalesia once," Ulath said. "He set out to map the country between Emsat and Husdal. At first he paced everything off very carefully, but after a day or so he bought himself a good horse and started guessing. His map doesn't even come close, but everybody uses it because nobody wants to take the trouble of drawing a new one."

The guards at the south gate of the city passed them after only the briefest of questions, and Sparhawk obtained the name and location of a respectable inn from one of them. "Talen," he said, "do you think you'll be able to find your way to that inn by yourself?"

"Of course. I can find any place in any town."

"Good. Stay here then, and keep your eyes on that road coming up from the south. Let's see if those Zemochs are still curious about us."

"No problem, Sparhawk." Talen dismounted and tied his horse at the side of the gate. Then he strolled back out and sat in the grass at the side of the road.

Sparhawk and the others rode on into the city with the wagon clattering along behind them. The cobbled streets of Paler were crowded, but people gave way to the Knights of the Church, and they reached the inn within perhaps half an hour. Sparhawk dismounted and went inside.

The innkeeper wore one of the tall, pointed hats common in Pelosia and had a slightly haughty expression.

"You have rooms?" Sparhawk asked him.

"Of course. This is an inn."

Sparhawk waited, his expression cold.

"What's your trouble?" the innkeeper asked.

"I was just waiting for you to finish your sentence. I think you left something out."

The innkeeper flushed. "Sorry, my Lord," he mumbled.

"Much better," Sparhawk congratulated him. "Now then, I have three injured friends. Does there happen to be a physician nearby?"

"Down at the end of this street, my Lord. He has a sign out."

"Is he any good?"

"I really couldn't say. I haven't been sick lately."

"We'll chance him, I guess. I'll bring my friends inside and go get him."

"I don't think he'll come, my Lord. He has a very high opinion of himself. He thinks it's beneath his dignity to leave his quarters. He makes the sick and injured come to him."

"I'll persuade him," Sparhawk said bleakly.

The innkeeper laughed a bit nervously at that. "How many in your party, my Lord?"

"Ten of us. We'll help the injured inside, and then I'll go have a chat with this self-important physician."

They aided Kalten, Tynian, and Bevier into the inn and up the stairs to their rooms. Then Sparhawk came back down and walked resolutely toward the end of the street, his black cape billowing out behind him.

The physician maintained his quarters on the second floor over a greengrocer's shop, and entry was gained by way of an outside stairway. Sparhawk clanked up the stairs and entered without knocking. The physician was a weaselly little fellow dressed in a flowing blue robe. His eyes bulged slightly when he looked up from his book to see a grim-faced man in black armor enter uninvited. "I *beg* your pardon," he objected.

Sparhawk ignored that. He had decided that the best course was to cut through any possible arguments. "You are the physician?" he asked in a flat voice.

"I am," the man replied.

"You will come with me." It was not a request.

"But—"

"No buts. I have three injured friends who require your attention."

"Can't you bring them here? I do not customarily leave my quarters."

"Customs change. Get what you'll need and come along. They're at the inn just up the street."

"This is outrageous, Sir Knight."

"We're not going to argue about this, are we, neighbor?" Sparhawk's voice was deadly quiet.

The physician flinched back. "Ah—no. I don't believe so. I'll make an exception in this case."

"I was hoping you'd feel that way."

The physician rose quickly. "I'll get my instruments and some medicines. What sort of injuries are we talking about?"

"One of them has some broken ribs. Another seems to be bleeding inside somewhere. The third suffers mostly from exhaustion."

"Exhaustion is easily cured. Just have your friend spend several days in bed."

"He doesn't have time. Just give him something that'll get him back on his feet."

"How did they receive these injuries?"

"Church business," Sparhawk said shortly.

"I'm always eager to serve the Church."

"You've got no idea of how happy that makes me."

Sparhawk led the reluctant physician back up the street to the inn and on up to the second floor. He drew Sephrenia aside as the healer began his examinations. "It's a little late," he said to her. "Why don't we hold off on visiting the tanner until morning? I don't think we want him to be rushed. He might forget things we need to know."

"Truly," she agreed. "Besides, I want to be sure this physician knows what he's doing. He looks a little unreliable to me."

"He'd better be reliable. He's already got a fair idea of what's going to happen to him if he isn't."

"Oh, Sparhawk," she said reprovingly.

"It's really a very simple arrangement, little mother. He fully understands that either they get healthy or he gets sick. That sort of encourages him to do his best."

Pelosian cooking, Sparhawk had noticed, leaned heavily in the direction of boiled cabbage, beets, and turnips, only lightly garnished with salt pork. The latter, of course was totally unacceptable to Sephrenia and Flute, and so the two made a meal of raw vegetables and boiled eggs. Kalten, however, ate everything in sight.

It was after dark when Talen arrived at the inn. "They're still following us, Sparhawk," he reported, "only there are a lot more of them now. I saw maybe forty of them on top of that hill just south of town, and they're on horses now. They stopped at the hilltop and looked things over. Then they pulled back into the woods."

"That's a little more serious than just four, isn't it?" Kalten said.

"It is indeed," Sparhawk agreed. "Any ideas, Sephrenia?"

She frowned. "We haven't really been moving all that fast," she said. "If they're on horseback, they could have caught up with us without much trouble. I'd guess that they're just following us. Azash seems to know something that we don't. He's been trying to kill you for months, but now he sends his people out with orders just to follow us at a distance.''

"Can you think of any reason for the change in tactics?''

"Several, but they're all pure speculation.''

"We'll have to be alert when we leave town,'' Kalten said.

"Maybe doubly alert,'' Tynian added. "They might be just biding their time until we come to a deserted stretch of road where they can ambush us.''

"That's a cheerful thought,'' Kalten said wryly. "Well, I don't know about the rest of you, but I'm going to bed.''

The sun was very bright again the following morning, and a freshening breeze blew in off the lake. Sparhawk dressed in his mail shirt, a plain tunic, and woolen leggings. Then he and Sephrenia rode out from the inn toward the north gate of Paler and the tanyard of the man named Berd. The people in the street appeared for the most part to be common workmen carrying a variety of tools. They wore sober blue smocks and the tall, pointed hats.

"I wonder if they realize just how silly those things look,'' Sparhawk murmured.

"Which things were those?'' Sephrenia asked him.

"Those hats. They look like dunce caps.''

"They're no more ridiculous than those plumed hats the courtiers in Cimmura wear.''

"I suppose you're right.''

The tanyard was some distance beyond the north gate, and it smelled vile. Sephrenia wrinkled her nose as they approached. "This is not going to be a pleasant morning,'' she predicted.

"I'll cut it as short as I can,'' Sparhawk promised.

The tanner was a heavy-set, bald man wearing a canvas apron stained with dark brown splotches. He was stirring at a large vat with a long paddle as Sparhawk and Sephrenia rode into his yard. "I'll be right with you,'' he said. His voice sounded like gravel being poured across a slate. He stirred for a moment or two longer, looking critically into the vat. Then he laid aside his paddle and came toward them, wiping his hands on his apron. "How can I help you?'' he asked.

Sparhawk dismounted and helped Sephrenia down from her white palfrey. "We were talking with a farmer named

Wat down in Lamorkand,'' he told the tanner. "He said you might be able to help us."

"Old Wat?" The tanner laughed. "Is he still alive?"

"He was three days ago. You're Berd, aren't you?"

"That's me, my Lord. What's this help you need?"

"We've been going around talking to people who know stories about that big battle they had around here some years back. There are some people up in Thalesia who are distantly related to the man who was their king during that battle. They want to find out where he's buried so they can take his bones back home."

"Never heard of no kings involved in the fights around here," Berd admitted. "Course that don't mean there wasn't a few. I don't imagine kings go around introducin' theirselves to common folks."

"Then there *were* battles up here?" Sparhawk asked him.

"I don't know as I'd call 'em battles exactly—more what you might call skirmishes an' the like. Y' see, my Lord, the main battle was down at the south end of the lake. That's where the armies drew up their lines of regiments an' battalions an' such. What was goin' through up here was small groups of men—Pelosians mostly at first, an' then later the Thalesians started to filter on down. Otha's Zemochs, they had out their patrols, an' there was a bunch of nasty little fights, but nothin' as you could really call a battle. They was a couple not far from here, but I don't know as any Thalesians was involved. Most of *their* fights went on up around Lake Venne, an' even as far north as Ghasek." He suddenly snapped his fingers. "Now *that's* the one you really ought to talk to," he said. "Can't think why I didn't remember that right off."

"Oh?"

"Of course. Can't imagine where my brain had went. That Count of Ghasek, he went to some university down in Cammoria, an' he got to studyin' up on history an' the like. Anyhow, all the books he read on that there battle, they sorta concentrated on what went on down to the south end of the lake. They didn't say hardly nothin' about what happened up here. Anyhow, when he finished up his studyin', he come back home, an' he started goin' around collectin' all the old stories he could come across. Wrote 'em all down, too. He's been at it for years now. I expect he's gathered up just about every story in northern Pelosia by now. He even come an' talked to me, an' it's some fair distance from Ghasek to here. He tole me that what he's tryin' to do is to fill in some mighty big gaps in what they teach at that there university. Yes, sir, you go talk to Count Ghasek. If anybody in all Pelosia knows anythin' about this king you're lookin' for, the count woulda found out about it an' wrote it down in that there book he's puttin' together."

"My friend," Sparhawk said warmly, "I think you've just solved our problem for us. How do we find the count?"

"Best way is to take the road to Lake Venne. The city of Venne itself is up at the north end of the lake. Then you go north from there. It's a real bad road, but it's passable—particularly at this time of year. Ghasek ain't no real town. Actual, it's just the count's estate. There's a few villages around it—mostly belongin' to the count hisself—but anybody up there can direct you to the main house—more like a palace, really, or maybe a castle. I've been past it a few times. Bleak-lookin' place it is, but I never went inside, though." He laughed a rusty-sounding laugh. "Me an' the count, we don't exactly move in the same circles, if you take my meanin'."

"I understand perfectly," Sparhawk said. He took out several coins. "Your work here looks hot, Berd."

"It purely is, my Lord."

"When you finish up for the day, why don't you get yourself something cool to drink?" He gave the tanner the coins.

"Why, thankee, my Lord. That's uncommon generous of you."

"I'm the one who should be thanking you, Berd. I think you've just saved me months of travel." Sparhawk helped Sephrenia back onto her horse and then remounted himself. "I'm more grateful to you than you can possibly imagine, Berd," he said to the tanner by way of farewell.

"Now that turned out extremely well, didn't it?" Sparhawk exulted as he and Sephrenia rode back into the city.

"I told you it would," she reminded him.

"Yes, as a matter of fact, you did. I shouldn't have doubted you for a moment, little mother."

"It's natural to have doubts, Sparhawk. We'll go on to Ghasek, then?"

"Of course."

"I think we'd better wait until tomorrow, though. That physician said that none of our friends is in any danger, but another day's rest won't hurt them."

"Will they be able to ride?"

"Slowly at first, I'm afraid, but they'll grow stronger as we go along."

"All right. We'll leave first thing tomorrow morning then."

The mood of the others brightened considerably when Sparhawk repeated what Berd had told him.

"Somehow this is beginning to seem too easy," Ulath muttered, "and easy things make me nervous."

"Don't be so pessimistic," Tynian told him. "Try to look on the bright side of things."

"I'd rather expect the worst. That way, if things turn out all right, I'm pleasantly surprised."

"I suppose you'll want me to get rid of the wagon then?" Talen said to Sparhawk.

"No. Let's take it along just to be on the safe side. If any one of these three takes a turn for the worse, we can always put him back in it."

"I'm going to check the supplies, Sparhawk," Kurik said. "It could be quite some time before we come to another town with a market place. I'll need some money."

Even that could not dampen Sparhawk's elation.

They spent the rest of the day quietly and retired early that evening.

Sparhawk lay in his bed staring up into the darkness. It was going to be all right; he was sure of that now. Ghasek was a long distance away, but if Berd had been right about the thoroughness of the count's research, he would have the answer they needed. Then all that would remain for them to do would be to go to the place where Sarak was buried and recover his crown. Then they hopefully would return to Cimmura with Bhelliom and—

There was a light tap on his door. He rose and opened it.

It was Sephrenia. Her face was ashen gray, and there were tears streaming down her cheeks. "Please, come with me, Sparhawk," she said. "I cannot face them alone any more."

"Face whom?"

"Just come with me. I'm hoping that I'm wrong, but I'm afraid I'm not." She led him down the hall and opened the room she shared with Flute, and once again Sparhawk smelled the familiar graveyard reek. Flute sat on the bed, her little face grave, but her eyes unafraid. She was looking at a shadowy figure in black armor. Then the figure turned, and Sparhawk saw the scarred face. "Olven," he said in a stricken voice.

The ghost of Sir Olven did not reply but simply extended its hands with its sword lying across them.

Sephrenia was weeping openly as she stepped forward to receive the sword.

The ghost looked at Sparhawk and raised one hand in a kind of half salute.

And then it vanished.

CHAPTER TWELVE

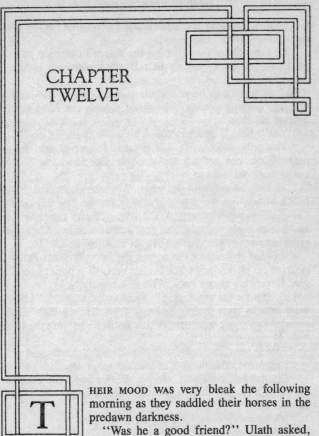

THEIR MOOD WAS very bleak the following morning as they saddled their horses in the predawn darkness.

"Was he a good friend?" Ulath asked, heaving Kalten's saddle up onto the back of the blond Pandion's horse.

"One of the best," Sparhawk answered. "He never said very much, but you always knew you could depend on him. I'm going to miss him."

"What are we going to do about those Zemochs following us?" Kalten asked.

"I don't think there's much we can do," Sparhawk replied. "We're a little under strength until you and Tynian and Bevier recover. As long as all they're doing is trailing along behind us, they're not much of a problem."

"I think I've told you before that I don't like having enemies behind me," Ulath said.

"I'd rather have them behind me where I can keep an eye on them instead of hiding in ambush somewhere ahead," Sparhawk said.

Kalten winced as he pulled his saddle cinch tight. "That's going to get aggravating," he noted, laying one hand gently against his side.

"You'll heal," Sparhawk told him. "You always do."

"The only problem is that it takes longer to heal every time. We're not getting any younger, Sparhawk. Is Bevier going to be all right to ride?"

"As long as we don't push him," Sparhawk replied. "Tynian's better, but we'll take it slowly for the first day or so. I'm going to put Sephrenia in the wagon. Every time she gets another of those swords, she gets a little weaker. She's carrying more than she's willing to let us know about."

Kurik led the rest of the horses out into the yard. He was wearing his customary black leather vest. "I suppose I should give Bevier his armor back," he said hopefully.

"Keep it for the time being," Sparhawk disagreed. "I don't want him to start feeling brave just yet. He's a little headstrong. Let's not encourage him until we're sure he's all right."

"This is very uncomfortable, Sparhawk," Kurik said.

"I explained the reasons to you the other day."

"I'm not talking about reasons. Bevier and I are close to the same size, but there are differences. I've got raw places all over me."

"It's probably only for a couple more days."

"I'll be a cripple by then."

Berit assisted Sephrenia out through the door of the inn. He helped her up into the wagon and then lifted Flute up beside her. The small Styric woman was wan-looking, and she cradled Olven's sword gently, almost as one would carry a baby.

"Are you going to be all right?" Sparhawk asked her.

"I just need some time to get used to it, that's all," she replied.

Talen led his horse out of the stable.

"Just tie him on behind the wagon," Sparhawk told the boy. "You'll be driving."

"Whatever you say, Sparhawk," Talen agreed.

"No arguments?" Sparhawk was a little surprised.

"Why should I argue? I can see the reason for it. Besides, that wagon seat's more comfortable than my saddle—much more comfortable, when you get right down to it."

Tynian and Bevier came out of the inn. Both wore mail shirts and walked a bit slowly.

"No armor?" Ulath asked Tynian lightly.

"It's heavy," Tynian replied. "I'm not sure I'm up to it just yet."

"Are you sure we didn't leave anything behind?" Sparhawk asked Kurik.

Kurik gave him a flat, unfriendly stare.

"Just asking," Sparhawk said mildly. "Don't get irritable this early in the morning." He looked at the others. "We're not going to push today," he told them. "I'll be satisfied with five leagues, if we can manage it."

"You're saddled with a group of cripples, Sparhawk," Tynian said. "Wouldn't it be better if you and Ulath went on ahead? The rest of us can catch up with you later."

"No," Sparhawk decided. "There are unfriendly people roaming about, and you and the others aren't in any condition to defend yourselves just yet." He smiled briefly at Sephrenia. "Besides," he added, "we're supposed to be ten. I wouldn't want to offend the Younger Gods."

They helped Kalten, Tynian, and Bevier to mount and then rode slowly out of the innyard into the still-dark and largely deserted streets of Paler. They proceeded at a walk to the north gate, and the gate guards hurriedly opened it for them.

"Bless you, my children," Kalten said grandly to them as he rode through.

"Did you have to do that?" Sparhawk asked him.

"It's cheaper than giving them money. Besides, who knows? My blessing might actually be worth something."

"I think he's going to get better," Kurik said.

"Not if he keeps that up, he won't," Sparhawk disagreed.

The sky to the east was growing lighter, and they moved at an easy pace along the road that ran northwesterly from Paler to Lake Venne. The land lying between the two lakes was rolling and given over largely to the growing of grain. Grand estates dotted the countryside, and here and there were villages of the long huts of the serfs. Serfdom had been abolished in western Eosia centuries before, but it still persisted here in Pelosia, since, as best as Sparhawk could tell, the Pelosian nobility lacked the administrative skills to make any other system work. They saw a few of those nobles, usually in bright satin doublets, supervising the work of the linen-shirted serfs from horseback. Despite everything Sparhawk had heard of the evils of serfdom, the workers in the fields seemed well fed and not particularly mistreated.

Berit was riding several hundred yards to the rear and he kept turning in his saddle to look back.

"He's going to wrench my armor completely askew if he keeps doing that," Kalten said critically.

"We can always stop by a smith and have it retailored for you," Sparhawk said. "Maybe we could have some of the seams let out at the same time, since you're so bent on stuffing yourself full of food every chance you get."

"You're in a foul humor this morning, Sparhawk."

"I've got a lot on my mind."

"Some people are just not suited for command," Kalten observed grandly to the others. "My ugly friend here seems to be one of them. He worries too much."

"Do you want to do this?" Sparhawk asked flatly.

"Me? Be serious, Sparhawk. I couldn't even herd geese, much less direct a body of knights."

"Then would you like to shut up and let me do it?"

Berit rode forward, his eyes narrowed and his hand slipping his ax up and down in the sling at the side of his saddle. "The Zemochs are back there, Sir Sparhawk," he said. "I keep catching glimpses of them."

"How far back?"

"About a half a mile. Most of them are hanging back, but they've got scouts out. They're keeping an eye on us."

"If we charged to the rear, they'd just scatter," Bevier advised. "And then they'd pick up our trail again."

"Probably," Sparhawk agreed glumly. "Well, I can't stop them. I don't have enough men. Let them trail along if it makes them happy. We'll get rid of them when we're all feeling a little better. Berit, drop back and keep an eye on them—and no heroics."

"I understand completely, Sir Sparhawk."

The day grew hot before noon, and Sparhawk began to sweat inside his armor.

"Am I being punished for something?" Kurik asked him, mopping his streaming face with a piece of cloth.

"You know I wouldn't do that."

"Then why am I locked up in this stove?"

"Sorry. It's necessary."

About midafternoon, when they were passing through a long, verdant valley, a dozen or so gaily dressed young men galloped from a nearby estate to bar their way. "Go no farther," one of them, a pale, pimply young fellow in a green velvet doublet and with a supercilious, self-important expression commanded, holding up one hand imperiously.

"I beg your pardon?" Sparhawk asked.

"I demand to know why you are trespassing on my father's lands." The young fellow looked around at his sniggering friends with a smugly self-congratulatory expression.

"We were led to believe that this is a public road," Sparhawk replied.

"Only at my father's sufferance." The pimply fellow puffed himself up, trying to look dangerous.

"He's showing off for his friends," Kurik muttered. "Let's just sweep them out of the way and ride on. Those rapiers they're carrying aren't really much of a threat."

"Let's try some diplomacy first," Sparhawk replied. "We really don't want a crowd of angry serfs on our heels."

"I'll do it. I've handled his sort before." Kurik rode forward deliberately, Bevier's armor gleaming in the afternoon sun and his white cape and surcoat resplendent. "Young man," he said in a stern voice, "you seem to be a bit unacquainted with the customary courtesies. Is it possible that you don't recognize us?"

"I've never seen you before."

"I wasn't talking about *who* we are. I was talking about *what*. It's understandable, I suppose. It's obvious that you're not widely travelled."

The young fellow's eyes bulged with outrage. "Not so. Not so," he objected in a squeaky voice. "I have been to the city of Venne at least twice."

"Ah," Kurik said. "And when you were there, did you perhaps hear about the Church?"

"We have our own chapel right here on the estate. I need no instruction in that foolishness." The young man sneered. It seemed to be his normal expression.

An older man in a black brocade doublet was riding furiously from the estate.

"It's always gratifying to speak with an educated man," Kurik was saying. "Have you ever by chance heard of the Knights of the Church?"

The young fellow looked a bit vague at that. The man in the black doublet was approaching rapidly from behind the group of young men. His face appeared white with fury.

"I'd strongly advise you to stand aside," Kurik continued smoothly. "What you're doing imperils your soul—not to mention your life."

"You can't threaten me—not on my father's own estate."

"Jaken!" the man in black roared, "have you lost your mind?"

"Father," the pimply young man faltered, "I was just questioning these trespassers."

"*Trespassers?*" the older man spluttered. "This is the king's highway, you jackass!"

"But—"

The man in the black doublet moved his horse in closer, rose in his stirrups, and knocked his son from the saddle with a solid blow of his fist. Then he turned to face Kurik. "My apologies, Sir Knight," he said. "My half-wit son didn't know to whom he was speaking. I revere the Church and honor her knights. I hope and pray that you were not offended."

"Not at all, my Lord," Kurik said easily. "Your son and I had very nearly resolved our differences."

The noble winced. "Thank God I arrived in time then. That idiot isn't much of a son, but his mother would have been distressed if you'd been obliged to cut off his head."

"I doubt that it would have gone that far, my Lord."

"Father!" the young man on the ground said in horrified shock. "You *hit* me!" There was blood streaming from his nose. "I'm going to tell Mother!"

"Good. I'm sure she'll be very impressed." The noble looked apologetically at Kurik. "Excuse me, Sir Knight. I think some long overdue discipline is in order." He glared at his son. "Return home, Jaken," he said coldly. "When you get there, pack up this covey of parasitic wastrels and send them away. I want them off the estate by sundown."

"But they're my *friends*!" his son wailed.

"Well, they're not mine. Get rid of them. You will also pack. Don't bother to take fine clothing, because you're going to a monastery. The brothers there are very strict, and they'll see to your education—which I seem to have neglected."

"Mother won't let you do that!" his son exclaimed, his face going very pale.

"She doesn't have anything to say about it. Your mother has never been more to me than a minor inconvenience."

"But—" The young brat's face seemed to disintegrate.

"You sicken me, Jaken. You're the worst excuse for a son a man has ever been cursed with. Pay close attention to the monks, Jaken. I have some nephews far more worthy than you. Your inheritance is not all that secure, and you could be a monk for the remainder of your life."

"You can't do that."

"Yes, actually, I can."

"Mother will punish you."

The noble's laugh was chilling. "Your mother has begun to tire me, Jaken," he said. "She's self-indulgent, shrewish, and more than a little stupid. She's turned you into something I'd rather not look at. Besides, she's not very attractive any more. I think I'll send her to a nunnery for the rest of her life. The prayer and fasting may bring her closer to heaven, and the amendment of her spirit is my duty as a loving husband, wouldn't you say?"

The sneer had slid off Jaken's face, and he began to shake violently as his world crashed down around his ears.

"Now, my son," the noble continued disdainfully, "will you do as I tell you, or shall I unleash this Knight of the Church to administer the chastisement you so richly deserve?"

Kurik took his cue from that and slowly drew Bevier's sword. It made a singularly unpleasant sound as it slid from its sheath.

The young man scrambled away on his hands and knees. "I have a dozen friends with me," he threatened shrilly.

Kurik looked the pampered boys up and down; then he spat derisively. "So?" he said, shifting his shield and flexing his sword arm. "Did you want to keep his head, my Lord?" he asked the noble politely, "as a keepsake naturally?"

"You wouldn't!" Jaken was very nearly in a state of collapse now.

Kurik moved his horse forward, his sword glinting ominously in the sunlight. "Try me," he said in a tone dreadful enough to make the very rocks shrink.

The young man's eyes bulged in horror, and he scrambled back into his saddle with his satin-dressed sycophants rushing along behind him.

"Was that more or less what you had in mind, my Lord?" Kurik asked the noble.

"It was perfect, Sir Knight. I've wanted to do that myself for years." Then he sighed. "Mine was an arranged marriage, Sir Knight," he said by way of explanation. "My wife's family had a noble title, but they were deeply in debt. My family had money and land, but our title was not impressive. Our parents felt that the arrangement was sound, but she and I scarcely speak to one another. I've avoided her whenever possible. I've solaced myself with other women, I'm ashamed to admit. There are many accommodating young ladies—if one has the price. My wife's solaced herself with that abomination you just saw. She has few other enthusiasms—aside from making my life as miserable as she possibly can. I've neglected my duties, I'm afraid."

"I have sons myself, my Lord," Kurik told him as they all rode on. "Most of them are good boys, but one has been a great disappointment to me."

Talen rolled his eyes heavenward, but didn't say anything.

"Do you travel far, Sir Knight?" the noble asked, obviously wanting to change the subject.

"We go toward Venne," Kurik replied.

"A journey of some distance. I have a summer house near the west end of my estate. Might I offer you its comfort? We should reach it by evening, and the servants there can see to your needs." He made a wry face. "I'd offer you the hospitality of the manor, but I'm afraid tonight may be a bit noisy there. My wife has a penetrating voice, and she's not going to take kindly to certain decisions I've made this afternoon."

"You're most kind, my Lord. We'll be happy to accept your hospitality."

"It's the least I can do in recompense for my son's behavior. I wish I could think of some appropriate form of discipline to salvage him."

"I've always gotten good results with a leather belt, my Lord," Kurik suggested.

The nobleman laughed wryly. "That might not be a bad idea, Sir Knight," he agreed.

They rode on through a lovely afternoon, and as the sun was just going down, they reached the "summer house," which appeared to be only slightly less opulent than a mansion. The nobleman gave instructions to the household servants and then remounted his horse. "I'd gladly stay, Sir Knight," he said to Kurik, "but I think I'd better get back home before my wife breaks every dish in the house. I'll find a comfortable cloister for her, and live out my life in peace."

"I quite understand, my Lord," Kurik replied. "Good luck."

"Godspeed, Sir Knight." And the noble turned and rode back the way they had come.

"Kurik," Bevier said gravely as they entered the marble-floored foyer of the house, "you did honor to my armor back there. I'd have had my sword through that young fellow after his second remark."

Kurik grinned at him. "It was much more fun this way, Sir Bevier."

The Pelosian noble's summer house was even more splendid in the inside than it had appeared from the exterior. Rare woods, exquisitely carved, panelled the walls. The floors and fireplaces were all of marble, and the furnishings were covered with the finest brocade. The serving staff was efficient and unobtrusive, and they saw to every need.

Sparhawk and his friends dined splendidly in a dining room only slightly smaller than a grand ballroom. "Now *this* is what I call living." Kalten sighed contentedly. "Sparhawk, why is it that *we* can't have a bit more luxury in our lives?"

"We're Knights of the Church," Sparhawk reminded him. "Poverty toughens us up."

"But do we have to have so much of it?"

"How are you feeling?" Sephrenia asked Bevier.

"Much better, thanks," the Arcian replied. "I haven't coughed up any blood since this morning. I think I'll be up to a canter tomorrow, Sparhawk. This leisurely stroll is costing us time."

"Let's go easy for one more day," Sparhawk said. "According to my map, the country beyond the city of Venne is a little rugged and very underpopulated. It's ideal for ambushes, and we're being followed. I want you and Kalten and Tynian fit to defend yourselves.''

"Berit," Kurik said.

"Yes?"

"Would you do me a favor before we leave here?"

"Of course."

"First thing in the morning, take Talen out into the court-yard and search him—thoroughly. The noble who owns this place was very hospitable, and I don't want to offend him.''

"What makes you think I'd steal anything?" Talen objected.

"What makes me think you wouldn't? It's just a precaution. There are a great number of small, valuable things in this house. Some of them might just accidentally find their way into your pockets.''

The beds in the house were down-filled, and they were deep and comfortable. They rose at dawn and ate a splendid breakfast. Then they thanked the servants, mounted their waiting horses, and rode on out. The new-risen sun was golden, and larks whirled and sang overhead. Flute, sitting in the wagon, accompanied them on her pipes. Sephrenia seemed stronger, but, at Sparhawk's insistence, she still rode in the wagon.

It was shortly before noon when a group of perhaps fifty fierce-looking men came galloping over a nearby hill. They were booted and dressed in leather, and their heads were all shaved.

"Tribesmen from the eastern marches," Tynian, who had been in Pelosia before, warned. "Be very careful, Sparhawk. These are reckless men.''

The tribesmen swooped down the hill with superb horse-manship. They had savage-looking sabers at their belts, carried short lances and wore round shields on their left arms. At a curt signal from their leader, most of them reined in so sharply that their horses' rumps skidded on the grass. With five cohorts, the leader, a lean man with narrow eyes and a scarred scalp, came forward. With ostentatious display, the advancing tribesmen moved their horses sideways, the proud stallions prancing in perfect unison. Then, plunging their lances into the earth, the warriors drew their flashing sabers with a grand flourish.

"No!" Tynian said sharply as Sparhawk and the others

instinctively went for their swords. "This is a ceremony. Stand fast."

The shaved-headed men came forward at a stately walk, and then at some hidden signal, their horses all went down on their front knees in a kind of genuflection as the riders raised their sabers to their faces in salute.

"Lord!" Kalten breathed. "I've never seen a horse do that before!"

Faran's ears flicked, and Sparhawk could feel him twitching irritably.

"Hail, Knights of the Church," the leather-garbed leader intoned formally. "We salute you, and stand at your service."

"Can I handle this?" Tynian suggested to Sparhawk. "I've had some experience."

"Feel free, Tynian," Sparhawk agreed, eyeing the pack of savage men on the hill.

Tynian moved forward, holding his black horse in tightly so that its pace was measured and slow. "Gladly we greet the Peloi," the Deiran declaimed formally. "Glad also are we of this meeting, for brothers should always greet each other with respect."

"You know our ways, Sir Knight," the scar-headed man approved.

"I have been in times past on the eastern marches, Domi," Tynian acknowledged.

"What's 'Domi' mean?" Kalten whispered.

"An ancient Pelosian word," Ulath supplied. "It means 'chief'—sort of."

"Sort of?"

"It takes a long time to translate."

"Will you take salt with me, Sir Knight?" the warrior asked.

"Gladly, Domi," Tynian replied, stepping slowly down from his saddle. "And might we season it with well-roasted mutton?" he suggested.

"An excellent suggestion, Sir Knight."

"Get it," Sparhawk said to Talen. "It's in that green pack. And don't argue."

"I'd sooner bite out my tongue," Talen agreed nervously, digging into the pack.

"Warm day, isn't it?" the Domi said conversationally, sitting cross-legged on the lush turf.

"We were saying the same thing just a few minutes ago," Tynian agreed, also sitting.

"I am Kring," the scarred man introduced himself, "Domi of this band."

"I am Tynian," the Deiran replied, "an Alcione Knight."

"I surmised as much."

Talen went a bit hesitantly to where the two men sat, carrying a roast leg of lamb.

"Well-prepared meat," Kring proclaimed, unhooking a leather bag of salt from his belt. "The Knights of the Church eat well." He ripped the lamb roast in two with teeth and fingernails and handed half to Tynian. Then he held out his leather bag. "Salt, brother?" he offered.

Tynian dipped his fingers into the bag, took out a generous pinch, and sifted it over his lamb. Then he shook his fingers in the direction of the four winds.

"You are well versed in our ways, friend Tynian," the Domi approved, imitating the gesture. "And is this excellent young fellow perhaps your son?"

"Ah, no, Domi." Tynian sighed. "He's a good lad, but he's addicted to thievery."

"Ho-ho!" Kring laughed, fetching Talen a clap on the shoulder that sent the boy rolling. "Thievery is the second most honorable profession in the world—next to fighting. Are you any good, boy?"

Talen smiled thinly, and his eyes went narrow. "Would you care to try me, Domi?" he challenged, coming to his feet. "Protect what you can, and I'll steal the rest."

The warrior rolled back his head, roaring with laughter. Talen, Sparhawk noticed, was already close to him, his hands moving fast.

"All right, my young thief," the Domi chortled, holding his widespread hands out in front of him, "steal what you can."

"Thank you all the same, Domi," Talen said with a polite bow, "but I already have. I believe I've got just about everything of value you own."

Kring blinked and began to pat himself here and there, his eyes filled with consternation.

Kurik groaned.

"It may turn out all right after all," Sparhawk muttered to him.

"Two brooches," Talen catalogued, handing them over, "seven rings—the one on your left thumb is really tight, you know. A gold bracelet—have that checked. I think there's brass mixed with it. A ruby pendant—I hope you didn't pay too much for it. It's really an inferior stone, you know. Then there's this jewelled dagger, and the pommel-stone off your sword." Talen brushed his hands together professionally.

The Domi roared with laughter. "I'll buy this boy, friend Tynian," he declared. "I'll give you a herd of the finest horses for him and raise him as my own son. Such a thief I've never seen before."

"Ah—sorry, friend Kring," Tynian apologized, "but he's not mine to sell."

Kring sighed. "Could you even steal horses, boy?" he asked wistfully.

"A horse is a little hard to fit in your pocket, Domi," Talen replied. "I could probably work it out, though."

"A lad of genius," the warrior said reverently. "His father is a man of great fortune."

"I hadn't noticed that very much," Kurik muttered.

"Ah, young thief," Kring said almost regretfully, "I seem to be also missing a purse—a fairly heavy one."

"Oh, did I forget that?" Talen said, slapping his forehead. "It must have completely slipped my mind." He fished a bulging leather bag out from under his tunic and handed it over.

"Count it, friend Kring," Tynian warned.

"Since the boy and I are now friends, I will trust his integrity."

Talen sighed and fished a large number of silver coins out of various hiding places. "I wish people wouldn't do that," he said, handing the coins over. "It takes all the fun out of it."

"*Two* herds of horses?" the Domi offered.

"Sorry, my friend," Tynian said regretfully. "Let us take salt and talk of affairs."

The two sat eating their salted lamb as Talen wandered back to the wagon. "He should have taken the horses," he muttered to Sparhawk. "I could have slipped away just after dark."

"He'd have chained you to a tree," Sparhawk told him.

"I can wriggle my way out of any chain in less than a minute. Do you have any idea of how much horses like he's got are worth, Sparhawk?"

"Training this boy may take longer than we'd expected," Kalten noted.

"Will you require an escort, friend Tynian?" Kring was asking. "We are engaged in no more than a slight diversion, and we will gladly put it aside to assist our holy mother Church and her revered knights."

"Thank you, friend Kring," Tynian declined, "but our mission involves nothing we can't deal with."

"Truly. The prowess of the Knights of the Church is legendary."

"What is this diversion you mentioned, Domi?" Tynian asked curiously. "Seldom have I seen the Peloi this far west."

"We normally haunt the eastern marches," Kring admitted, ripping a large chunk of lamb off the bone with his teeth, "but from time to time over the past few generations, Zemochs have been trying to slip across the border into Pelosia. The king pays a gold half crown for their ears. It's an easy way to make money."

"Does the king demand both ears?"

"No, just the right ones. We still have to be careful with our sabers, though. You can lose the whole bounty with a misaimed stroke. Anyway, my friends and I flushed a fair-sized group of Zemochs near the border. We took a number of them, but the rest fled. They were coming this way last we saw them, and some were wounded. Blood leaves a good trail. We'll run them down and collect their ears—and the gold. It's just a question of time."

"I think I might be able to save you a bit of that, my friend," Tynian said with a broad smile. "From time to time in the last day or so, we've seen a fairly large party of Zemochs riding to our rear. It might just be that they're the ones you're seeking. In any case, though, an ear is an ear, and the king's gold spends just as sweetly, even if it chances to be mistakenly dispensed."

Kring laughed delightedly. "It does indeed, friend Tynian," he agreed. "And who knows, it could just be that there are *two* bags of gold available out here. How many are they, would you say?"

"We've seen forty or so. They're coming up the road from the south."

"They won't come much farther," Kring promised, grinning a wolflike grin. "This was indeed a fortunate meeting, Sir Tynian—at least for me and my comrades. But why didn't you and your companions turn around and collect the bounty?"

"We weren't really aware of the bounty, Domi," Tynian confessed, "and we're on Church business of some urgency." He made a wry face. "Besides, even if we did gain that bounty, our oaths would require that we hand it over to the Church. Some fat abbot somewhere would profit from our labors. I don't propose to sweat that much to enrich a man who's never done an honest day's work in his life. I'd far rather point a friend in the direction of honest gain."

Impulsively, Kring embraced him. "My brother," he said, "you are a true friend. It's an honor to have met you."

"The honor is mine, Domi," Tynian said gravely.

The Domi wiped his greasy fingers on his leather breeches. "Well, I suppose we should be on our way, friend Tynian," he said. "Slow riding earns no bounty." He paused. "Are you sure you don't want to sell that boy?"

"He's the son of a friend of mine," Tynian said. "I wouldn't mind getting rid of the boy, but the friendship's valuable to me."

"I understand perfectly, friend Tynian." Kring bowed. "Commend me to God next time you talk with Him." He vaulted into his saddle from a standing start, and his horse was running before he was even settled.

Ulath walked up to Tynian and gravely shook his hand. "You're fast on your feet," he observed. "That was absolutely brilliant."

"It was a fair trade," Tynian said modestly. "We get the Zemochs off our backs, and Kring gets the ears. No bargain between friends is fair unless both sides get something they want."

"Very, very true," Ulath agreed. "I've never heard of selling ears before, though. Usually it's heads."

"Ears are lighter," Tynian said professionally, "and they don't stare at you every time you open your saddlebags."

"Would you gentlemen *mind*?" Sephrenia said tartly. "We have children with us, after all."

"Sorry, little mother," Ulath apologized easily. "Just talking shop."

She stalked back to the wagon, muttering. Sparhawk was fairly certain that some of the Styric words she was saying under her breath were never used in polite society.

"Who were they?" Bevier asked, looking at the warriors who were rapidly disappearing toward the south.

"They're of the Peloi," Tynian replied, "nomadic horse herders. They were the first Elenes in this region. The Kingdom of Pelosia is named after them."

"Are they as fierce as they look?"

"Even fiercer. Their presence on the border was probably why Otha invaded Lamorkand instead of Pelosia. No one in his right mind attacks the Peloi."

They reached Lake Venne late the following day. It was a large, shallow body of water into which nearby peat bogs continually drained, making the water turbid and brown-stained. Flute seemed strangely agitated as they made camp some distance back from the marshy lake shore. As soon as Sephrenia's tent was erected, she darted inside and refused to come out.

"What's the matter with her?" Sparhawk asked Sephrenia, absently rubbing the ring finger on his left hand. It seemed to be throbbing for some reason.

"I really don't know," Sephrenia frowned. "It's almost as if she's afraid of something."

After they had eaten and Sephrenia had carried Flute's supper in to her, Sparhawk closely questioned each of his injured companions. They all claimed perfect health, a claim he was sure was spurious. "All right, then." He gave up finally. "We'll go back to doing it the old way. You gentlemen can have your armor back, and we'll try a canter tomorrow. No galloping; no running; and if we run into any trouble, try to hold back unless things get serious."

"He's just like an old mother hen, isn't he?" Kalten observed to Tynian.

"If he scratches up a worm, you get to eat it," Tynian replied.

"Thanks all the same, Tynian," Kalten declined, "but I've already had my supper."

Sparhawk went to bed.

It was about midnight, and the moon was very bright outside the tent. Sparhawk sat bolt upright in his blankets, jolted awake by a hideous, roaring bellow.

"Sparhawk!" Ulath said sharply from outside the tent. "Rouse the others! Fast!"

Sparhawk shook Kalten awake and pulled on his mail shirt. He grabbed up his sword and ducked out of the tent. He looked around quickly and saw that the others needed no rousing. They were already struggling into their mail and were taking up weapons. Ulath stood at the edge of camp, his round shield in place and his ax in his hand. He was looking off intently into the darkness.

Sparhawk joined him. "What is it?" he asked quietly. "What makes a noise like that?"

"Troll," Ulath replied shortly.

"Here? In Pelosia? Ulath, that's impossible. There aren't any Trolls in Pelosia."

"Why don't you go out there and explain that to *him*?"

"Are you absolutely sure it's a Troll?"

"I've heard that sound too many times to miss it. It's a Troll, all right, and he's absolutely enraged about something."

"Maybe we should build up the fire," Sparhawk suggested as the others joined them.

"It wouldn't do any good," Ulath said. "Trolls aren't afraid of fire."

"You know their language, don't you?"

Ulath grunted.

"Why don't you call to him and tell him that we mean him no harm?"

"Sparhawk," Ulath said with a pained look, "in this situation, it's the other way around. If he attacks, try to strike at his legs," he warned them all. "If you swing at his body, he'll jerk your weapons out of your hands and feed them to you. All right, I'll try to talk with him." He lifted his head and bellowed something in a horrid, guttural language.

Something out there in the darkness replied, snarling and spitting.

"What did it say?" Sparhawk asked.

"He's cursing. It may take him an hour or so to get finished. Trolls have a lot of swearwords in their language." Ulath frowned. "He doesn't really seem all that sure of himself," he said, sounding puzzled.

"Perhaps our numbers are making it cautious," Bevier suggested.

"They don't know what the word means," Ulath disagreed. "I've seen a lone Troll attack a walled city."

There was another snarling bellow from out in the darkness, this time a little closer.

"Now, what's *that* supposed to mean?" Ulath said in bafflement.

"What?" Sparhawk asked.

"He's demanding that we turn the thief over to him."

"Talen?"

"I don't know. How could Talen pick a Troll's pocket? They don't *have* pockets."

Then they heard the sound of Flute's pipes coming from Sephrenia's tent. Her melody was stern and vaguely threatening. After a moment, the beast out in the darkness howled—a sound partially of pain and partially of frustration. Then the howling faded off into the distance.

"Why don't we all go to Sephrenia's tent and kiss that little girl about the head and shoulders for a while?" Ulath suggested.

"What happened?" Kalten asked.

"Somehow she ran him off. I've never seen a Troll run from anything. I saw one try to attack an avalanche once. I think we'd better talk with Sephrenia. Something's going on here that I don't understand."

Sephrenia, however, was as puzzled as they. She was holding Flute in her arms, and the little girl was crying. "Please, gentlemen," the Styric woman said softly, "just leave her alone for now. She's very, very upset."

"I'll stand watch with you, Ulath," Tynian said as they came out of the tent. "That bellow froze my blood. I'll never get back to sleep now."

They reached the city of Venne two days later. Once the Troll had been frightened away, they neither saw nor heard any further sign of him. Venne was not a very attractive city. Because local taxes were based on the number of square feet on the ground floor of each house, the citizens had circumvented the law by building overhanging second stories. In most cases, the overhang was so extreme that the streets were like narrow, dark tunnels, even at noon. They put up at the cleanest inn they could find, and Sparhawk took Kurik and went in search of information.

For some reason, however, the word *Ghasek* made the citizens of Venne very nervous. The answers Sparhawk and Kurik received were vague and contradictory, and the citizens usually went away from them very fast.

"Over there," Kurik said shortly, pointing at a man staggering from the door of a tavern. "He's too drunk to run."

Sparhawk looked critically at the reeling man. "He could also be too drunk to talk," he added.

Kurik's methods, however, were brutally direct. He crossed the street, seized the drunkard by the scruff of the neck, dragged him to the end of the street, and shoved his head into the fountain that stood there. "Now, then," he said pleasantly, "I think we understand each other. I'm going to ask you some questions, and you're going to give me the answers—unless you can figure out a way to sprout gills."

The fellow was spluttering and coughing. Kurik pounded on his back until the paroxysm passed.

"All right," Kurik said, "the first question is, 'Where is Ghasek?' "

The drunken man's face went pasty white, and his eyes bulged in horror.

Kurik shoved his head under water again. "This is starting to make me very tired," he said conversationally to Sparhawk, looking across the bubbles coming up out of the fountain. He pulled the fellow out by the hair. "This isn't going to get any more enjoyable, friend," he warned. "I really think you ought to start to cooperate. Let's try again. Where is Ghasek?"

"N-north," the fellow choked, spewing water all over the street. He seemed to be almost sober now.

"We know that. Which road do we take?"

"Go out the north gate. A mile or so after you get out of town, the road branches. Take the left fork."

"You're doing fine. See, you're even staying sort of dry. How far is it to Ghasek?"

"A-about forty leagues." The man writhed in Kurik's iron grip.

"Last question," Kurik promised. "Why does everybody in Venne wet himself whenever he hears the name Ghasek?"

"I-it's a horrible place. Things happen there that are too hideous to describe."

"I've got a strong stomach," Kurik assured him. "Go ahead. Shock me."

"They drink blood up there—and bathe in it—and even feed on human flesh. It's the most awful place in the world. Even to mention its name brings down a curse on your head." The man shuddered and began to weep.

"There, there," Kurik said, releasing him and patting him gently on the shoulder. He gave the man a coin. "You seem to have gotten all wet, friend," he added. "Why don't you go back to the tavern and see if you can get dry?"

The fellow scurried off.

"Doesn't sound like too pleasant a place, does it?" Kurik said.

"No, not really," Sparhawk admitted, "but we're going there all the same."

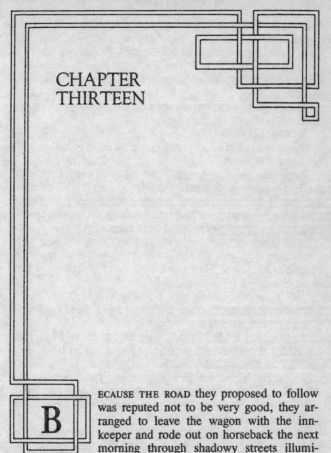

CHAPTER
THIRTEEN

ECAUSE THE ROAD they proposed to follow was reputed not to be very good, they arranged to leave the wagon with the innkeeper and rode out on horseback the next morning through shadowy streets illuminated by torches. Sparhawk had passed on the information Kurik had wrung out of the drunken man the day before, and they all looked around warily as they passed out through the north gate of Venne.

"It's probably just some local superstition," Kalten scoffed. "I've heard awful stories about places before, and they usually turned out to be about things that had happened generations before."

"It doesn't really make much sense," Sparhawk agreed. "That tanner back in Paler said that Count Ghasek's a scholar.

That's not usually the sort of man who goes in for exotic entertainments. Let's stay alert anyway. We're a long way from home, and it might be a little hard to call in help.''

"I'll hold back a bit," Berit volunteered. "I think we'd all feel better if we're sure those Zemochs aren't still trailing us."

"I think we can count on the Domi's efficiency," Tynian said.

"Still—" Berit said.

"Go ahead, Berit," Sparhawk agreed. "It's just as well not to take chances."

They rode at an easy canter; as the sun was rising, they reached the fork in the road. The left fork was rutted, narrow, and poorly maintained. The rain that had swept through the area for some days back had left it muddy and generally unpleasant, and thick brush lined both sides of it.

"It's going to be slow going," Ulath noted. "I've seen smoother roads, and it's not going to get better once we get up into those hills." He looked toward the low range of forested mountains lying just ahead.

"We'll do the best we can," Sparhawk said, "but you're right. Forty leagues is quite a distance, and a bad road isn't going to make it seem any shorter."

They started up the muddy road at a trot. As Ulath had predicted, it grew steadily worse. After about an hour, they entered the forest. The trees were evergreens, and they cast a somber shade, but the air was cool and damp, a welcome relief for the armored knights. They stopped briefly for a meal of bread and cheese at noon and then pressed on, climbing higher and higher into the mountains.

The region was ominously deserted, and even most of the birds seemed muted, the only exception being the sooty ravens, who seemed to croak from every tree. As evening began to settle over the gloomy wood, Sparhawk led the others some distance away from the road, and they made camp for the night.

The dismal forest had subdued even the irrepressible Kalten, and they were all very quiet as they ate their evening meal. After they had eaten, they went to their beds.

It was about midnight when Ulath woke Sparhawk to take his turn on watch. "There seem to be a lot of wolves out there," the big Genidian said quietly. "It might not be a bad idea to put your back to a tree."

"I've never heard of a wolf attacking a man," Sparhawk replied, also speaking softly to avoid waking the others.

"They usually don't," Ulath agreed, "unless they're rabid."

"That's a cheerful thought."

"I'm glad you liked it. I'm going to bed. It's been a long day."

Sparhawk left the circle of firelight and stopped about fifty yards back in the forest to allow his eyes to adjust to the darkness. He heard the howling of wolves back off in the woods. He thought he had found the source of many of the stories that had been circulating about Ghasek. This gloomy forest alone would be sufficient to stir up the fears in superstitious people. Add to that the flocks of ravens— always a bird of ill omen—and the chill howling of packs of wolves, and it was easy to see how the stories had gotten started. Sparhawk carefully circled the camp, his eyes and ears alert.

Forty leagues. Given the worsening condition of the road, it would be unlikely that they could cover more than ten leagues a day. Sparhawk chafed at their slow pace, but there was nothing he could do about it. They had to go to Ghasek. The thought came to him that the count might very well not have found anyone who knew the whereabouts of King Sarak's grave, and that this tedious and time-consuming trek might all be for nothing. He quickly pushed that thought out of his mind.

Idly, still watching the surrounding woods, he began to wonder what his life would be like if they were successful in curing Ehlana. He had known her only as a child, but she was no longer a little girl. He had received a few hints about her adult personality, but nothing definite enough to make him feel that he really knew her. She would be a good Queen, of that he was certain, but exactly what kind of a woman was she?

He saw a movement out in the shadows and stopped, his hand going to his sword as he searched the darkness. Then he saw a pair of blazing green eyes that reflected back the light of their fire. It was a wolf. The animal stared at the flames for a long time, then turned to slink silently back into the forest.

Sparhawk realized that he had been holding his breath, and he let it out explosively. No one is ever really prepared for a meeting with a wolf, and even though he knew it was irrational, he nonetheless felt the instinctive chill.

The moon rose, casting its pale light over the dark forest. Sparhawk looked up and saw the clouds coming in. Gradually, they obscured the moon and inexorably continued to build up. "Oh, fine," he muttered. "That's all we need—more rain." He shook his head and walked on, his eyes probing the darkness around him.

Somewhat later, Tynian relieved him, and he went back to his tent.

"Sparhawk." It was Talen, and his shaking of Sparhawk's shoulder was light as he woke the big Pandion.

"Yes." Sparhawk sat up, recognizing the note of urgency in the boy's voice.

"There's something out there."

"I know. Wolves."

"This wasn't a wolf—unless they've learned to walk on their hind legs."

"What did you see?"

"It was back in the shadows under those trees. I couldn't see it very well, but it seemed to have a kind of robe over it, and the robe didn't fit very well."

"The Seeker?"

"How would I know? I only caught a glimpse of it. It came to the edge of the woods and then dropped back into the shadows. I probably wouldn't even have seen it except for the glow coming off its face."

"Green?"

Talen nodded.

Sparhawk started to swear.

"When you run out of words, let me know," Talen offered. "I'm a pretty good swearer."

"Did you warn Tynian?"

"Yes."

"What were you doing out of bed?"

Talen sighed. "Grow up, Sparhawk," he said in a tone far older than his years. "No thief ever sleeps more than two hours at a time without going out to look around."

"I didn't know that."

"You should have. It's a nervous life, but it's a lot of fun."

Sparhawk cupped his hand about the back of the young

fellow's neck. "I'm going to make a normal boy out of you yet," he said.

"Why bother? I outgrew all that a long time ago. It might have been nice to run and play—if things had been different—but they weren't, and this is much more fun. Go back to sleep, Sparhawk. Tynian and I'll keep an eye on things. Oh, by the way, it's going to rain tomorrow."

But it was not raining the following morning, though murky clouds obscured the sky. About midafternoon, Sparhawk reined Faran in.

"What's the trouble?" Kurik asked him.

"There's a village down there in that little valley."

"What could they possibly be doing out here in these woods? You can't farm with all these trees in the way."

"We could ask them, I suppose. I want to talk with them anyway. They're closer to Ghasek than the people back in Venne were, and I'd like to get a little more up-to-date information. There's no point in riding into something blind if you don't have to. Kalten," he called.

"Now what?" Kalten demanded.

"Take the others and keep on going. Kurik and I are going down to that village to ask a few questions. We'll catch up with you."

"All right." Kalten's tone was abrupt and slightly surly.

"What's the matter?"

"These woods depress me."

"They're only trees, Kalten."

"I know, but do there have to be so many of them?"

"Keep your eyes open. That Seeker's out there someplace."

Kalten's eyes brightened. He drew his sword and tested its edge with his thumb.

"What have you got in mind?" Sparhawk asked him.

"This might just be the chance we've been waiting for to get that thing off our backs once and for all. Otha's bug is very skinny. One good stroke should cut it in two. I think I'll just hang back a little bit and set up an ambush of my own."

Sparhawk thought very quickly at that point. "Nice plan," he seemed to agree, "but somebody has to lead the others to safety."

"Tynian can do that."

"Maybe, but do you feel like trusting Sephrenia's well-being to somebody we've only known for six months and who's still recovering from an injury?"

Kalten called his friend a number of obscene names.

"Duty, my friend," Sparhawk said calmly. "Duty. Its stern call pulls us away from various entertainments. Just do as I asked you to do, Kalten. We'll take care of the Seeker later."

Kalten continued to swear. Then he wheeled his horse and rode off to join the others.

"You were right on the edge of a fight there," Kurik commented.

"I noticed that."

"Kalten's a good man in a fight, but he's a hothead sometimes."

Then the two of them turned their horses and rode on down the hill toward the village.

The houses were made of logs, and they had sod roofs. The villagers had made some effort to clear the trees surrounding their community, creating stump-dotted fields extending perhaps a hundred paces back from their houses.

"They've cleared the land," Kurik observed, "but about all I see are kitchen gardens. I still wonder what they're doing out here."

That question was answered as soon as they rode into the place. A number of villagers were laboriously sawing boards from logs lying atop crude trestles. Stacks of warped green lumber beside the houses explained the purpose of the village.

One of the men stopped sawing, mopping at his brow with a dirty rag. "There's no inn here," he said to Sparhawk in an unfriendly tone.

"We're not really looking for an inn, neighbor," Sparhawk said, "just some information. How much farther is it to the house of Count Ghasek?"

The villager's face went slightly pale. "Not far enough away to suit me, my Lord," he replied, eyeing the big man in black armor nervously.

"What's the trouble, friend?" Kurik asked him.

"No sensible man goes near Ghasek," the villager replied. "Most people don't even want to talk about it."

"We heard some of the same sort of thing back in Venne,"

Sparhawk said. "What's going on at the count's house, anyway?"

"I couldn't really say, my Lord," the man said evasively. "I've never been there. I've heard some stories, though."

"Oh?"

"People have been disappearing around there. They're never seen again, so nobody really knows for sure what happened to them. The count's serfs have been running away, though, and he's not reputed to be a hard master. Something evil is going on in his house, and all the people who live nearby are terrified."

"Do you think the count's responsible?"

"It's not very likely. The count's been away from home for the past year. He travels around a lot."

"We heard that about him." Sparhawk thought of something. "Tell me, neighbor, have you seen any Styrics lately?"

"Styrics? No, they don't come into this forest. People up here don't like them, and we make the fact well known."

"I see. How far did you say it is to the count's house?"

"I didn't say. It's about fifteen leagues, though."

"A fellow in Venne said that it was forty leagues from there to Ghasek," Kurik told him.

The villager snorted derisively. "City folk don't even know how far a league is. It can't be much over thirty from Venne to Ghasek."

"We happened to see somebody back in the woods last night," Kurik said in a mildly conversational tone. "He was wearing a black robe and had his hood up. Could that have been one of your neighbors?"

The sawyer's face went very, very pale. "Nobody around here wears that kind of clothes," he said shortly.

"Are you sure?"

"You heard me. I said nobody in this district dresses like that."

"It must have been some traveller then."

"That must be it." The villager's tone had become unfriendly again, and his eyes were a little wild.

"Thank you for your time, neighbor," Sparhawk said, turning Faran around to leave the village.

"He knows more than he's saying," Kurik observed as the two of them were passing the last houses.

"Right," Sparhawk agreed. "The Seeker doesn't own him,

but he's very, very much afraid. Let's move right along. I want to catch up with the others before dark."

They overtook their friends just as the sky to the west took on the ruddy glow of sunset, and they made camp beside a silent mountain lake not far from the road.

"You think it's going to rain?" Kalten asked after they had eaten supper and were sitting around the fire.

"Don't say that," Talen said. "I only just got dry from all that rain in Lamorkand."

"It's always possible, of course," Kurik said in reply to Kalten's question. "It's the time of year for it, but I don't smell very much moisture in the air."

Berit came back from where they had picketed the horses. "Sir Sparhawk," he said quietly, "there's somebody coming."

Sparhawk came to his feet. "How many?"

"I only heard one horse. Whoever it is is coming down the road from the direction we're going." The novice paused. "He's pushing his horse very hard," he added.

"That's not too wise," Ulath grunted, "considering the dark and the condition of that road."

"Should we put out the fire?" Bevier asked.

"I think he's already seen it, Sir Bevier," Berit replied.

"Let's see if he decides to stop," Sparhawk said. "One man all by himself isn't much of a threat."

"Unless it's the Seeker," Kurik said, shaking out his chain mace. "All right, gentlemen," he said in his gruff, drill sergeant's voice, "spread out and get ready."

The knights automatically responded to that note of command. They all instinctively recognized the fact that Kurik probably knew more about close fighting than any man in the four orders. Sparhawk drew his sword, suddenly feeling an enormous pride in his friend.

The traveller reined in his horse on the road not too far from their camp. They could all hear the horse panting and gasping for breath. "May I approach?" the man out in the darkness pleaded. His voice was shrill and seemed to hover on the very brink of hysteria.

"Come on in, stranger," Kalten replied easily after a quick glance at Kurik.

The man who came riding out of the darkness was flamboyantly, even gaudily dressed. He wore a wide-brimmed, plumed hat, a red satin doublet, blue hose, and knee-length leather boots. He had a lute slung across his back; except for a small dagger at his waist, he carried no weapons. His horse lurched and staggered with exhaustion, and the rider himself appeared to be in much the same condition. "Thank God," the man said when he saw the armored knights standing around the fire. He swayed dangerously in his saddle and would have fallen had not Bevier jumped forward to catch him.

"The poor fellow seems to be just about played out," Kalten said. "I wonder what's chasing him."

"Wolves, maybe." Tynian shrugged. "I expect he'll tell us just as soon as he gets his breath."

"Get him some water, Talen," Sephrenia instructed.

"Yes, ma'am." The boy took a pail and went down to the lake.

"Just lie back for a few moments," Bevier told the stranger. "You're safe now."

"There's no time," the man gasped. "There's something of vital urgency I must tell you."

"What's your name, friend?" Kalten asked him.

"I am Arbele, a minstrel by profession," the stranger replied. "I write poetry and compose the songs I sing for the entertainment of lords and ladies. I have just come from the house of that monster, Count Ghasek."

"That doesn't sound too promising," Ulath muttered.

Talen brought the pail of water, and Arbele drank greedily.

"Take his horse down to the lake," Sparhawk told the boy. "Don't let him drink too much right at first."

"Right," Talen said.

"Why do you call the count a monster?" Sparhawk asked then.

"What else would you call a man who seals up a fair damsel in a tower?"

"Who is this fair damsel?" Bevier asked, his voice strangely intent.

"His own sister!" Arbele choked in a tone of outrage. "A lady incapable of wrongdoing."

"Did he happen to tell you why?" Tynian asked.

"He rambled out some nonsense, accusing her of foul misdeeds. I refused to listen to him."

"Are you sure about this?" Kalten's tone was skeptical. "Did you ever see the lady?"

"Well, no, not really, but the count's servants told me about her. They said that she's the greatest beauty in the district, and that the count sealed her in that tower when he returned from a journey. He drove me and all the servants from the castle, and now he proposes to keep his sister in that tower for the rest of her life."

"Monstrous!" Bevier exclaimed, his eyes afire with indignation.

Sephrenia had been watching the minstrel very closely. "Sparhawk," she said urgently, motioning him away from the fire. The two of them walked off, and Kurik followed them.

"What is it?" Sparhawk asked once they were out of earshot.

"Don't touch him," she replied, "and warn the others to avoid him as well."

"I don't quite follow."

"Something's wrong with him, Sparhawk," Kurik said. "His eyes aren't right, and he's talking a little too fast."

"He's infected with something," Sephrenia said.

"A disease?" Sparhawk shuddered back from the word. In a world where plagues were rampant, that word rang in human imagination like the clap of doom.

"Not in the sense you mean," she replied. "This is not a physical disease. Something has contaminated his mind— something evil."

"The Seeker?"

"I don't think so. The symptoms aren't the same. I've got a strong feeling that he might be contagious, so keep everybody away from him."

"He's talking," Kurik said, "and he doesn't have that wooden face. I think you're right, Sephrenia. I don't believe it's the Seeker. It's something else."

"He's very dangerous just now," she said.

"Not for long," Kurik said bleakly, reaching for his mace.

"Oh, Kurik," she said in a resigned tone of voice, "stop that. What would Aslade say if she found out you were assaulting helpless travellers?"

"We really don't have to tell her, Sephrenia."

"When will the day come when Elenes stop thinking with

their weapons?'' she said in exasperation. Then she said something in Styric that Sparhawk did not recognize.

"I beg your pardon?'' he said.

"Never mind.''

"There's a problem, though,'' Kurik said seriously. "If the minstrel's infectious, then Bevier's got it too. He touched him when he fell off his horse.''

"I'll keep an eye on Bevier,'' she said. "Perhaps his armor protected him. I'll know better in a little while.''

"And Talen?'' Sparhawk asked. "Did he touch the minstrel when he brought him that pail of water?''

"I don't think so,'' she said.

"Could you cure Bevier if he's caught it?'' Kurik asked.

"I don't even know what it is yet. All I know is that something has taken possession of that minstrel. Let's go back and try to keep the others away from him.''

"I charge you, Knights of the Church,'' the minstrel was saying in strident tones, "ride forthwith to the house of the wicked count. Punish him for his cruelty, and free his beautiful sister from her undeserved punishment.''

"Yes!'' Bevier said fervently.

Sparhawk looked quickly at Sephrenia, and she gravely nodded to advise him that Bevier had been infected. "Stay with him, Bevier,'' he told the Arcian. "The rest of you, come with me.''

They walked a short distance from the fire, and Sephrenia quietly explained.

"And now Bevier's got it too?'' Kalten asked her.

"I'm afraid so. He's already beginning to behave irrationally.''

"Talen,'' Sparhawk said seriously, "when you gave him that pail of water, did you touch him?''

"I don't think so,'' the boy replied.

"Are you feeling any urges to run around rescuing ladies in distress?'' Kurik asked him.

"Me? Kurik, be serious.''

"He's all right,'' Sephrenia said with a sound of relief in her voice.

"All right,'' Sparhawk said, "what do we do?''

"We ride to Ghasek as quickly as we can,'' she replied. "I have to find out what's causing the infection before I can cure it. We absolutely *have* to get into that castle—even if it involves force.''

''We can handle that,'' Ulath said, ''but what are we going to do about that minstrel? If he can infect others just by touching them, he's likely to come back at the head of an army.''

''There's a simple way to deal with it,'' Kalten said, putting his hand on his sword hilt.

''No,'' Sephrenia said sharply. ''I'll put him to sleep instead. A few days' rest might do him some good anyway.'' She looked sternly at Kalten. ''Why is your first answer to any problem always a sword?''

''Overtrained, I guess.'' He shrugged.

Sephrenia began to speak the incantation, weaving the spell with her fingers and quietly releasing it.

''What about Bevier?'' Tynian asked. ''Wouldn't it be a good idea for him to go to sleep too?''

She shook her head. ''He has to be able to ride. We can't leave him behind. Just don't get close enough to him to let him touch you. I've got problems enough already.''

They walked back to the fire.

''The poor fellow's gone to sleep,'' Bevier reported. ''What are we going to do about this?''

''Tomorrow morning, we're going to ride on to Ghasek,'' Sparhawk replied. ''Oh, one thing, Bevier,'' he added. ''I know you're outraged about this, but try to keep your emotions under control when we get there. Keep your hand away from your sword, and keep your tongue under control. Let's feel this situation out before we take any action.''

''That's the course of prudence, I suppose,'' Bevier admitted grudgingly. ''I'll feign illness when we get there. I'm not sure I could restrain my anger if I have to look this monstrous count in the face too many times.''

''Good idea,'' Sparhawk agreed. ''Put a blanket over our friend here, and then get to bed. Tomorrow's going to be a hard day.''

After Bevier had gone to his tent, Sparhawk spoke quietly with his fellow knights. ''Don't wake Bevier to stand watch tonight,'' he cautioned. ''I don't want him getting any ideas about riding out on his own in the middle of the night.''

They all nodded and went to their blankets.

It was still cloudy the following morning, a dense, gray

overcast that filled the dismal wood with a kind of murky twilight. After they had finished breakfast, Kurik erected a sheet of canvas on poles over the sleeping minstrel. "Just in case it rains," he said.

"Is he all right?" Bevier asked.

"Just exhausted," Sephrenia replied evasively. "Let him sleep."

They mounted and rode back out to the rutted track. Sparhawk led them at first at a trot to warm up the horses, and then, after about a half hour, he pushed Faran into a gallop. "Keep your eyes on the road," he shouted to the others. "Let's not cripple any of the horses."

They rode hard through the murky wood, slowing briefly from time to time to rest their mounts. As the day progressed, they began to hear rumbles of thunder off to the west, and the impending storm increased their desire to reach the questionable safety of the house at Ghasek.

As they drew closer to the count's castle, they passed deserted villages that had fallen into ruin. The storm clouds roiled overhead, and the distant thunder marched steadily toward them.

Late in the afternoon, they rounded a curve and saw the large castle perched atop a crag on the far side of a desolate field where ruined houses stood huddled together as if fearful of the bleak structure glowering down at them. Sparhawk reined Faran in. "Let's not just go charging up there," he said to the others. "We don't want the people in the castle to misunderstand our intentions." He led them at a trot across the field. They passed the village and approached the base of the craggy hill.

There was a narrow track leading up the side of the crag, and they rode up it in single file.

"Gloomy-looking place," Ulath said, craning his neck to look up at the brooding structure atop the crag.

"It doesn't really help to generate much enthusiasm for this visit," Kalten agreed.

The track they followed led ultimately to a barred gate. Sparhawk reined in, leaned over in his saddle, and pounded on the gate with one steel-clad fist.

They waited, but nothing happened.

Sparhawk pounded again.

After some time, a small panel in the center of the gate slid open. "What is it?" a hollow voice demanded shortly.

"We are travellers," Sparhawk replied, "and we seek shelter from the storm which approaches."

"The house is closed to strangers."

"Open the gate," Sparhawk said flatly. "We are Knights of the Church, and failure to comply with our reasonable request for shelter is an offense against God."

The unseen man on the other side of the gate hesitated. "I must ask the count's permission," he said grudgingly in a deep, rumbling voice.

"Do so at once then."

"Not a very promising beginning, is it?" Kalten said.

"Gatekeepers sometimes take themselves too seriously," Tynian told him. "Keys and locks do strange things to some people's sense of proportion."

They waited while lightning streaked the purple sky to the west.

Then, after what seemed a very long time, they heard the rattling of a chain followed by the sound of a heavy iron bar sliding through massive rings. Grudgingly, the gate groaned open.

The man inside was huge. He wore bullhide armor, and his eyes were deep-sunk beneath heavy brows. His lower jaw protruded, and his face was bleak.

Sparhawk knew him. He had seen him once before.

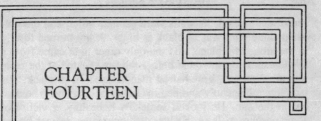

CHAPTER
FOURTEEN

HE CORRIDOR INTO which the surly gate guard led them was draped with cobwebs and dimly lighted by flickering torches set in iron rings at widely spaced intervals. Sparhawk quite deliberately lagged behind to fall in beside Sephrenia. "You recognized him too?" he whispered to her.

She nodded. "There's more going on here than we realized," she whispered back. "Be very careful, Sparhawk. This is dangerous."

"Right," he grunted.

At the far end of the cobwebbed hallway stood a large, heavy door. When their silent escort pulled it open, the rusty hinges squealed in protest. They came out at the head of a curved stairway that led down into a very large room. The room was vaulted, its walls were painted white, and the polished stone floor was as black as night. A fire burned fitfully in the arched fireplace, and the only other light came from a single candle on the table before the fire. Seated at the table was a pale-faced, gray-haired man dressed all in black. His face was melancholy and had the pallor of one who is seldom out in the sun. He looked somehow unhealthy, a victim of some obscure malaise. He was reading a large, leather-bound book by the light of his single candle.

"The people I spoke of, Master," the lantern-jawed man in the bullhide armor said deferentially in his deep, hollow voice.

"Very well, Occuda," the man at the table replied in a weary voice. "Prepare chambers for them. They will stay until the storm abates."

"It shall be as you say, Master." The big servant turned and went back up the stairs.

"Very few people travel into this part of the kingdom," the man in black informed them. "The region is desolate and unpopulated. I am Count Ghasek, and I offer you the meager shelter of my house until the weather clears. In time, you may wish that you had not found my gate."

"My name is Sparhawk," the big Pandion told him, and then he introduced the others.

Ghasek nodded politely to each. "Seat yourselves," he invited his guests. "Occuda will return shortly and prepare refreshments for you."

"You are very kind, my Lord of Ghasek," Sparhawk said, removing his helmet and gauntlets.

"You may not think so for long, Sir Sparhawk," Ghasek said ominously.

"That's the second time you've hinted at some kind of trouble within your walls, my Lord," Tynian said.

"And it may not be the last, Sir Tynian. The word 'trouble,' however, is far too mild, I'm afraid. To be quite honest with you, had you not been Knights of the Church, my gates would have remained closed to you. This is an unhappy house, and I do not willingly inflict its sorrows on strangers."

"We passed through Venne a few days ago, my Lord," Sparhawk said carefully. "All manner of rumors are going about concerning your castle."

"I'm not in the least surprised," the count replied, passing a trembling hand across his face.

"Are you unwell, my Lord?" Sephrenia asked him.

"Advancing age perhaps, and there's only one cure for that."

"We saw no other servants in your house, my Lord," Bevier said, obviously choosing his words carefully.

"Occuda and I are the only ones here now, Sir Bevier."

"We encountered a minstrel in the forest, Count Ghasek," Bevier told him almost accusingly. "He mentioned the fact that you have a sister."

"You must mean the fool called Arbele," the count replied. "Yes, I do in fact have a sister."

"Will the lady be joining us?" Bevier's tone was sharp.

"No," the count replied shortly. "My sister is indisposed."

"Lady Sephrenia here is highly skilled in the healing arts," Bevier pressed.

"My sister's malady is not susceptible to cure." The count said it with a note of finality.

"That's enough, Bevier," Sparhawk told the young Cyrinic in a tone of command.

Bevier flushed and rose from his chair to walk to the far end of the room.

"The young man seems distraught," the count observed.

"The minstrel Arbele told him some things about your house," Tynian said candidly. "Bevier's an Arcian, and they're an emotional people."

"I see," the melancholy nobleman replied. "I can imagine the kind of wild tales Arbele is telling. Fortunately, few will believe him."

"I'm afraid you're in error, my Lord," Sephrenia disagreed. "The tales Arbele tells are a symptom of a disorder that clouds his reason, and the disorder is infectious. For a time at least, everyone he encounters will accept what he says as absolute truth."

"My sister's arm grows longer, I see."

From somewhere far back in the house there came a hideous shriek, followed by peal upon peal of mindless laughter.

"Your sister?" Sephrenia asked gently.

Ghasek nodded, and Sparhawk could see the tears brimming in his eyes.

"And her malady is not physical?"

"No."

"Let us not pursue this further, gentlemen," Sephrenia said to the knights. "The subject is painful to the count."

"You're very kind, Madame," Ghasek said gratefully. He sighed, then said, "Tell me, Sir Knights, what brings you into this melancholy forest?"

"We came expressly to see you, my Lord," Sparhawk told him.

"Me?" The count looked surprised.

"We are on a quest, Count Ghasek. We seek the final resting place of King Sarak of Thalesia, who fell during the Zemoch invasion."

"The name is vaguely familiar to me."

"I thought it might be. A tanner in the town of Paler—a man named Berd—"

"Yes. I know him."

"Anyway, he told us of the chronicle you're compiling."

The count's eyes brightened, bringing life to his face for the first time since they had entered the room. "The labor of a lifetime, Sir Sparhawk."

"So I understand, my Lord. Berd told us that your research has been more or less exhaustive."

"Berd may be a bit overgenerous in that regard." The count smiled modestly. "I have, however, gathered *most* of the folklore in northern Pelosia and even in some parts of Deira. Otha's invasion was far more extensive than is generally known."

"Yes, so we discovered. With your permission, we'd like to examine your chronicle for clues that might lead us to the place where King Sarak is buried."

"Certainly, Sir Sparhawk, and I'll help you myself, but the hour grows late, and my chronicle is weighty." He smiled self-deprecatingly. "Once I begin, we could be up for most of the night. I lose all track of time once I immerse myself in those pages. Suppose we wait until morning before we begin."

"As you wish, my Lord."

Then Occuda entered, bringing a large pot of thick stew and a stack of plates. "I fed her, Master," he said quietly.

"Is there any change?" the count asked.

"No, Master. I'm afraid not."

The count sighed, and his face became melancholy again.

Occuda's skills in the kitchen appeared to be limited. The stew he provided was marginal at best, but the count was so immersed in his studies that he appeared to be indifferent to what was set before him.

After they had eaten, the count bade them good night, and Occuda led them up the stairs and down a long corridor toward the rooms he had prepared. As they approached the chambers, they heard the shrieks of the madwoman once again. Bevier suppressed a sob. "She's suffering," he said in an anguished voice.

"No, Sir Knight," Occuda disagreed. "She's completely insane, and people in her condition cannot comprehend their circumstances."

"I'd be interested to know how a servant came to be such an expert in diseases of the mind."

"That's enough, Bevier," Sparhawk said again.

"No, Sir Knight," Occuda said. "Your friend's question is pertinent." He turned toward Bevier. "In my youth, I was a monk," he said. "My order devoted itself to caring for the infirm. One of our abbeys had been converted into a hospice for the deranged, and that's where I served. I have had much experience with the insane. Believe me when I tell you that Lady Bellina is hopelessly mad."

Bevier looked a little less certain of himself, but then his face hardened again. "I don't believe you," he snapped.

"That's entirely up to you, Sir Knight," Occuda said. "This will be your chamber." He opened a door. "Sleep well."

Bevier went into the room and slammed the door behind him.

"You know that as soon as the house grows quiet, he'll go in search of the count's sister, don't you?" Sephrenia murmured.

"You're probably right," Sparhawk agreed. "Occuda, is there some way you can lock that door?"

The huge Pelosian nodded. "I can chain it shut, my Lord," he said.

"You'd better do it then. We don't want Bevier wandering around the halls in the middle of the night." Sparhawk thought a moment. "We'd better post a guard outside his door as well," he told the others. "He's got his Lochaber ax with him, and if he gets desperate enough, he might try to chop the door down.''

''That could get a little tricky, Sparhawk,'' Kalten said dubiously. ''We don't want to hurt him, but we don't want him coming at us with that gruesome ax of his either.''

''If he tries to get out, we'll just have to overpower him,'' Sparhawk said.

Occuda showed the others to their rooms, and Sparhawk's was the last. ''Will that be all, Sir Knight?'' the servant asked politely as they entered.

''Stay a moment, Occuda,'' Sparhawk said.

''Yes, my Lord.''

''I've seen you before, you know.''

''Me, my Lord?''

''I was in Chyrellos some time ago, and Sephrenia and I were watching a house belonging to some Styrics. We saw you accompany a woman into that house. Was that Lady Bellina?''

Occuda sighed and nodded.

''It was what happened in that house that drove her mad, you know.''

''I'd guessed as much.''

''Can you tell me the whole story? I don't want to bother the count with painful questions, but we've got to rid Sir Bevier of his obsession.''

''I understand, my Lord. My first loyalty is to the count, but perhaps you *should* know the details. At least that way you may be able to protect yourselves from that madwoman.'' Occuda sat down, his rugged face mournful. ''The count is a scholarly man, Sir Knight, and he's frequently away from home for long periods, pursuing the stories he's been collecting for decades. His sister, Lady Bellina, is—or was—a plain, rather dumpy woman of middle years with very little prospect of ever catching a husband. This is a remote and isolated house, and Bellina suffered from loneliness and boredom. Last winter, she begged the count to permit her to visit friends in Chyrellos, and he gave her his consent, provided that I accompany her.''

''I'd wondered how she got there,'' Sparhawk said, sitting on the edge of the bed.

''Anyway,'' Occuda continued, ''Bellina's friends in Chyrellos are giddy, senseless ladies, and they filled her ears with stories about a Styric house where a woman's youth and beauty could be restored by magic. Bellina became inflamed with a wild desire to go to the house. Women do things for strange reasons sometimes.''

"Did she in fact grow younger?''

"I wasn't permitted to accompany her into the room where the Styric magician was, so I can't say what happened in there, but when she came out, I scarcely recognized her. She had the body and face of a sixteen-year-old, but her eyes were dreadful. As I told your friend, I've worked with the insane before, so I recognize the signs. I bundled her up and brought her straight back to this house, hoping that I might be able to treat her here. The count was away on one of his journeys, so he had no way of knowing what began to happen after I got her home.''

"And what was that?''

Occuda shuddered. "It was horrible, Sir Knight," he said in a sick voice. "Somehow, she was able to dominate the other servants completely. It was as if they were powerless to resist her commands.''

"All except you?''

"I think the fact that I had been a monk may have protected me—either that or she didn't think I was worth the trouble.''

"What exactly did she do?'' Sparhawk asked him.

"Whatever it was that she encountered in that house in Chyrellos was totally evil, Sir Knight, and it possessed her utterly. She would send the servants who were her slaves out to surrounding villages by night, and they would abduct innocent serfs for her. I discovered later that she'd had a torture chamber set up in the cellar of this house. She gloried in blood and agonies.'' Occuda's face twisted with revulsion. "Sir Knight, she fed on human flesh and bathed her naked body in human blood. I saw her with my own eyes.''

He paused and then continued. "It was no more than a week ago when the count returned to the castle. It was late one night when he arrived, and he sent me to the cellar for a bottle of wine, though he seldom drinks anything but water. When I was down there, I heard what sounded like a scream. I went to investigate, and opened the door to her secret chamber. I wish to God I never had!'' He covered his face with his hands, and a racking sob escaped him. "Bellina was naked,'' he continued after he had regained his composure, ''and she had a serf girl chained down on a table. Sir Knight, she was cutting the poor girl to pieces while the girl was still alive, and she was cramming quivering pieces of flesh into her own mouth!'' Occuda made a retching sound, then clenched his teeth together.

Sparhawk never knew what impelled him to ask the question. ''Was she alone in there?''

''No, my Lord. The servants who were her slaves were there as well, lapping the blood from those dank stones. And—'' The lantern-jawed man hesitated.

''Go on.''

''I cannot swear to this, my Lord. My head was reeling, but it seemed that at the back of the chamber there was a hooded figure all in black, and its presence chilled my soul.''

''Can you give me any details about it?'' Sparhawk asked.

''Tall, very thin, totally enshrouded in a black robe.''

''And?'' Sparhawk pressed, knowing with icy certainty what came next.

''The room was dark, my Lord,'' Occuda apologized, ''except for the fires in which Bellina heated her torturing irons, but from that back corner I seemed to see a glow of green. Is that in any way significant?''

''It may be,'' Sparhawk replied bleakly. ''Go on with the story.''

''I ran to inform the count. At first he refused to believe me, but I forced him to go to the cellar with me. I thought at first he would kill her when he saw what she was doing. Would to God that he had! She started screeching when she saw him in the doorway and tried to attack him with the knife she'd been using on the serf girl, but I wrested it from her.''

''Was that when he locked her in the tower?'' Sparhawk was shaken by the horrible story.

''That was my idea, actually,'' Occuda said grimly. ''At the hospice where I served, the violent ones were always confined. We dragged her to the tower, and I chained the door shut. She will remain there for the rest of her life if there's any way I can manage it.''

''What happened to the other servants?''

''At first they made attempts to free her, and I had to kill several of them. Then, yesterday, the count heard a few of them telling a wild story to that silly fool of a minstrel. He instructed me to drive them all out of the castle. They milled around outside the gate for a while, and then they all ran off."

"Was there anything strange about them?"

"They all had absolutely blank faces," Occuda replied, "and the ones I killed died without making a sound."

"I was afraid of that. We've encountered that before."

"What happened to her in that house, Sir Knight? What drove her mad?"

"You've been trained as a monk, Occuda," Sparhawk said, "so you've probably had some theological instruction. Are you familiar with the name Azash?"

"The God of the Zemochs?"

"That's him. The Styrics in that house in Chyrellos were Zemochs, and it's Azash who owns Lady Bellina's soul. Is there any way she could possibly have gotten out of that tower?"

"Absolutely impossible, my Lord."

"Somehow she managed to infect that minstrel, and he was able to pass it on to Bevier."

"She could not have gotten out of the tower, Sir Knight," Occuda said adamantly.

"I'll need to talk with Sephrenia," Sparhawk said. "Thank you for being so honest, Occuda."

"I told you all this in the hope that you could help the count." Occuda rose to his feet.

"We'll do what we can."

"Thank you. I'll go chain your friend's door shut." He started toward the door, then turned back. "Sir Knight," he said in a somber tone, "do you think I should kill her? Might that not be better?"

"It may come to that, Occuda," Sparhawk said frankly, "and if you do, you'll have to cut off her head. Otherwise, she'll just rise again."

"I can do that if I have to. I have an ax, and I'll do anything to spare the count more suffering."

Sparhawk put a comforting hand on the servant's shoulder. "You're a good and true man, Occuda," he said. "The count's lucky to have you in his service."

"Thank you, my Lord."

Sparhawk removed his armor and went down the corridor to Sephrenia's door.

"Yes?" she said in response to his knock.

"It's me, Sephrenia," he said.

"Come in, dear one," she said.

He entered her room. "I had a talk with Occuda," he said.
"Oh?"

"He told me what's been happening here. I'm not sure if you want to hear it."

"If I'm to cure Bevier, I'm afraid I'll have to."

"We were right," Sparhawk began. "The Pelosian woman we saw going into that Zemoch house in Chyrellos was the count's sister."

"I was sure of it. What else?"

Briefly, Sparhawk repeated what Occuda had told him, glossing over the more gory details.

"It's consistent," she said almost clinically. "That form of sacrifice is a part of the worship of Azash."

"There's more," Sparhawk told her. "When he entered the chamber in the cellar, Occuda saw a shadowy figure back in one of the corners. It was robed and hooded, and its face glowed green."

She drew in her breath sharply.

"Could Azash have more than one Seeker out there?" Sparhawk asked.

"With an Elder God, anything is possible."

"It couldn't be the same one," he said. "Nothing can be in two places at the same time."

"As I said, dear one, with an Elder God, anything is possible."

"Sephrenia," he said in a strained voice, "I hate to say it, but all this is beginning to frighten me just a little."

"And me as well, dear Sparhawk. Keep the spear of Aldreas close to you. The power of Bhelliom may protect you. Now go to bed. I need to think."

"Will you bless me before I sleep, little mother?" he asked, dropping to his knees. He suddenly felt like a small, helpless child. He gently kissed her palms.

"With all my heart, my dear one," she replied, enfolding his head in her arms and drawing him to her. "You are the best of them all, Sparhawk," she said to him, "and if you be but strong, not even the gates of Hell can prevail against you."

As he rose to his feet, Flute slid down off her bed and

gravely came to him. He felt suddenly unable to move. The little girl took him by the wrists in a gentle grasp that he was powerless to resist. She turned his hands over and gently kissed each of his palms, and her kisses burned in his blood like holy fire. Shaken, Sparhawk left the room without a further word.

He slept fitfully, waking often and stirring uneasily in his bed. The night seemed interminable, and the rumble of thunder shook the very foundations of the castle. The rain the storm had brought with it clawed at the window of the room in which Sparhawk tried to sleep, and water ran in torrents from the slate roof to hammer the stones of the courtyard. It must have been well past midnight when he finally gave up. He threw off his blankets and sat moodily on the edge of the bed. What were they going to do about Bevier? He knew that the Arcian's faith was strong, but the Cyrinic Knight did not have Occuda's iron will. He was young and ingenuous, and he had the native passion of all Arcians. Bellina could use that to her advantage. Even if Sephrenia could rid Bevier of his obsessive compulsion, what guarantee would there be that Bellina could not reimpose it upon him at any time it pleased her? Although he shrank from the idea, Sparhawk was forced to admit that the course Occuda had suggested might be the only one available to them.

Then, quite suddenly, he was almost overcome by a sense of dread. Something overpoweringly evil was nearby. He rose from the bed, seeking his sword in the darkness. Then he went to the door and opened it.

The hallway outside his room was dimly lit by a single torch. Kurik sat dozing in the chair outside Bevier's room, but otherwise, the hallway was empty. Then Sephrenia's door opened, and she came hurrying out with Flute directly behind her. "Did you feel it, too?"

"Yes. Can you locate it?"

She pointed at Bevier's door. "It's in there."

"Kurik," Sparhawk said, touching his squire's shoulder.

Kurik's eyes came open immediately. "What's the trouble?" he asked.

"Something's in there with Bevier. Be careful." Sparhawk unhooked Occuda's chain, slipped the latch, and slowly pushed the door open.

The room was filled with an eerie light. Bevier lay tossing

on his bed, and over him hovered the misty, glowing shape of a naked woman. Sephrenia drew in her breath sharply. "Succubus," she whispered. She immediately began an incantation, motioning sharply to Flute. The little girl lifted her pipes and began to play a melody so complex that Sparhawk could not even begin to follow it.

The glowing and indescribably beautiful woman at the bedside turned toward the door, drawing its lips back to reveal its dripping fangs. It hissed at them spitefully and the hiss seemed overlaid by an insectlike stridulation, but the glowing figure seemed unable to move. The spell continued, and the succubus began to shriek, clutching at its head. Flute's song grew more stern, and Sephrenia's incantation grew louder. The succubus began to writhe, screaming imprecations so vile that Sparhawk flinched back from them. Then Sephrenia lifted one hand and spoke, surprisingly in Elene rather than Styric. "Return to the place from which you came!" she commanded, "and venture forth no more this night!"

The succubus vanished with a disjointed howl of frustration, leaving behind it the foul odor of decay and corruption.

CHAPTER
FIFTEEN

OW DID SHE get out of that tower?'' Sparhawk asked in a hushed voice. ''There's only one door, and Occuda's got it chained shut.''

''She didn't get out,'' Sephrenia replied absently, her brow creased with a frown. ''I've only seen this happen once before,'' she added. Then she smiled a bit wryly. ''We're lucky I remembered the spell.''

''You're not making any sense, Sephrenia,'' Kurik said. ''She was right here.''

''No, actually she wasn't. The succubus is not of the flesh. It's the spirit of the one who sends it. Bellina's body is still confined in that tower, but her spirit roams the halls of this melancholy house, infecting everything it touches.''

''Bevier's lost then, isn't he?'' Sparhawk asked bleakly.

219

"No. I've at least partially freed him of her influence. If we move quickly enough, I can clear his mind entirely. Kurik, go find Occuda. I need to ask him some questions."

"Right away," the squire replied, going out the door.

"Won't she come back tomorrow night and infect Bevier again?" Sparhawk asked.

"I think there's a way to prevent that, but I've got to question Occuda to be sure. Don't talk so much, Sparhawk. I need to think." She sat on the bed, rather absently laying her hand on Bevier's forehead. He stirred restlessly. "Oh, stop that," she snapped at the sleeping man. She muttered a few words in Styric, and the young Arcian suddenly sank back into his pillow.

Sparhawk waited nervously as the small woman pondered the situation. Several minutes later, Kurik returned with Occuda. Sephrenia rose to her feet. "Occuda," she began, but then seemed to change her mind. "No," she said, almost to herself. "There's a faster way. Here's what I want you to do. I want you to think back to the moment you opened that door in the cellar—only the moment when you opened it. Don't dwell on what Bellina was doing."

"I don't quite understand, my Lady," Occuda said.

"You don't have to. Just do it. We don't have much time." She murmured briefly to herself and then reached up to touch his shaggy brow. She had to stand on her tiptoes. "Why are you people all so tall?" she complained. She kept her fingers lightly on Occuda's forehead for a moment and then let out an explosive breath. "Just as I thought," she said exultantly. "It *had* to be there. Occuda, where's the count right now?"

"I believe he's still in that central room, Lady. He usually reads for most of the night."

"Good." She looked at the bed and snapped her fingers. "Bevier, get up."

The Arcian rose stiffly, his eyes blank.

"Kurik," she said, "you and Occuda help him. Don't let him fall down. Flute, you go back to bed. I don't want you to see this."

The little girl nodded.

"Come along, gentlemen," Sephrenia said crisply. "We haven't much time left."

"Just exactly what are we doing?" Sparhawk asked as he

followed her down the hall. For a small person she moved very fast.

"There isn't time to explain," she said. "We need the count's permission to go to the cellar—and his presence, I'm afraid."

"The cellar?" Sparhawk was baffled.

"Don't ask foolish questions, Sparhawk." She stopped and looked at him critically. "I told you to keep your hands on that spear," she scolded him. "Now go back to your room and get it."

He threw his hands helplessly in the air and turned around.

"Run, Sparhawk!" she shouted after him.

He caught up with them just as they entered the doorway that opened out onto the stairs leading down into the sunken room near the center of the castle. Count Ghasek still sat hunched over his book in the flickering light of his guttering candle. His fire had burned down to embers, and the wind from the storm outside howled fitfully in the chimney.

"You're going to ruin your eyes, my Lord," Sephrenia told him. "Put aside the book. We have things to do."

He stared at her in astonishment.

"I need to ask a favor of you, my Lord."

"A favor? Of course, Madame."

"Don't be too quick to agree, Count Ghasek—not until you know what I'm going to ask you. There's a room in the cellar of your house. I need to visit it with Sir Bevier here, and I'll need to have you accompany us. If we move quickly enough, I can cure Bevier and rid this house of its curse."

Ghasek stared at Sparhawk, his face totally baffled.

"I'd advise doing as she says, my Lord," Sparhawk told him. "You'll do it in the end anyway, and it's a lot less embarrassing if you just agree gracefully."

"Is she like this often?" the count asked, rising to his feet.

"Frequently."

"Time is passing, gentlemen," Sephrenia said, her foot tapping impatiently on the floor.

"Come with me, then," the count said, giving up. He led them up the stairs and into the cobwebby corridor. "The entrance to the cellar is this way." He pointed down a narrow side hall and then led the way again. He took a large iron key from his doublet and unlocked a narrow door. "We'll need light," he said.

Kurik took a torch down from its ring and handed it to him.

The count lifted the torch and started down a long flight of narrow stone stairs. Occuda and Kurik supported the somnolent Bevier to keep him from falling as they descended. At the foot of the stairs, the count turned to his left. "One of my ancestors considered himself to be quite a connoisseur of fine wines," he said, pointing at dusty casks and bottles lying on their sides on wooden racks back in the dimness as they passed. "I have little taste for wine myself, so I seldom come down here. It was only by chance that I happened to send Occuda down here one night, and he came upon that dreadful room."

"This is not going to be very pleasant for you, my Lord," Sephrenia warned him. "Perhaps you might want to wait outside the room."

"No, Madame," he said. "If you can endure it, I can as well. It's only a room now. What happened in it is in the past."

"It's the past which I intend to resurrect, my Lord."

He looked at her sharply.

"Sephrenia is an adept in the secrets," Sparhawk explained. "She can do many things."

"I have heard of such people," the count admitted, "but there are few Styrics in Pelosia, so I've never seen those arts performed."

"You may not wish to, my Lord," she warned him ominously. "It's necessary for Bevier to see the full extent of your sister's perversions for him to be cured of his obsession. Your presence as the owner of the house is necessary, but if you stand just outside the room, it will suffice."

"No, Madame, witnessing what happened here may stiffen my resolve. If my sister cannot be restrained by confinement, I may find it necessary to take sterner measures."

"Let's hope it doesn't come to that."

"This is the door to the room," the count said, producing another key. He unlocked the door and opened it wide. The sickening stench of blood and decaying flesh washed out over them.

By the flickering light of the torch, Sparhawk saw immediately why this chamber had inspired such horror. A rack stood in the center of the bloodstained floor, and cruel hooks jutted from the walls. He winced when he saw that many of the hooks had gobbets of blackened flesh clinging to them. On one wall hung the gruesome implements of the torturer's trade, knives, pincers, branding irons, and needle-sharp hooks. There were also thumbscrews and an iron boot, as well as assorted whips.

"This may take some time," Sephrenia said, "and we must complete the task before morning. Kurik, take the torch and hold it as high over your head as you can. Sparhawk, hold the spear in readiness. Something may try to interfere." She took Bevier's arm and led him toward the rack. "All right, Bevier," she said to him, "wake up."

Bevier blinked and looked around in confusion. "What is this place?" he said.

"You're here to watch, not to talk, Bevier," she told him crisply. She began to speak in Styric, her fingers moving rapidly in the air in front of her. Then she pointed at the torch to release the spell.

At first nothing seemed to happen, but then Sparhawk saw a faint movement near the brutal rack. The figure was dim and hazy at first, but then the torch flared up, and he could see it more clearly. It was the form of a woman, and he recognized her face. She was the Pelosian woman he had seen emerging from the Styric house in Chyrellos. Her face was also the face of the succubus that had hovered over Bevier's bed earlier this night. She was naked, and her face was exultant. In one hand she held a long, cruel knife, in the other, a hook. Gradually, another figure began to appear, strapped down on the rack. The second figure appeared to be that of a serf girl, judging from her clothing. Her face was contorted into an expression of mindless terror, and she struggled futilely with her bonds.

The woman with the knife approached the bound figure on the rack and with deliberate slowness began to cut her victim's clothing away. When the serf girl had been stripped, the count's sister methodically began on her flesh, muttering all the while in an alien Styric dialect. The serf girl was screaming, and the look of cruel exultation on Lady Bellina's face locked into a hideous grin. Sparhawk saw with revulsion that her teeth had been filed to points. He looked away, unable to watch any longer, and he saw Bevier's face. The Arcian watched in horrified disbelief as Bellina gorged herself on the girl's flesh.

When it was done, blood was running from the corners of Bellina's mouth, and her body was smeared with it.

Then the images changed. This time Bellina's victim was a male, and he writhed on one of the hooks protruding from the wall while Bellina slowly carved small chunks from his body and ate them with relish.

One after another, the procession of victims continued. Bevier was sobbing now and trying to cover his eyes with his hands.

"No!" Sephrenia said sharply, pulling his hands down. "You must see it all."

On and on the horror went as victim after victim came under Bellina's knife. The worst were all the children. Sparhawk could not bear that.

And then, after an eternity of blood and agony, it was over. Sephrenia looked intently into Bevier's face. "Do you know who I am, Sir Knight?" she asked him.

"Of course," he sobbed. "Please, Lady Sephrenia," he begged, "no more, I pray you."

"How about this man?" She pointed at Sparhawk.

"Sir Sparhawk of the Pandion Order, my brother knight."

"And him?"

"Kurik, Sparhawk's squire."

"And this gentleman?"

"Count Ghasek, the owner of this unhappy house."

"And him?" She pointed at Occuda.

"He's the count's servant, a good and honest man."

"Is it still your intention to release the count's sister?"

"Release her? Are you mad? That fiend belongs in the deepest pit in Hell."

"It's worked," Sephrenia said to Sparhawk. "We won't have to kill him now." There was a great relief in her voice.

Sparhawk cringed back from the implication in her matter-of-fact tone.

"Please, my Lady," Occuda said in a shaking voice, "can we go out of this horrible place now?"

"We're not finished yet. Now we come to the dangerous part. Kurik, take the torch to the back of the room. Go with him, Sparhawk, and be ready for anything."

Shoulder to shoulder the two slowly walked to the back of

the chamber. And then in the flickering torchlight they saw the small stone idol set in a niche in the back wall. It was grotesquely misshapen and had a hideous face.

"What is it?" Sparhawk gasped.

"That is Azash," Sephrenia replied.

"Does he actually look like *that*?"

"Approximately. There are some things about him that are too horrible for any sculptor to capture."

The air in front of the idol seemed to waver, and a tall, skeletal figure in a hooded black robe suddenly appeared between the image of Azash and Sparhawk. The green glow coming out of the hood grew brighter and brighter.

"Don't look at its face!" Sephrenia warned them sharply. "Sparhawk, slide your left hand up the shaft of the spear until you're holding the blade."

He vaguely understood, and when his hand reached the blade socket, he felt an enormous surge of power.

The Seeker shrieked and flinched back from him, and the glow from its face flickered and began to fade. Grimly, step by step, Sparhawk advanced on the hooded creature, holding the spear blade out in front of him like a knife. The Seeker shrieked again and then vanished.

"Destroy the idol, Sparhawk," Sephrenia commanded.

Still holding the spear, he reached forward with one hand and took the idol from its niche. It seemed terribly heavy, and it was hot to the touch. He raised it overhead and dashed it to the floor where it shattered into hundreds of pieces.

From high up in the house came a shriek of unutterable despair.

"Done!" Sephrenia said. "Your sister is powerless now, Count Ghasek. The destruction of the image of her God has bereft her of all supernatural capabilities, and I think that, were you to look at her, you'd find that she once again appears as she did before she entered the Styric house in Chyrellos."

"I will never be able to thank you enough, Lady Sephrenia," he said with gratitude.

"Was that the same thing that's been following us?" Kurik asked.

"Its image," Sephrenia replied. "Azash summoned it when he realized that the idol was in danger."

"If it was only an image, then it wasn't really dangerous, was it?"

"Don't ever make that mistake, Kurik. The images Azash summons are sometimes even more dangerous than the real things." She looked around with distaste. "Let us leave this revolting place," she suggested. "Lock the door again, Count Ghasek—for the time being. Later on, it might be wise to wall up the entrance."

"I'll see to it," he promised.

They went back up the narrow stairs and returned to the vaulted room where they had found the count. The others had already gathered there.

"What was all that awful screaming?" Talen asked. The boy's face was pale.

"My sister, I'm afraid," Count Ghasek replied sadly.

Kalten looked warily at Bevier. "Is it safe to talk about her in front of him?" he quietly asked Sparhawk.

"He's all right now," Sparhawk answered, "and Lady Bellina has been stripped of her powers."

"That's a relief. I wasn't sleeping too well under the same roof with her." He looked at Sephrenia. "How did you manage it?" he asked. "Cure Bevier, I mean?"

"We found out how the lady was influencing others," she said. "There's a spell that temporarily counteracts that sort of thing. Then we went to a room in the cellar and completed the cure." She frowned. "There's still a problem, though," she said to the count. "That minstrel's still out there. He's infected, and the servants you sent away probably are as well. They can infect others, and they could return with a large number of people. I cannot remain here to cure them all. Our quest is far, far too important for such delay."

"I will send for armed men," the count declared. "I have enough resources for that, and I will seal up the gates of this castle. If necessary, I will kill my sister to prevent her escape."

"You may not have to go that far, my Lord," Sparhawk told him, remembering something Sephrenia had said in the cellar. "Let's go have a look at this tower."

"You have a plan, Sir Sparhawk?"

"Let's not get our hopes up until I see the tower."

The count led them out into the courtyard. The storm had largely passed. The lightning was flickering on the eastern horizon now, and the pounding rain had diminished to intermittent tatters that raked the shiny stones of the yard. "It's that one, Sir Sparhawk,'' the count said, pointing at the southeast corner of the castle.

Sparhawk took a torch from beside the entryway, crossed the rainy courtyard, and began his examination of the tower. It was a squat, round structure perhaps twenty feet high and fifteen or so in diameter. A stone stairway wound halfway around the side of it to a solidly barred and chained door at the top. The windows were no more than narrow slits. There was a second door at the base of the tower, and it was unlocked. Sparhawk opened it and went inside. It appeared to be a storeroom. Boxes and bags were piled along the walls, and the room appeared dusty and unused. Unlike the tower, however, the room was not round but semicircular. Buttresses jutted out from the walls to hold up the stone floor of the chamber above. Sparhawk nodded with satisfaction and went back outside again. "What's behind that wall in this storeroom, my Lord?'' he asked the count.

"There's a wooden staircase that runs up from the kitchen, Sir Sparhawk. In times when the tower had to be defended, the cooks could take food and drink to the men up there. Occuda uses it now to feed my sister.''

"Do the servants you sent away know about the stairway?''

"Only the cooks knew, and they were among the ones Occuda killed.''

"Better and better. Is there a door at the top of those stairs?''

"No. Just a narrow slot to push the food through.''

"Good. The lady's misbehaved a bit, but I don't think any of us would want to starve her to death.'' He looked around at the others. "Gentlemen,'' he said to them, "we're going to learn a new trade.''

"I don't quite follow you, Sparhawk,'' Tynian admitted.

"We're now going to be stonemasons. Kurik, do you know how to lay brick and stone?''

"Of course I do, Sparhawk,'' Kurik said disgustedly. "You should know that.''

"Good. You'll be our foreman then. Gentlemen, what I'm going to suggest may shock you, but I don't think we have any choice.'' He looked at Sephrenia. "If Bellina ever gets out of that tower, she's probably going to go looking for Zemochs or the Seeker. Would they be able to restore her powers?''

"Yes, I'm sure they could."

"We can't allow that. I don't want that cellar ever to be used that way again."

"What are you proposing, Sir Sparhawk?" the count asked.

"We're going to wall up that door at the top of those stairs," Sparhawk replied. "Then we'll tear the stairway down and use the stones to wall in this door at the base of the tower as well. Then we'll conceal the door that leads from the kitchen to that stairway inside the tower. Occuda will still be able to feed her, but if the minstrel or those servants ever manage to get inside the castle, they'll never figure out how to get to that room up there. Lady Bellina will live out the rest of her life right where she is."

"That's a rather horrible thing to suggest, Sparhawk," Tynian said.

"Would you rather kill her?" Sparhawk asked bluntly.

Tynian's face blanched.

"That's it, then. We brick her up inside."

Bevier's smile was chill. "Perfect, Sparhawk," he said. Then he looked at the count. "Tell me, my Lord, which of the structures inside your walls can you spare?"

The count gave him a puzzled look.

"We're going to need building stone," Bevier explained. "Quite a bit of it, I think. I want the wall across that door up there good and thick."

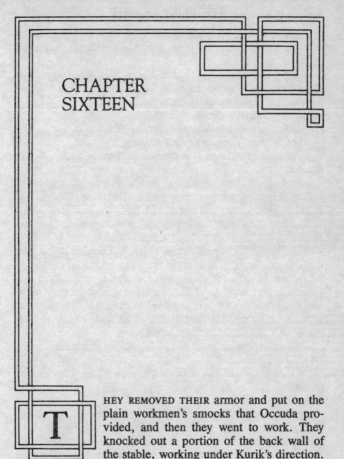

CHAPTER
SIXTEEN

HEY REMOVED THEIR armor and put on the plain workmen's smocks that Occuda provided, and then they went to work. They knocked out a portion of the back wall of the stable, working under Kurik's direction. Occuda mixed a large tub of mortar, and they began to carry building stones up the curved stairway to the door at the top of the tower.

"Before you begin, gentlemen," Sephrenia said, "I'll need to see her."

"Are you sure of that?" Kalten asked her. "She might still be dangerous, you know."

"That's what I have to find out. I'm positive that she's powerless, but it's best to be certain, and I can't do that unless I see her."

"And I'd like to see her face one last time as well," Count Ghasek added. "I can't bear what she's become, but I did love her once."

They mounted the stairs, and Kurik pried the heavy chain away from the door with a steel bar. Then the count took yet another key and unlocked the door.

Bevier drew his sword.

"Is that really necessary?" Tynian asked him.

"It may be," Bevier replied bleakly.

"All right, my Lord," Sephrenia said to the count, "open the door."

The Lady Bellina stood just inside. Her wildly contorted face was pouchy and her neck wrinkled. Her tangled hair was streaked with gray, and her naked body sagged in unlovely folds. Her eyes were totally insane, and she pulled back her lips from her pointed teeth in a snarl of hate.

"Bellina," the count began sadly, but she hissed at him and lunged forward with her fingers extended like claws.

Sephrenia spoke a single word, pointing her finger, and Bellina reeled back as if she had been struck a heavy blow. She howled in frustration and tried to rush at them again, but suddenly stopped, clawing at the air in front of her as if at some wall that none of them could see.

"Close it again, my Lord," Sephrenia instructed sadly. "I've seen enough."

"So have I," the count replied in a choked voice and with tear-filled eyes as he closed the door. "She's hopelessly mad now, isn't she?"

"Completely. Of course she's been mad since she left that house in Chyrellos, but she's absolutely gone now. She's no longer a danger to anyone but herself." Sephrenia's voice was filled with pity. "There are no mirrors in that room, are there?"

"No. Would that pose some threat?"

"Not really, but at least she'll be spared the sight of herself. That would be too cruel." She paused thoughtfully. "There are some common weeds hereabouts, I've noticed. There's a way to extract their juices, and they have a calming effect. I'll talk with Occuda and give him instructions for putting them in her food. They won't cure her, but they'll make it less likely that she'll hurt herself. Lock the door, my Lord. I'll go back inside while you gentlemen do what needs to be done. Let me know when you're finished." Flute and Talen trailed after her as she walked back toward the castle.

"Hold it right there, young man," Kurik said to his son.

"Now what?" Talen said.

"You stay here."

"Kurik, I don't know anything about bricklaying."

"You don't have to know all that much to carry stones up those stairs."

"You're not serious!"

Kurik reached for his belt, and Talen hurried over to the pile of squared-off stones at the back of the stable.

"Good lad there," Ulath noted. "He grasps reality almost immediately."

Bevier insisted upon being in the forefront of their work. The young Cyrinic laid building stones almost in a frenzy.

"Keep them level," Kurik barked at him. "This is a permanent structure, so let's make a workmanlike job of it."

In spite of himself, Sparhawk laughed.

"Something amusing, my Lord?" Kurik asked him coldly.

"No. I just remembered something, that's all."

"You'll have to share it with us later. Don't just stand there, Sparhawk. Help Talen carry stones."

The embrasure into which the door was set was quite thick, since this tower was a part of the castle's fortifications. They built one wall flush against the door as the count's sister shrieked insanely inside and pounded wildly against the door that they were sealing. Then they began a second wall tightly against the first. It was midmorning when Sparhawk went into the castle to tell Sephrenia that they had finished.

"Good," she said. The two of them went back out into the courtyard. The rain had ceased now, and the sky had begun to clear. Sparhawk looked upon that as a good omen. He led Sephrenia to the stair that half encircled the tower.

"Very nice, gentlemen," Sephrenia called up to the others, who were putting the finishing touches on the wall they had constructed. "Now, come down from there. I have one last thing to do."

They trooped down, and the small woman went on up. She began to chant in Styric. When she released the spell, the fresh-built wall seemed to shimmer for a moment. Then the shimmering was gone. She came back down. "All right," she said, "you can knock down the stairs now."

"What did you do?" Kalten asked curiously.

She smiled. "Your work was much better than you might have thought, dear one," she told him. "The wall you built is totally impregnable now. That minstrel or the servants can pound on it with sledges until they're old and gray without damaging it in the slightest."

Kurik, who had gone back up the steps, leaned out and looked down at them. "The mortar's completely dry," he reported. "That usually takes days."

Sephrenia pointed at the door at the base of the tower. "Let me know when you finish this one. It's a bit damp and chilly out there. I think I'll go back inside where it's warm."

The count, who had been more saddened by the necessary entombment of his sister than he had readily admitted, accompanied her back inside while Kurik instructed his makeshift work crew on how to proceed.

It took them most of the rest of the day to knock down the stone stairway leading to the now-walled-in upper door and to seal off the lower one. Then Sephrenia came out, repeated the spell, and went back into the castle.

Sparhawk and the others adjourned to the kitchen, which was located in a wing of the castle abutting the tower.

Kurik considered the small door leading to the inside staircase.

"Well?" Sparhawk asked him.

"Don't rush me, Sparhawk."

"It's getting late, Kurik."

"Do you want to do this?"

Sparhawk closed his mouth and watched without saying a word as Talen slipped away. The boy looked tired, and Kurik was a hard taskmaster. Sparhawk was like that on occasion.

Kurik consulted with Occuda for a few moments, then looked at his mortar-spattered crew. "Time to learn a new trade, gentlemen," he said. "You're now going to become carpenters. We're going to build a china cabinet out from that door. The hinges will still work, and I can fashion a hidden latch. The door will be completely concealed." He thought a moment, cocking his head to listen to the muffled shrieks coming from above. "I think I'll need some quilts, Occuda," he said thoughtfully. "We'll nail them to the other side of the door to keep the noise from being too loud in here."

"Good idea," Occuda agreed. "With no other servants

around, I'll be spending a fair amount of time in here, and that screaming might get on my nerves."

"That's not the only reason we're doing it, but that's all right. Very well, gentlemen, let's get to work." Kurik grinned. "I'll make useful people out of you all yet," he said.

When they were done, the china cabinet was a solid piece of work. Kurik rather liberally laid a dark stain over it, then stepped back and viewed the new woodwork critically. "Wax it a couple times after the stain dries," he said to Occuda, "and then scuff it up a bit. You'd probably better scratch it in a few places as well and blow dust into the corners. Then load it with crockery. Nobody will ever know that it hasn't been here for a century or more."

"That is a very good man you've got there, Sparhawk," Ulath noted. "Would you consider selling him?"

"His wife would kill me," Sparhawk replied. "Besides, we don't sell people in Elenia."

"We're not *in* Elenia."

"Why don't we go back to that main room?"

"Not just yet, Sir Knights," Kurik said firmly. "First you have to sweep the sawdust up from the floor and put the tools away."

Sparhawk sighed and went looking for a broom.

After they had cleaned up the kitchen, they washed the mortar and sawdust off themselves, changed back into tunics and hose, and returned to the large room with the vaulted ceiling, where they found the count and Sephrenia deep in conversation while Talen and Flute sat not far away. The boy appeared to be teaching the little girl how to play draughts.

"You look much neater now," Sephrenia told them approvingly. "You were all really very messy out there in the courtyard."

"You can't lay brick or stone without getting mud on you." Kurik shrugged.

"I seem to have picked up a blister," Kalten mourned, looking at the palm of his hand.

"It's the first honest work he's done since he was knighted," Kurik said to the count. "With a little training, he might not make a bad carpenter, but the rest of them have a long way to go, I'm afraid."

"How did you conceal the door in the kitchen?" the count asked him.

"We built a china cabinet against it, my Lord. Occuda's going to do a few things to it to make it look old and then fill it with dishes. We padded the back of it to muffle the sound of your sister's screaming."

"Is she still doing that?" The count sighed.

"It will not diminish as the years go by, my Lord," Sephrenia told him. "I'm afraid she'll scream until the day she dies. When she stops, you'll know that it's over."

"Occuda's fixing us something to eat," Sparhawk said to the count. "It's going to take him awhile, so this might not be a bad time to have a look at the chronicle you've compiled."

"Excellent idea, Sir Sparhawk," the count said, rising from his chair. "Will you excuse us, Madame?"

"Of course."

"Perhaps you might care to accompany us?"

She laughed. "Ah, no, my Lord. I'd be of no use in a library."

"Sephrenia doesn't read," Sparhawk explained. "It has something to do with her religion, I think."

"No," she disagreed. "It has to do with language, dear one. I don't want to get into the habit of thinking in Elene. It might interfere at some point when I need to think—and speak—very rapidly in Styric."

"Bevier, Ulath, why don't you come with the count and me?" Sparhawk suggested. "Between you, you might be able to fill in some details that will help him pinpoint the story we need."

They went back up the stairs and left the room. The three knights followed the count through the dusty hallways of the castle until they reached a door in the west wing. The count opened the door and led them into a dark room. He fumbled around on a large table for a moment, took up a candle, and went back into the hallway to light it from the torch burning outside.

The room was not large, and it was crammed with books. They stood on shelves stretching from floor to ceiling and were piled in the corners.

"You are well read, my Lord," Bevier said to him.

"It's what scholars do, Sir Bevier. The soil hereabouts is

poor—except for growing trees—and the cultivation of trees is not a very stimulating activity for a civilized man.'' He looked around fondly. "These are my friends," he said. "I'll need their companionship now more than ever, I'm afraid. I won't be able to leave this house ever again. I'll have to stay here to guard my sister."

"The insane don't usually live for very long, my Lord," Ulath assured him. "Once they go mad, they begin to neglect themselves. I had a cousin who lost her mind one winter. She was gone by spring."

"It's a painful thing to hope for the death of a loved one, Sir Ulath, but God help me, I find that I do." The count put his hand on a foot-thick stack of unbound paper lying on his desk. "My life's work, gentlemen." He seated himself. "To business then. Exactly what are we looking for?"

"The grave of King Sarak of Thalesia," Ulath told him. "He didn't reach the battlefield down in Lamorkand, so we assume he fell in some skirmish up here in Pelosia or in Deira—unless his ship was lost at sea."

Sparhawk had never thought of that. The possibility that Bhelliom lay at the bottom of the Straits of Thalesia or the Sea of Pelos chilled him.

"Can you generalize a bit?" the count asked. "Which side of the lake was the king's destination? I've broken my chronicle down by districts to give it some organization."

"In all probability, King Sarak was bound for the east side," Bevier replied. "That's where the Thalesian army engaged the Zemochs."

"Are there any clues at all about where his ship landed?"

"Not any that I've ever heard," Ulath admitted. "I've made a few guesses, but they could be off by a hundred leagues or so. Sarak might have sailed to some seaport along the north coast, but Thalesian ships don't always do that. We're reputed to be pirates in some quarters, and Sarak might have wanted to avoid the tiresome questions and just driven his prow up onto some deserted beach."

"That makes it a little more difficult," Count Ghasek said. "If I knew where he'd landed, I'd know which districts he might have passed through. Does Thalesian tradition provide any description of the king?"

"Not in very much detail," Ulath replied, "only that he was about seven feet tall."

"That helps a bit. The common people probably wouldn't have known his name, but a man of that size would have been remembered." He began to leaf through his manuscript. "Could he possibly have landed on the north coast of Deira?" he asked.

"It's possible, but unlikely," Ulath said. "Relations between Deira and Thalesia were a bit strained in those days. Sarak probably wouldn't have put himself in a position to have been captured."

"Let's begin up around the port of Apalia then. The shortest route to the east side of Lake Randera would run south from there." He began to leaf through the pages in front of him. He frowned. "There doesn't seem to be anything useful here," he said. "How large was the king's party?"

"Not very sizeable," Ulath rumbled. "Sarak left Emsat in a hurry, and he only took a few retainers with him."

"All of the accounts I picked up in Apalia mention large bodies of Thalesian troops. Of course, it could be as you suggested, Sir Ulath. King Sarak might have landed on some lonely beach and bypassed Apalia entirely. Let's try the port of Nadera before we start combing beaches and isolated fishing villages." He consulted a map and then turned to a place about halfway through the manuscript and began to skim through it. "I think we've got something!" he exclaimed with a scholar's enthusiasm. "A peasant up near Nadera told me about a Thalesian ship that slipped past the city during the night early in the campaign and sailed several leagues up the river before she landed. A number of warriors disembarked, and one of them stood head and shoulders above the rest. Was there anything unusual about Sarak's crown?"

"It had a large blue jewel on top of it," Ulath said, his face intent.

"That was him, then," the count said exultantly. "The story makes particular mention of that jewel. They say that it was the size of a man's fist."

Sparhawk let out an explosive breath. "At least Sarak's ship didn't sink at sea," he said with relief.

The count took a length of string and stretched it diagonally across the map. Then he dipped his pen into his inkwell and made a number of notes. "All right, then," he said crisply. "Assuming King Sarak took the shortest course from Nadera to the battlefield, he'd have passed through the districts on this list. I've done research in all of them. We're getting closer, Sir Knights. We'll track down this king of yours yet." He began to leaf through rapidly. "No mention of him here," he muttered, half to himself, "but there weren't any engagements in that district." He read on, his lips pursed. "Here!" he said, his face breaking into a smile of triumph. "A group of Thalesians rode through a village twenty leagues to the north of Lake Venne. Their leader was a very large man wearing a crown. We're narrowing it down."

Sparhawk found that he was actually holding his breath. He had been on many missions and quests in his life, but this searching out a trail through paper had a strange excitement to it. He began to understand how a man could devote his life to scholarship with absolute contentment.

"And here it is!" the count said excitedly. "We've found him."

"Where?" Sparhawk demanded eagerly.

"I'll read you the entire passage," the count replied. "You understand, of course, that I've cast the account in more gentlemanly language that that of the man who told it to me." He smiled. "The language of peasants and serfs is colorful, but hardly suitable for a scholarly work." He squinted at the page. "Oh, yes. Now I remember. This fellow was a serf. His master told me that the fellow liked to tell stories. I found him breaking up clods with a mattock in a field near the east side of Lake Venne. This is what he told me:

" 'It was early in the campaign, and the Zemochs under Otha had penetrated the eastern border of Lamorkand and were devastating the countryside as they marched. The western Elenian kings were rushing to meet them with all the forces they could muster, and large bodies of troops were crossing into Lamorkand from the west, but they were primarily farther south than Lake Venne. The troops coming down from the north were mostly Thalesians. Even before the Thalesian army landed, however, an advance party of them rode south past Lake Venne.

" 'Otha, as we all know, had sent out skirmishers and patrols well in advance of his main force. It was one of those patrols that intercepted the party of Thalesians mentioned above at a place called Giant's Mound.' "

"Was the place named before or after the battle?" Ulath asked.

"It almost had to have been after," the count replied. "Pelosians don't erect burial mounds. That's a Thalesian custom, isn't it?"

"Right, and the word *giant* describes Sarak rather well, wouldn't you say?"

"Exactly my thought. There's more, though." The count continued to read. " 'The engagement between the Thalesians and the Zemochs was short and very savage. The Zemochs vastly outnumbered the small band of northern warriors and soon swarmed them under. Among the last to fall was the leader, a man of enormous proportions. One of his retainers, though sorely wounded, took something from his fallen leader's body and fled west toward the lake with it. There is no clear account of what it was that he took or what he did with it. The Zemochs pursued the retainer hotly, and he died of his wounds on the shore of the lake. However, a column of Alcione Knights, men who had been returned to their mother house in Deira to recuperate from wounds received in the campaign in Rendor, happened by on their way to Lake Randera and exterminated the Zemoch patrol to the last man. They buried the faithful retainer and rode on, by purest chance missing the site of the original engagement.

" 'As it happened, a sizeable force of Thalesians had been following the first party by no more than a day. When the local peasants informed them of what had transpired, they buried their countrymen and erected the mound over their graves. This second Thalesian force never reached Lake Randera, since they were ambushed two days later, and all were slain.' "

"And that explains why no one ever knew what had happened to Sarak," Ulath said. "There was no one left alive to tell anybody about it."

"This retainer," Bevier mused, "might it have been the king's crown he took?"

"It's possible," Ulath conceded. "More likely, though, it would have been his sword. Thalesians put great value on royal swords."

"It won't be hard to find out," Sparhawk said. "We'll go to Giant's Mound and Tynian can raise Sarak's ghost. He'll be able to tell us what happened to his sword—and his crown."

"Here's something odd," the count said. "I remember

that I almost didn't write it down because it happened *after* the battle. The serfs have been seeing a monstrously deformed shape in the marshes around Lake Venne for centuries now."

"Some swamp creature?" Bevier suggested. "A bear perhaps?"

"I think that serfs would recognize a bear," the count said.

"Maybe a moose," Ulath said. "The first time I ever saw a moose, I couldn't believe anything could get that big, and a moose hasn't got the prettiest face in the world."

"I remember that the serfs said that the thing walks on its hind legs."

"Could it possibly be a Troll?" Sparhawk asked. "That one who was roaring outside our camp down by the lake?"

"Did the serfs describe it as shaggy and very tall?" Ulath asked.

"It's shaggy, right enough, but they say it's squat, and its limbs are all twisted."

Ulath frowned. "That doesn't sound like any Troll I've ever heard about—except maybe—" His eyes suddenly went wide. "Ghwerig!" he shouted, snapping his fingers. "It *has* to be Ghwerig. That nails it down, Sparhawk. Ghwerig's looking for Bhelliom, and he knows right where to look."

"I think we'd better go back to Lake Venne," Sparhawk said, "and just as fast as we can. I don't want Ghwerig to find Bhelliom before I do. I definitely don't want to have to wrestle him for it."

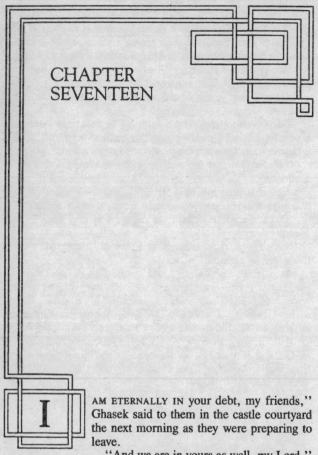

CHAPTER
SEVENTEEN

I AM ETERNALLY IN your debt, my friends,"
Ghasek said to them in the castle courtyard
the next morning as they were preparing to
leave.

"And we are in yours as well, my Lord,"
Sparhawk assured him. "Without your aid, we'd have had no
chance of finding what we seek."

"Godspeed then, Sir Sparhawk," Ghasek said, shaking the
big Pandion's hand warmly.

Sparhawk led the way out of the courtyard and back down
the narrow track to the foot of the crag.

"I wonder what's going to happen to him," Talen said
rather sadly as they rode along.

"He has no choice," Sephrenia said. "He has to stay there

until his sister dies. She's no longer a danger, but she still has to be guarded and cared for."

"I'm afraid the rest of his life is going to be very lonely." Kalten sighed.

"He has his books and chronicles," Sparhawk disagreed. "That's all the company a scholar really needs."

Ulath was muttering under his breath.

"What's the trouble?" Tynian asked him.

"I should have known that the Troll at Lake Venne was there for some specific reason," Ulath replied. "I could have saved us some time if I'd investigated."

"Would you have recognized Ghwerig if you'd seen him?"

Ulath nodded. "He's dwarfed, and there aren't very many dwarfed Trolls about. She-Trolls usually eat deformed cubs as soon as they're born."

"That's a brutal practice."

"Trolls aren't famous for their gentle dispositions. They don't even get along with each other most of the time."

The sun was very bright that morning, and the birds sang in the bushes near the deserted village in the center of the field below Count Ghasek's castle. Talen turned aside to ride into the village.

"There won't be anything in there to steal," Kurik called after him.

"Just curious is all," Talen called back. "I'll catch up with you in a couple of minutes."

"Do you want me to go get him?" Berit asked.

"Let him look around," Sparhawk said. "He'll complain all day if we don't."

Then Talen came galloping out of the village. His face was deathly pale, and his eyes were wild. When he reached them, he tumbled from his horse and lay on the ground retching and unable to speak.

"We'd better go have a look," Sparhawk said to Kalten. "The rest of you wait here."

The two knights rode warily into the deserted village with their lances at the ready.

"He went this way," Kalten said quietly, pointing to the tracks of Talen's horse in the muddy street with the tip of his lance.

Sparhawk nodded, and they followed the tracks to a house

that was somewhat larger than the others in the village. The two dismounted, drew their swords and entered.

The rooms inside were dusty and devoid of any furniture. "Nothing at all in here," Kalten said. "I wonder what frightened him so much."

Sparhawk opened the door to a room at the back of the house and looked inside. "You'd better go get Sephrenia," he said bleakly.

"What is it?"

"A child. It's not alive, and it's been dead for a long time."

"Are you sure?"

"Look for yourself."

Kalten looked into the room and made a gagging sound. "Are you sure you want her to see that?" he asked.

"We need to know what happened."

"I'll go get her then."

The two went back outside. Kalten remounted and rode out to where the others waited while Sparhawk stood near the door of the house. A few minutes later, the blond knight returned with Sephrenia.

"I told her to leave Flute with Kurik," Kalten said. "We wouldn't want her to see what's in there."

"No," Sparhawk replied somberly. "Little mother," he apologized to Sephrenia, "this will not be pleasant."

"Few things are," she said resolutely.

They took her inside the house to that back room.

She took one quick look and then turned aside. "Kalten," she said, "go dig a grave."

"I don't have a shovel," he objected.

"Then use your hands!" Her tone was intense, almost savage.

"Yes, Sephrenia." He seemed awed by her uncharacteristic vehemence. He left the house quickly.

"Oh, poor thing," Sephrenia mourned, hovering over the desiccated little body.

The body of the child was withered and dry. Its skin was gray, and its sunken eyes were open.

"Bellina again?" Sparhawk asked. His voice seemed loud, even to himself.

"No," she replied. "This is the work of the Seeker. This is how it feeds. Here," she pointed at dry puncture marks on the child's body, "and here, here, and here. This is where the Seeker fed. It draws out the body's fluids and leaves only a dry husk.''

"Not any more," Sparhawk said, his fist closing about the haft of Aldreas' spear. "The next time we meet, it dies."

"Can you afford to do that, dear one?"

"I can't afford not to. I'll avenge this child—against the Seeker or Azash or even against the gates of Hell itself."

"You're angry, Sparhawk."

"Yes. You could say that." It was stupid and served no purpose, but Sparhawk suddenly tore his sword from its scabbard and destroyed an unoffending wall with it. It didn't accomplish anything, but it made him feel a little better.

The others came silently down into the village and to the open grave Kalten had grubbed out of the earth with his bare hands. Sephrenia came out of the house with the dry body of the child in her arms. Flute came forward with a light linen cloth, and the two carefully wrapped the dead child in it. Then they deposited it in the rude grave.

"Bevier," Sephrenia said, "would you? This is an Elene child, and you are the most devout among these knights."

"I am unworthy." Bevier was weeping openly.

"Who *is* worthy, dear one?" she said. "Will you send this unknown child into the darkness alone?"

Bevier stared at her and then fell to his knees beside the grave and began to recite the ancient prayer for the dead of the Elene church.

Rather peculiarly, Flute came up beside the kneeling Arcian. Her fingers gently wove through his curly blue-black hair in a strangely comforting way. For some reason, Sparhawk began to feel that the strange little girl might be far, far older than any of them realized. Then she raised her pipes. The hymn was an ancient one, almost at the core of the Elene faith, but there was a minor Styric overtone to it. Briefly, in the sound of the little girl's song, Sparhawk began to perceive some unbelievable possibilities.

When the burial was complete, they mounted and rode on. They were all very quiet for the rest of that day, and they stopped for the night at the campsite beside the small lake where they had encountered the wandering minstrel. The man was gone.

"I was afraid of that," Sparhawk said. "It was too much to hope that he'd still be here."

"Maybe we'll catch up with him farther south," Kalten suggested. "That horse of his wasn't in very good shape."

"What can we do about him even if we do catch him?" Tynian said. "You weren't planning to kill him, were you?"

"Only as a last resort," Kalten replied. "Now that Sephrenia knows how Bellina influenced him, she could probably cure him."

"Your confidence is very nice, Kalten," she said, "but it might be misplaced."

"Will the spell she put on him ever wear off?" Bevier asked.

"To some degree. He'll grow less desperate as time goes on, but he'll never be entirely free of it. It might even make him write better poetry, though. The important thing is that he'll grow less and less infectious. Unless he meets a fair number of people in the next week or so, he won't be much of a danger to the count, and neither will those servants."

"That's something at least," the young Cyrinic said. He frowned slightly. "Since I was already infected, why did that creature come to me that night? Wasn't that just a waste of her time?" Bevier seemed still strongly shaken by the funeral service for the dead child.

"It was for reinforcement, Bevier," she told him. "You were agitated, but you wouldn't have gone so far as to attack your companions. She had to make sure you'd go to any lengths to free her from that tower."

As they were setting up their night's camp, something occurred to Sparhawk. He went over to where Sephrenia sat by the fire with her teacup in her hands. "Sephrenia," he said, "what's Azash up to? Why is he suddenly going out of his way to corrupt Elenes? He's never done that before, has he?"

"Do you remember what the ghost of King Aldreas said to you that night in the crypt?" she said. "That the time had come for Bhelliom to re-emerge?"

"Yes."

"Azash knows that too, and he's growing desperate. I'd guess that he's found that his Zemochs aren't reliable. They follow orders, but they're not very bright. They've been digging up that battlefield for centuries now and they just keep plowing over the same ground. We've found out more about Bhelliom's location in the past few weeks than they've found out in the past five hundred years."

"We were lucky."

"That's not entirely true, Sparhawk. I know that I tease you sometimes about Elene logic, but that was precisely what's gotten us so close to Bhelliom. A Zemoch is incapable of logic. That's Azash's weakness. A Zemoch doesn't think because he doesn't have to. Azash does all his thinking for him. That's why Azash so desperately needs Elene converts. He doesn't need their adoration; he needs their minds. He has Zemochs all over the western kingdoms gathering old stories—in the same way that we did. I think he believes that one of them will stumble over the right story and that then his Elene converts will be able to piece together the meaning of it."

"That's the long way around, isn't it?"

"Azash has time. He's not pressed by the same sense of urgency that we are."

Later that night, Sparhawk was standing watch some distance away from the fire, looking out over the small lake that glittered in the moonlight. Again, the howls of wolves echoed back in the dismal woods, but now for some reason the sound did not seem so ominous. The ghastly spirit that had haunted this forest was locked away forever, and the wolves were only wolves now and not harbingers of evil. The Seeker, of course, was an entirely different matter. Grimly Sparhawk promised himself that the next time they encountered it, he would bury the spear of Aldreas in the hideous creature.

"Sparhawk, where are you?" It was Talen. He spoke quietly and stood near the fire peering out into the darkness.

"Over here."

The boy came toward him, putting his feet down carefully to avoid hidden obstructions on the ground.

"What's the problem?" Sparhawk asked him.

"I couldn't sleep. I thought you might like some company."

"I appreciate that, Talen. Standing watch is a lonely business."

"I'm certainly glad to be away from that castle," Talen said. "I've never been so scared in my life."

"I was a little nervous myself," Sparhawk admitted.

"Do you know something? There were all sorts of very nice things in Ghasek's castle, and I didn't once think of stealing any of them. Isn't that odd?"

"Maybe you're growing up."

"I've known some very old thieves," Talen disagreed. Then he sighed disconsolately.

"Why so mournful, Talen?"

"I wouldn't tell just anyone this, Sparhawk, but it's not as much fun as it used to be. Now that I know I can take just about anything I want from almost anybody, the thrill has sort of gone out of it."

"Maybe you should look for another line of work."

"What else am I suited for?"

"I'll give it some thought and let you know what I come up with."

Talen laughed suddenly.

"What's so funny?" Sparhawk asked him.

"I might have just a little trouble getting references," the boy replied, still laughing. "My customers didn't usually know they were doing business with me."

Sparhawk grinned. "It could be a problem," he agreed. "We'll work something out."

The boy sighed again. "It's almost over, isn't it, Sparhawk? We know where that king's buried now. All we have left to do is go dig up his crown, and then we'll go back to Cimmura. You'll go to the palace, and I'll go back to the streets."

"I don't think so," Sparhawk said. "Maybe we can come up with an alternative to the streets."

"Maybe, but the minute it gets tedious, I'll just run away again. I'm going to miss all this, you know? There've been a few times when I was so scared I almost wet myself, but there have been good times, too. Those are the ones I'll remember."

"At least we gave you something." Sparhawk put his hand on the boy's shoulder. "Go back to bed, Talen. We'll be getting up early tomorrow."

"Whatever you say, Sparhawk."

They set out at dawn, riding carefully along the rutted road to avoid injury to the horses. They passed the woodcutters' village without stopping and pressed on.

"How far do you make it?" Kalten asked about mid-morning.

"Three, maybe four more days—five more at the most,"

Sparhawk replied. "Once we get out of this forest, the roads improve and we'll make better time."

"Then all we have to do is find Giant's Mound."

"That shouldn't be much of a problem. From what Ghasek said, the local peasantry uses it as a landmark. We'll ask around."

"Then we get to start digging."

"It's not really the sort of thing you want to have somebody to do for you."

"Do you remember what Sephrenia said at Alstrom's castle back in Lamorkand?" Kalten said seriously. "The business about Bhelliom's re-emergence ringing through the whole world?"

"Vaguely," Sparhawk replied.

"Then the minute we dig it up, Azash is going to know about it, and the road back to Cimmura could be lined on both sides with Zemochs. It could be a very nervous trip."

Ulath was riding directly behind them. "Not really," he disagreed. "Sparhawk's already got the rings. I can teach him a few words in the language of the Trolls. Once he's got Bhelliom in his hands, there's almost nothing he won't be able to do. He'll be able to bowl over whole regiments of Zemochs."

"Is it really that powerful?"

"Kalten, you have no idea. If even half the stories are true, Bhelliom can do almost anything. Sparhawk could probably stop the sun with it, if he wanted to."

Sparhawk looked back over his shoulder at Ulath. "Do you have to know Troll language to use Bhelliom?" he asked.

"I'm not really sure," Ulath replied, "but they say that it's infused with the power of the Troll-Gods. They might not respond to words spoken in Elene or Styric. The next time I talk with a Troll-God, I'll ask him."

They camped in the forest again that night. After supper, Sparhawk walked away from the fire to do some thinking. Bevier quietly joined him. "Will we stop in Venne when we reach it?" the Cyrinic asked.

"More than likely," Sparhawk replied. "I doubt that we'd be able to get much farther tomorrow."

"Good. I'll need to find a church."

"Oh?"

"I've been contaminated by evil. I need to pray for a while."

"It wasn't really your fault, Bevier. It could have happened to any one of us."

"But it was me, Sparhawk," Bevier sighed. "The witch probably sought me out because she knew that I'd be susceptible."

"Nonsense, Bevier. You're the most devout man I've ever met."

"No," Bevier disagreed sadly. "I know my own weaknesses. I am powerfully attracted to members of the fair sex."

"You're young, my friend. What you feel is only natural. It subsides in time—or so I'm told."

"Do you still feel those urges? I'd hoped that by the time I reached your age, they would no longer trouble me."

"It doesn't work exactly that way, Bevier. I've known some very old men whose heads could still be turned by a pretty face. It's part of being human, I suppose. If God didn't want us to feel that way, He wouldn't permit it. Patriarch Dolmant explained it to me once when I was having a problem with it. I'm not sure I entirely believed him, but it made me feel a little less guilty."

Bevier chuckled. "You, Sparhawk? This is a side of you I hadn't seen. I thought you were totally consumed with your sense of duty."

"Not entirely, Bevier. I still have a little time for other thoughts as well. I'm sorry you didn't get the chance to meet Lillias."

"Lillias?"

"A Rendorish woman. I lived with her while I was in exile."

"Sparhawk!" Bevier gasped.

"It was part of a necessary disguise."

"But surely you didn't—" Bevier left it hanging. Sparhawk was sure that the young man was blushing furiously, but the darkness concealed it.

"Oh, yes," he assured his friend. "Lillias would have left me otherwise. She's a woman of strong appetites. I needed her to help conceal my real identity, so I more or less had to try to keep her happy."

"I'm shocked at you, Sparhawk, truly shocked."

"The Pandions are a more pragmatic order than the Cyrinics, Bevier. We do what has to be done in order to get the job finished. Don't worry, my friend. Your soul hasn't been damaged—at least not very much.''

''I still need to spend some time in a church.''

''Why? God is everywhere, isn't he?''

''Of course.''

''Talk with Him here, then.''

''It wouldn't be quite the same.''

''Whatever makes you feel right, I suppose.''

They set out again at first light. The road now tended downward, for they were coming down out of the low range of forested hills. On occasion, when rounding a curve or cresting a hill, they could see Lake Venne sparkling in the spring sun off in the distance; by midafternoon, they reached the fork in the road. The main road was much better than had been the one leading down from Ghasek, and they reached the north gate of Venne just before the sunset filled the western sky with its fire.

Once again they rode through the narrow streets with the overhanging houses casting a premature darkness, and arrived back at the inn where they had previously stayed. The innkeeper, a jovial fat Pelosian, welcomed them and led them upstairs to the second floor where the sleeping rooms were located. ''Well, my Lords,'' he said, ''how was your sojourn in those accursed woods?''

''Quite successful, neighbor,'' Sparhawk replied, ''and I think you can begin to pass the word around that Ghasek's no longer a place to be feared. We found out what was causing the problem and took care of it.''

''Thanks be to God for the Knights of the Church!'' the innkeeper cried enthusiastically. ''The stories that have been going around have been very bad for business here in Venne. People have been choosing other routes because they didn't want to go into those woods.''

''It's all taken care of now,'' Sparhawk assured him.

''Was it some kind of monster?''

''In a manner of speaking,'' Kalten replied.

''Did you kill it?''

''We entombed it.'' Kalten shrugged, starting to remove his armor.

''Good for you, my Lord.''

''Oh, by the way,'' Sparhawk said, ''we need to find a

place called Giant's Mound. Do you by any chance happen to know where we should start looking?''

''I think it's on the east side of the lake,'' the innkeeper replied. ''There are some villages down there. They're back a ways from the lake shore because of all those peat bogs.'' He laughed. ''The villages won't be hard to find. The peasants down there burn peat in their stoves. It puts out quite a bit of smoke, so about all you have to do is follow your noses.''

''What are you planning to offer for supper tonight?'' Kalten asked eagerly.

''Is that all you ever think about?'' Sparhawk said.

''It's been a long trip, Sparhawk. I need some real food. You gentlemen are good companions, but your cooking leaves a bit to be desired.''

''I've had a haunch of beef turning on the spit since this morning, my Lord,'' the innkeeper said. ''It should be well-done by now.''

Kalten smiled beatifically.

True to his word, Bevier spent the night in a nearby church and rejoined them in the morning. Sparhawk chose not to question him concerning the state of his soul.

They rode out of Venne and took the road south along the lake. They made much better time than they had when they had made the trip to the city. On that occasion, Kalten, Bevier, and Tynian had been recovering from their encounter with the monstrous thing that had emerged from the burial mound at the north end of Lake Randera, but now they were wholly restored and able to ride at a gallop.

It was late afternoon when Kurik pulled up beside Sparhawk. ''I just caught a trace of peat smoke in the air,'' he reported. ''There's a village of some kind around here.''

''Kalten,'' Sparhawk called.

''Yes?''

''There's a village nearby. Kurik and I are going to go have a look. Set up camp and build a good fire. It might be after dark before the two of us get back, and we'll need something to guide us in.''

''I know what to do, Sparhawk.''

''All right. Do it then.'' Sparhawk and his squire turned aside from the road and galloped across an open field toward a low band of trees a mile or so to the east.

The smell of burning peat grew stronger—a strangely homelike scent. Sparhawk leaned back in his saddle, feeling strangely at ease.

"Don't get too confident," Kurik warned. "The smoke does strange things to their heads. Peat burners are not always very reliable. In some ways, they're worse than Lamorks."

"Where did you get all this information, Kurik?"

"There are ways, Sparhawk. The Church and the nobility get their information in dispatches and reports. The commons go to the heart of things."

"I'll remember that. There's the village."

"You'd better let me do most of the talking when we get there," Kurik advised. "No matter how hard you try, you don't sound much like a commoner."

It was a low village. Shallow, wide houses built of gray fieldstone and roofed with thatch lined both sides of the single street. A thick-bodied peasant sat on a stool in an open-sided shed, milking a brown cow.

"Hello there, friend," Kurik called to him, slipping down from his horse.

The peasant turned and stared at him in slack-lipped stupidity.

"Do you happen to know about a place called Giant's Mound?" Kurik asked him.

The fellow continued to gape at him without answering.

Then a lean man with squinting eyes came out of a nearby house. "Won't do you no good to talk to him," he said. "He got kicked in the head by a horse when he was young, and he ha'n't been right since."

"Oh," Kurik said. "Sorry to hear about that. Maybe you could help us. We're looking for a place called Giant's Mound."

"You're not plannin' to go there at night, are you?"

"No, we thought we'd wait until daylight."

"That's a little better, but not much. It's haunted, you know."

"No, I didn't know that. Whereabouts is it?"

"You see that lane as runs off toward the southeast?" The lean man pointed.

Kurik nodded.

"Come sunup, follow that. It runs right past the mound— four, maybe five mile from here."

"Have you ever seen anybody poking around it? Maybe somebody digging?"

"Never heard tell of nothin' like that. People as has good sense don't poke around haunted places."

"We've heard that you've got a Troll in this area."

"What's a Troll?"

"Ugly brute all covered with hair. This one is pretty badly deformed."

"Oh, that thing. It's got a lair someplace out in the bogs. It only comes out at night. It wanders up an' down the lake shore. It makes awful noises for a while an' then pounds on the ground with its front paws as if it was real mad about somethin'. I seen it a couple times myself when I was cuttin' peat. I'd stay away from it if it was me. It seems like it's got a awful bad temper."

"Sounds like good advice to me. Ever see any Styrics hereabouts?"

"No. They don't come around here. People in this district don't hold with heathens much. You sure are full of questions, friend."

Kurik shrugged. "Best way to learn things is to ask questions," he said easily.

"Well, go ask somebody else. I got work to do." The fellow's expression had turned unfriendly. He scowled at the stupid fellow in the shed. "You done with the milkin' yet?" he demanded.

The slack-lipped idiot shook his head apprehensively.

"Well, get at it. You don't get no supper till yer done."

"Thanks for your time, friend," Kurik said, remounting.

The lean man grunted and went back into the house.

"Useful," Sparhawk said as they rode out of the village in the ruddy light of the setting sun. "At least there aren't any Zemochs around."

"I'm not so sure, Sparhawk," Kurik disagreed. "I don't think that fellow was the best source of information in the world. He doesn't seem to take too much interest in what's going on around him. Besides, Zemochs aren't the only ones we have to worry about. That Seeker thing could set just about anybody on us, and we've also got to keep an eye out for that Troll. If Sephrenia's right about that jewel's making its re-emergence known, the Troll would be one of the first ones to know, wouldn't he?"

"I don't know. We'll have to ask her."

"I think we'd better assume that he will. If we dig the crown up, we should more or less expect a visit from him."

"That's a cheery thought. At least we found out where the mound is located. Let's go see if we can find Kalten's camp before it gets dark."

Kalten had set up for the night in a copse of beech trees a mile or so back from the lake, and he had built a large fire at the edge of the grove. He was standing beside it when Sparhawk and Kurik rode in. "Well?" he asked.

"We got directions to the mound," Sparhawk replied, climbing down from his saddle. "It's not very far. Let's go talk with Tynian."

The heavily armored Alcione was standing by the fire, talking with Ulath.

Sparhawk related the information Kurik had obtained from the villager, then looked at Tynian. "How are you feeling?" he asked directly.

"I'm fine. Why? Am I looking unwell?"

"Not really. I was just wondering if you felt up to necromancy again. The last time took quite a bit out of you, as I recall."

"I'm up to it, Sparhawk," Tynian assured him, "provided you don't want me to raise whole regiments."

"No, just one. We need to talk with King Sarak before we dig him up. He'll probably know what happened to his crown, and I want to be sure he's not going to object to being taken back to Thalesia. I don't want an angry ghost trailing along behind us."

"Truly," Tynian agreed fervently.

They rose before dawn the next morning and waited impatiently for the first sign of daylight along the horizon to the east. When it came, they were ready and they set out across the still-dark fields.

"I think we should have waited for more light, Sparhawk," Kalten grumbled. "We're likely to run around in circles out here."

"We're going east, Kalten. That's where the sun comes up. All we have to do is ride toward the lightest part of the sky."

Kalten muttered something to himself.

"I didn't quite catch that," Sparhawk said.

"I wasn't talking to you."

"Oh. Sorry."

The pale predawn light gradually increased, and Sparhawk looked around to get his bearings. "That's the village over there," he said, pointing. "The lane we want to follow is on the far side of it."

"Let's not rush too much," Sephrenia cautioned, drawing her white robe about Flute. "I want the sun to be up when we reach the mound. The talk of haunting may be just a local superstition, but let's not take any chances."

Sparhawk curbed his impatience with some difficulty.

They rode through the silent village at a walk and entered the lane the surly villager had pointed out. Sparhawk nudged Faran into a trot. "It's not all that fast, Sephrenia," he said in response to her disapproving expression. "The sun will be well up by the time we get there."

The lane was lined on both sides by low fieldstone walls and, like all country lanes, it wandered. Farmers, by and large, took little interest in straight lines and usually followed the path of least resistance. Sparhawk's impatience grew greater with each passing mile.

"There it is," Ulath said finally, pointing ahead. "I've seen hundreds like it in Thalesia."

"Let's wait until the sun gets a little higher," Tynian said, squinting at the sunrise. "I don't want any shadows around when I do this. Where's the king likely to be buried?"

"In the center," Ulath replied, "with his feet pointed toward the west. His retainers will be in ranks on either side of him."

"It helps to know that."

"Let's ride around it," Sparhawk said. "I want to see if anybody's been digging, and I definitely want to make sure that nobody's around. This is the sort of thing we want lots of privacy for." They cantered around the mound. It was quite high, and it was perhaps a hundred feet long and twenty wide. Its sides were covered with grass, and it was smoothly symmetrical. There were no signs of any excavations.

"I'm going up on top," Kurik said when they returned to the road. "That's the highest point around here. If anybody's in the area, I should be able to see them from up there."

"You would actually walk on a grave?" Bevier's tone was shocked.

"We're all going to be walking on it in a little while, Bevier," Tynian said. "I'll need to be fairly close to where King Sarak's buried to raise his ghost."

Kurik clambered up the side of the mound and stood atop it, peering around. "I don't see anybody," he called down, "but there are some trees off to the south. It might not hurt to have a look before we get started."

Sparhawk ground his teeth together, but he had to admit to himself that his squire was probably right.

Kurik slid down the grassy side of the mound and remounted.

"Sephrenia," Sparhawk said, "why don't you stay here with the children?"

"No, Sparhawk," she refused. "If there are people hiding in those trees, we don't want them to know that we have any particular interest in this mound."

"Good point," he agreed. "Let's just ride on down to those trees as if we intended to keep going south."

They moved out, following the winding country lane across the fields.

"Sparhawk," Sephrenia said quietly as they approached the edge of the trees, "there are people in those woods, and they aren't friendly."

"How many?"

"A dozen at least."

"Hold back a little bit with Talen and Flute," he told her. "All right, gentlemen," he said to the others, "you know what to do."

But before they could enter the woods, a group of poorly armed peasants dashed out from under the trees. They had that vacant look that immediately identified them. Sparhawk lowered his lance and charged with his companions thundering along at either side of him.

The fight did not last for very long. The peasants were unskilled with their weapons and they were on foot. It was all over in a few minutes.

"Nicely done, Sssir Knightsss," a chillingly metallic voice said sardonically from the shadows back under the trees. Then the robed and hooded Seeker rode out into the morning sunlight. "But no matter," it continued. "I know where ye are now."

Sparhawk handed his lance to Kurik and drew Aldreas'

spear out from under his saddle skirt. "And we know where you are as well, Seeker," he said in an ominously quiet voice.

"Do not be foolisssh, Sssir Sssparhawk," it hissed. "Thou art no match for me."

"Why don't we try it and find out?"

The hooded figure's hidden face began to glow green. Then the light flickered and faded. "Thou hassst the ringsss!" it hissed, seeming much less sure of itself now.

"I thought you already knew that."

Then Sephrenia joined them.

"It hasss been quite sssome time, Sssephrenia," the thing said in its hissing voice.

"Not nearly long enough to suit me," she replied coldly.

"I will ssspare thy life if thou wilt fall down and worssship me."

"No, Azash. Never. I will remain faithful to my Goddess."

Sparhawk stared at her and then at the Seeker in astonishment.

"Thinkessst thou that Aphrael canssst protect thee if I decide that thy life ssservesss no further purpossse?"

"You've decided that before without much noticeable effect. I will still serve Aphrael."

"Asss thou ssseesssst fit, Sssephrenia."

Sparhawk moved Faran forward at a walk, sliding his ringed hand up the shaft of the spear until it rested on the metal shank. Once again he felt that enormous surge of power.

"The game isss almossst played out, and itsss conclusssion isss foregone. We will meet once again, Sssephrenia, and for the lassst time." Then the hooded creature wheeled its horse and fled from Sparhawk's menacing approach.

PART THREE

THE
TROLL
CAVE

The Troll Cave

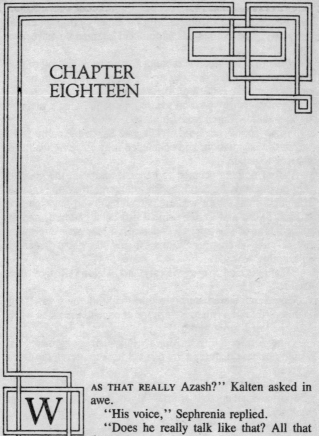

CHAPTER
EIGHTEEN

AS THAT REALLY Azash?" Kalten asked in awe.

"His voice," Sephrenia replied.

"Does he really talk like that? All that hissing?"

"Not really. The Seeker's mouth parts distort things."

"I gather that you've met him before," Tynian said, shifting the shoulder plates of his bulky armor.

"Once," she said shortly, "a very long time ago." Sparhawk got the distinct impression that she didn't really want to talk about it. "We may as well go back to the mound," she added. "Let's get what we came for and leave before the Seeker comes back with reinforcements."

They turned their horses and rode back along the winding lane. The sun had fully risen by now, but Sparhawk nonetheless felt cold. The encounter with the Elder God, even though by proxy, had chilled his blood and seemed to have even dulled the sun.

When they reached the mound, Tynian took his coil of rope and laboriously led the way up the steep side. Again he laid out the peculiar pattern on the ground.

"Are you sure you won't raise one of the king's retainers by mistake?" Kalten asked him.

Tynian shook his head. "I'll call Sarak by name." He began the incantation, and concluded it by clapping his hands sharply together.

At first nothing seemed to happen, and then the ghost of the long-dead King Sarak began to emerge from the mound. His chain-mail armor was archaic and showed huge rents in it from sword and ax. His shield had been battered, and his ancient sword was nicked and scarred. He was enormous, but he wore no crown. "Who art thou?" the ghost demanded in a hollow voice.

"I am Tynian, your Majesty, an Alcione Knight from Deira."

King Sarak stared sternly at him with hollow eyes. "This is unseemly, Sir Tynian. Return me at once to the place where I sleep, lest I grow wroth."

"Pray forgive me, your Majesty," Tynian apologized. "We would not have disturbed thy rest but for a matter of desperate urgency."

"Nothing hath sufficient urgency to concern the dead."

Sparhawk stepped forward. "My name is Sparhawk, your Majesty," he said.

"A Pandion, judging from thine armor."

"Yes, your Majesty. The Queen of Elenia is gravely ill, and only Bhelliom can heal her. We have come to entreat thee to permit us to use the jewel to restore her health. We will return it to thy grave when we have completed our task."

"Return it or keep it, Sir Sparhawk," the ghost said indifferently. "Thou shalt not find it in my grave, however."

Sparhawk felt as if he had been struck a sharp blow to the pit of the stomach.

"This Queen of Elenia, what malady hath she so grave that only Bhelliom can heal it?" There was only the faintest hint of curiosity in the ghost's voice.

"She was poisoned, your Majesty, by those who would seize her throne."

Sarak's expression, which had been blankly indifferent, suddenly became angry. "A treasonous act, Sir Sparhawk," he said harshly. "Knowest thou the perpetrators?"

"I do."

"And hast thou punished them?"

"Not as yet, your Majesty."

"They still have their heads? Have the Pandions become weaklings over the centuries?"

"We thought it best to return the Queen to health, your Majesty, so that *she* might have the pleasure of pronouncing their doom upon them."

Sarak seemed to consider that. "It is fitting," he approved finally. "Very well then, Sir Sparhawk, I will aid thee. Despair not that Bhelliom is not in the place where I lie, for I can direct thee to the place where it lies hidden. When I fell upon this field, my kinsman, the Earl of Heid, seized up my crown and fled with it to keep it out of the hands of our foes. Hard was he pressed and gravely wounded. He reached the shores of yon lake ere he died, and he hath sworn to me in the House of the Dead that with his dying breath, he cast the crown into the murky waters, and that our foes found it not. Seek ye, therefore, in that lake, for doubtless Bhelliom still lies there."

"Thank you, your Majesty," Sparhawk replied with profound gratitude.

Then Ulath pushed forward. "I am Ulath of Thalesia," he declared, "and I claim distant kinship with thee, my King. It is unseemly that thy final resting place be in foreign soil. As God gives me strength, I vow to thee that with thy permission I will return thy bones to our homeland and lay thee to rest in the royal sepulcher at Emsat."

Sarak regarded the braided Genidian with some approval. "Let it be so then, my kinsman, for in truth, my sleep hath been unquiet in this rude place."

"Sleep here but for a short while longer, my King, for as soon as our task is completed, I will return here and take thee home." There were tears in Ulath's ice-blue eyes. "Let him rest, Tynian," he said. "His final journey will be long."

Tynian nodded and let King Sarak sink back into the earth.

"That's it then, isn't it?" Kalten said eagerly. "We ride to Lake Venne and go swimming."

"It's easier than digging," Kurik told him. "All we have to worry about is the Seeker and that Troll." He frowned slightly. "Sir Ulath," he said, "if Ghwerig knows exactly where Bhelliom is, why hasn't he retrieved it in all these years?"

"The way I understand it, Ghwerig can't swim," Ulath replied. "His body's too twisted. We'll probably still have to fight him, though. As soon as we bring Bhelliom out of the lake, he'll attack us."

Sparhawk looked toward the west where the light from the newly risen sun sparkled on the waters of the lake. The tall, summer-green grass of the fields near the mound moved in long waves in the fitful morning breeze, and the fields were bounded near the lake by the grayish sedge and marsh grass that covered the peat bogs. "We'll worry about Ghwerig when we see him," he said. "Let's go have a closer look at this lake."

They all slid down the grassy side of the mound and climbed into their saddles. "Bhelliom shouldn't be too far out from shore," Ulath said as they rode toward the lake. "Crowns are made of gold, and gold's heavy. A dying man couldn't throw something like that very far." He scratched at his chin. "I've looked for things underwater before," he said. "You have to be very methodical about it. Just floundering around doesn't accomplish very much."

"When we get there, show us how it's done," Sparhawk replied.

"Right. Let's ride due west until we come to the lake. If the Earl of Heid was dying, he wouldn't have taken any side trips."

They rode on. Sparhawk's elation was overshadowed with some anxiety. There was no way to know how long it would be before the Seeker returned with a horde of numb-faced men at its back, and he knew that he and his friends could not wear armor while they probed the depths of the lake. They would be defenseless. Not only that, as soon as the spirit of Azash saw them in the lake, he would know exactly what they were doing, and for that matter, so would Ghwerig.

The light breeze was still blowing as they rode west, and

puffy white clouds marched at a stately pace across the deep blue sky.

"There's a grove of cedar trees up ahead," Kurik said, pointing to a low, dark green patch of vegetation a quarter of a mile away. "We're going to need to build a raft when we get to the lake. Come along, Berit. Let's go start chopping." He led his string of packhorses toward the grove with the novice close behind him.

Sparhawk and his friends reached the lake about midmorning and stood looking out over the water rippling in the breeze. "That's going to make looking for something on the bottom very difficult," Kalten said, pointing toward the murky, peat-stained depths.

"Any notion of where the Earl of Heid might have come out on the lake shore?" Sparhawk asked Ulath.

"Count Ghasek's story said that some Alcione Knights came along and buried him," the Genidian replied. "They were in a hurry, so they probably wouldn't have moved his body very far from where he fell. Let's look around for a grave."

"After five hundred years?" Kalten said skeptically. "There won't be much to mark it, Ulath."

"I think you're wrong, Kalten," Tynian disagreed. "Deirans build cairns over graves when they bury somebody. The earth might flatten out over a grave, but rocks are a bit more permanent."

"All right," Sparhawk said, "let's spread out and start looking for a pile of rocks."

It was Talen who found the grave, a low mound of brown-stained stones partially covered by muddy silt that had accumulated over centuries of high water. Tynian marked it by sinking the butt of his pennon-tipped lance into the mud at the foot of the grave.

"Shall we get started?" Kalten asked.

"Let's wait for Kurik and Berit," Sparhawk said. "The lake bottom's a little too soupy for wading. We're going to need that raft."

It was perhaps a half hour later when the squire and the novice joined them. The packhorses were laboriously pulling a dozen cedar logs behind them.

It was shortly after noon when they finished lashing the logs together with ropes to form a crude raft. The knights had discarded their armor and worked in loincloths, sweating in the hot sun.

"You're getting sunburned," Kalten told the pale-skinned Ulath.

"I always do," Ulath replied. "Thalesians don't tan very well." He straightened as he finished tying the last knot in the rope that held one end of the raft together. "Well, let's launch it and see if it floats," he suggested.

They pushed the raft down the slippery mud beach into the water. Ulath looked at it critically. "I wouldn't want to make a sea voyage on that thing," he said, "but it's good enough for our purposes here. Berit, go over to that willow thicket and cut yourself a couple of saplings."

The novice nodded and returned a few minutes later with two long, springy wands.

Ulath went to the grave and picked up two stones somewhat larger than his fist. He hefted them a couple of times, one in each hand, then tossed one to Sparhawk. "What do you think?" he asked. "Does that feel to be about the same weight as a gold crown?"

"How would I know?" Sparhawk asked. "I've never worn a crown."

"Guess, Sparhawk. The day's wearing on, and the mosquitoes are going to come out before long."

"All right, that's probably about the weight of a crown, give or take a few pounds."

"That's what I thought. All right, Berit, take your saplings and pole the raft out into the lake. We're going to mark the area we want to search."

Berit looked a little puzzled, but did as he was told.

Ulath hefted one of his rocks. "That's far enough, Berit," he called. He gave the rock an underhand toss toward the shaky raft. "Mark that place!" he bellowed.

Berit wiped the water the rock had splashed on him from his face. "Yes, Sir Ulath," he said, poling the raft toward the widening circles on the surface of the lake. Then he took one of his willow saplings and sank one end of it down into the muddy bottom.

"Now pole the raft off to the left," Ulath shouted. "I'll throw the next rock a ways beyond you."

"Your left or mine, Sir Ulath?" Berit asked politely.

"Take your pick. I just don't want to brain you with this."

Ulath was tossing his rock from one hand to the other and squinting out at the brown-stained waters of the lake.

Berit pushed the raft out of the way, and Ulath launched his rock with a mighty heave.

"Lord!" Kalten said. "No dying man could ever throw anything that far."

"That was the idea," Ulath said modestly. "That's the absolute outer limit of the area we search. Berit!" he bellowed in a shattering voice, "mark that spot and then go down. I need to know how deep we're going and what kind of bottom we've got to work with."

Berit hesitated after he marked the place where the second rock had struck the water. "Would you please ask Lady Sephrenia to turn her back?" he asked plaintively, his face suddenly bright red.

"If anyone laughs, he'll spend the rest of his life as a toad," Sephrenia threatened, resolutely turning her back on the lake and pulling the curious little girl Flute around at the same time.

Berit stripped and went over the edge of the raft like an otter. He re-emerged a minute later. Everyone on shore, Sparhawk noticed, had held his breath while the agile novice had been down. Berit exhaled explosively, spraying water. "It's about eight feet deep, Sir Ulath," he reported, clinging to the end of the raft, "but the bottom's muddy—two feet of it at least—mucky and not very nice. The water's dark brown. You can't see your hand in front of your face."

"I was afraid of that," Ulath muttered.

"How's the water?" Kalten called out to the young man in the lake.

"Very, very cold," Berit chattered.

"I was afraid of that, too," Kalten said glumly.

"Well, gentlemen," Ulath said, "time to get wet."

The rest of the afternoon was distinctly unpleasant. As Berit had announced, the water was cold and murky, and the soft bottom was thick with brown mud from the nearby peat bogs. "Don't try to dig around in that with your hands," Ulath instructed. "Probe with your feet."

They found nothing. By the time the sun went down, they were all exhausted and blue with the cold.

"We have a decision to make," Sparhawk said soberly after they had dried themselves and put on tunics and mail shirts. "How long is it going to be safe for us to stay here? The Seeker knows almost exactly where we are, and our scent will lead it right to us. As soon as it sees us in the lake, Azash will know where Bhelliom is. That's something we can't let him find out."

"You're right, Sparhawk," Sephrenia agreed. "It will take the Seeker awhile to gather its forces, and awhile longer to lead them back here, but I think we'll need to set a time limit on how long we stay in this place."

"But we're so close," Kalten objected.

"It's not going to do us any good to find Bhelliom just to turn it over to Azash," she pointed out. "If we ride off, we'll lead the Seeker away from this spot. We know where Bhelliom is now. We can always come back later when it's safe."

"Noon tomorrow?" Sparhawk asked her.

"I don't think we should stay any longer."

"That's it then," Sparhawk said. "At noon we'll pack up and go back to the city of Venne. I get the feeling that the Seeker won't take its men into a town. They'd be very conspicuous the way they shamble around."

"A boat," Ulath said, his face ruddy in the light of their fire.

"Where?" Kalten asked, peering out at the night-shrouded lake.

"No. What I mean is, why don't we ride to Venne and hire a boat? The Seeker will follow our trail to Venne, but it won't be able to sniff our tracks over water, will it? It'll camp outside Venne waiting for us to come out, but we'll be back here by then. We'll be free to search for Bhelliom until we find it."

"It's a good idea, Sparhawk," Kalten said.

"Is he right?" Sparhawk asked Sephrenia. "Will travelling by water throw the Seeker off our trail?"

"I believe it will," she replied.

"Good. We'll try it then."

They ate a meager supper and went to their beds.

They rose at sunrise the following morning, took a quick breakfast, and poled the raft back out to the markers that indicated where they had left off the previous day. They anchored the raft and once again went into the chill waters to probe at the muddy bottom with their feet.

It was almost noon when Berit surfaced not far from where

Sparhawk was treading water and catching his breath. "I think I've found something," the novice said, gasping for air. Then he upended himself and swam down headfirst. After a painfully long minute, he came up again. It was not a crown he held in his hand, though, but a brown-stained human skull. He swam to the raft and laid the skull up on the logs. Sparhawk squinted up at the sun and swore. Then he followed Berit to the raft. He hauled himself up on the logs. "That's it," he called to Kalten, whose head had just popped up out of the water. "We can't stay here any longer. Gather up the others, and let's get back to shore."

When they reached the shore, the sunburned Ulath curiously examined the skull. "Seems awfully long and narrow for some reason," he said.

"That's because he was a Zemoch," Sephrenia told him.

"Did he drown?" Berit asked.

Ulath scraped some of the mud off the skull and then poked one finger into an aperture in the left temple. "Not with this hole in the side of his head, he didn't." He went down to the lake shore and sloshed the skull around in the water to rinse centuries of accumulated mud out of it. Then he brought it back and shook it. Something rattled inside. The big Thalesian laid it on the mounded-up stones of the grave of the Earl of Heid, took up a rock, and cracked the skull open as casually as a man might crack a walnut. Then he picked something up out of the fragments. "I thought so," he said. "Somebody put an arrow in his brainpan, probably from shore." He handed the rusty arrowhead to Tynian. "Do you recognize it?"

"It's Deiran forging," Tynian said after examining it.

Sparhawk thought back for a moment. "Ghasek's account said that Alcione Knights from Deira came along and wiped out the Zemochs who'd been pursuing the Earl of Heid. We can be fairly certain that the Zemochs saw the earl throw the crown into the lake. They'd have gone out after it, wouldn't they? And to the exact spot where it hit the water. Now we find this one with a Deiran arrow in his head. It's not too hard to reconstruct what happened. Berit, can you pinpoint the precise spot where you found the skull?"

"To within a few feet, Sir Sparhawk. I was taking bearings on things along the shore. It was straight out from that dead snag over there and about thirty feet out into the lake."

"That's it, then," Sparhawk said exultantly. "The Zemochs were diving after the crown, and the Alciones came along and raked them with arrows from shore. That skull was probably lying no more than a few yards from Bhelliom."

"We know where it is now," Sephrenia said. "We'll come back for it later."

"But—"

"We must leave immediately, Sparhawk, and it would be far too dangerous to have Bhelliom in our possession with the Seeker right behind us."

Grudgingly, Sparhawk had to admit that she was probably right. "All right, then," he said in a disappointed tone, "let's break down the camp and get out of here. We'll wear mail instead of armor so we won't be so conspicuous. Ulath, push that raft back out into the lake. We'll wipe out any traces that we've been here and ride on up to Venne."

It took them about a half an hour; then they moved out. They rode north along the lake, moving at a gallop. As usual, Berit rode to the rear, watching for signs of pursuit.

Sparhawk was melancholy. Somehow it seemed that for weeks he had been trying to run in soft sand. No matter how close he got to the one thing that would save his Queen, something always seemed to interfere, to force him away from the goal. He began to have darkly superstitious feelings. Sparhawk was an Elene and a Church Knight. He was at least nominally committed to the Elene faith and its rigid rejection of anything remotely related to what the Church called "heathenism." Sparhawk had been abroad in the world too long, however, and seen far too many things to accept the dictates of his Church at face value. He realized that in many ways he hung suspended between absolute faith and total skepticism. Something somewhere was desperately trying to keep him away from the Bhelliom, and he was fairly certain he knew who it was—but why would Azash bear such enmity toward the young Queen of Elenia? Sparhawk grimly began to think of armies and invasions. If Ehlana died, he vowed to himself that he would obliterate Zemoch and leave Azash weeping alone in the ruins without one single human to worship him.

They reached the city of Venne not long after noon the following day and returned through the gloomy streets to the now-familiar inn. "Why don't we just buy this place?" Kalten suggested as they dismounted in the courtyard. "I'm starting to feel as if I've lived here all my life."

"Go ahead and make the arrangements," Sparhawk told him. "Kurik, let's walk down to the lake shore and see if we can find a boat before the sun goes down."

The knight and his squire walked out of the innyard and down the cobbled street that led toward the lake. "This town doesn't get any prettier when you get to know it," Kurik observed.

"We're not here for the scenery," Sparhawk growled.

"What's the matter, Sparhawk?" Kurik asked. "You've been in a foul humor for the last week or more."

"Time, Kurik." Sparhawk sighed. "Time. Sometimes it's almost as if I can feel it dribbling through my fingers. We were within no more than a few feet of Bhelliom, and then we had to pack up and leave. My Queen is dying inch by inch, and things keep getting in my way. I'm starting to feel a very powerful urge to hurt some people."

"Don't look at me."

Sparhawk smiled faintly. "I think you're safe, my friend," he said, putting his hand affectionately on Kurik's shoulder. "If nothing else, I'd hate to make wagers on the outcome if you and I ever had a really serious disagreement."

"There's that, too," Kurik agreed. Then he pointed. "Over there," he said.

"Over there what?"

"That tavern. People with boats go in there."

"How do you know that?"

"I just saw one go in. Boats tend to leak, and the men who own them try to seal up the seams with tar. Anytime you see a man with tar on his tunic, you can be fairly sure that he has something to do with boats."

"You're an absolute sink of information sometimes, Kurik."

"I've been around in the world for quite a long time, Sparhawk. If a man keeps his eyes open, he can learn a great deal. When we go inside, let me do the talking. It'll be faster." Kurik's stride suddenly took on a peculiar roll, and he banged open the tavern door with unnecessary force. "Hello there, mates," he said in a raspy voice. "Have we chanced by luck on a place where men as works on the water be accustomed to gather?"

"You've found the right place, friend," the barman said.

"Praise be," Kurik said. "I hate to drink with landsmen. All they can talk about is the weather an' their crops, an' once you've said it's cloudy an' that the turnips is growin', you've exhausted the possibilities of conversation."

The men in the tavern laughed appreciatively.

"Forgive me if I seem to pry," the barman apologized, "but you seem to have the speech of a salt-water man."

"Indeed," Kurik said, "an' sore do I miss the smell of brine an' the gentle kiss of spray upon my cheek."

"You're a long way from any salt water, mate," one tar-smeared fellow sitting at a table in the corner said with an odd note of respect in his voice.

Kurik sighed deeply. "Missed me boat, mate," he said. "We made port in Apalia, sailin' down from Yosut up in Thalesia, an' I went out on the town an' got sore took by the grog. The cap'n was not one to wait for stragglers, so he upped an' sailed with the mornin' tide an' left me beached. As luck had it, I fell in with this man," he clapped Sparhawk familiarly on the shoulder, "an' he give me employment. Says he needs to hire a boat here in Venne an' he needed someone as knew the way of boats to make sure he doesn't wind up on the bottom of the lake."

"Well, now, mate," the tarry man in the corner said with narrowed eyes, "what would your employer be willing to pay for the hire of a boat?"

" 'Twould only be for a couple of days," Kurik said. He looked at Sparhawk. "What thinkee, Cap'n? Would a half crown strain your purse?"

"I could manage a half crown," Sparhawk replied, trying to conceal his amazement at Kurik's sudden alteration.

"Two days, you say?" the man in the corner said.

"Dependin' on the wind and weather, mate, but it's always that way on the water, isn't it?"

"Truly. It could just be that we can do some business here. I happen to own a fair-sized fishing boat, and the fishing hasn't been very good of late. I could hire out the boat to you and spend the two days mending my nets."

"Why don't we just nip on down to the water's edge an' have a look at your vessel?" Kurik suggested. "It might just could be that we could strike a bargain."

The tar-smeared fellow drained his tankard and rose to his feet. "Come along then," he said, moving toward the door.

"Kurik," Sparhawk said quietly in a pained tone, "don't spring surprises like that on me. My nerves aren't as good as they used to be."

"Variety keeps life interestin', Cap'n." Kurik grinned as they left the tavern in the wake of the fisherman.

The boat was perhaps thirty feet long, and it sat low in the water.

"She appears to have a leak or two, mate," Kurik noted, pointing at the foot or so of water standing in the hull.

"We were just patching her," the fisherman apologized. "I hit a submerged log and sprung a seam. The men as works for me wanted to get something to eat before they came back to finish up and bail her out." He patted the boat's rail affectionately. "She's a good old tub," he said modestly. "She responds to the helm well, an' she can take whatever kind of weather this lake can throw at her."

"An' you'll have her patched by mornin'?"

"Shouldn't be no trouble, mate."

"What thinkee, Cap'n?" Kurik asked Sparhawk.

"Looks all right to me," Sparhawk replied, "but I'm no expert. That's what I hired you for."

"All right then, we'll try her, mate," Kurik told the fisherman. "We'll come back down sunup an' settle up then." He spat on his hand, and he and the fisherman slapped their palms together. "Come along, Cap'n," Kurik told his lord. "Let's find us some grog an' supper an' then a bed. 'Twill be a long day tomorrow." And then with that rolling swagger, he led the way up from the lake front.

"Would you like to explain all that?" Sparhawk asked when they were some distance away from the boat owner.

"It's not too difficult, Sparhawk," Kurik said. "Men who sail on lakes always have a great deal of respect for salt-water sailors, and they'll go out of their way to be accommodating."

"So I noticed, but how did you ever learn to talk that way?"

"I went to sea once when I was about sixteen. I've told you that before."

"Not that I remember, no."

"I must have."

"Maybe it slipped my mind. What possessed you to go to sea?"

"Aslade." Kurik laughed. "She was about fourteen then and just blossoming out. She had that marrying sort of look in her eye. I wasn't ready yet, so I ran away to sea. Biggest mistake I ever made. I hired on as a deckhand on the leakiest bucket on the west coast of Eosia. I spent six months bailing water out of the bilges. When I got back to shore, I swore I'd never set foot on a ship again. Aslade was very happy to see me again, but then she's always been an emotional girl."

"Was that when you decided to marry her?"

"Shortly after that. When I got home, she took me up to her father's hayloft and did some fairly serious persuading. Aslade can be very, very persuasive when she sets her mind to it."

"*Kurik!*" Sparhawk was actually shocked.

"Grow up, Sparhawk. Aslade's a country girl, and most country girls have already started to swell when they get married. It's a relatively direct form of courtship, but it has its compensations."

"In a *hayloft*?"

Kurik smiled. "Sometimes you have to improvise, Sparhawk."

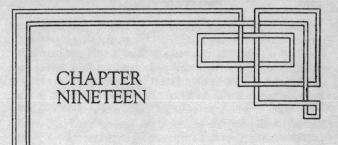

CHAPTER
NINETEEN

S PARHAWK SAT IN the room he shared with Kalten, poring over his map while his friend snored on a nearby bed. Ulath's idea of a boat was a good one. Sephrenia's statement that it would indeed evade the Seeker's most dangerous means of tracking them down was reassuring. They could return to that lonely mud beach where the Earl of Heid slumbered and resume their interrupted search without looking over their shoulders for signs of a hooded figure sniffing at the ground behind them. The Zemoch skull Berit had found on the murky bottom had almost precisely pinpointed Bhelliom's location. With only a little luck, they would be able to find it within the space of a single afternoon. They'd have to return here to Venne for the horses, however, and that was the problem. If, as they had surmised, the Seeker's blank-minded cohorts likely would be lurking in the fields and woods around the town, they'd have to fight their way out. Under ordinary circumstances, fighting would not have concerned Sparhawk; it was what he had trained a lifetime to do. If he had Bhelliom in his possession, however, it would not only be his own life he would be risking, but Ehlana's as well, and that was unacceptable. Moreover, as soon as Azash sensed Bhelliom's re-emergence, the Seeker would hurl whole armies against them in a desperate attempt to seize the jewel.

The solution was simple, of course. All they had to do was to come up with a way to convey the horses to the west side of the lake. Then the Seeker could haunt the region around Venne until it grew old and died without causing Sparhawk and his friends any further inconvenience. The boat that he and Kurik had hired, though, would not be capable of carrying more than two horses at a time. The notion of making eight or nine separate trips halfway down the lake to deposit the horses on some lonely beach on the west side of the lake made Sparhawk almost want to scream with impatience. Hiring several boats was an alternative, though not a very good one. A single boat probably would not attract attention; a fleet of them, though, would. Perhaps they could find someone dependable enough to herd the horses down the west shore. The only problem with that was that Sparhawk was not sure whether the Seeker could identify the smell of the horses as well as that of the people who rode them. He scratched absently at the finger that bore his ring. The finger seemed to be tingling and throbbing for some reason.

There was a light tap at the door.

"I'm busy," he said irritably.

"Sparhawk." The voice was light and musical, and it had that peculiar lilt that identified the speaker as Styric. Sparhawk frowned. He didn't recognize the voice.

"Sparhawk, I need to talk with you."

He rose and went to the door. To his astonishment, it was Flute. She slipped into the room and closed the door behind her.

"So you *can* talk?" he asked, surprised.

"Of course I can."

"Why haven't you then?"

"It wasn't necessary before. You Elenes babble far too

much." Although her voice was that of a little girl, her words and inflections were peculiarly adult. "Listen to me, Sparhawk. This is very important. We must all leave immediately."

"It's the middle of the night, Flute," he objected.

"How terribly observant of you," she said, looking toward the darkened window. "Now please be still and listen. *Ghwerig has retrieved Bhelliom!* We have to intercept him before he can get to the north coast and sneak aboard a ship bound for Thalesia. If he evades us, we'll have to follow him to his cave in the mountains of Thalesia, and that would take quite a while."

"According to Ulath, nobody even knows where the cave is."

"I know where it is. I've been there before."

"You *what?*"

"Sparhawk, you're wasting time. I have to get out of this city. There's too much distraction here. I can't feel what's happening. Put on your iron suit and let's go." Her tone was abrupt, even imperious. She looked at him, her large, dark eyes grave. "Is it possible that you're such a total lump that you can't feel Bhelliom moving through the world? Isn't that ring telling you anything?"

He started slightly and looked at the ruby ring on his left hand. It still seemed to be throbbing. The small child standing in front of him seemed to know far too much. "Does Sephrenia know about all this?"

"Of course. She's getting our things together."

"Let's go talk with her."

"You're beginning to irritate me, Sparhawk." Her dark eyes flashed, and the corners of her bowlike pink mouth turned down.

"I'm sorry, Flute, but I still have to talk with Sephrenia."

She rolled her eyes upward. "Elenes," she said in a tone so like Sephrenia's that Sparhawk almost laughed. He took her hand and led her from the room and down the hallway.

Sephrenia was busily stowing clothing, both hers and Flute's, in the canvas bag sitting on the bed in her room. "Come right in, Sparhawk," she said to him as he paused in the doorway. "I've been expecting you."

"What's going on, Sephrenia?" he asked in a baffled tone of voice.

"Didn't you tell him?" she asked Flute.

"Yes, but he doesn't seem to believe me. How can you tolerate these stubborn people?"

"They have a certain charm. Believe her, Sparhawk," she said gravely to him. "She knows what she's talking about. Bhelliom has emerged from the lake. I felt it myself, and now Ghwerig has it. We have to get out into open country so that Flute and I can sense which way he's going with it. Go rouse the others and have Berit saddle our horses."

"You're sure about this?"

"Yes. Hurry, Sparhawk, or Ghwerig will get away."

He turned quickly and went back out into the hall. This was all moving so rapidly that he did not have time to think. He went from room to room, waking the others and instructing them all to gather in Sephrenia's room. He sent Berit to the stable to saddle the horses and, last of all, he woke Kalten.

"What's the problem?" the blond Pandion asked, sitting up and rubbing sleepily at his eyes.

"Something's come up," Sparhawk replied. "We're leaving."

"In the middle of the night?"

"Yes. Get dressed, Kalten, and I'll pack our things."

"What's going on, Sparhawk?" Kalten swung his legs over the edge of the bed.

"Sephrenia will explain it. Hurry, Kalten."

Grumbling, Kalten began to dress while Sparhawk jammed their spare clothing into the pack they had brought up to their room. Then the two of them went back down the hall, and Sparhawk rapped on the door to Sephrenia's room.

"Oh, *do* come in, Sparhawk. This is no time to stand on ceremony."

"Who's that?" Kalten asked.

"Flute," Sparhawk replied, opening the door.

"Flute? She can talk?"

The others had already gathered in the room, and they were all looking at the little girl they had thought was mute with some astonishment.

"To save time," she said, "yes, I *can* talk, and no, I didn't want to before. Does that answer all the tiresome questions? Now listen very carefully. The Troll-Dwarf Ghwerig has managed to get his hands on Bhelliom again, and he's trying to take it to his cave up in the mountains of Thalesia. Unless we hurry, he'll get away from us.''

''How did he get it out of the lake when he hasn't ever been able to do it before?'' Bevier asked.

''He had help.'' She looked around at their faces and muttered a naughty word in Styric. ''You'd better show them, Sephrenia. Otherwise they'll stand here all night asking foolish questions.''

There was a large mirror—a sheet of polished brass, actually—on one wall of Sephrenia's room. ''Would you all come over here, please?'' Sephrenia said, going to the mirror.

They gathered around the mirror, and she began an incantation Sparhawk had not heard before. Then she gestured. The mirror became momentarily cloudy. When it cleared, they seemed to be looking down at the lake.

''There's the raft,'' Kalten said in astonishment, ''and that's Sparhawk coming to the surface. I don't understand, Sephrenia.''

''We're looking at things that happened just before noon yesterday,'' she told him.

''We already know what happened.''

''We knew what *we* were doing,'' she corrected. ''There were others there as well, however.''

''I didn't see anybody.''

''They didn't want you to see them. Just keep watching.''

The perspective in the mirror seemed to change, moving away from the lake toward the sedge that grew thickly on the peat bog. A dark-robed shape was crouched down, hidden in the marsh grass.

''The Seeker!'' Bevier exclaimed. ''It was watching us!''

''It wasn't the only one,'' Sephrenia told him.

The perspective changed again, sliding several hundred yards north along the lake to a clump of scrubby trees. A shaggy, grotesquely deformed shape was hidden in the grove.

''And that's Ghwerig,'' Flute told them.

''That's a *dwarf*?'' Kalten exclaimed. ''It's as big as Ulath. How big is a normal one?''

"About twice as big as Ghwerig." Ulath shrugged. "Ogres are even bigger."

The mirror clouded again as Sephrenia spoke rapidly in Styric. "Nothing important went on for quite a while, so we're skipping that part," she explained.

The mirror cleared again. "There we go, riding away from the lake," Kalten said.

Then the Seeker rose from the marsh grass, and with it about ten wooden-faced men who appeared to be Pelosian serfs. Numbly, the serfs shambled down to the lake shore and waded into the water.

"We were afraid that might happen," Tynian said.

The mirror clouded again. "They continued the search all through yesterday, last night, and today," Sephrenia told them. "Then, just over an hour ago, one of them found Bhelliom. This part might be a little hard to see, because it was dark. I'll lighten the image as much as I can for you."

It was a bit hard to make out, but it seemed that one of the serfs emerged from the lake carrying a mud-caked object in his hand. "King Sarak's crown," Sephrenia identified the object.

The black-robed Seeker rushed along the lake shore, its scorpionlike claws extended and clicking eagerly, but Ghwerig reached the serf before Azash's creature could. With a mighty blow of his gnarled fist, he crushed in the side of the serf's head and seized the crown. Then he turned and ran before the Seeker could summon its followers out of the lake. Ghwerig's run was a peculiar loping gait involving both legs and one extraordinarily long arm. A man might be able to run faster, but not by very much.

The image faded.

"What happened next?" Kurik asked.

"Ghwerig stopped from time to time when one of the serfs began to overtake him," Sephrenia replied. "It looked as if he were deliberately slowing down. He killed them one by one."

"Where's Ghwerig now?" Tynian asked.

"We can't tell," Flute told him. "It's very hard to follow a Troll in the dark. That's why we have to get out into the open countryside. Sephrenia and I can feel Bhelliom, but only if we can get clear of all these townsmen."

Tynian considered it. "The Seeker's more or less out of the picture now," he said. "It's going to have to go out and gather more people before it can go after Ghwerig."

"That's a comforting thought," Kalten said. "I wouldn't want to have to take them both on at once."

"We'd better get started," Sparhawk told them. "Put on your armor, gentlemen," he suggested. "When we run across Ghwerig, we might need it."

They went back to their rooms to gather their belongings and to dress themselves in steel. Sparhawk clanked down the stairs to settle up with the fat innkeeper, who stood leaning against the doorway of the empty taproom, sleepy-eyed and yawning.

"We're going to be leaving now," Sparhawk said to him.

"It's still dark outside, Sir Knight."

"I know, but something came up."

"You've heard the news then, I gather."

"What news was that?" Sparhawk asked him cautiously.

"There's trouble down in Arcium. I haven't been able really to get the straight of it, but there's even been talk that it might be a war of some kind."

Sparhawk frowned. "That doesn't make much sense, neighbor. Arcium's not like Lamorkand. The Arcian nobles foreswore their blood feuds generations ago at the king's command."

"I can only repeat what I heard, Sir Knight. The word that I've picked up is that the kingdoms of western Eosia are all mobilizing. Earlier tonight some fellows came through Venne in quite a hurry—fellows who weren't very interested in going off to fight in a foreign war—and they say that there's a huge army gathering to the west of the lake conscripting every man they run across."

"The western kingdoms wouldn't mobilize because of a civil war in Arcium," Sparhawk told him. "That kind of thing is an internal matter."

"That's what puzzles me too," the innkeeper agreed, "but what puzzles me even more is that some of those timid fellows have said that a fair portion of that army is made up of Thalesians."

"They must have been wrong," Sparhawk said. "King Wargun drinks quite a bit, but he still wouldn't invade a friendly kingdom. If these men you mentioned were trying to avoid being conscripted, they probably wouldn't have stopped to examine the men who were chasing them, and one man in a mail shirt looks much like another.''

"That's probably very true, Sir Knight.''

Sparhawk paid for their night's lodging. "Thank you for the information, neighbor,'' he said to the innkeeper as the others began to come down the stairway. He turned and went out to the courtyard.

"What's going on, Sir Sparhawk?'' Berit asked, handing Sparhawk Faran's reins.

"The Seeker was watching us while we were in the lake,'' Sparhawk replied. "One of its men found Bhelliom, but Ghwerig the Troll took it away from him. Now we have to go find Ghwerig.''

"That might be a little difficult, Sir Sparhawk. There's fog rolling in off the lake.''

"Hopefully, it'll burn off before Ghwerig gets this far north.''

The others came out of the inn. "Let's all get mounted,'' Sparhawk said to them. "Which way do we go, Flute?''

"North for now,'' she replied as Kurik lifted her up to Sephrenia.

Berit blinked. "She knows how to talk!'' he exclaimed.

"Please, Berit,'' she said to him, "don't repeat the obvious. Let's go, Sparhawk. I can't pinpoint Bhelliom's location until we get away from here.''

They rode out of the innyard and into the foggy street. The fog was thick, hovering just this side of rainy drizzle, and it carried with it the acidic reek of the peat bogs that surrounded the lake.

"This isn't a good night for coming up against a Troll,'' Ulath said, falling in beside Sparhawk.

"I doubt very much that we'll run across Ghwerig tonight,'' Sparhawk said. "He's on foot, and it's a long way from here to where he found Bhelliom—that's assuming he's even coming this way.''

"He almost has to, Sparhawk,'' the Genidian said. "He wants to get to Thalesia, and that means he's got to get to a seaport on the north coast.''

"We'll know better which way he's moving once we get Sephrenia and Flute out of town.''

"My guess would be Nadera," Ulath speculated. "It's a bigger seaport than Apalia, and there are more ships there. Ghwerig's going to have to sneak on board one. It's not likely that he could book passage. Most sea captains are superstitious about sailing with Trolls aboard."

"Would Ghwerig understand enough of our language to find out which ships are going to Thalesia by eavesdropping?"

Ulath nodded. "Most Trolls have a smattering of Elene and even Styric. They usually can't speak any language but their own, but they can understand a few words of ours."

They passed through the city gate and reached the fork in the road north of Venne shortly before daybreak. They looked dubiously at the rutted track that led up into the mountains toward Ghasek and ultimately to the seaport at Apalia. "I hope he doesn't decide to go that way," the white-cloaked Bevier said with a shudder. "I don't really want to go back to Ghasek."

"Is he moving at all?" Sparhawk asked Flute.

"Yes," she replied. "He's coming north along the lake shore."

"I don't quite understand this," Talen said to the little girl. "If you can sense where Bhelliom is, why didn't we just stay at the inn until he got closer with it?"

"Because there are too many people in Venne," Sephrenia told him. "We can't get a clear picture of Bhelliom's location in the middle of all that welter of thoughts and emotions."

"Oh," the boy said, "that makes sense—I guess."

"We could ride down the lake shore and meet him," Kalten suggested. "Save us all a lot of time."

"Not in the fog," Ulath said firmly. "I want to be able to see him coming. I don't want to get surprised by a Troll."

"He's going to have to pass through here," Tynian said, "or at least very close to here, if he's headed toward the north coast. He can't swim across the lake, and he can't go into Venne. Trolls are a little conspicuous, or so I'm told. When he gets closer, we can ambush him."

"It's got some possibilities, Sparhawk," Kalten said. "If we've got his probable line of travel pinpointed, we can catch him unawares up here. We can kill him and be halfway to Cimmura with Bhelliom before anyone is the wiser."

"Oh, Kalten," Sephrenia sighed.

"Killing is what we do, little mother," he told her. "You don't have to watch if you don't want to. One Troll more or less in the world isn't going to make all that much difference."

"There could be a problem, though," Tynian said to Flute. "The Seeker's going to be hot on Ghwerig's heels just as soon as it gathers up enough men, and it can probably sense Bhelliom in the same way you and Sephrenia can, can't it?"

"Yes," she admitted.

"Then you're forgetting that we may have to face it just as soon as we dispose of Ghwerig, aren't you?"

"And you're forgetting that we'll have Bhelliom at that point and that Sparhawk has the rings."

"Would Bhelliom eliminate the Seeker?"

"Quite easily."

"Let's pull back into those trees a ways," Sparhawk suggested. "I don't know how long it's going to take Ghwerig to get here, and I don't want him coming up on us while we're all standing in the middle of the road talking about the weather and other things."

They withdrew into the shadowy cover of a stand of trees and dismounted.

"Sephrenia," Bevier said in a puzzled tone of voice, "if Bhelliom can destroy the Seeker with magic, couldn't you use ordinary Styric magic to do the same thing?"

"Bevier," she replied patiently, "if I could do that, don't you think I'd have done it a long time ago?"

"Oh," he said, sounding a bit abashed, "I didn't think of that, I guess."

The sun came up blearily that morning. The pervading fog from the lake and the heavy mist out of the forest to the north half clouded the air at ground level, although the sky above was clear. They set out watches and checked over saddles and equipment. After that, most of them dozed in the muggy heat, frequently changing watch. A man on short sleep in sultry weather is not always very alert.

It was not long after noon when Talen woke Sparhawk. "Flute wants to talk to you," he said.

"I thought she'd be asleep."

"I don't think she ever really sleeps," the boy said. "You can't get near her without her eyes popping open."

"Someday maybe we'll ask her about that." Sparhawk threw off his blanket, rose to his feet, and splashed some water from a nearby spring on his face. Then he went to where Flute cuddled comfortably next to Sephrenia.

The little girl's huge eyes opened immediately. "Where have you been?" she asked.

"It took me a moment to get fully awake."

"Stay alert, Sparhawk," she said. "The Seeker's coming."

He swore and reached for his sword.

"Oh, don't do that," she said disgustedly. "It's still a mile or so away."

"How did it get this far north so fast?"

"It didn't stop to pick up any people the way we thought it would. It's alone, and it's killing its horse. The poor beast is dying right now."

"And Ghwerig's still a good ways away?"

"Yes, Bhelliom's still south of the city of Venne. I can get snatches of the Seeker's thought." She shuddered. "It's hideous, but it has much the same idea that we have. It's trying to get far enough ahead of Ghwerig to set up an ambush for him. It can pick up local people to do its work for it up here. I think we'll have to fight it."

"Without Bhelliom?"

"I'm afraid so, Sparhawk. It doesn't have any people to help it, and that might make it easier to deal with."

"Can we kill it with ordinary weapons?"

"I don't think so. There's something that might work, though. I've never tried it, but my older sister told me how to do it."

"I didn't think you had any family."

"Oh, Sparhawk!" She laughed. "My family is far, far larger than you could possibly imagine. Get the others. The Seeker will be coming up that road in just a few minutes. Confront it, and I'll bring Sephrenia. It will stop to think—which is to say that Azash will, since Azash is really its mind. But Azash is far too arrogant to avoid a chance to taunt Sephrenia, and that's when I'll strike at the Seeker."

"Are you going to kill it?"

"Of course not. We don't kill things, Sparhawk. We let nature do that. Now go. We don't have much time."

"I don't understand."

"You don't have to. Just go get the others."

They ranged out across the road at the fork, their lances set.

"Does she really know what she's talking about?" Tynian asked dubiously.

"I certainly hope so," Sparhawk murmured.

And then they heard the labored breathing of a horse very near to fatal exhaustion, the unsteady thudding of staggering hooves, and the savage whistle and crack of a whip. The Seeker, black-robed and hunched in its saddle, came around the bend, flogging unmercifully at its dying horse.

"Stay, hound of Hell!" Bevier cried out in a ringing voice, "for here ends your reckless advance!"

"We're going to have to talk to that boy someday," Ulath muttered to Sparhawk.

The Seeker, however, had reined in cautiously.

Then Sephrenia, with Flute at her side, stepped out of the trees. The small Styric woman's face was even paler than usual. Oddly enough, Sparhawk had never fully realized how tiny his teacher really was—scarcely taller than Flute herself. Her presence had always been so commanding that somehow in his mind she had seemed even taller that Ulath. "And is this the meeting thou hast promised, Azash?" she demanded contemptuously. "If so, then I am ready."

"Ssso, Sssephrenia," the hateful voice said, "we meet again and all unexsspectedly. Thisss may be thy lassst day of life."

"Or thine, Azash," she replied with calm courage.

"Thou canssst not dessstroy me." The laugh was hideous.

"Bhelliom can," she told the thing, "and we will deny Bhelliom unto thee and turn it to our own ends. Flee, Azash, if thou wouldst cling to thy life. Pull the rocks of this world over thine head and cower in fear before the wrath of the Younger Gods."

"Isn't she pushing this a little?" Talen said in a strangled voice.

"They're up to something," Sparhawk murmured. "Sephrenia and Flute are deliberately goading that thing into doing something rash."

"Not while I have breath!" Bevier declared fervently, couching his lance.

"Hold your ground, Bevier!" Kurik barked. "They know what they're doing! God knows, none of the rest of us do."

"And art thou ssstill continuing thine unwholesssome dalliancce with these Elene children, Sssephrenia?" the voice of Azash said. "If thine appetite isss ssso vassst, come thou unto me, and I ssshall give thee sssurfeit."

"That is no longer within thy power, Azash, or hast thou forgotten thy unmanning? Thou art an abomination in the sight of all the Gods, and that is why they cast thee out, emasculated thee, and confined thee in thy place of eternal torment and regret."

The thing on the exhausted horse hissed in fury, and Sephrenia nodded calmly to Flute. The little girl lifted her pipes to her lips and began to play. Her melody was rapid, a series of skittering, discordant notes, and the Seeker seemed to shrink back. "It ssshall avail thee not, Sssephrenia," Azash declared in a shrill voice. "There isss yet time."

"Thinkest thou so, mighty Azash?" she said in a taunting voice. "Then thine endless centuries of confinement have bereft thee of thy wits as well as thy manhood."

The Seeker's shriek was one of sheer rage.

"Impotent godling," Sephrenia continued her goading, "return to foul Zemoch and gnaw upon thy soul in vain regret for the delights now eternally denied thee."

Azash howled, and Flute's song grew even faster.

Something was happening to the Seeker. Its body seemed to be writhing under its black robe, and terrible, inarticulate noises came out from under its hood. With an awful jerking motion it clambered down from its dying horse. It half staggered forward, its scorpion claws extended.

Instinctively, the Church Knights moved to protect Sephrenia and the little girl.

"Stay back!" Sephrenia snapped. "It cannot stop what is happening now."

The Seeker fell squirming to the road, tearing off the black robe. Sparhawk surpressed a powerful urge to retch. The Seeker had an elongated body divided in the middle by a waist like that of a wasp, and it glistened with a puslike grayish slime. Its spindly limbs were jointed in many places, and it did not have what one could really call a face, but only two bulging eyes and a gaping maw surrounded by a series of sharp-pointed, fanglike appendages.

Azash shrieked something at Flute. Sparhawk recognized the inflection as Styric, but—and he was forever grateful for the fact—he recognized none of the words.

And then the Seeker began to split apart with an awful ripping sound. There was something inside of it, something that squirmed and wriggled, trying to break free. The rip in the Seeker's body grew wider, and that which was inside began to emerge. It was shiny black and wet. Translucent wings hung from its shoulders. It had two huge protruding eyes, delicate antennae, and no mouth. It shuddered and struggled, pulling itself free of the now-shrunken husk of the Seeker. Then, finally fully emerging, it crouched in the dirt of the road, rapidly fanning its insect wings to dry them. When the wings were dry and flushed with something that might even have been blood, they began to whir, moving so rapidly now that they seemed to blur, and the creature that had been so hideously born before their eyes rose into the air and flew off toward the east.

"Stop it!" Bevier shouted. "Don't let it get away!"

"It's harmless now," Flute told him calmly, lowering her pipes.

"What did you do?" he asked in awe.

"The spell simply speeded up its maturing," she replied. "My sister was right when she taught me that spell. It's an adult now, and all of its instincts are bent on breeding. Not even Azash can override its desperate search for a mate."

"What was the purpose of that little exchange of insults?" Kalten asked Sephrenia.

"Azash had to be so enraged that he would begin to lose his control of the Seeker so that Flute's spell would work," she explained. "That's why I threw certain unpleasant realities in his face."

"Wasn't that a little dangerous?"

"Very," she admitted.

"Will the adult find a mate?" Tynian asked Flute in an awed voice. "I'd hate to see the world crawling with Seekers."

"It will find no mate," she told him. "It is the only one of its kind on the surface of the earth. It no longer has a mouth, so it can no longer feed. It will fly around in its desperate search for a week or so."

"And then?"

"And then? And then it will die." She said it in a chillingly indifferent voice.

CHAPTER
TWENTY

T HEY DRAGGED THE husk of the Seeker off the road and returned to the trees to await Ghwerig. "Where is he now?" Sparhawk asked Flute.

"Not far from the north end of the lake," she replied. "He's not moving right now. It's my guess that now that the fog has burned off, the serfs have gone to the fields. There are probably so many people about that he has to hide."

"That means that he's likely to come through here after nightfall, doesn't it?"

"It's probable, yes."

"I'm really not very excited about meeting a Troll in the dark."

"I can make light, Sparhawk—enough for our purposes, anyway."

"I'd appreciate it." He frowned. "If you could do that to the Seeker, why didn't you do it before?"

"There wasn't time. It always came on us by surprise. It takes awhile to prepare oneself for that particular spell. Do you really have to talk so much, Sparhawk? I'm trying to concentrate on Bhelliom."

"Sorry. I'll go talk with Ulath. I want to find out exactly how to go about attacking a Troll."

He found the big Genidian Knight dozing under a tree. "What's happening?" Ulath said, one of his blue eyes opening.

"Flute says that Ghwerig's probably hiding right now. He's not moving, at any rate. He's likely to come past here sometime tonight."

Ulath nodded. "Trolls like to move around in the dark," he said. "It's their customary hunting time."

"What's the best way to deal with him?"

"Lances might work—if we all charge him at the same time. One of us might be able to get in a lucky thrust."

"This is a little too serious to be trusting to luck."

"It's worth a try—for a start, anyway. We'll probably still have to fall back on swords and axes. We'll need to be very careful, though. You have to watch out for a Troll's arms. They're very long, and Trolls are much more agile than they look."

"You seem to know a great deal about them. Have you ever fought one?"

"A few times, yes. It's not really the sort of thing you want to make a habit of. Has Berit still got that bow of his?"

"I think so, yes."

"Good. That's usually the best way to start on a Troll—slow him down with a few arrows and then move in to finish up."

"Will he have any weapons?"

"Maybe a club. Trolls don't really have the knack of working in iron or steel."

"How did you ever learn their language?"

"We had a pet Troll in our chapterhouse at Heid. Found him when he was a cub, but Trolls are born knowing how to speak their language. He was an affectionate little rascal—at least at first. Turned mean on us later on, though. I learned the language from him while he was growing up.''

''You say he turned mean?''

''It wasn't really his fault, Sparhawk. When a Troll grows up, he starts to get these urges, and we didn't have time to hunt down a female for him. And then his appetite started to get out of hand. He'd eat a couple of cows or a horse every week.''

''What finally happened to him?''

''One of our brothers went out to feed him, and he attacked. The brothers couldn't have that, so we decided that we'd have to kill him. It took five of us, and most of us had to take to our beds for a week or so afterward.''

''Ulath,'' Sparhawk said suspiciously, ''are you pulling my leg?''

''Would I do that? Trolls aren't really too bad—as long as you've got plenty of armed men around you. An arrow in the belly usually makes them kind of cautious. It's the Ogres you've got to watch out for. They don't have enough brains to be cautious.'' He scratched at his cheek. ''There was an Ogress once who developed an unreasoning passion for one of the brothers at Heid,'' he said. ''She wasn't too bad looking—for an Ogress. She kept her fur fairly clean and her horns shiny. She even used to polish her fangs. They chew granite to do that, you know. Anyhow, as I was saying, she was wildly in love with this knight at Heid. She used to lurk in the woods and sing to him—most awful sound you ever heard. She could sing all the needles off a pine tree at a hundred paces. The knight finally couldn't stand it any more, and he entered a monastery. She just pined away after that.''

''Ulath, I *know* you're pulling my leg now.''

''Why, Sparhawk,'' Ulath protested mildly.

''Then the best way to get Ghwerig out of the way is to stand back and shoot him full of arrows?''

''For a start. We'll still have to get in close, though. Trolls have very tough hide and thick fur. Arrows don't usually penetrate very deep, and trying to do it in the dark is going to make it very tricky.''

''Flute says she can make enough light for us.''

''She's a very strange person, isn't she—even for a Styric?''

''That she is, my friend.''

''How old do you think she really is?''

"I have no idea. Sephrenia won't even give me a clue. I do know that she's much, much older than she appears to be, and much wiser than any of us can guess."

"After the way she got that Seeker off our backs, I don't think it would hurt us to do as she says for a while."

"I'd agree to that," Sparhawk said.

"Sparhawk," the little girl called sharply, "come here."

"I just wish she wouldn't be so imperious all the time," Sparhawk muttered, turning around to answer the summons.

"Ghwerig's doing something I don't understand," she said when he rejoined her.

"What's that?"

"He's moving out onto the lake."

"He must have found a boat," Sparhawk said. "Ulath tells us that he can't swim. Which way's he going?"

She closed her eyes in concentration. "More or less to the northwest. He'll miss the city of Venne and come out on the west side of the lake. We're going to have to ride on down there if we're going to intercept him."

"I'll tell the others," Sparhawk said. "How fast is he moving?"

"Very slowly right now. I don't think he knows how to row a boat very well."

"That might give us a little time to get there before he does."

They broke their minimal encampment and rode south along the west side of Lake Venne as twilight settled over western Pelosia.

"Will you be able to pinpoint his approximate landing place by the sense you're picking up from Bhelliom?" Sparhawk asked Flute, who rode in Sephrenia's arms.

"To within a half mile or so," she replied. "It gets more precise as he gets closer to shore. There are currents and winds and that sort of thing, you understand."

"Is he still moving slowly?"

"Even more so. Ghwerig has certain difficulties with his shoulders and hips. It would make rowing very difficult for him."

"Can you make any kind of guess about when he'll make it to shore here on the west side of the lake?"

"In his present condition, not until well after daybreak tomorrow. At this point he's fishing. He needs food."

"With his hands?"

"Trolls are very, very fast with their hands. The lake surface confuses him. Most of the time, he's not even sure which way he's going. Trolls have a very poor sense of direction—except for north. They can feel the pull of the pole through the earth. On water, though, they're almost helpless."

"We've got him then."

"Don't plan the victory celebration until after you've won the fight, Sparhawk," she said tartly.

"You're a very disagreeable little girl, Flute. Do you know that?"

"But you do love me, don't you?" she said with disarming ingenuousness.

"What can you do?" he helplessly asked Sephrenia. "She's impossible."

"Answer her question, Sparhawk," his tutor suggested. "It's more important than you realize."

"Yes, God help me," he said to Flute, "I do. There are times when I want to spank you, but I *do* love you."

"That's all that's important." She sighed. Then she snuggled up in Sephrenia's protective robe and went promptly to sleep.

They patrolled a long stretch of the western shore of Lake Venne, peering out into the darkness that had settled over the lake. Gradually during the long night, Flute narrowed the area of their patrol, bringing them closer and closer together.

"How can you tell?" Kalten demanded of her a few hours past midnight.

"Would he understand?" Flute asked Sephrenia.

"Kalten? Probably not, but you can try to explain it, if you'd like." Sephrenia smiled. "We all need a bit of frustration in our lives from time to time."

"It feels different when Bhelliom's moving at a diagonal than when it's coming at you head-on," Flute tried.

"Oh," he said dubiously, "that makes sense, I suppose."

"See," Flute said triumphantly to Sephrenia, "I knew I could make him understand."

"Only one question," Kalten added. "What's a diagonal?"

"Oh dear," she said, pressing her face against Sephrenia in a gesture of despair.

"Well, what is it?" Kalten appealed to his fellow knights.

"Let's swing south a bit, Kalten, and keep an eye on the lake," Tynian said. "I'll explain it to you as we go along."

"You!" Sephrenia said to Ulath, who had a faint smile on his face. "Not a word."

"I didn't say anything."

Sparhawk turned Faran and rode slowly back toward the north, looking out at the dark waters.

The moon rose late that night, and it cast a long, glittering path across the surface of the lake. Sparhawk relaxed a bit then. Looking for a Troll in the dark had been a very tense business. It seemed somehow almost too easy now. All they had to do was wait for Ghwerig to reach the lake shore. After all the difficulties and setbacks that had dogged them since they had set out in search of Bhelliom, the idea of just being able to sit and wait for it to be delivered to them made Sparhawk a little nervous. He had an ominous suspicion that something was going to go wrong. If all the things that had happened in Lamorkand and here in Pelosia were any indication, something was bound to go wrong. Their quest had been dogged by near-disaster almost from the moment they had left the chapterhouse at Cimmura, and Sparhawk saw no reason to hope that this situation would be any different.

Once again, the sun rose in a rusty sky, a coppery disk hanging low over the brown-stained waters of the lake. Sparhawk rode wearily back through the grove of trees from which they kept watch to where Sephrenia and the children were waiting. "How far away is he now?" he asked Flute.

"He's about a mile out in the lake," she replied. "He's stopped again."

"Why *does* he keep stopping?" Sparhawk was growing increasingly irritated about these periodic halts in the Troll's progress across the lake.

"Would you like to hear a guess?" Talen asked.

"Go ahead."

"I stole a boat once because I had to get across the Cimmura River. The boat leaked. I had to stop every five minutes or so to bail out the water. Ghwerig's been stopping about every half hour. Maybe his boat doesn't leak as much as mine did."

Sparhawk stared at the boy for a moment, and then he suddenly burst out laughing. "Thanks, Talen," he said, feeling suddenly much better.

"No charge," the boy replied impudently. "You see, Sparhawk, the easiest answer is usually the right one."

"Then I've got a Troll out there in a leaky boat, and I've got to wait here on shore until he gets all the water out of it."

"That pretty well sums it up, yes."

Tynian rode in at a canter. "Sparhawk," he said quietly, "we've got some riders coming in from the west."

"How many?"

"Too many to count conveniently."

"Let's take a look." The two rode back through the trees to where Kalten, Ulath, and Bevier were sitting their horses, looking off to the west. "I've been watching them, Sparhawk," Ulath said. "I think they're Thalesians."

"What are Thalesians doing here in Pelosia?"

"Remember what that innkeeper told you back in Venne?" Kalten said, "about a war going on down in Arcium? Didn't he say that the western kingdoms are mobilizing?"

"I'd forgotten about that," Sparhawk admitted. "Well, it's none of our concern—at least not for the moment."

Kurik and Berit rode up. "I think we've seen him, Sparhawk," Kurik reported. "At least Berit has."

Sparhawk looked quickly at the novice.

"I climbed a tree, Sir Sparhawk," Berit explained. "There's a small boat some distance off shore. I couldn't make out too many details, but it looks as if it's just drifting, and there seems to be some splashing going on."

Sparhawk laughed wryly. "I guess Talen was right," he said.

"I don't quite follow, Sir Sparhawk."

"He said that Ghwerig probably stole a leaky boat, and that he has to stop every so often to bail out the water."

"You mean we've been waiting all night while Ghwerig scoops the water out of his boat?" Kalten asked.

"It looks that way," Sparhawk said.

"They're getting closer, Sparhawk," Tynian said, pointing to the west.

"And they're definitely Thalesians," Ulath added.

Sparhawk swore and went to the edge of the trees. The approaching men were formed up in a column; at the head of the column rode a large man in a mail shirt and a purple cape. Sparhawk recognized him. It was King Wargun of

Thalesia, and he appeared to be roaring drunk. Beside him rode a pale, slender man in a highly decorated but somewhat delicate suit of armor.

"The one beside Wargun is King Soros of Pelosia," Tynian said quietly. "I don't think he poses much of a danger. He spends most of his time praying and fasting."

"We do have a problem, though, Sparhawk," Ulath said gravely. "Ghwerig's going to be coming ashore very shortly, and he's got the royal crown of Thalesia with him. Wargun would give his very soul to get that crown back. I hate to say it, but we'd better lead him away from here before Ghwerig reaches the lake shore."

Sparhawk began to swear in frustration. His suspicions of the previous night had turned out to be all too correct.

"We'll be all right, Sparhawk," Bevier assured him. "Flute can follow Bhelliom's trail. We'll get King Wargun some distance away and then take our leave of him. We can come back later and chase down the Troll."

"It doesn't look as if we have much choice," Sparhawk conceded. "Let's go get Sephrenia and the children and draw Wargun away from here."

They mounted quickly and rode back to where Sephrenia, Talen, and Flute waited. "We're going to have to leave," Sparhawk said tersely. "There are some Thalesians coming, and King Wargun's with them. Ulath says that if Wargun finds out what we're here for, he'll try to take the crown away from us as soon as we get our hands on it. Let's ride."

They left the trees on the margin of the lake at a gallop, headed north. As they had anticipated, the column of Thalesian troops moved in pursuit. "We need a couple of miles at least," Sparhawk shouted to the others. "We've got to give Ghwerig a chance to get away."

They reached the road that bore northeasterly back toward the city of Venne and galloped along, rather ostentatiously not looking back at the pursuing Thalesians.

"They're coming up fast," Talen, who could look back over his shoulder without seeming to, called to Sparhawk.

"I'd like to get them a little farther away from Ghwerig," Sparhawk said regretfully, "but I guess this is as far as we can go."

"Ghwerig's a Troll, Sparhawk," Ulath said. "He knows how to hide."

"All right," Sparhawk agreed. He made some show of looking back over his shoulder and then held up one hand in the signal for a halt. They reined in and turned their horses to face the oncoming Thalesians.

The Thalesians also halted, and one of their number came forward at a walk. "King Wargun of Thalesia would have words with you, Sir Knights," he said respectfully. "He will join us presently."

"Very well," Sparhawk said curtly.

"Wargun's drunk," Ulath muttered to his friend. "Try to be diplomatic, Sparhawk."

King Wargun and King Soros rode up and reined in their horses. "Ho-ho, Soros!" Wargun roared, swaying dangerously in his saddle. "We seem to have snared us a covey of Church Knights." He blinked and peered at the knights. "I know that one," he said. "Ulath, what are you doing here in Pelosia?"

"Church business, your Majesty," Ulath replied blandly.

"And that one with the broken nose is the Pandion Sparhawk," Wargun added to King Soros. "Why were you running so hard, Sparhawk?"

"Our mission is of a certain urgency, your Majesty," Sparhawk said.

"And what mission is that?"

"We're not at liberty to discuss it, your Majesty. Standard Church practice, you understand."

"Politics then," Wargun snorted. "I wish the Church would keep her nose out of politics."

"Will you ride along with us for a ways, your Majesty?" Bevier inquired politely.

"No, I think it's going to be the other way around, Sir Knight—and it's going to be more than just a ways." Wargun looked at them all. "Do you know what's been going on in Arcium?"

"We've heard a few garbled rumors, your Majesty," Tynian said, "but nothing very substantial."

"All right," Wargun said, "I'll give you some substance. The Rendors have invaded Arcium."

"That's impossible!" Sparhawk exclaimed.

"Go tell the people who used to live in Coombe about impossible. The Rendors sacked and burned the town. Now they're marching north toward the capital at Larium. King

Dregos has invoked the mutual defense treaties. Soros here and I are gathering up every able-bodied man we can lay our hands on. We're going to ride south and stamp out the Rendorish infection once and for all.''

"I wish we could accompany your Majesty," Sparhawk said, "but we have another commitment. Perhaps, once our task is finished, we may be able to join you."

"You already have, Sparhawk," Wargun said bluntly.

"We have another urgent commitment, your Majesty," Sparhawk repeated.

"The Church is eternal, Sparhawk, and she's very patient. Your other commitment will have to wait."

That did it. Sparhawk, whose temper was never really all that much under control, looked the monarch of Thalesia full in the face. Unlike the anger of other men, whose rage was dissipated in shouting and oaths, Sparhawk's grew more and more icy calm. "We are Church Knights, your Majesty," he said in a flat, unemotional voice. "We are not subject to earthly kings. Our responsibility is to God and to our mother, the Church. We will obey *her* commands, not yours."

"I have a thousand picked men at my back," Wargun blustered.

"And how many are you prepared to lose?" Sparhawk asked in his deadly quiet voice. He drew himself up in his saddle and slowly lowered his visor. "Let's save some time, Wargun of Thalesia," he said formally, removing his right gauntlet. "I find your attitude unseemly, even irreligious, and it offends me." With a negligent-appearing toss, he threw his gauntlet into the dust of the road in front of the Thalesian king.

"*That's* his idea of diplomacy?" Ulath murmured to Kalten in some dismay.

"That's about as close as he can usually get," Kalten said, loosening his sword in its sheath. "You may as well go ahead and draw your ax, Ulath. This promises to be an interesting morning. Sephrenia, take the children to the rear."

"Are you mad, Kalten?" Ulath exploded. "You want me to draw my ax on my own king?"

"Of course not," Kalten grinned, "only on his funeral cortege. If Wargun goes up against Sparhawk, he'll be drinking heavenly mead after the first pass."

"Then I'll have to fight Sparhawk," Ulath said regretfully.

"That's up to you, my friend," Kalten said with equal regret, "but I don't advise it. Even if you get past Sparhawk, you'll still have to face me, and I cheat a lot."

"I will not permit this!" a booming voice roared. The man who shouldered his horse through the surrounding Thalesians was huge, bigger even than Ulath. He wore a mail shirt, and an Ogre-horned helmet, and carried a massive ax. A wide black ribbon about his neck identified him as a churchman. "Pick up your gauntlet, Sir Sparhawk, and withdraw your challenge! This is the command of our mother, the Church!"

"Who's that?" Kalten asked Ulath.

"Bergsten, the Patriarch of Emsat," Ulath replied.

"A *patriarch*? Dressed like that?"

"Bergsten's not your average churchman."

"Your Grace," King Wargun faltered. "I—"

"Put up your sword, Wargun," Bergsten thundered, "or would you face *me* in single combat?"

"*I* wouldn't," Wargun said almost conversationally to Sparhawk. "Would *you*?"

Sparhawk looked appraisingly at the Patriarch of Emsat. "Not if I could help it," he admitted. "How *did* he get that big?"

"He was an only child," Wargun said. "He didn't have to fight with nine brothers and sisters for his supper every night. What's your feeling about a truce at this point, Sparhawk?"

"It sounds like the course of prudence to me, your Majesty. We really have something important to do, though."

"We'll talk about it later—when Bergsten's at prayers."

"This is the command of the Church!" the Patriarch of Emsat roared. "The Church Knights will join us in this holy mission. The Eshandist heresy is an offense against God. It will die on the rocky plains of Arcium. As God gives us strength, my children, let us proceed with this great work that we are about." He wheeled his horse to face south. "Don't forget your gauntlet, Sir Sparhawk," he said over his shoulder. "You might need it when we get to Arcium."

"Yes, your Grace," Sparhawk replied through clenched teeth.

CHAPTER
TWENTY-ONE

ROMPTLY AT NOON, King Soros of Pelosia called a halt. He instructed his servants to erect his pavilion, and he and his private chaplain retired inside for noon prayers.

"Choirboy," King Wargun muttered under his breath. "Bergsten!" he bellowed.

"Right here, your Majesty," the militaristic patriarch said mildly from behind his king.

"Have you gotten over your siege of bad temper yet?"

"I wasn't really bad tempered, your Majesty. I was merely trying to save lives—yours included."

"What's that supposed to mean?"

"Had you been foolish enough to accept Sir Sparhawk's challenge, you'd be dining in Heaven tonight—or supping in Hell, depending on Divine Judgment."

"That's direct enough."

"Sir Sparhawk's reputation precedes him, your Majesty, and you would be no match for him. Now, what was it you had on your mind?"

"How far is Lamorkand from here?"

"The south end of the lake, my Lord—about two days."

"And the closest Lamork city?"

"That would be Agnak, your Majesty. It's just across the border and a bit to the east."

"All right. We'll go there then. I want to get Soros out of his own country and away from all these religious shrines. If he stops to pray one more time, I'm going to strangle him. We'll pick up the bulk of the army late today. They're already marching south. I'm going to send Soros on down to mobilize the Lamork barons. You go with him, and if he tries to pray more than once a day, you have my permission to brain him."

"That could have some interesting political ramifications, your Majesty," Bergsten noted.

"Lie about it," Wargun growled. "Say it was an accident."

"How can you brain somebody by accident?"

"Think something up. Now, listen to me, Bergsten. I need those Lamorks. Don't let Soros get side-tracked on some religious pilgrimage. Keep him moving. Quote sacred texts to him if you have to. Pick up every Lamork you can lay your hands on and then swing into Elenia. I'll meet you on the Arcian border. I've got to go to Acie in Deira. Obler's called a council of war." He looked around. "Sparhawk," he said disgustedly, "go someplace and pray. A Church Knight should be above eavesdropping."

"Yes, your Majesty," Sparhawk replied.

"That's a very ugly horse you've got there, you know?" Wargun said, looking critically at Faran.

"We're a matched set, your Majesty."

"I'd be careful, King Wargun," Kalten advised over his shoulder as he and Sparhawk started back to where their friends had dismounted. "He bites."

"Which one? Sparhawk or the horse?"

"Take your pick, your Majesty."

The two swung down from their horses and joined their friends. "What's Ghwerig doing?" Sparhawk asked Flute.

"He's still hiding," the little girl replied. "At least I think he is. Bhelliom's not moving. He's probably going to wait until dark before he starts out again.''

Sparhawk grunted.

Kalten looked at Ulath. "What's the story behind Bergsten?" he asked. "I've never seen a churchman in armor before.''

"He used to be a Genidian Knight," Ulath replied. "He'd be preceptor by now if he hadn't entered the priesthood.''

Kalten nodded. "He *did* seem to be carrying that ax as if he knew how to use it. Isn't it a bit unusual for a member of one of the militant orders to take the cloth?''

"Not that unusual, Kalten," Bevier disagreed from nearby. "A fair number of the high churchmen in Arcium used to be Cyrinics. Someday I myself may leave our order so that I can serve God more personally.''

"We're going to have to find some nice accommodating girl for that boy, Sparhawk," Ulath muttered. "Let's get him involved in some serious sin so that he gives up that notion. He's too good a man to waste by putting him in a cassock.''

"How about Naween?" Talen, who was standing beside them, suggested.

"Who's Naween?" Ulath asked.

Talen shrugged. "The best whore in Cimmura. She's enthusiastic about her work. Sparhawk's met her.''

"Really?" Ulath said, looking at Sparhawk with one raised eyebrow.

"It was on business," Sparhawk said shortly.

"Of course—but yours or hers?''

"Do you suppose we could drop this?" Sparhawk cleared his throat and then looked around to make sure that none of King Wargun's soldiers was within earshot. "We've got to get clear of this lot before Ghwerig gets too far ahead of us," he said.

"Tonight," Tynian suggested. "Rumor has it that King Wargun drinks himself to sleep every night. We should be able to slip away without too much problem.''

"We surely cannot disobey the direct command of the Patriarch of Emsat," Bevier said in a shocked tone.

"Of course not, Bevier," Kalten said easily. "We'll just slip out and find some country vicar or the abbot of a monastery and get him to order us to go back to what we were doing.''

"That's immoral!" Bevier gasped.

"I know." Kalten smirked. "Disgusting, isn't it?"

"But it *is* technically legitimate, Bevier," Tynian assured the young Cyrinic. "A bit devious, I'll admit, but still legitimate. We're oath-bound to follow the orders of consecrated members of the clergy. The order of a vicar or an abbot would supersede the order of Patriarch Bergsten, wouldn't it?" Tynian's eyes were wide and innocent.

Bevier looked at him helplessly, and then he began to laugh.

"I think he's going to be all right, Sparhawk," Ulath said, "but let's keep your friend Naween in reserve—just in case."

"Who's Naween?" Bevier asked, puzzled.

"An acquaintance of mine," Sparhawk replied distantly. "Someday I may introduce you."

"I'd be honored," Bevier said sincerely.

Talen went off some distance and collapsed in helpless laughter.

They caught up with the mob of disconsolate-looking Pelosian conscripts late that afternoon. As Sparhawk had feared, the perimeter of their encampment was being patrolled by Wargun's heavily armed thugs.

The soldiers set up a pavilion for them just before sunset, and they went inside. Sparhawk removed his armor and put on a mail shirt instead. "The rest of you wait here," he said. "I want to take a look around before it gets dark." He put on his sword belt and stepped out of the tent.

There were two evil-looking Thalesians outside. "Where do you think you're going?" one of them demanded.

Sparhawk gave him a flat, unfriendly stare and waited.

"My Lord," the fellow grudgingly added.

"I want to check on my horses," Sparhawk said.

"We have farriers to do that, Sir Knight."

"We're not going to have an argument about this, are we, neighbor?"

"Ah—no, I don't think so, Sir Knight."

"Good. Where are the horses picketed?"

"I'll show you, Sir Sparhawk."

"There's no need of that. Just tell me."

"I have to accompany you anyway, Sir Knight. The king's orders."

"I see. Lead on then."

As they started out, Sparhawk heard a sudden boisterous voice. "Ho there, Sir Knight!" He looked around.

"I see they got you and your friends, too." It was Kring, the Domi of the marauding band of Peloi.

"Hello, my friend," Sparhawk greeted the shaved-headed tribesman. "Did you catch up with those Zemochs?"

Kring laughed. "I've got a whole sackful of ears," he said. "They tried to make a stand. Stupid people, the Zemochs. But then King Soros took up with this ragtag army, and we had to follow along in order to collect the bounty." He rubbed at his shaved head. "That's all right, though. We didn't have anything pressing to do back home anyway, now that the mares have all foaled. Tell me, do you still have that young thief with you?"

"Last time I looked he was still around. Of course, he might have stolen a few things and then bolted. He bolts very well when the occasion demands it."

"I'll wager he does, Sir Knight. I'll wager he does. How's my friend Tynian? I saw you all when you rode in, and I was just on my way to visit him."

"He's well."

"Good." The Domi looked seriously at Sparhawk then. "Perhaps you can give me some information about military etiquette, Sir Knight. I've never been a part of a formal army before. What are the general rules about pillage?"

"I don't think anybody would get too concerned," Sparhawk replied, "as long as you limit your plundering to the enemy dead. It's considered bad form to loot the bodies of our own soldiers."

"Stupid rule, that one," Kring sighed. "What does a dead man care about possessions? How about rape?"

"It's frowned on. We'll be in Arcium, and that's a friendly country. Arcians are sensitive about their womenfolk. Wargun's gathered up a fair number of camp followers if those urges are bothering you."

"Camp followers always act so bored. Give me a nice young virgin every time. You know, this campaign is turning out to be less and less enjoyable. How about arson? I love a good fire."

"I'd definitely advise against it. As I said, we'll be in Arcium, and all the towns and houses belong to the people who live there. I'm sure they'd object."

"Civilized warfare leaves a lot to be desired, doesn't it, Sir Knight?"

"What can I say, Domi?" Sparhawk apologized, spreading his hands helplessly.

"If you don't mind my saying so, it's the armor, I think. You people are so encased in steel that you lose sight of the main things—booty, women, horses. It's a failing, Sir Knight."

"It is a failing, Domi," Sparhawk conceded. "Centuries of tradition, you understand."

"There's nothing wrong with tradition—as long as it doesn't get in the way of important things."

"I'll bear that in mind, Domi. Our tent's right over there. Tynian will be glad to see you." Sparhawk followed the Thalesian sentry on through the camp to where the horses were picketed. He made some pretense of checking Faran's hooves, looking intently out into the twilight at the perimeter of the camp. As he had noted earlier, there were dozens of men riding around the outside. "Why so many patrols?" he asked the Thalesian.

"The Pelosian conscripts are unenthusiastic about this campaign, Sir Knight," the warrior replied. "We didn't go to all the trouble of gathering them up only to have them sneak off in the middle of the night."

"I see," Sparhawk said. "We can go back now."

"Yes, my Lord."

Wargun's patrols seriously complicated things, not to mention the presence of the two sentries outside their tent. Ghwerig was getting farther and farther away with Bhelliom, and it seemed that there was very little Sparhawk could do about it. He knew that by himself, using a mixture of stealth and main force, he could escape from the camp, but what would that accomplish? Without Flute, he'd have little chance of tracking down the fleeing Troll, and to take her along without the others to help guard her would be to place her in unacceptable danger. They were going to have to come up with some other idea.

The Thalesian warrior was leading him past the tent of some Pelosian conscripts when he saw a familiar face. "Occuda?" he said incredulously, "is that you?"

The lantern-jawed man in bullhide armor rose to his feet,

his bleak face showing no particular pleasure at the meeting. "I'm afraid it is, my Lord," he said.

"What happened? What forced you to leave Count Ghasek?"

Occuda looked briefly at the men who shared the tent with him. "Might we discuss this privately, Sir Sparhawk?"

"Certainly, Occuda."

"Over there, my Lord."

"I'll be in plain sight," Sparhawk told his escort. Together Sparhawk and Occuda walked away from the tent and stopped near a grove of sapling fir trees that stood so closely together that they precluded the possibility of anyone's pitching a tent among them.

"The count has fallen ill, my Lord," Occuda said somberly.

"And you left him alone with that madwoman? I'm disappointed in you, Occuda."

"The circumstances have changed somewhat, my Lord."

"Oh?"

"The Lady Bellina is dead now."

"What happened to her?"

"I killed her." Occuda said it in a numb voice. "I could no longer bear her endless screaming. At first the herbs the Lady Sephrenia advised quieted Bellina somewhat, but after a short while, she seemed to shake off their effects. I tried to increase the dosage, but to no avail. Then one night, as I was pushing her supper through that slot in the tower wall, I saw her. She was raving and frothing at the mouth like a rabid dog. She was obviously in agony. That's when I made the decision to put her to rest."

"We all knew it might come to that," Sparhawk said gravely.

"Perhaps. I could not bring myself simply to slaughter her, however. The herbs no longer quieted her. The nightshade, however did. She stopped screaming shortly after I gave it to her." There were tears in Occuda's eyes. "I took my sledge and broke a hole in the tower wall. Then I did as you instructed with my ax. I've never done anything so difficult in my life. I wrapped her body in canvas and took her outside the castle. There I burned her. After what I had done, I could not face the count. I left him a note confessing my crime and then went to a woodcutter's village not far from the castle. I hired servants there to care for the count. Even after I told them there was no longer any danger at the castle, I had to pay them double wages to get them to agree. Then I came away from that place and joined this army. I hope the fighting starts soon. Everything in my life is over. All I want now is to die.''

''You did what you had to, Occuda.''

''Perhaps, but that does not absolve me of my guilt.''

Sparhawk made a decision at that point. ''Come with me,'' he said.

''Where are we going, my Lord?''

''To see the Patriarch of Emsat.''

''I could not enter the presence of a high churchman with Lady Bellina's blood on my hands.''

''Patriarch Bergsten is a Thalesian. I doubt that he's very squeamish. We need to see the Patriarch of Emsat,'' he told his Thalesian escort. ''Take us to his tent.''

''Yes, my Lord.''

The sentry led them through camp to the pavilion of Patriarch Bergsten. Bergsten's brutish face looked particularly Thalesian by candlelight. He had heavy bone ridges across his brows, and his cheekbones and jaw were prominent. He was still wearing his mail shirt, although he had removed his Ogre-horned helmet and stood his ax in the corner.

''Your Grace,'' Sparhawk said with a bow, ''my friend here has a problem of a spiritual nature. I wonder if you could help him?''

''That is my calling, Sir Sparhawk,'' the patriarch replied.

''Thank you, your Grace. Occuda here was at one time a monk. Then he entered the service of a count in northern Pelosia. The count's sister became involved with an evil cult, and she began to practice rites involving human sacrifice, which gave her certain powers.''

Bergsten's eyes widened.

''At any rate,'' Sparhawk continued, ''when the count's sister was finally stripped of those powers, she went mad, and her brother was forced to confine her. Occuda took care of her until he could no longer bear her agonies. Then, out of compassion, he poisoned her.''

''That's a dreadful story, Sir Sparhawk,'' Bergsten said in his deep voice.

''It was a dreadful series of events,'' Sparhawk agreed.

"Occuda feels overcome with guilt now, and he's convinced that his soul is lost. Can you absolve him so that he can face the rest of his life?"

The armored Patriarch Bergsten looked thoughtfully at Occuda's suffering face, his eyes at once shrewd and compassionate. He seemed to consider the matter for several moments, then he straightened, and his expression grew hard. "No, Sir Sparhawk, I can't," he said flatly.

Sparhawk was about to protest, but the patriarch raised one thick hand. He looked at the hulking Pelosian. "Occuda," he said sternly, "you were once a monk?"

"I was, your Grace."

"Good. This shall be your penance then. You will resume your monk's habit, Brother Occuda, and you will enter my service. When I have decided that you have paid for your sin, I will grant you absolution."

"Y-your Grace," Occuda sobbed, falling to his knees, "how can I ever thank you?"

Bergsten smiled bleakly. "You may change your mind in time, Brother Occuda. You will find that I'm a very hard master. You'll pay for your sin many times over before your soul is washed clean. Now, go gather your possessions. You'll be moving in here with me."

"Yes, your Grace." Occuda rose and left the tent.

"If you don't mind my saying so, your Grace," Sparhawk said, "you are a very devious man."

"No, not really, Sir Sparhawk." The huge churchman smiled. "It's just that I've had enough experience to know that the human spirit is a very complex thing. Your friend feels that he must suffer in order to expiate his sin, and if I were simply to absolve him, he would always doubt that he had been throughly cleansed. He feels that he has to suffer, so I'll make sure that he suffers—in moderation, of course. I'm not a monster, after all."

"Was what he did really a sin?"

"Of course not. He acted out of mercy. He'll make a very good monk, and after I think he's suffered long enough, I'll find a nice quiet monastery some place and make him the abbot. He'll be too busy to brood about things, and the Church will get a good, faithful abbot. This is not to mention all those years when I'll have his services at no cost."

"You're not really a very nice man, your Grace."

"I have never pretended to be, my son. That will be all, Sir Sparhawk. Go with my blessing." The patriarch winked slyly.

"Thank you, your Grace," Sparhawk said without cracking a smile.

He felt somehow very pleased with himself as he and the sentry walked back across the camp. He might not always be able to solve his own problems, but he certainly seemed able to solve those of others.

"Kring was telling us that the outside of the camp is being patrolled," Tynian said when Sparhawk re-entered the tent. "That's going to make it more difficult to get away, isn't it?"

"Much more," Sparhawk agreed.

"Oh," Tynian added. "Flute's been asking some questions about distances. Kurik looked in the packs, but he couldn't find your map."

"It's in my saddlebag."

"I should have thought of that, I suppose," Kurik said.

"What is it you want to know?" Sparhawk asked the little girl, opening his saddlebag for the map.

"How far is it from this Agnak place to Acie?"

Sparhawk spread his map out on the table in the center of the pavilion.

"It's a very pretty picture, but it doesn't answer my question," she said.

Sparhawk measured it off. "It's about three hundred leagues," he replied.

"That still doesn't answer my question, Sparhawk. I need to know how long it will take."

He computed it. "About twenty days."

She frowned. "Perhaps I can shorten that a bit," she said.

"What are we talking about here?" he asked her.

"Acie's on the coast, isn't it?"

"Yes."

"We're going to need a boat to get us to Thalesia. Ghwerig's taking Bhelliom to his cave up in the mountains there."

"There are enough of us to overpower the sentries," Kalten said, "and dealing with a patrol in the middle of the night's not all that hard. We're still not so far behind Ghwerig that we can't catch him."

"We have something to do in Acie," she told him. "At least I do—and it must be done before we go after Bhelliom.

We know where Ghwerig's going, so he won't be hard to find. Ulath, go tell Wargun that we'll accompany him to Acie. Think up some plausible reason.''

"Yes, lady," he said with the faintest hint of a smile.

"I wish you'd all stop doing that," she complained. "Oh, by the way, on your way to Wargun's tent, ask someone to bring us some supper.''

"What would you like?"

"Goat would be nice, but anything will do as long as it's not pork.''

They reached Agnak just before sunset the following day and set up their huge camp. The local citizenry immediately closed the city gates. King Wargun insisted that Sparhawk and the other Church Knights accompany him under a flag of truce to the north gate. "I am Wargun of Thalesia," he roared at the city walls. "I have King Soros of Pelosia with me—as well as these Knights of the Church. The Kingdom of Arcium has been invaded by the Rendors, and I call upon every able-bodied man with faith in God to join with us in our efforts to stamp out the Eshandist heresy. I'm not here to inconvenience you in any way, my friends, but if that gate isn't open by the time the sun goes down, I'll reduce your walls to rubble and drive you all into the wilderness where you can watch your city burn down to ashes.''

"Do you think they heard him?" Kalten asked.

"They probably heard him in Chyrellos," Tynian replied. "Your king has a most penetrating voice, Sir Ulath.''

"It's a long way from one mountain top to another in Thalesia." Ulath shrugged. "You have to talk very loud if you want to be heard.''

King Wargun grinned crookedly at him. "Would anyone care to wager on whether or not that gate opens before the sun slips behind yon hill?" he asked.

"We are Church Knights, your Majesty," Bevier replied piously. "We take a vow of poverty, so we're not really in a position to gamble on sporting events.''

King Wargun roared with laughter.

The city gate opened somewhat hesitantly.

"Somehow I knew they'd see it my way," Wargun said, leading the way into the city. "Where will I find your chief magistrate?" he asked one of the trembling gate guards.

"I-I believe he's in the council house, your Majesty," the guard stammered. "Probably hiding in the cellar."

"Be a good fellow and go fetch him for me."

"At once, your Majesty." The guard threw down his pike and ran off down the street.

"I like Lamorks," Wargun said expansively. "They're always so eager to be obliging."

The chief magistrate was a pudgy man. His face was pale, and he was sweating profusely as the gate guard bodily dragged him into Wargun's presence.

"I will require suitable quarters for King Soros, myself, and our entourage, your Excellency," Wargun informed him. "This won't inconvenience your citizens all that much, because they'll be up all night equipping themselves for an extended military campaign anyway."

"As your Majesty commands," the magistrate replied in a squeaky voice.

"You see what I mean about Lamorks?" Wargun said. "Soros will have smooth going down here. He'll sweep the whole kingdom clean in a week—if he doesn't stop to pray too often. Why don't we go someplace and get something to drink while his excellency here empties a dozen or so houses for us?"

After a consultation with King Soros and Patriarch Bergsten the following morning, Wargun took a troop of Thalesian cavalry and led them toward the west with Sparhawk riding at his side. It was a fine morning. The sunlight sparkled on the lake, and there was a light breeze blowing in from the west.

"I suppose you're still not going to tell me what you were doing in Pelosia?" Wargun said to Sparhawk. The Thalesian King seemed relatively sober this morning, so Sparhawk decided to risk his mood.

"You know about Queen Ehlana's illness, of course," he began.

"The whole world knows about it. That's why her bastard cousin is trying to seize power."

"There's a bit more to it than that, your Majesty. We've finally isolated the cause of the illness. Primate Annias needed access to her treasury, so he had her poisoned."

"He did *what*?"

Sparhawk nodded. "Annias is not overburdened with scruples and he'll do anything to reach the Archprelacy."

"The man's a scoundrel," Wargun growled.

"At any rate, we've discovered a possible cure for Ehlana. It involves the use of magic, and we need a certain talisman to make it work. We found out that the talisman is in Lake Venne."

"What is this talisman?" Wargun asked, his eyes narrowed.

"It's a kind of an ornament," Sparhawk replied evasively.

"Do you really put that much store in all that magic nonsense?"

"I've seen it work a few times, your Majesty. Anyhow, that's why we objected so much when you insisted that we join you. We weren't trying to be disrespectful. Ehlana's life is being sustained by a spell, but it's only good for just so long. If she dies, Lycheas will take the throne."

"Not if I can help it, he won't. I don't want any throne in Eosia occupied by a man who doesn't know his own father."

"The idea doesn't appeal to me either, but I think Lycheas does in fact know who his father is."

"Oh? Who is it? Do you know?"

"The Primate Annias."

Wargun's eyes went wide. "Are you sure of that?"

Sparhawk nodded. "I have it on the very best authority. The ghost of King Aldreas told me. His sister was a bit profligate."

Wargun made the sign to ward off evil, a peasant gesture that looked peculiar coming from a reigning monarch. "A ghost, you say? The word of a ghost won't stand up in any court, Sparhawk."

"I wasn't planning to take it to court, your Majesty," Sparhawk said grimly, resting his hand on his sword hilt. "As soon as I have the leisure, the principals will be standing before a higher judgment."

"Good man," Wargun approved. "I wouldn't have thought that a churchman would have succumbed to Arissa, though."

"Arissa can be very persuasive sometimes. Anyway, this campaign of yours is directed at another one of Annias' plots. I strongly suspect that the Rendorish invasion is being led by a man named Martel. Martel works for Annias, and he's been trying to stir up enough trouble to draw the Church Knights away from Chyrellos during the election. Our preceptors could probably keep Annias off the Archprelate's throne, so he had to get them out of his way.''

''The man's a real snake, isn't he?''

''That's a pretty fair description.''

''You've given me a lot to think about this morning, Sparhawk. I'll mull it over, and we'll talk some more about it later.''

A sudden light sprang into Sparhawk's eyes.

''Don't get your hopes up too much, though. I still think I'm going to need you when I get to Arcium. Besides, the militant orders have already marched south. You're Vanion's right arm, and I think he'd miss you if you stayed away.''

Time and distance seemed to drag on interminably as they rode west. They crossed into Pelosia again and rode across the unending plains in bright summer sunlight.

One night when they were still some distance from the border of Deira, Kalten was in a bad humor. ''I thought you said you were going to speed this trip up,'' he said accusingly to Flute.

''I did,'' she replied.

''Really?'' he said with heavy sarcasm. ''We've been on the road for a week already, and we haven't even reached Deira yet.''

''Actually, Kalten, we've only been on the road for two days. I have to make it *seem* longer so that Wargun doesn't get suspicious.''

He looked at her disbelievingly.

''I've got another question for you, Flute,'' Tynian said. ''Back at the lake, you were very eager to catch Ghwerig and take Bhelliom away from him. Then you suddenly changed your mind and said that we have to go to Acie. What happened?''

''I received word from my family,'' she told him. ''They told me about this task I have to complete at Acie before we can go after Bhelliom.'' She made a wry face. ''I probably would have thought of it myself.''

''Let's get back to this other thing,'' Kalten said impatiently. ''How did you squeeze time together the way you said you have?''

''There are ways,'' she said evasively.

''I wouldn't pursue it, Kalten,'' Sephrenia advised. ''You

wouldn't understand what she's been doing, so why worry about it? Besides, if you keep asking her questions, she might decide to answer you, and the answers would probably upset you very much.''

CHAPTER
TWENTY-TWO

I T SEEMED THAT it took them two more weeks to reach the foothills above Acie, the bleak, ugly capital of Deira, which perched on an eroded bluff overlooking the original harbor and the long, narrow Gulf of Acie. Flute advised them that evening, however, that no more than five days had passed since they had left the city of Agnak in Lamorkand. Most of them chose to take her at her word, but Sir Bevier, who was of a scholarly and resolutely Elenian frame of mind, questioned her about how this seeming miracle had come to pass. Her explanation was patient, although dreadfully obscure. Bevier finally excused himself and went outside the tent for a time to look at the stars and to reestablish his relations with things he had always considered immutable and eternal.

314

"Did you understand anything she said at all?" Tynian asked him when he returned, pale and sweating, to the tent.

"A little," Bevier replied, sitting down again. "Just around the edges." He looked at Flute with frightened eyes. "I think perhaps that Patriarch Ortzel was right. We should have no dealings with these Styric people. Nothing is sacred to them."

Flute crossed the tent on her grass-stained little feet and laid a consoling hand on his cheek. "Dear Bevier," she said sweetly, "so serious and so devout. We must get to Thalesia quickly—just as soon as I can finish what I have to do in Acie. We simply did not have the time to plod halfway across the continent at the usual pace. That's why I did it the other way."

"I understand the reasons," he said, "but—"

"I will never hurt you, you know, and I won't let anybody else hurt you either, but you must try not to be so rigid. It makes it so very hard to explain things to you. Does that help at all?"

"Not appreciably."

She raised up on her tiptoes and kissed him. "Now then," she said brightly, "everything's all right again, isn't it?"

He gave up. "Do as you will, Flute," he said to her with a gentle, almost shy smile. "I can't refute your arguments and your kisses at the same time."

"He's such a *nice* boy," she said delightedly to the others.

"We sort of feel the same way about him ourselves," Ulath said blandly, "and we have some plans for him."

"You, however," she said critically to the Genidian Knight, "are most definitely *not* a nice boy."

"I know," he admitted, unruffled, "and you have no idea how much that disappointed my mother—and a number of other ladies from time to time as well."

She gave him a dark look and stalked away, muttering to herself in Styric. Sparhawk recognized some of the words, and he wondered if she really knew what they meant.

As had become his custom, Wargun asked Sparhawk to ride beside him the following morning as they trekked down the long, rocky slope from the foothills of the Deiran mountains toward the coast. "I should really get out more often," the King of Thalesia confided. "After almost three weeks coming from Agnak, I should be nearly ready to fall out of my saddle, but I feel as if we've been on the road for only a few days."

"Perhaps it was the mountains," Sparhawk suggested carefully. "Mountain air is always invigorating."

"Maybe that's it," Wargun agreed.

"Have you given any more thought to the discussion we had awhile back, your Majesty?" Sparhawk asked cautiously.

"I've had a lot on my mind, Sparhawk. I appreciate your personal concern about Queen Ehlana, but, from a political standpoint, the important thing now is to crush this Rendorish invasion. Then the preceptors of the militant orders will be able to return to Chyrellos and block the Primate of Cimmura. If Annias fails to gain the Archprelacy, Lycheas the bastard won't have any chance of ascending the throne of Elenia. I realize that it's a hard choice, but politics is a hard game."

A little later, when Wargun was conferring with his troop commander, Sparhawk relayed the gist of their conversation to his companions.

"He's not any more reasonable when he's sober, is he?" Kalten said.

"From his own standpoint, he's right, though," Tynian observed. "The politics of the situation dictate that we do everything we can to get all the preceptors back to Chyrellos before Cluvonus dies. I doubt that he cares much one way or the other about Ehlana. There's one other possibility, though. We're in Deira now, and Obler's the king here. He's a very wise old man. If we explain the situation to him, he might overrule Wargun."

"I don't think I'd care to hang Ehlana's life on that slim a possibility," Sparhawk said. He turned to rejoin Wargun.

Despite Flute's assurances concerning the actual elapsed time their journey had consumed, Sparhawk was still impatient. The apparent slow pace nagged at him. While he could intellectually accept what she said, he could not come to grips with it emotionally. Twenty days is twenty days to one's senses, and Sparhawk's senses were strung wire-taut just now. He began to have dark thoughts. Things had been going wrong so consistently that seeming premonitions tugged at his mind. He began to think about the forthcoming encounter with Ghwerig with a great deal less certainty about the outcome.

About noon they reached Acie, the capital city of the Kingdom of Deira. The Deiran army was encamped around the city, and their camp was bustling with activity as they prepared for the march south.

Wargun had been drinking again, but he looked around with satisfaction. "Good," he said, "they're almost ready. Come along, Sparhawk, and bring your friends. Let's go talk to Obler."

As they rode through the narrow, cobbled streets of Acie, Talen pulled his horse in beside Sparhawk's. "I'm going to drop behind a ways," he said very quietly. "I want to look around. Getting away in the open countryside's very hard. This is a town, though, and there are always lots of places to hide in towns. King Wargun's not going to miss me. He hardly knows I'm along. If I can find us a good hiding place, maybe we can slip away to it and stay there until the army moves out. Then we can make a run for Thalesia."

"Just be very careful."

"Naturally."

A few streets farther on, Sephrenia reined in sharply and pulled her white palfrey off to the side of the street. She and Flute quickly dismounted and went to the entrance of a narrow alley to greet an aged Styric with a long, snowy beard who wore an intensely white robe. Some sort of ritual ceremony seemed to take place among the three of them, but Sparhawk could not quite make out the details. Sephrenia and Flute spoke earnestly to the old man at some length, and then he bowed in acknowledgment and went back on up the alley.

"What was that all about?" Wargun asked suspiciously when Sephrenia and the little girl rejoined them.

"He's an old friend, your Majesty," Sephrenia replied, "and the most revered and wise man in all of western Styricum."

"A king, you mean?"

"That's a word that has no meaning in Styricum, your Majesty," she told him.

"How can you have a government if you don't have a king?"

"There are other ways, your Majesty, and besides, Styrics have outgrown the need for government."

"That's absurd."

"Many things seem that way—at first. It may come to you Elenes in time."

"That's a very infuriating woman sometimes, Sparhawk," Wargun growled, pushing his horse back to the front of the column.

"Sparhawk," Flute said very lightly.

"Yes?"

"The task here in Acie is complete. We can leave for Thalesia at any time now."

"How do you propose to manage that?"

"I'll tell you later. Go keep Wargun company. He gets lonesome without you."

The palace was not a particularly imposing building. It looked to be more like a complex of administrative offices than something built for ostentation and display. "I don't know how Obler can live in this hovel," Wargun said disdainfully, swaying in his saddle. "You there," he bellowed at one of the guards posted at the main door, "go tell Obler that Wargun of Thalesia has arrived. We need to confer about a few things."

"At once, your Majesty." The guard saluted and went inside.

Wargun dismounted and unhooked the wineskin from the skirt of his saddle. He uncorked it and took a long drink. "I hope Obler's got some chilled ale," he said. "This wine's beginning to sour my stomach."

The guard returned. "King Obler will receive you, your Majesty," he said. "Please follow me."

"I know the way," Wargun replied. "I've been here before. Have somebody see to our horses." He blinked his bloodshot eyes at Sparhawk. "Come along then," he commanded. He did not appear to have missed Talen.

They trooped through the unadorned hallways of King Obler's palace and found the aged king of Deira sitting behind a large table littered with maps and papers.

"Sorry to be so late, Obler," Wargun said, untying his purple cloak and dropping it on the floor. "I made a swing through Pelosia to pick up Soros and a sort of an army." He sprawled out in a chair. "I've been sort of out of touch. What's been going on?"

"The Rendors have laid siege to Larium," the white-haired King of Deira replied. "The Alciones, Genidians, and Cyrinics are holding the city, and the Pandions are out in the countryside dealing with Rendorish raiding parties."

"That's more or less what I'd expected," Wargun grunted. "Can you send for some ale, Obler? My stomach's been bothering me for the past few days. You remember Sparhawk, don't you?"

"Of course. He's the man who saved Count Radun down in Arcium."

"And this one is Kalten. The big one there is Ulath. The one with the dark skin is Bevier, and I'm sure you know Tynian. The Styric woman is called Sephrenia—I'm not really sure about her real name. I'm sure neither one of us could even pronounce it. She teaches the Pandions magic, and that adorable child there is her little girl. The other two work for Sparhawk. I wouldn't aggravate either one of them." He looked around, his eyes bleary. "What happened to that boy you had with you?" he asked Sparhawk.

"Probably exploring," Sparhawk replied blandly. "Political discussions bore him."

"Sometimes they bore me as well," Wargun said. He looked back at King Obler. "Have the Elenes mobilized yet?"

"My agents have found no evidence of it."

Wargun started to swear. "I think I'll stop in Cimmura on my way south and hang that young bastard Lycheas."

"I'll lend you a rope, your Majesty," Kalten offered.

Wargun laughed. "What's happening in Chyrellos, Obler?"

"Cluvonus is in delirium," Obler replied. "He can't last much longer, I'm afraid. Most of the major churchmen are already there preparing for the election of his successor."

"The Primate of Cimmura, most likely," Wargun growled sourly. He took a tankard of ale from a servant. "That's all right, boy," he said. "Just leave the keg." His voice was slurred. "This is the way I see it, Obler. We'd better get to Larium as quickly as we can. We'll push the Rendors back into the sea so that the militant orders can go to Chyrellos and keep Annias from becoming Archprelate. If that happens, we may have to declare war."

"On the Church?" Obler sounded startled.

"Archprelates have been deposed before, Obler. Annias won't have any use for a miter if he doesn't have a head. Sparhawk has already volunteered to use his knife."

"You'll start a general civil war, Wargun. No one has directly confronted the Church for centuries."

"Then maybe it's about time. Anything else happening?"

"The Earl of Lenda and Preceptor Vanion of the Pandion order arrived no more than an hour ago," Obler said. "They wanted to get cleaned up. I sent for them just as soon as I'd heard that you'd arrived. They'll join us in a bit."

"Good. We'll be able to settle a lot of things here then. What's the date?"

King Obler told him.

"Your calendar must be wrong, Obler," Wargun said after counting days off on his fingers.

"What did you do with Soros?" Obler asked.

"I came close to killing him," Wargun growled. "I've never seen anybody pray so much when there was work to be done. I sent him into Lamorkand to pick up the barons down there. He's riding at the head of the army, but Bergsten's actually the one in charge. Bergsten would make a good Archprelate, if we could ever get him out of that armor." He laughed. "Can you imagine the reaction of the Hierocracy to an Archprelate in a mail shirt and a horned helmet, and with a battle-ax in his hands?"

"It might enliven the Church a bit, Wargun," Obler conceded with a faint smile.

"God knows she needs it," Wargun said. "She's been acting like a frigid old maid since Cluvonus fell ill."

"Would your Majesties excuse me?" Sparhawk asked deferentially. "I'd like to look in on Vanion. We haven't seen each other for a while, and there are things I need to report to him."

"More of this everlasting Church business?" Wargun asked.

"You know how it is, your Majesty."

"No, thank God, I don't. Go ahead, Knight of the Church. Talk with your father superior, but don't keep him too long. We've got important business here."

"Yes, your Majesty." Sparhawk bowed to the two kings and quietly left the room.

Vanion was trying to struggle into his armor when Sparhawk entered the room. He stared at his subordinate in some astonishment. "What are you doing here, Sparhawk?" he demanded. "I though you were in Lamorkand."

"Just passing through, Vanion," Sparhawk replied. "Some

things have changed. I'll give you the gist of it now, and we can fill you in on more detail after King Wargun goes to bed." He looked critically at his preceptor. "You're looking tired, my friend."

"Old age," Vanion said ruefully, "and all of those swords I made Sephrenia give me are getting heavier every day. You know that Olven died?"

"Yes. His ghost brought his sword to Sephrenia."

"I was afraid of that. I'll take it away from her."

Sparhawk tapped Vanion's breastplate with one knuckle. "You don't have to wear this, you know. Obler's fairly informal, and Wargun doesn't even know what the word formal means."

"Appearances, my friend," Vanion said, "and the honor of the Church. Sometimes it's boring, I'll admit, but—" He shrugged. "Help me into this contraption, Sparhawk. You can talk while you're tightening straps and buckling buckles."

"Yes, my Lord Vanion." Sparhawk began to assist his friend into the suit of armor, briefly summarizing the events that had taken place in Lamorkand and Pelosia.

"Why didn't you chase down the Troll?" Vanion asked him.

"Some things came up," Sparhawk said, fastening Vanion's black cape to his shoulder plates. "Wargun, for one thing. I even offered to fight him, but Patriarch Bergsten interfered."

"You challenged a *king*?" Vanion looked stunned.

"It seemed appropriate at the time, Vanion."

"Oh, my friend." Vanion sighed.

"We'd better get going," Sparhawk said. "There's a lot more to tell you, but Wargun's getting impatient." Sparhawk squinted at Vanion's armor. "Brace yourself," he said. "You're lopsided." Then he banged both of his fists down on Vanion's shoulder plates. "There," he said. "That's better."

"Thanks," Vanion said dryly, his knees buckling slightly.

"The honor of the order, my Lord. I don't want you to look as if you were dressed in cheap tin plates."

Vanion decided not to answer that.

The Earl of Lenda was in the room when Sparhawk and Vanion entered.

"There you are, Vanion," King Wargun said. "Now we can get started. What's happening down in Arcium?"

"The situation hasn't changed all that much, your Majesty. The Rendors are still besieging Larium, but the Genidians, Cyrinics, and Alciones are inside the walls along with most of the Arcian army."

"Is the city in any real danger?"

"Hardly. It's built like a mountain. You know the Arcian fondness for stonework. It could probably hold out for twenty years." Vanion looked over at Sparhawk. "I saw an old friend of yours down there," he said. "Martel appears to be in command of the Rendorish army."

"I'd sort of guessed that. I thought I'd nailed his feet to the floor down in Rendor, but apparently he managed to talk his way around Arasham."

"He really didn't have to," King Obler said. "Arasham died a month ago—under highly suspicious circumstances."

"It sounds as if Martel's had his hand in the poison jar again," Kalten said.

"Who's the new spiritual leader in Rendor then?" Sparhawk asked.

"A man named Ulesim," King Obler replied. "I gather he was one of Arasham's disciples."

Sparhawk laughed. "Arasham didn't even know he existed. I've met Ulesim. The man's an idiot. He won't last six months."

"Anyway," Vanion continued, "I have the Pandion order out in the countryside dealing with Rendorish foraging parties. Martel's going to start getting hungry before long. That's about all, your Majesty," he concluded.

"Nice and to the point. Thanks, Vanion. Lenda, what's going on in Cimmura?"

"Things are about the same, your Majesty—except that Annias has gone to Chyrellos."

"And he's probably perched on the foot of the Archprelate's bed like a vulture," Wargun surmised.

"I wouldn't be at all surprised, your Majesty," Lenda agreed. "He left Lycheas in charge. I have a number of people in the palace who work for me, and one of them managed to hear Annias giving Lycheas his final instructions. He ordered Lycheas to withhold the Elenian army from the campaign in Rendor. As soon as Cluvonus dies, the army—and the Church soldiers in Cimmura—are supposed to march on Chyrellos. Annias wants to flood the Holy City with his own men to help intimidate the uncommitted members of the Hierocracy.''

"The Elenian army's mobilized then?''

"Fully, your Majesty. They have an encampment about ten leagues south of Cimmura.''

"We'll probably have to fight them, your Majesty,'' Kalten said. "Annias dismissed most of the old generals and replaced them with men loyal to him.''

Wargun started to swear.

"It may not be quite as serious as it sounds, your Majesty,'' the Earl of Lenda said. "I've made an extended study of the law. In times of religious crisis, the militant orders are empowered to take command of all forces in Western Eosia. Wouldn't you say that an invasion by the Eshandist heresy qualifies as a religious crisis?''

"By God, you're right, Lenda. Is that Elenian law?''

"No, your Majesty. Church law.''

Wargun suddenly howled with laughter. "Oh, that's too rare!'' he roared, pounding on the arm of his chair with one beefy fist. "Annias is trying to become the head of the Church, and we use Church law to spike his wheel. Lenda, you're a genius.''

"I have my moments, your Majesty,'' Lenda replied modestly. "I'd imagine that Preceptor Vanion here can persuade the General Staff to join your forces—particularly in view of the fact that Church law empowers him to resort to extreme measures should any officer refuse to accept his authority in such situations.''

"I'd imagine that a few beheadings might prove instructional to the General Staff,'' Ulath said. "If we shorten four or five generals, the rest will probably fall in line.''

"Quickly,'' Tynian added with a grin.

"Keep your ax good and sharp then, Ulath,'' Wargun said.

"Yes, your Majesty.''

"About the only problem remaining is what we're going to do about Lycheas,'' the Earl of Lenda said.

"I've already decided that,'' Wargun said. "As soon as we get to Cimmura, I'm going to hang him.''

"Splendid notion,'' Lenda said smoothly, "but I think we

might want to consider that just a bit. You *do* know that Annias is the Prince Regent's father, don't you?''

"So Sparhawk tells me, but I don't really care who his father is; I'm going to hang him anyway."

"I'm not really sure just how fond Annias is of his son, but he *did* go to some fairly extreme measures to put him on the Elenian throne. It might just be that the militant orders can use him to some advantage when they get to Chyrellos. An offer to put him to the torture might just persuade Annias to move his troops out of Chyrellos so that the election can proceed without their interference."

"You're taking all the fun out of this, Lenda," Wargun complained. He scowled. "You're probably right, though. All right, when we get to Cimmura, we'll throw him in the dungeon—along with all his toadies. Are you up to taking charge at the palace?"

"If your Majesty wishes," Lenda sighed. "But wouldn't Sparhawk or Vanion be a better choice?"

"Maybe, but I'm going to need them when I get to Arcium. What do you think, Obler?"

"I have absolute confidence in the Earl of Lenda," King Obler replied.

"I'll do my best, your Majesties," Lenda said, "but keep in mind the fact that I'm getting very old."

"You're not as old as I am, my friend," King Obler reminded him, "and nobody's offered to let *me* evade my responsibilities."

"All right, that's settled then," Wargun said. "Now, let's get down to cases. We'll march south to Cimmura, imprison Lycheas, and bully the Elenian General Staff into joining us with their army. We may as well pick up the Church soldiers as well. Then we join Soros and Bergsten on the Arcian border. We march south to Larium, encircle the Rendors, and exterminate the lot of them."

"Isn't that a bit extreme, your Majesty?" Lenda objected.

"No, as a matter of fact, it's not. I want it to be at least ten generations before the Eshandist heresy raises its head again." He grinned crookedly at Sparhawk. "If you serve well and faithfully, my friend, I'll even let you kill Martel."

"I'd appreciate that, your Majesty," Sparhawk replied politely.

"Oh, dear," Sephrenia sighed.

"It needs to be done, little lady," Wargun told her. "Obler, is your army ready to move?"

"They're only awaiting orders, Wargun."

"Good. If you don't have anything else planned, why don't we start for Elenia tomorrow?"

"We might as well." Old King Obler shrugged.

Wargun stood up and stretched, yawning broadly. "Let's all get some sleep then," he said. "We'll be starting early tomorrow."

Later, Sparhawk and his friends gathered in Vanion's room to tell the preceptor in much greater detail what had happened in Lamorkand and Pelosia.

When they had finished, Vanion looked curiously at Flute. "Just exactly what's your part in all this?" he asked her.

"I was sent to help," she replied with a shrug.

"By Styricum?"

"In a manner of speaking."

"And what is this task you have to perform here in Acie?"

"I've already done it, Vanion. Sephrenia and I had to talk with a certain Styric here. We saw him in the street on our way to the palace and took care of it."

"What did you have to say to him that was more important than getting the Bhelliom?"

"We had to prepare Styricum for what is about to happen."

"The invasion by the Rendors, you mean?"

"Oh, that's nothing, Vanion. This is much, much more serious."

Vanion looked at Sparhawk. "You're going to Thalesia then?"

Sparhawk nodded. "Even if I have to walk on water to get there."

"All right, I'll do what I can to help you get out of the city. There's one thing that concerns me, though. If you *all* leave, Wargun's going to notice that you're gone. Sparhawk and one or two others might be able to get away without alerting Wargun, but that's about all."

Flute stepped into the middle of the room and looked them over. "Sparhawk," she said, pointing, "and Kurik. Sephrenia and me—and Talen."

"That's absurd!" Bevier exploded. "Sparhawk's going to need knights with him if he's going to come up against Ghwerig."

"Sparhawk and Kurik can take care of it," she said complacently.

"Isn't it dangerous to take Flute along?" Vanion asked Sparhawk.

"Maybe so, but she's the only one who knows the way to Ghwerig's cave."

"Why Talen?" Kurik said to Flute.

"There's something he has to do in Emsat," she replied.

"I'm sorry, my friends," Sparhawk told the other knights, "but we're more or less committed to doing things her way."

"Are you going to leave now?" Vanion said.

"No, we have to wait for Talen."

"Good. Sephrenia, go get Olven's sword."

"But—"

"Just do it, Sephrenia. Please don't argue with me."

"Yes, dear one." She sighed.

After she had delivered Olven's sword to him, Vanion was so weak he could barely stand.

"You're going to kill yourself doing this, you know," she told him.

"Everybody dies from something. Now then, gentlemen," he said to the knights, "I have a troop of Pandions with me. Those of you who are staying behind should mingle yourselves in among them when we ride out. Lenda and Obler are both quite old. I'll suggest to Wargun that we put them in a carriage and that he ride along with them. That should keep him from being able to count noses. I'll try to keep him occupied." He looked at Sparhawk. "A day or two is probably all I'll be able to manage for you," he apologized.

"That should be enough," Sparhawk said. "Wargun's likely to think that I'm going back to Lake Venne. He'll send any pursuit in that direction."

"The only problem now is getting you out of the palace," Vanion said.

"I'll take care of that," Flute told him.

"How?"

"Maa-gic," she said, comically drawing the word out and wiggling her fingers at him.

He laughed. "How did we ever get along without you?"

She sniffed. "Badly, I'd imagine."

It was about an hour later when Talen slipped into the room.

"Any problems?" Kurik asked him.

"No." Talen shrugged. "I made a few contacts and found us a place to hide."

"Contacts?" Vanion asked him. "With whom?"

"A few thieves, some beggars, and a couple of murderers. They sent me to the man who controls the underside of Acie. He owes Platime a few favors, so when I mentioned Platime's name, he became very helpful."

"You live in a strange world, Talen," Vanion said.

"No stranger than the one you live in, my Lord," Talen said with an extravagant bow.

"That may be entirely true, Sparhawk," Vanion said. "We may all be thieves and brigands when you get right down to it. All right," he said to Talen, "where is this hiding place?"

"I'd rather not say," Talen replied evasively. "You're sort of an official person, and I gave my word."

"There's honor in your profession?"

"Oh yes, my Lord. It's not based on any knightly code, though. It's based on not getting your throat cut."

"You have a very wise son, Kurik," Kalten said.

"You had to go ahead and say it, didn't you, Kalten?" Kurik asked acidly.

"Are you ashamed of me, Father?" Talen asked in a small voice, his face downcast.

Kurik looked at him. "No, Talen," he said, "actually I'm not." He put his burly arm about the boy's shoulders. "This is my son, Talen," he said defiantly, "and if anybody wants to make an issue of it, I'll be more than happy to give him satisfaction, and we can throw out the nonsense about the nobility and the commons not being allowed to fight each other."

"Don't be absurd, Kurik," Tynian said with a broad grin. "Congratulations to you both."

The other knights gathered about the husky squire and his larcenous son, clapping them on the shoulders and adding their congratulations to Tynian's.

Talen looked around at them, his eyes suddenly very wide

and filled with tears at his sudden acknowledgment. Then he fled to Sephrenia, fell to his knees, buried his face in her lap, and wept.

Flute smiled.

CHAPTER
TWENTY-THREE

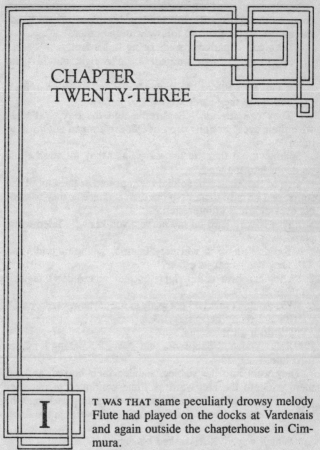

I T WAS THAT same peculiarly drowsy melody
Flute had played on the docks at Vardenais
and again outside the chapterhouse in Cimmura.

"What's she doing now?" Talen whis-
pered to Sparhawk as they all crouched behind the balustrade
of the wide porch at the front of King Obler's palace.

"She's putting Wargun's sentries to sleep," Sparhawk replied. There was no point in extended explanations. "They'll
ignore us as we pass them." Sparhawk wore his mail shirt
and his traveller's cloak.

"Are you sure about that?" Talen sounded dubious.

"I've seen it work a few times before."

Flute stood up and walked to the wide staircase leading

down to the courtyard. Still holding her pipes in one hand, she motioned for them to follow with the other.

"Let's go," Sparhawk said, rising to his feet.

"Sparhawk," Talen warned, "you're right out in plain sight."

"It's all right, Talen. They won't pay any attention to us."

"You mean they can't see us?"

"They can see us," Sephrenia told the boy, "at least with their eyes, but our presence doesn't mean anything to them."

Sparhawk led them to the stairs, and they followed Flute on down into the yard.

One of the Thalesian soldiers was posted at the foot of the stairs, and he gave them no more than a glance as they passed, his eyes dull and uninterested.

"This is very hard on my nerves, you know," Talen whispered.

"You don't have to whisper, Talen," Sephrenia told him.

"They can't hear us either?"

"They can hear us all right, but our voices don't register on them."

"You wouldn't mind if I got ready to run anyhow, would you?"

"It's not really necessary."

"I'll do it all the same."

"Relax, Talen," Sephrenia said. "You're making it harder for Flute."

They went into the stables, saddled their horses, and led them out into the courtyard as Flute continued to play her pipes. Then they walked out through the gate past King Obler's indifferent sentries and King Wargun's patrol in the street outside the palace.

"Which way?" Kurik asked his son.

"That alley just down the street."

"Is this place very far?"

"About halfway across town. Meland doesn't like to get too close to the palace because the streets around here are patrolled."

"Meland?"

"Our host. He controls all the thieves and beggars here in Acie."

"Is he dependable?"

"Of course not, Kurik. He's a thief. He won't betray us

though. I asked for thieves' sanctuary. He's obliged to take us in and hide us from anybody who might come looking for us. If he had refused, he'd have had to answer to Platime at the next meeting of the thieves' council in Chyrellos.''

''There's a whole world out there that we don't know anything about,'' Kurik said to Sparhawk.

''I've noticed,'' Sparhawk replied.

The boy led them through the crooked streets of Acie to a shabby section not too far from the city gates. ''Stay here,'' he said when they reached a seedy-looking tavern. He went inside and emerged a moment later with a ferret-like man. ''He's going to take care of our horses.''

''Watch out for this one, neighbor,'' Sparhawk warned the fellow as he handed him Faran's reins. ''He's playful. Faran, behave yourself.''

Faran flicked his ears irritably as Sparhawk carefully pulled the spear of Aldreas out from under his saddle skirt.

Talen led them into the tavern. It was lighted by smoky tallow candles and had long, scarred tables flanked by rickety-looking benches. There were a number of rough-looking men sitting at the tables. None of them paid any particular attention to Sparhawk and his friends, though their eyes were busy. Talen went to a stairway at the back. ''It's up here,'' he said, pointing up the stairs.

The loft at the top of the stairs was very large, and it looked oddly familiar to Sparhawk. It was sparsely furnished and there were straw pallets on the floor along the walls. It seemed somehow very similar to Platime's cellar back in Cimmura.

Meland was a thin man with an evil-looking scar running down his left cheek. He was sitting at a table with a sheet of paper and an inkpot in front of him. There was a heap of jewelry near his left hand, and he seemed to be cataloguing the pieces.

''Meland,'' Talen said as they approached the table, ''these are the friends I told you about.''

''I thought you said there would be ten of you.'' Meland had a nasal, unpleasant voice.

''The plans have changed. This is Sparhawk. He's the one who's more or less in charge.''

Meland grunted. ''How long do you plan to be here?'' he asked Sparhawk shortly.

"If I can find a ship, only until tomorrow morning."

"You shouldn't have any trouble finding a ship. There are ships from all over western Eosia down at the harbor, Thalesian, Arcian, Elenian, and even a few from Cammoria."

"Are the city gates open at night?"

"Not usually, but there's that army camped outside the walls. The soldiers are going in and out of town, so the gates are open." Meland looked critically at the knight. "If you're going down to the harbor, you'd better not wear that mail—or the sword. Talen says that you'd prefer not to be noticed. The people down there would remember someone dressed the way you are. There are some clothes hanging on those pegs over there. Find something that fits." Meland's tone was abrupt.

"What's the best way to get down to the harbor?"

"Go out the north gate. There's a wagon track that leads down to the water. It branches off the main road on the left about a half mile out of town."

"Thank you, neighbor," Sparhawk said.

Meland grunted and went back to his catalogue.

"Kurik and I are going to go down to the harbor to see about a ship," Sparhawk told Sephrenia. "You'd better stay here with the children."

"As you wish," she said.

Sparhawk found a somewhat shabby blue doublet hanging on one of the pegs that looked as if it might fit. He took off his mail shirt and sword and put it on. Then he pulled on his cloak again.

"Where are all of your people?" Talen was asking Meland.

"It's nighttime," Meland replied. "They're out working—or at least they'd better be."

"Oh, I hadn't thought of that, I guess."

Sparhawk and Kurik went back downstairs to the tavern.

"You want me to get our horses?" Kurik asked.

"No. Let's walk. People pay attention to mounted men."

"All right."

They went out through the city gate and on along the main road until they came to the wagon road Meland had mentioned. Then they walked on down to the harbor.

"Shabby-looking sort of place, isn't it?" Sparhawk noted, looking around at the settlement surrounding the harbor.

"Waterfronts usually are," Kurik said. "Let's ask a few questions." He accosted a passerby who appeared to be a seagoing man. "We be lookin' for a ship as is bound for Thalesia," he said, reverting to the sailor language he had used in Venne. "Tell me, mate, could y' maybe tell us if there be a tavern hereabouts where the ship captains gather?"

"Try the Bell and Anchor," the sailor replied. "It's that way a couple of streets—right near the water."

"Thanks, mate."

Sparhawk and Kurik walked down toward the long wharves jutting out into the dark, garbage-strewn waters of the Gulf of Acie. Kurik suddenly stopped. "Sparhawk," he said, "doesn't there seem to be something familiar about that ship out at the end of this wharf?"

"She does seem to have a familiar rake to her masts, doesn't she?" Sparhawk agreed. "Let's go have a closer look."

They walked a ways out on the wharf. "She's Cammorian," Kurik advised.

"How can you tell?"

"By the rigging and the slant of her masts."

"You don't think—" Then Sparhawk broke off, looking incredulously at the vessel's name painted on her bow. "Well, I'll be," he said. "That's Captain Sorgi's ship. What's he doing all the way up here?"

"Why don't we see if we can find him and ask him? If it's really Sorgi and not just somebody who bought his ship from him, this could solve our problem."

"Provided he plans to sail in the right direction. Let's go find the Bell and Anchor."

"Do you remember all the details of that story you told Sorgi?"

"Enough to get by, I think."

The Bell and Anchor was a tidy, sedate tavern, as befitted a place frequented by ship captains. The taverns visited by common sailors tended to be rowdier and usually showed evidence of hard use. Sparhawk and Kurik entered and stood in the doorway, looking around. "Over there," Kurik said, pointing at a husky man with silver-shot, curly hair drinking with a group of substantial-looking men at a table in the corner. "It's Sorgi, all right."

Sparhawk looked at the man who had conveyed them from

Madel in Cammoria to Cippria in Rendor and nodded his agreement. "Let's drift on over there," he said. "It might be best if he saw us first." They went across the room, doing their best to appear to be only casually looking around.

"Why, strike me blind if it isn't Master Cluff!" Sorgi exclaimed. "What are you doing up here in Deira? I thought you were going to stay down in Rendor until all those cousins got tired of looking for you."

"Why, I believe it's Captain Sorgi," Sparhawk said in mock astonishment to Kurik.

"Join us, Master Cluff," Sorgi invited expansively. "Bring your man as well."

"You're very kind, Captain," Sparhawk murmured, taking a chair at the seamen's table.

"What happened to you, my friend?" Sorgi asked.

Sparhawk put on a mournful expression. "Somehow the cousins tracked me down," he said. "I was lucky enough to see one of them in a street in Cippria before he saw me, and I bolted. I've been on the run ever since."

Sorgi laughed. "Master Cluff here has a bit of a problem," he told his companions. "He made the mistake of paying court to an heiress before he got a look at her face. The lady turned out to be remarkably ugly, and he ran away from her screaming."

"Well, I didn't exactly scream, Captain," Sparhawk said. "I'll admit that my hair stood on end for a week or so, though."

"Anyway," Sorgi continued, grinning broadly, "as it turns out, the lady has a multitude of cousins, and they've been pursuing poor Master Cluff for months now. If they catch him, they're going to drag him back and force him to marry her."

"I think I'd rather kill myself first," Sparhawk said in a mournful tone of voice. "But what are you doing this far north, Captain? I thought you plied the Arcian Strait and the Inner Sea."

"I happened to be in the port of Zenga on the south coast of Cammoria," Sorgi explained, "and I ran across the opportunity to buy a cargo of satins and brocade. There's no market for that sort of merchandise in Rendor. They all wear those ugly black robes, you know. The best market for Cammorian fabrics is in Thalesia. You wouldn't think so, considering the climate, but Thalesian ladies are passionate for satins and brocades. I stand to make a tidy profit on the cargo.''

Sparhawk felt a sudden surge of elation. "You're going to Thalesia then?" he said. "Might you have room for some passengers?"

"Do you want to go to Thalesia, Master Cluff?" Sorgi asked with some surprise.

"I want to go *anywhere*, Captain Sorgi,' Sparhawk told him in a desperate-sounding voice. "I've got a group of those cousins no more than two days behind me. If I can get to Thalesia, maybe I can go up and hide in the mountains."

"I'd be careful, my friend," one of the other captains advised. "There are robbers up in the mountains of Thalesia— not to mention the Trolls."

"I can outrun robbers, and Trolls can't be any uglier than the lady in question," Sparhawk said, feigning a shudder. "What do you say, Captain Sorgi," he pleaded. "Will you help me out of my predicament again?"

"Same price?" Sorgi asked shrewdly.

"Anything," Sparhawk said in apparent desperation.

"Done then, Master Cluff. My ship is at the end of the third wharf down from here. We sail for Emsat with the morning tide."

"I'll be there, Captain Sorgi," Sparhawk promised. "Now, if you'll excuse us, my man and I have to go pack a few things." He rose to his feet and extended his hand to the seaman. "You've saved me again, Captain," he said with genuine gratitude. Then he and Kurik quietly left the tavern.

Kurik was frowning as they went back out into the street. "Do you get the feeling that somebody may be tampering with things?" he asked.

"How do you mean?"

"Isn't it peculiar that we just happened to run across Sorgi again—the one man we can usually count on to help us? And isn't it even more peculiar that he just happens to be going to Thalesia—the one place we really want to go?"

"I think your imagination's getting away with you, Kurik. You heard him. It's perfectly logical that he should be here."

"But at just the right time for us to run across him?"

That was a somewhat more troubling question. "We can ask Flute about it when we get back up to the city," he said.

"You think she might be responsible?"

"Not really, but she's the only one I know of who might have been able to arrange something like this—although I doubt if even *she* could have managed it."

There was, however no chance to speak with Flute when they returned to the loft above the seedy tavern, because a familiar figure sat across the table from Meland. Large and grossly bearded and wearing a nondescript cloak, Platime was busily haggling. "Sparhawk!" the huge man roared his greeting.

Sparhawk stared at him in some astonishment. "What are you doing in Acie, Platime?"

"Several things, actually," Platime said. "Meland and I always trade stolen jewelry. He sells what I steal in Cimmura, and I take what he steals around here back to Cimmura and sell it there. People tend to recognize their own jewelry, and it's not always safe to sell things in the same town where you stole them."

"This piece isn't worth what you're asking for it, Platime," Meland said flatly, holding up a jewel-studded bracelet.

"All right, make me an offer," Platime suggested.

"Another coincidence, Sparhawk?" Kurik asked suspiciously.

"We'll see," Sparhawk said.

"The Earl of Lenda's here in Acie, Sparhawk," Platime said seriously. "He's the closest thing to an honest man on the royal council, and he's attending some kind of conference at the palace. Something's afoot, and I want to know about it. I don't like surprises."

"I can tell you what's going on," Sparhawk told him.

"You can?" Platime looked a little surprised.

"If the price is right." Sparhawk grinned.

"Money?"

"No, a little more than that, I think. I sat in on the conference you mentioned. You know about the war in Arcium, of course?"

"Naturally."

"And what I tell you will go no further?"

Platime motioned Meland away from the table, then looked closely at Sparhawk and grinned. "Only in the way of business, my friend."

This was not a particularly reassuring reply. "You've professed some degree of patriotism in the past," Sparhawk said carefully.

"I have those feelings from time to time," Platime admitted grudgingly. "As long as they don't interfere with honest profit."

"All right, I need your co-operation."

"What have you got in mind?" Platime asked suspiciously.

"My friends and I are seeking to restore Queen Ehlana to her throne."

"You have been for quite some time, Sparhawk, but can that pale little girl really manage a kingdom?"

"I think she can, yes, and I'll be right behind her."

"That gives her a certain edge. What are you going to do about Lycheas the bastard?"

"King Wargun wants to hang him."

"I don't normally approve of hangings; but in the case of Lycheas, I'd make an exception. Do you think I could reach an accommodation with Ehlana?"

"I wouldn't wager any money on it."

Platime grinned. "It was worth a try," he said. "Just tell my Queen that I am her most faithful servant. She and I can work out the details later."

"You're a bad man, Platime."

"I never pretended to be anything else. All right, Sparhawk, what do you need? I'll go along with you—up to a point."

"I need information more than anything. You know Kalten?"

"Your friend? Of course."

"He's at the palace right now. Put on something that makes you look more or less respectable. Go there and ask for him. Make arrangements with him to pass on information. I gather that you have ways to pick up details about most of the things that are going on in the known world?"

"Would you like to know what's going on in the Tamul Empire right now?"

"Not really. I've got enough trouble here in Eosia at the moment. We'll deal with the Daresian continent when the time comes."

"You're ambitious, my friend."

"Not really. For the moment, I just want our Queen back on her throne."

"I'll settle for that," Platime said. "Anything to get rid of Lycheas and Annias."

"We're all working in the same direction then. Talk with Kalten. He can set up ways for you to get information to him, and he'll pass it on to people who can use it."

"You're turning me into a spy, Sparhawk," Platime said in a pained voice.

"It's at least as honorable a profession as thievery."

"I know. The only problem, though, is that I don't know how well it pays. Where are you going from here?"

"We have to go to Thalesia."

"Wargun's own kingdom? After you just ran away from him? Sparhawk, you're either braver or stupider than I thought you were."

"You know that we slipped out of the palace then?"

"Talen told me." Platime thought a moment. "You'll probably make port at Emsat, won't you?"

"That's what our captain says."

"Talen, come here," Platime called.

"What for?" the boy replied flatly.

"Haven't you broken him of that habit yet, Sparhawk?" Platime asked sourly.

"It was only for old times' sake, Platime." Talen grinned.

"Listen carefully," Platime said to the boy. "When you get to Emsat, look up a man named Stragen. He more or less runs things there—the same way I do in Cimmura and Meland does here in Acie. He'll be able to give you whatever help you'll need."

"All right," Talen said.

"You think of everything, don't you, Platime?" Sparhawk said.

"In my business, you sort of have to. People who don't tend to wind up dangling unpleasantly."

They reached the harbor shortly after sunrise the following morning and, after they had seen to the loading of the horses, they went on board.

"You seem to have picked up another retainer, Master Cluff," Captain Sorgi said to Sparhawk when he saw Talen.

"My man's youngest son," Sparhawk replied truthfully.

"Just as an indication of the friendship I bear you, Master

Cluff, there won't be any extra charge for the boy. Speaking of that, why don't we settle up before we set sail?''

Sparhawk sighed and reached for his purse.

There was a good following wind as they sailed out of the Gulf of Acie and around the promontory that lay to the north. Then they entered the Straits of Thalesia and left the land behind. Sparhawk stood on deck talking with Sorgi. "How long do you think it's going to take to get to Emsat?" he asked the curly-haired seaman.

"We'll probably make port by noon tomorrow," Sorgi replied, "if the wind holds. We'll furl sail and rig sea-anchors tonight. I'm not as familiar with these waters as I am with the Inner Sea or the Arcian Strait, so I'd rather not take chances."

"I like prudence in the captain of a ship I'm sailing on," Sparhawk told him. "Oh, and speaking of prudence, do you imagine we might be able to find some secluded cove before we reach Emsat? Towns make me very nervous for some reason."

Sorgi laughed. "You see those cousins around every corner, don't you, Master Cluff? Is that why you're under arms?" Sorgi looked meaningfully at Sparhawk's mail shirt and sword.

"A man in my circumstances can't be too careful."

"We'll find you a cove, Master Cluff. The coast of Thalesia is one long secluded cove. We'll find you a quiet beach and put you ashore so you can sneak north to visit the Trolls without the inconvenience of having cousins dogging your heels."

"I appreciate that, Captain Sorgi."

"You up there!" Sorgi bellowed to one of the sailors aloft, "look lively! You're up there to work, not to daydream!"

Sparhawk walked a ways up the deck and leaned on the rail, idly watching the intensely blue rollers sparkling in the midday sun. Kurik's questions were still troubling him. Had the chance meetings with Sorgi and Platime indeed been co-incidence? Why should they both have been in Acie at pre-cisely the same time that Sparhawk and his friends had made good their escape from the palace? If Flute indeed could tam-per with time, could she also reach out over tremendous dis-tances to draw in people they needed at precisely the right moment? How powerful was she?

Almost as if his thought had summoned her, Flute came up the companionway and looked around. Sparhawk crossed the deck to meet her. "I have a question or two for you," he said.

"I thought you might have."

"Did you have anything to do with bringing both Platime and Sorgi to Acie?"

"Not personally, no."

"But you knew they'd be there?"

"It saves time when you deal with people who already know you, Sparhawk. I made some requests, and certain members of my family arranged the details."

"You keep mentioning your family. Just exactly—"

"What on earth is that?" she exclaimed, pointing off to starboard.

Sparhawk looked. A huge surging was just beneath the surface, and then a great flat tail burst up out of the water and crashed down, sending up a great cloud of spray. "A whale, I think," he said.

"Do fish really get that big?"

"I don't think they're actually fish—at least that's what I've heard."

"He's *singing*!" Flute said, clapping her hands in delight.

"I don't hear anything."

"You're not listening, Sparhawk." She ran forward and leaned out over the bow of the ship.

"Flute!" he shouted. "Be careful!" He rushed to the rail at the bow and took hold of her.

"Stop that," she said. She lifted her pipes to her lips, but a sudden lurch of the ship made her lose her grip on them, and they fell from her hands into the sea. "Oh, bother," she said. Then she made a face. "Oh, well, you'll find out soon enough anyway." Then she lifted her small face. The sound that came from her throat was the sound of those rude shepherd's pipes. Sparhawk was stunned. The pipes had been simply for show. What they had been hearing all along had been the sound of Flute's own voice. Her song soared out over the waves.

The whale rose again and rolled slightly over on one side, his vast eye curious. Flute sang to him, her voice trilling. The enormous creature swam closer, and one of the sailors aloft shouted with alarm, "There be whales here, Captain Sorgi!"

And then there were other whales rising from the deep as if in response to the little girl's song. The ship rocked and bobbed in their surging wake as they gathered about the bow, sending huge clouds of mist from great blowholes in the tops of their heads.

One sailor ran forward with a long boat hook, his eyes filled with panic.

"Oh, don't be silly," Flute told him. "They're only playing."

"Uh—Flute," Sparhawk said in an awed voice, "don't you think you should tell them to go home?" He realized even as he said it just how foolish it sounded. The whales *were* home.

"But I *like* them," she protested. "They're beautiful."

"Yes, I know, but whales don't make very good pets. As soon as we get to Thalesia, I'll buy you a kitten instead. Please, Flute, say good-bye to your whales and make them go away. They're slowing us down."

"Oh." Her face was disappointed. "All right, I guess." She lifted her voice again with a peculiar trilling sound of regret. The whales moved off and then sounded, their vast flukes crashing against the surface of the sea, tearing it to frothy tatters.

Sparhawk glanced around. The sailors were gaping open-mouthed at the little girl. Explanations at this point would be extremely difficult. "Why don't we go back to our cabin and have some lunch?" he suggested.

"All right," she agreed. Then she lifted her arms to him. "You can carry me, if you'd like."

It was the quickest way to get her out from under the awed stares of Sorgi's crew, so he picked her up and carried her to the companionway.

"I really wish you wouldn't wear this," she said, picking at his mail shirt with one small fingernail. "It smells absolutely awful, you know."

"In my business, it's sort of necessary. Protection, you understand."

"There are other ways to protect yourself, Sparhawk, and they're not nearly so offensive."

When they reached the cabin, they found Sephrenia sitting, pale-faced and shaken, with a ceremonial sword in her lap. Kurik, who looked a little wild about the eyes, hovered over her. "It was Sir Gared, Sparhawk," he said quietly. "He walked right straight through the door as if it wasn't even there and gave his sword to Sephrenia.''

Sparhawk felt a sharp wrench of pain. Gared had been a friend. Then he straightened and sighed. If all went well, this would be the last sword Sephrenia would be forced to bear. "Flute," he said, "can you help her to sleep?"

The little girl nodded, her face grave.

Sparhawk lifted Sephrenia in his arms. She seemed to have almost no weight. He carried her to her bunk and gently laid her down. Flute came to the bunk and began to sing. It was a lullaby such as one would sing to a small child. Sephrenia sighed and closed her eyes.

"She'll need to rest," Sparhawk told Flute. "It's going to be a long ride to Ghwerig's cave. Keep her asleep until we reach the coast of Thalesia."

"Of course, dear one."

They reached the Thalesian coast about noon of the following day, and Captain Sorgi hove to in a small cove just to the west of the port city of Emsat.

"You have no idea of how much I appreciate your help, Captain," Sparhawk said to Sorgi as he and the others were preparing to disembark.

"My pleasure, Master Cluff," Sorgi told him. "We bachelors need to stick together in these affairs."

Sparhawk grinned at him.

The little group led their horses down a long gangway and out onto the beach. They mounted as the sailors were carefully maneuvering the ship out of the cove.

"Do you want to go with me into Emsat?" Talen asked. "I have to go talk with Stragen."

"I'd probably better not," Sparhawk said. "Wargun might have had time to get a messenger to Emsat by now, and I'm fairly easy to describe."

"I'll go with him," Kurik volunteered. "We're going to need supplies anyway."

"All right. Let's go back into the woods a ways and set up for the night first, though."

They made camp in a small glade in the forest, and Kurik and Talen rode out about midafternoon.

Sephrenia was wan, and her face was drawn-looking as she sat by the fire cradling Sir Gared's sword.

"This is not going to be easy for you, I'm afraid," Sparhawk said regretfully. "We're going to have to ride fast if we want to reach Ghwerig's cave before he seals it up. Is there any way you could give me Gared's sword?"

She shook her head. "No, dear one. You weren't present in the throne room. Only one of us who was there when we cast the spell can keep Gared's sword."

"I was afraid that might be the case. I guess I'd better see about some supper."

It was about midnight when Kurik and Talen returned.

"Any problems?" Sparhawk asked.

"Nothing worth mentioning." Talen shrugged. "Platime's name opens all kinds of doors. Stragen told us that the countryside north of Emsat is infested with robbers, though. He's going to provide us with an armed escort and spare horses— the horses were my father's idea."

"We can move faster if we change horses every hour or so," Kurik explained. "Stragen's also going to send supplies along with the men who'll be riding with us."

"You see how nice it is to have friends, Sparhawk?" Talen asked impudently.

Sparhawk ignored that. "Are Stragen's men going to come here?" he asked.

"No," Talen replied. "Before sunrise we'll meet them a mile or so up the road that runs north out of Emsat." He looked around. "What's for supper? I'm starving."

CHAPTER
TWENTY-FOUR

THEY RODE OUT at first light, circled through the forest lying to the north of Emsat, and stopped not far from the north road. "I hope this Stragen keeps his word," Kurik muttered to Talen. "I've never been in Thalesia before, and I don't like the notion of riding into hostile country without knowing what's going on."

"We can trust Stragen, Father," Talen replied confidently. "Thalesian thieves have this peculiar sense of honor. It's the Cammorians you have to watch out for. They'd cheat themselves if they could figure out a way to make a profit out of it."

"Sir Knight," a soft voice said from back in the trees.

Sparhawk immediately went for his sword.

"There's no need of that, my Lord," the voice said. "Stragen sent us. There are robbers out there in the foothills, and he told us to get you safely past them.''

"Come out of the shadows then, neighbor," Sparhawk said.

"Neighbor." The man laughed. "I like that. You have a very wide neighborhood, neighbor."

"Most of the world lately," Sparhawk admitted.

"Welcome to Thalesia then, neighbor." The man who rode out of the shadows had pale, flaxen hair. He was clean-shaven and roughly dressed and he carried a brutal-looking pike and had an ax slung to his saddle. "Stragen says you want to go north. We're to accompany you as far as Heid."

"Will that work out?" Sparhawk asked Flute.

"Perfectly," she replied. "We'll be leaving the road a mile or so beyond there."

"You take orders from a child?" the flaxen-haired man asked.

"She knows the way to the place where we're going." Sparhawk shrugged. "Never argue with your guide."

"That's probably true, Sir Sparhawk. My name is Tel—if it makes any difference. I've got a dozen men and spare horses—along with the supplies your man Kurik requested." He rubbed one hand over his face. "This sort of baffles me, Sir Knight," he admitted. "I've never seen Stragen so eager to accommodate a stranger."

"Have you ever heard of Platime?" Talen asked him.

Tel looked at the boy sharply. "The chief down in Cimmura?" he asked.

"That's the one," Talen said. "Stragen owes Platime some favors, and I work for Platime."

"Oh, that explains it, I guess," Tel admitted. "The day's wearing on, Sir Knight," he said to Sparhawk. "Why don't we go to Heid?"

"Why don't we?" Sparhawk agreed.

Tel's men were all dressed in utilitarian Thalesian peasant garb, and they all carried weapons as if they knew how to use them. They were uniformly blond and had the bleak faces of men with little concern for the politer amenities of life.

When the sun came up, they increased their pace. Sparhawk knew that having Tel and his cutthroats along might slow them considerably, but he was grateful for the additional safety they provided for Sephrenia and Flute. He had been more than a little concerned about their vulnerability in the event of an ambush in the mountains.

They passed briefly through farm country, and neat farmsteads stood here and there along the road. An attack was unlikely in such well-populated country. The danger would come when they reached the mountains. They rode hard that day and covered considerable distance. They camped some distance from the road and left again early the following morning.

"I'm starting to feel a little saddle-weary," Kurik admitted as they set out at first light.

"I thought you'd be used to it by now," Sparhawk said.

"Sparhawk, we've been riding almost constantly for the last six months. I think I'm starting to wear out my saddle with my backside."

"I'll buy you a new one."

"So I can have all the entertainment of breaking it in? No thanks."

The country became more rolling, and they could clearly see the dark green mountains to the north now. "If I can make a suggestion, Sparhawk," Tel said, "why don't we make camp before we get up into the hills? There are robbers up there, and a night attack could cause us some inconvenience. I doubt that they'd come down onto this plain, though."

Sparhawk had to admit that Tel was probably right, even though he chafed at the delay. The safety of Sephrenia and Flute was of far more importance than any arbitrary time limits.

They stopped for the night before the sun set and took shelter in a shallow dell. Tel's men were very good at concealment, Sparhawk noticed.

The next morning they waited for daylight before setting out. "All right," Tel said as they rode along at a trot. "I know some of the fellows who hide up here in the mountains, and they've got some favorite places for their ambushes. I'll let you know when we start to get close to those places. The best way to get through them is to ride at a gallop. It takes people hiding in ambush by surprise, and they usually need a minute or two to get on their horses. We can be well past them before they can give chase."

"How many of them are there likely to be?" Sparhawk asked him.

"About twenty or thirty altogether. They'll split up, though. They've got more than one place, and they'll probably want to cover them all."

"Your plan isn't bad, Tel," Sparhawk said, "but I think I've got a better one. We ride through the ambush at a gallop the way you suggested until they start to come after us. Then we turn on them. There's no point in letting them join forces with others farther up on the trail."

"You're a bloodthirsty one, aren't you, Sparhawk?"

"I've got a friend from up here in Thalesia who keeps telling me that you should never leave live enemies behind you."

"He may have a point there."

"How did you learn so much about those fellows up here?"

"I used to be one of them, but I got tired of sleeping out of doors in bad weather. That's when I went to Emsat and started working for Stragen."

"How far is it from here to Heid?"

"About fifty more leagues. We can make it by the end of the week if we hurry along."

"Good. Let's go then."

They rode up into the mountain at a trot, keeping a wary eye on the trees and bushes at the side of the road.

"Just ahead," Tel said quietly. "That's one of their places. The road goes through a gap there."

"Then let's ride," Sparhawk said. He led the way at the gap. They heard a startled shout from the top of the bluff on the left side of the road. A single man stood up there.

"He's there alone," Tel shouted, looking back over his shoulder. "He watches the road for travellers and then lights a fire to signal on up ahead."

"Not this time he won't," one of Tel's men growled, unslinging a longbow from across his back. He stopped his horse and smoothly shot an arrow at the lookout atop the bluff. The lookout doubled over when the arrow took him in the stomach and toppled off the bluff to lie motionless in the dusty road.

"Good shot," Kurik said.

"Not too bad," the archer said modestly.

"Do you think anyone heard him yell?" Sparhawk asked Tel.

"That depends on how close they are. They probably won't know what it meant, but a few of them might ride down here to investigate."

"Let them," the man with the bow said grimly.

"We'd better go a little slowly along here," Tel advised. "It wouldn't do to go around a corner and come face to face with them."

"You're very good at this, Tel," Sparhawk said.

"Practice, Sparhawk, and I know the ground. I lived up here for more than five years. That's why Stragen sent me instead of somebody else. You'd better let me have a look around that bend in the road just ahead." He slipped down off his horse and took his pike. He ran ahead at a crouch; just before he reached the bend, he eased his way into the bushes and disappeared. A moment later he reappeared and made a few obscure gestures.

"Three of them," the man with the bow translated in a muted voice. "They're coming at a trot." He set an arrow to his bowstring and raised the bow.

Sparhawk drew his sword. "Guard Sephrenia," he told Kurik.

The first man around the bend toppled out of his saddle with an arrow in his throat. Sparhawk shook his reins and Faran charged.

The two other men were staring at their fallen companion in blank amazement. Sparhawk cut one of them out of the saddle, and the other turned to flee. Tel, however, stepped out of the bushes and drove his pike at an angle up into the man's body. The man gave a gurgling groan and fell from his horse.

"Get the horses!" Tel barked to his men. "Don't let them get back to where the other brigands are hiding!"

His men galloped after the fleeing horses and brought them back a few minutes later.

"A nice piece of work," Tel said, pulling his pike free of the body lying in the road. "No yelling, and none of them got away." He rolled the body over with his foot. "I know this one," he said. "Those other two must be new. The life expectancy of a highway robber isn't really very good, so Dorga has to find new recruits every so often."

"Dorga?" Sparhawk asked, dismounting.

"He's the chief of this band. I never really cared for him very much. He's a little too self-important."

"Let's drag these into the bushes," Sparhawk said. "I'd rather not have the little girl see them."

"All right."

After the bodies had been concealed, Sparhawk stepped back around the bend and signalled Sephrenia and Kurik to come on ahead.

They rode on carefully.

"This may be much easier than I'd thought," Tel said. "I think they're splitting up into very small groups so they can watch more of the road. We should go into the woods a ways on the left side of the road just ahead. There's a rockslide coming down on the right side, and Dorga usually has a few archers there. Once we get past them, I'll send a few men around behind them to deal with them."

"Is that really necessary?" Sephrenia asked.

"I'm just following Sir Sparhawk's advice, lady," Tel said. "Don't leave live enemies behind you—particularly not ones armed with bows. I don't really need an arrow in my back, and neither do you."

They rode into the woods before they reached the rockslide and continued at a very careful walk. One of Tel's men crept out to the edge of the trees and rejoined them a few minutes later. "Two of them," he reported quietly. "They're about fifty paces up the slide."

"Take a couple of men," Tel instructed. "There's cover about two hundred paces up ahead. You'll be able to get across the road there. Work your way up along the edge of the slide and get behind them. Try not to let them make any noise."

The stubble-faced blond cutthroat grinned, signalled to two of his companions, and rode on ahead.

"I'd forgotten how much fun this is," Tel said. "At least in good weather. It's miserable in the winter, though."

They had ridden perhaps half a mile past the slide when the three ruffians caught up with them.

"Any problems?" Tel asked.

"They were half-asleep." One of the men chuckled. "They're all the way asleep now."

"Good." Tel looked around. "We can gallop for a ways

now, Sparhawk. The roadsides are too open for ambushes for the next few miles.''

They galloped until almost noon, when they reached the crest of the ridge where Tel signalled for a halt. ''The next part might be tricky,'' he told Sparhawk. ''The road runs down a ravine, and there's no way for us to work our way around it from this end. The place is one of Dorga's favorites, so he's likely to have quite a few men there. I'd say that the best thing for us to do is to go through it at a dead run. An archer has a little trouble shooting downhill at moving targets—at least I always did.''

''How far is it until we come out of the ravine?''

''About a mile.''

''And we'll be in plain sight all the way?''

''More or less, yes.''

''We don't have much choice, though, do we?''

''Not unless you want to wait until dark, and that would make the rest of the road to Heid twice as dangerous.''

''All right,'' Sparhawk decided. ''You know the country, so you lead the way.'' He unhooked his shield from his saddlehorn and strapped it on his arm. ''Sephrenia, you ride right beside me. I can cover you and Flute with the shield. Lead on, Tel.''

Their plunging run down the ravine took the concealed brigands by surprise. Sparhawk heard a few startled shouts from the top of the ravine, and a single arrow fell far behind them.

''Spread out!'' Tel shouted. ''Don't ride all clustered together!''

They plunged on. More arrows came whizzing down into the ravine, dropping among them now. One arrow shattered on the shield that Sparhawk was holding protectively over Sephrenia and Flute. He heard a muffled cry and glanced back. One of Tel's men was swaying in his saddle, his eyes filled with pain. Then he slumped over and fell heavily to the ground.

''Keep going!'' Tel ordered. ''We're almost clear now!''

The road ahead came out of the ravine, passed through a stretch of trees, and then curved along the side of a cliff that dropped steeply down into a gorge.

A few more arrows arced down from the top of the ravine, but they were falling far behind now.

They galloped through the stretch of trees and on out along the side of the cliff. "Keep going!" Tel commanded again. "Let them think we're going to run all the way through here."

They galloped on along the face of the cliff. Then the wide ledge upon which the road was built bent sharply inward to the point where the cliff face ended and the road ran steeply down into the forest again. Tel reined in his panting horse. "This looks like a good place," he said. "The road narrows a little ways back there, so they'll only be able to come at us a couple at a time."

"You really think they'll try to follow us?" Kurik asked.

"I know Dorga. He may not know exactly who we are, but he definitely doesn't want us to get to the authorities in Heid. Dorga's very nervous about the notion of having large groups of the sheriff's men sweeping though these mountains. They have a very stout gallows in Heid."

"Is that forest down there safe?" Sparhawk asked, pointing down the road.

Tel nodded. "The brush is too thick to make ambushes feasible. That ravine was the last stretch that's really dangerous on this side of the mountains."

"Sephrenia," Sparhawk said, "ride on down there. Kurik, you go with her."

Kurik's face showed that he was about to protest, but he said nothing. He led Sephrenia and the children on down the road toward the safety of the forest.

"They'll come fast," Tel said. "We went past them at a dead run, and they'll be trying to catch up." He looked at the ruffian with a longbow. "How fast can you shoot that thing?" he asked.

"I can have three arrows in the air at the same time." The fellow shrugged.

"Try for four. It doesn't matter if you hit the horses. They'll fall off the edge of the cliff and take their riders with them. Get as many as you can, and then the rest of us will charge. Does that sound all right, Sparhawk?"

"It's workable," Sparhawk agreed. He shifted the shield on his left arm and then drew his sword.

Then they heard the clatter of horses' hooves coming fast along the rocky ledge on the other side of the sharp curve. Tel's archer climbed down from his horse and hung his quiver of arrows on a stunted tree at the roadside where they would be close at hand. "These are going to cost you a quarter crown apiece, Tel," he said calmly, drawing an arrow from the quiver and setting it to his bowstring. "Good arrows are expensive."

"Take your bill to Stragen," Tel suggested.

"Stragen pays very slowly. I'd rather collect from you and let you argue with him."

"All right." Tel's tone was slightly sulky.

"Here they come," one of the other cutthroats said without any particular excitement.

The first two brigands to come around the curve probably didn't even see them. Tel's laconic archer was at least as good as he had claimed to be. The two men fell from their saddles, one at the side of the road and the other vanishing into the gorge. Their horses ran on a few yards and then pulled up when they saw Tel's mounted men blocking the road.

The archer missed one of the next pair that came around the sharp curve. "He ducked," he said. "Let's see him try to get out of the way of this one." He pulled his bow and shot again, and his arrow took the fellow in the forehead. The man tumbled over backward and lay in the road kicking.

Then the brigands came around the curve in a cluster. The archer loosed several arrows into their midst. "You'd better go now, Tel," he said. "They're coming on a little too fast."

"Let's ride!" Tel shouted, settling his pike under his arm in a manner curiously reminiscent of that used by armored knights. Tel's men had a peculiar assortment of weapons, but they handled them in a professional manner.

Because Faran was by far the strongest and fastest horse they had, Sparhawk outdistanced the others in the fifty-pace intervening stretch of road. He crashed into the center of the startled group of men, swinging his sword to the right and left in broad overhand strokes. The men he was attacking wore no mail to protect them, and so Sparhawk's blade bit deep into them. A couple of them feebly tried to hold rusty swords up to ward off his ruthless blows, but Sparhawk was a trained swordsman who could alter his point of aim even in midswing, and the two fell howling into the road, clutching at the stumps of missing right hands.

A red-bearded man had been riding at the back of the ambushers. He turned to flee, but Tel plunged past Sparhawk, his blond hair flying, his pike lowered, and the two disappeared around the curve.

Tel's men followed along behind Sparhawk, cleaning up with brutal efficiency.

Sparhawk trotted Faran around the curve. Tel, it appeared, had picked the red-bearded man out of the saddle with his pike, and the fellow lay writhing on the road with the pike protruding from his back. Tel dismounted and squatted beside the mortally wounded man. "It didn't turn out so well, did it, Dorga?" he said in an almost friendly tone. "I told you a long time ago that waylaying travellers was a risky business." Then he pulled the pike out of his former chieftain's back and calmly kicked him off the edge of the cliff. Dorga's despairing shriek faded down into the gorge.

"Well," Tel said to Sparhawk, "I guess that takes care of all this. Let's go on down. It's still some distance to Heid."

Tel's men were disposing of the bodies of the dead and wounded ambushers by casually throwing them into the gorge.

"It's safe now," Tel told them. "Some of you stay here and round up those people's horses. We ought to be able to get a good price for them. The rest of you, come with us. Coming, Sparhawk?" He led the way on down the road.

The days seemed to drag on as they moved through the unpopulated mountains of central Thalesia. At one point, Sparhawk reined Faran back to ride beside Sephrenia and Flute. "To me it seems as if we've been out here on this road for five days at least," he said to the little girl. "How long has it really been?"

She smiled and raised two fingers.

"You're playing with time again, aren't you?" he accused.

"Of course," she said. "You didn't buy me that kitten the way you promised you would, so I have to play with something."

He gave up at that point. Nothing in the world was more immutable than the rising and setting of the sun, but Flute seemed able to alter those events at will. Sparhawk had seen Bevier's consternation when she had patiently explained the inexplicable to him. He decided that he did not wish to experience that personally.

It seemed to be several days later—though Sparhawk would not have taken an oath to that effect—when, at sunset, the flaxen-haired Tel pulled his horse in beside Faran. "That smoke down there is coming from the chimneys at Heid," he said. "My men and I'll be turning back here. I believe there's still a price on my head in Heid. It's all a misunderstanding, of course, but explanations are tiresome—particularly when you're standing on a ladder with a noose around your neck."

"Flute," Sparhawk said back over his shoulder, "has Talen done what he came here to do?"

"Yes."

"I sort of thought so. Tel, would you do me a favor and take the boy back to Stragen? We'll pick him up on our way back. Tie him very tightly and loop a rope about his ankles and under his horse's belly. Jump him from behind and be careful, he's got a knife in his belt."

"There's a reason, I suppose," Tel said.

Sparhawk nodded. "Where we're going is very dangerous. The boy's father and I would rather not expose him to that."

"And the little girl?"

"She can take care of herself—probably better than any of the rest of us."

"You know something, Sparhawk," Tel said skeptically, "when I was a boy, I always wanted to become a Church Knight. Now I'm glad I didn't. You people don't make any sense at all."

"It's probably all the praying," Sparhawk told him. "It tends to make a man a little vague."

"Good luck, Sparhawk," Tel said shortly. Then he and two of his men roughly jerked Talen from his saddle, disarmed him, and tied him on the back of his horse. The names Talen called Sparhawk as he and his captors rode off to the south were wide-ranging and, for the most part, very unflattering.

"She doesn't really understand all those words, does she?" Sparhawk asked Sephrenia, looking meaningfully at Flute.

"Will you stop talking as if I weren't here?" the little girl snapped. "Yes, as a matter of fact, I do know what the words mean, but Elene is such a puny language to swear in. Styric is more satisfying, but if you really want to curse, try Troll."

"You speak Troll?" He was surprised.

"Of course. Doesn't everyone? There's no point in going into Heid. It's a depressing place—all mud and rotting logs and mildewed thatching. Circle it to the west, and we'll find the valley we want to follow."

They bypassed Heid and moved up into steeper mountains. Flute watched intently and finally pointed one finger. "There," she said. "We turn left here."

They stopped at the entrance to the valley and peered with some dismay at the track to which she had directed them. It was a path more than a road, and it seemed to wander quite a bit.

"It doesn't look too promising," Sparhawk said dubiously, "and it doesn't look as if anybody's been on it for years."

"People don't use it," Flute told him. "it's a game trail— sort of."

"What kind of game?"

"Look there." She pointed.

It was a boulder with one flat side, and an image had been crudely chiselled into it. The image looked very old and weathered, and it was hideous.

"What's that?" Sparhawk asked.

"It's a warning," she replied calmly. "That's a picture of a Troll."

"You're taking us into Troll country?" he asked in alarm.

"Sparhawk, Ghwerig's a Troll. Where else do you think he'd live?"

"Isn't there any other way to get to his cave?"

"No, there isn't. I can frighten off any Trolls we happen to run across, and the Ogres don't come out in the daytime, so they shouldn't be any problem."

"Ogres, too?"

"Of course. They always live in the same country with Trolls. Everybody knows that."

"I didn't."

"Well, now you do. We're wasting time, Sparhawk."

"We'll have to go in single file," the knight told Kurik and Sephrenia. "Stay as close behind me as you can. Let's not get spread out." He started up the trail at a trot with the spear of Aldreas in his hand.

The valley to which Flute had led them was narrow and gloomy. The steep walls were covered with tall fir trees so dark as to look nearly black, and the sides of the valley were so high that the sun seldom shone into this murky place. A mountain river rushed down the center of the narrow gap, roaring and foaming. "This is worse than the road to Ghasek," Kurik shouted over the noise of the river.

"Tell him to be still," Flute told Sparhawk. "Trolls have very sharp ears."

Sparhawk turned in his saddle and laid a finger across his lips. Kurik nodded.

There seemed to be an inordinate number of dead white snags dotting the dark forest that rose steeply on either side. Sparhawk leaned forward and put his lips close to Flute's ear. "What's killing the trees?" he asked.

"Ogres come out at night and gnaw on the bark," she said. "Eventually the tree dies."

"I thought Ogres were meat eaters."

"Ogres eat anything. Can't you go any faster?"

"Not through here I can't. This is a very bad trail. Does it get any better on up ahead?"

"After we go up out of this valley, we'll come to a flat place in the mountains."

"A plateau?"

"Whatever you want to call it. There are a few hills, but we can go around those. It's all covered with grass."

"We'll be able to make better time there. Does the plateau stretch all the way to Ghwerig's cave?"

"Not quite. After we cross that, we'll have to go up into the rocks."

"Who brought you all the way up here? You said you'd been here before."

"I came alone. Somebody who knew the way told me how to get to the cave."

"Why would you want to?"

"I had something to do there. Do we really have to talk so much? I'm trying to listen for Trolls."

"Sorry."

"Hush, Sparhawk." She put her finger to his lips.

It was a day later when they reached the plateau. As Flute had told them, it was a vast, rolling grassland with snow-covered peaks lining the horizon on all sides.

"How long is it going to take us to get across this?" Sparhawk asked.

"I'm not sure," Flute replied. "The last time I was here I was on foot. The horses should be able to go much faster."

"You were up here alone and on foot with Trolls and Ogres about?" he asked incredulously.

"I didn't see any of those. There was a young bear that

followed me for a few days, though. I think he was only curious, but I got tired of having him behind me, so I made him go away."

Sparhawk decided not to ask her any more questions. The answers were far too disturbing.

The high grassland seemed interminable. They rode for hours, but the skyline did not appear to change. The sun sank low above the snowy peaks, and they made their camp in a small clump of stunted pines.

"It's big country up here," Kurik said, looking around. He pulled his cloak closer about him. "Cold too, once the sun goes down. Now I can see why most Thalesians wear fur."

They hobbled the horses to keep them from straying and built up the fire.

"There's no real danger here in this meadow," Flute assured them. "Trolls and Ogres like to stay in the forest. The hunting's easier for them when they can hide behind trees."

The next morning dawned cloudy, and a chilly wind swept down from the mountain peaks, bending the tall grass in long waves. They rode hard that day, and by evening they had reached the foot of the peaks that towered white above them. "We can't make any fire tonight," Flute said. "Ghwerig may be watching."

"Are we that close?" Sparhawk asked.

"You see that ravine just ahead?"

"Yes."

"Ghwerig's cave is at the upper end of it."

"Why didn't we just go on up there, then?"

"That wouldn't have been a good idea. You can't sneak up on a Troll at night. We'll wait until the sun's well up tomorrow before we start out. Trolls usually doze in the daytime. They don't actually ever really sleep, but they're a little less alert when the sun's out."

"You seem to know a great deal about them."

"It's not too hard to find things out—if you know the right people to ask. Make Sephrenia some tea and some hot soup. Tomorrow's likely to be very difficult for her, and she'll need all her strength."

"It's a little hard to make hot soup without a fire."

"Oh, Sparhawk, I know that. I'm small, but I'm not stupid. Heap up a pile of rocks in front of the tent. I'll take care of the rest.''

Grumbling to himself, he did as she directed.

"Get back from it," she said. "I don't want to burn you."

"Burn? How?"

She began to sing softly, and then she made a brief gesture with one small hand. Sparhawk immediately felt the heat radiating out from his pile of rocks.

"That's a useful spell," he said admiringly.

"Start cooking, Sparhawk. I can't keep the rocks hot all night."

It was very strange, Sparhawk thought as he set Sephrenia's teakettle up against one of the heated rocks. Somehow in the past weeks, he had almost begun to stop thinking of Flute as a child. Her tone and manner were adult, and she ordered him around like a lackey. Even more surprising was the fact that he automatically obeyed her. Sephrenia was right, he decided. This little girl was in all probability one of the most powerful magicians in all of Styricum. A disturbing question came to him. Just how old *was* Flute anyway? Could Styric magicians control or modify their ages? He knew that neither Sephrenia nor Flute would answer those questions, so he busied himself with cooking and tried not to think about it.

They awoke at dawn, but Flute insisted that they wait until midmorning before they attempted to ascend the ravine. She also instructed them to leave the horses at the camp, since the sound of their hoofs on the rocks might alert the sharp-eared Troll lurking inside the cave.

The ravine was narrow with sheer sides, and it was filled with dense shadows. The four of them moved slowly up its rocky floor, placing their feet carefully to avoid dislodging any loose stones. They spoke but rarely and then only in whispers. Sparhawk carried the ancient spear. For some reason it seemed right.

The climb grew steeper, and they were forced to clamber over rounded boulders now in order to continue their ascent. As they neared the top, Flute motioned them to a halt and crept on ahead a few yards. Then she came back. "He's inside," she whispered, "and he's already started his enchantments."

"Is the cave mouth blocked?" Sparhawk whispered back.

"In a manner of speaking. When we get up there, you won't be able to see it. He's created an illusion to make it look as if the mouth of the cave is just a part of the cliff face. The illusion is solid enough so that we won't be able just to walk through it. You'll need to use the spear to break though." She whispered for a moment to Sephrenia, and the small woman nodded. "All right, then," Flute said, taking a deep breath, "let's go."

They climbed up the last few yards and entered a bleak, unwholesome-looking basin choked with brambles and dead white snags. On one side of the basin there was a steep overhanging cliff that did not appear to have any openings in it.

"There it is," Flute whispered.

"Are you sure this is the right place?" Kurik murmured. "It looks like solid rock."

"This is the place," she replied. "Ghwerig's hiding the entrance." She led the way along a scarcely defined path to the face of the cliff. "It's right here," she said softly, laying one small hand on the rock. "Now, this is what we're going to do. Sephrenia and I are going to cast a spell. When we release it, it's going to pour into you, Sparhawk. You'll feel very strange for a moment, and then you'll feel the power starting to build up inside you. At the right moment, I'll tell you what to do." She began to sing very softly, and Sephrenia spoke in Styric almost under her breath. Then, in unison, they both gestured at Sparhawk.

His eyes went suddenly dim, and he almost fell. He felt very weak, and the spear he held in this left hand seemed almost too heavy to bear. Then, just as quickly, it seemed to have no weight at all. He felt his shoulders surging with the force of the spell.

"Now," Flute said to him. "Point the spear at the face of the cliff."

He lifted his arm and did as she had told him.

"Walk forward until the spear touches the wall."

He took two steps and felt the spear point touch the unyielding rock.

"Release the power—*through* the spear."

He concentrated, gathering the power within him. The ring on his left hand seemed to throb. Then he sent the power along the shaft of the spear into the broad blade.

The seemingly solid rock in front of him wavered; then it was gone, revealing an irregularly shaped opening.

"And there it is," Flute said in a triumphant whisper, "Ghwerig's cave. Now let's go find him."

CHAPTER TWENTY-FIVE

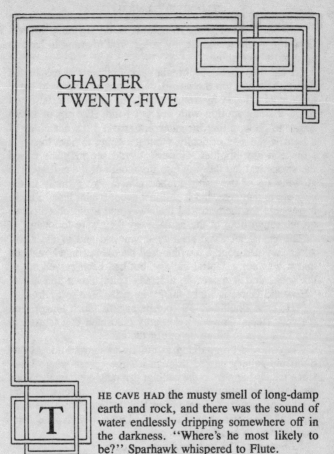

T HE CAVE HAD the musty smell of long-damp earth and rock, and there was the sound of water endlessly dripping somewhere off in the darkness. "Where's he most likely to be?" Sparhawk whispered to Flute.

"We'll start in his treasure chamber," she replied. "He likes to look at his hoard. It's down there." She pointed at the opening of a passageway.

"It's completely dark back in there," he said dubiously.

"I'll take care of that," Sephrenia told him.

"But quietly," Flute cautioned. "We don't know exactly where Ghwerig is, and he can hear and feel magic." She looked closely at Sephrenia. "Are you all right?" she asked.

"It's not as bad as it was," Sephrenia replied, shifting Sir Gared's sword to her right hand.

"Good. I'm not going to be able to do anything in here. Ghwerig would recognize my voice. You're going to have to do almost everything."

"I can manage," Sephrenia said, but her voice sounded weary. She held up the sword. "As long as I have to carry this anyway, I may as well use it." She muttered briefly and made a small motion with her left hand. The tip of sword began to glow, a tiny incandescent spark. "It's not much of a light," she said critically, "but it's going to have to do. If I made it any brighter, Ghwerig would see it." She raised the sword and led the way into the mouth of the gallery. The glowing tip of the sword looked almost like a firefly in the oppressive darkness, but it cast just enough faint light to make it possible for them to find their way and avoid obstructions on the rough floor of the passageway they were following.

The passage curved steadily downward and to the right. After they had gone a few hundred paces, Sparhawk realized that it was not a natural gallery, but had been carved out of the rock, and it moved in a steady spiral down and down. "How did Ghwerig make this?" he whispered to Flute.

"He used Bhelliom. The old passage is much longer, and it's very steep. Ghwerig's so badly deformed that it used to take him days to climb up out of the cave."

They moved on, walking as quietly as they could. At one point the gallery passed through a large cavern where limestone icicles hung from the ceiling, dripping continually. Then the passage continued on into the rock. Occasionally, their faint light disturbed a colony of bats hanging from the ceiling, and the creatures chittered shrilly as they flapped frantically away in huge, dark clouds.

"I *hate* bats," Kurik said with an oath.

"They won't hurt you," Flute whispered. "A bat will never run into you, not even in total darkness."

"Are their eyes that good?"

"No, but their ears are."

"Do you know *everything*?" Kurik's whisper sounded a little grumpy.

"Not yet," she said quietly, "but I'm working on that. Do you have anything to eat? I'm a little hungry for some reason."

"Some dried beef," Kurik replied, reaching inside the tunic that covered his black leather vest. "It's very salty, though."

"There's plenty of water in this cave." She took the chunk of leather-hard beef he offered and bit into it. "It *is* a little salty, isn't it?" she admitted, swallowing hard.

They moved on. Then they saw a light coming from somewhere ahead, faint at first but growing steadily stronger as they moved on down the spiral gallery. "His treasure cave is just ahead," Flute whispered. "Let me have a look." She crept on ahead and then returned. "He's there," she said, her face breaking into a smile.

"Is he making that light?" Kurik whispered.

"No. It comes down from the surface. There's a stream that drops down into the cavern. It catches the sunlight at certain times of the day." She was speaking in a normal tone now. "The sound of the waterfall will muffle our voices. We still have to be careful, though. His eyes will catch any movement." She spoke briefly to Sephrenia, and the small Styric woman nodded. She reached up and extinguished the spark at the tip of the sword between two fingers. Then she began to weave an incantation.

"What's she doing?" Sparhawk asked Flute.

"Ghwerig's talking to himself," she replied, "and it might just be that he'll say something useful to us. He's speaking in the language of the Trolls, so Sephrenia's making it possible for us to understand him."

"You mean that she's going to make him speak in Elene?"

"No. The spell isn't directed at him." She smiled that impish little smile of hers. "You're learning many things, Sparhawk. Now you'll understand the language of the Trolls— for a time at least."

Sephrenia released the spell, and quite suddenly Sparhawk could hear much more than he had during their long descent through the spiralling gallery. The rushing sound of the waterfall dropping into the cavern ahead became almost a roar, and Ghwerig's rasping mutter came clearly over it.

"We'll wait here for a time," Flute told them. "Ghwerig's an outcast, so he talks to himself most of the time, and he says whatever is crossing his mind. We can find out a great deal by eavesdropping. Oh, by the way, he has Sarak's crown, and Bhelliom's still attached to it."

Sparhawk felt a sudden rush of excitement. The thing he

had sought for so long was no more than a few hundred paces away. "What's he doing?" he asked Flute.

"He's sitting at the edge of the chasm that the waterfall has carved out of the rock. All his treasures are piled up around him. He's cleaning the peat stains off of Bhelliom with his tongue. That's why we can't understand him at the moment. Let's move a little closer, but stay back from the mouth of the gallery."

They crept on down toward the light and stopped a few yards from the opening. The reflected light from the waterfall shimmered and seemed to waver liquidly. It was peculiarly like a rainbow.

"Stealers! Thieves!" The voice was harsh, far harsher than any Elenian or Styric throat could have produced. "Dirty. She all dirty." There was more of the slobbering sound as the Troll-Dwarf licked at his treasure. "Stealers all dead now," Ghwerig chortled hideously. "All dead. Ghwerig not dead, and his rose come home at last."

"He sounds as if he's mad," Kurik muttered.

"He always has been," Flute told him. "His mind's as twisted as his body."

"Talk to Ghwerig, blue rose!" the unseen monstrosity commanded. Then he howled out a hideous oath directed at the Styric Goddess Aphrael. "Bring back rings! Bring back rings! Bhelliom not talk to Ghwerig if Ghwerig not got rings!" There was a blubbering sound, and Sparhawk realized with revulsion that the beast was crying. "Lonely," the Troll sobbed. "Ghwerig so lonely!"

Sparhawk felt a wrench of almost unbearable pity for the misshapen dwarf.

"Don't do that," Flute said sharply. "It will weaken you when you face him. You're our only hope now, Sparhawk, and your heart must be like stone."

Then Ghwerig spoke for a time in terms so vile that there were no counterparts in the Elenian language.

"He's invoking the Troll-Gods," Flute explained quietly. She cocked her head. "Listen," she said sharply. "The Troll-Gods are answering him."

The muted roar of the waterfall seemed to change tone, becoming deeper, more resonant.

"We'll have to kill him very soon," the little girl said in a chillingly matter-of-fact tone. "He still has some fragments of the original sapphire left in his workshop. The Troll-Gods instructed him to make new rings. Then they'll infuse them with the force to unlock the power of Bhelliom. He'll be able to destroy us at that point.''

Then Ghwerig chuckled hideously. ''Ghwerig beat you, Azash. Azash a God, but Ghwerig beat him. Azash not ever see Bhelliom now.''

''Can Azash possibly hear him?'' Sparhawk asked.

''Probably,'' Sephrenia said calmly. ''Azash knows the sound of his own name. He listens when somebody says something to him.''

''Man-things swim in lake to find Bhelliom,'' Ghwerig rambled on. ''Bug-thing belong Azash watch from weeds and see them. Man-things go away. Bug-thing bring man-things with no minds. Man-things swim in water. Many drown. One man-thing find Bhelliom. Ghwerig kill man-thing and take blue rose. Azash want Bhelliom? Azash come seek Ghwerig. Azash cook in Troll-God fire. Ghwerig never eat God-meat before. Ghwerig wonder how God-meat taste.''

Deep within the earth there was a rumbling sound, and the floor of the cave seemed to shudder.

''Azash definitely heard him,'' Sephrenia said. ''You almost have to admire that twisted creature out there. No one has ever thrown that kind of insult into the face of one of the Elder Gods.''

''Azash mad at Ghwerig?'' the Troll was saying. ''Or maybe-so Azash shake from fear. Ghwerig have Bhelliom now. Soon make rings. Ghwerig not need Troll-Gods then. Cook Azash in Bhelliom fire. Cook slow so juice not burn away. Ghwerig eat Azash. Who is pray to Azash when Azash deep in Ghwerig's belly?''

The rumble this time was accompanied by sharp cracking sounds as rocks deep in the earth shattered.

''He's sticking his neck out, wouldn't you say?'' Kurik said in a strained voice. ''Azash isn't the sort you want to play with.''

''The Troll-Gods are protecting Ghwerig,'' Sephrenia replied. ''Not even Azash would risk a confrontation with them.''

''Stealers! All stealers!'' the Troll howled. ''Aphrael steal rings! Adian-of-Thalesia steal Bhelliom! Now Azash and

Sparhawk-from-Elenia try to steal her from Ghwerig again! Talk to Ghwerig, blue rose! Ghwerig lonely!"

"How did he find out about me?" Sparhawk was startled by the breadth of the Troll-Dwarf's knowledge.

"The Troll-Gods are old and very wise," Sephrenia replied. "There's very little that happens in the world that they don't know, and they'll pass it on to those who serve them—for a price."

"What sort of price would satisfy a God?"

"Pray that you never have to know, dear one," she said with a shudder.

"Take Ghwerig ten years to carve one petal here, blue rose. Ghwerig love blue rose. Why she not talk to Ghwerig?" He mumbled inaudibly for a time. "Rings. Ghwerig make rings so Bhelliom speak again. Burn Azash in Bhelliom fire. Burn Sparhawk in Bhelliom fire. Burn Aphrael in Bhelliom fire. All burn. All burn. Then Ghwerig eat."

"I think it's time for us to get to it," Sparhawk said grimly. "I definitely don't want him getting into his workshop." He reached for his sword.

"Use the spear," Flute told him. "He can grab your sword out of your hand, but the spear has enough power to hold him off. Please, my noble father, try to stay alive. I need you."

"I'm doing my very best," he told her.

"Father?" Kurik asked in a tone of surprise.

"It's a Styric form of address," Sephrenia said rather quickly, throwing a look at Flute. "It has to do with respect—and love."

At that point Sparhawk did something he had seldom done before. He set his palms together in front of his chest and bowed to this strange Styric child.

Flute clasped her hands together in delight, then hurled herself into his arms and kissed him soundly with her rosebud little mouth. "Father," she said. For some reason, Sparhawk felt profoundly embarrassed. Flute's kiss was not that of a little girl.

"How hard is a Troll's head?" Kurik asked Flute gruffly, obviously as disturbed as Sparhawk by the little girl's open display of affection that seemed far beyond her years. He was shaking out his brutal chain mace.

"Very, very hard," she told him.

"We've heard that he's deformed," Kurik continued. "How good are his legs?"

"Weak. It's all he can do to stand."

"All right then, Sparhawk," Kurik said in a professional tone. "I'll edge around to the side of him and whip him across the knees, hips, and ankles with this." He swung his mace whistling through the air. "If I can put him down, shove the spear into his guts and then I'll try to brain him."

"*Must* you be so graphic, Kurik?" Sephrenia protested in a sick voice.

"This is business, little mother," Sparhawk told her. "We have to know exactly what we're going to do, so don't interfere. All right, Kurik, let's go." Quite deliberately he walked to the mouth of the gallery and stepped out into the cavern, making no attempt to conceal himself.

The cavern was a place of wonder. Its roof was lost in purple shadow, and the seething waterfall plunged in glowing, golden mist into an unimaginably deep chasm from which the hollow roar of falling water echoed up in endless babble. The walls, stretching out as far as the eye could reach, glittered with flecks and veins of gold, and gems more precious than the ransom of kings sparkled in the shifting, rainbow-hued light.

The misshapen Troll-Dwarf, shaggy and grotesque, squatted at the edge of the chasm. Piled around him were lumps and chunks of pure gold and heaps of gems of every hue. In his right hand Ghwerig held the stained gold crown of King Sarak, and surmounting that crown was Bhelliom, the sapphire rose. The jewel seemed to glow as it caught and reflected the light that came tumbling down with the falling water. Sparhawk looked for the first time at the most precious object on earth, and for a moment a kind of wonder almost overcame him. Then he stepped forward, the ancient battle spear held low in his left hand. He wasn't sure if Sephrenia's spell would make it possible for the grotesque Troll to understand him, but he felt a peculiar moral compunction to speak. Simply to destroy this deformed monstrosity without a word was not in Sparhawk's nature. "I have come for Bhelliom," he said. "I am not Adian, King of Thalesia, so I will not try to trick you. I will take what I want from you by main force. Defend yourself if you can." It was as close as Sparhawk could come to a formal challenge under the circumstances.

Ghwerig came to his feet, his twisted body hideous, and his flat lips peeled back from his yellow fangs in a snarl of hatred. "You not take Ghwerig's Bhelliom from him, Sparhawk-from-Elenia. Ghwerig kill first. Here you die, and Ghwerig eat—not even pale Elene God save Sparhawk now."

"That hasn't been decided yet," Sparhawk replied coolly. "I need the use of Bhelliom for a time, and then I will destroy it to keep it out of the hands of Azash. Surrender it up to me or die."

Ghwerig's laughter was hideous. "Ghwerig die? Ghwerig immortal, Sparhawk-from-Elenia. Man-thing cannot kill."

"That also hasn't been decided yet." Quite deliberately, Sparhawk took the spear in both hands and advanced on the Troll-Dwarf. Kurik, his spiked chain mace hanging from his right fist, came out of the mouth of the gallery and edged around his lord to come at the Troll from the side.

"Two?" Ghwerig said. "Sparhawk should have brought a hundred." He bent and lifted a huge stone club bound with iron out of a pile of gems. "You not take Ghwerig's Bhelliom from him, Sparhawk-from-Elenia. Ghwerig kill first. Here you die, and Ghwerig eat. Not even Aphrael save Sparhawk now. Little man-things doomed. Ghwerig feast this night. Roasted man-things have much juice." He smacked his lips grossly. He straightened, his rough-furred shoulders bulking ominously. The term "dwarf" as applied to a Troll, Sparhawk saw, was grossly deceptive. Ghwerig, despite his deformity, was at least as tall as he, and the Troll's arms, twisted like old stumps, hung down below his knees. His face was furred rather than bearded, and his green eyes seemed to glow malevolently. He shambled forward, his vast club swinging in his right hand. In his left he still clutched Sarak's crown with Bhelliom glowing at its apex.

Kurik stepped in and swung his whistling chain mace at the monster's knees, but Ghwerig almost disdainfully blocked the blow with his club. "Flee, weak man-thing," he said, his voice grating horribly. "All flesh is food for me." He swung his horrid club at that point, and the reach of his abnormally long arms made him doubly dangerous. Kurik jumped back as the ironbound stone cudgel whistled past his face.

Sparhawk lunged in, driving the spear at the Troll's chest, but again Ghwerig deflected the stroke. "Too slow, Sparhawk-from-Elenia." He laughed.

Then Kurik's mace caught him high on the left hip. Ghwerig fell back, but, with catlike speed, smashed his club into a pile of glittering gems, spraying them out like missiles. Kurik winced and put his free hand to his face to wipe the blood from a gash in his forehead out of his eyes.

Sparhawk jabbed again with his spear, lightly slicing the off-balance Troll across the chest. Ghwerig roared with rage and pain, then stumbled forward with vast swings of his club. Sparhawk jumped back, coolly watching for an opening. He saw that the Troll was totally without fear. No injury short of one that was mortal would make the thing retreat. Ghwerig was actually foaming at the mouth now, and his green eyes glowed with madness. He spat out hideous curses and lurched forward again, swinging his horrid club.

"Keep him away from the edge!" Sparhawk shouted to Kurik. "If he goes over, we may never find the crown!" Then he quite clearly realized that he had found the key. Somehow they had to make the deformed Troll drop the crown. It was obvious by now that not even the two of them could prevail against this shaggy creature with its long arms and its eyes ablaze with insane rage. Only a distraction would give them the opportunity to leap in and deliver a mortal wound. He shook his right hand to get Kurik's attention, then reached over and clapped the hand on his left elbow. Kurik's eyes looked puzzled for a moment, but then they narrowed, and he nodded. He circled around to Ghwerig's left, his mace at the ready.

Sparhawk tightened his grip on the spear with both hands again and feinted with it. Ghwerig swung his club at the extended weapon, and Sparhawk jerked it back.

"Ghwerig's rings!" the Troll shouted in triumph. "Sparhawk-from-Elenia brings the rings back to Ghwerig. Ghwerig feel their presence!" With a hideous roar he leaped forward, his club tearing at the air.

Kurik struck, his spiked chain mace tearing a huge chunk of flesh from the Troll's massive left arm. Ghwerig, however, paid little heed to the injury, but continued his rush, his club whistling as he bore down on Sparhawk. His left hand was still tightly locked on the crown.

Sparhawk gave ground grudgingly. He had to keep the Troll away from the brink of the chasm for as long as he held the crown.

Kurik swung his mace again, but Ghwerig shied away, and the blow missed the shaggy elbow. It appeared that the first stroke had caused the Troll more pain than had been evident. Sparhawk took advantage of that momentary flinch and stabbed quickly, opening a gash in Ghwerig's right shoulder. Ghwerig howled, more in rage than in pain, and immediately swung the club again.

Then, from behind him, Sparhawk heard the sound of Flute's voice rising clear and bell-like above the muted roar of the waterfall. Ghwerig's eyes went wide, and his brutish mouth gaped. "You!" he shrieked. "Now Ghwerig pay you back, girl-child! Girl-child's song ends here!"

Flute continued to sing, and Sparhawk risked a quick glance over his shoulder. The little girl stood in the mouth of the gallery with Sephrenia hovering behind her. Sparhawk sensed that the song was not in fact a spell but rather was intended to distract the dwarf so that either he or Kurik could catch the monster off guard. Ghwerig hobbled forward again, swinging his club to force Sparhawk out of his path. The Troll's eyes were fixed on Flute, and his breath hissed between his tightly clenched fangs. Kurik crashed his mace into the monster's back, but Ghwerig gave no indication that he even felt the stroke as he bore down on the Styric child. Then Sparhawk saw his opportunity. As the Troll passed him, the wide swings of the stone club left the hairy flank open. He struck with all his strength, driving the broad blade of the ancient spear into Ghwerig's body just beneath the ribs. The Troll-Dwarf howled as the razor-sharp blade penetrated his leathery hide. He tried to swing his club, but Sparhawk jumped back, jerking the spear free. Then Kurik whipped his chain mace at the deformed side of Ghwerig's right knee, and Sparhawk heard the sickening sound of breaking bone. Ghwerig toppled, losing his grip on his club. Sparhawk reversed his grip on the spear and drove it down into the Troll's belly.

Ghwerig screamed, clutching at the spear with his right hand as Sparhawk wrenched it back and forth, slicing the sharp blade through the Troll's entrails. The crown, however, still remained tightly clenched in that twisted left hand. Only death, Sparhawk saw, would release that iron grip.

The Troll rolled away from the spear, gashing himself open even more horribly as he did so. Kurik smashed him in the face with the mace, crushing out one of his eyes. With a hideous howl, the monster rolled toward the brink of the chasm, scattering his hoarded jewels in the process. Then, with a scream of triumph, he toppled over the edge with Sarak's crown still in his grip!

Filled with chagrin, Sparhawk rushed to the brink of the abyss and stared down in dismay. Far below he could see the deformed body plunging down and down into unimaginable darkness. Then he heard the light patter of bare feet on the stony floor of the cavern, and Flute sped past him, her glossy black hair flying. To his horror, the little girl did not hesitate nor falter, but ran directly off the edge and plunged down after the falling Troll. "Oh, my God!" he choked, reaching vainly out toward her even as Kurik, his face aghast, came up beside him.

And then Sephrenia was there, Sir Gared's sword still in her hand.

"Do something, Sephrenia," Kurik pleaded.

"There's no need, Kurik," she replied calmly. "Nothing can happen to her."

"But—"

"Hush, Kurik. I'm trying to listen."

The light from the glowing waterfall seemed to dim somewhat as if far overhead a cloud had passed over the sun. The roar of the falling water seemed mocking now, and Sparhawk realized that tears were streaming down his cheeks.

Then, in the deep darkness of that unimaginable abyss, he saw what appeared to be a spark of light. It grew steadily brighter, rising, or so it seemed, from that ghastly chasm. And as it rose, he could see it more clearly. It appeared to be a brilliant shaft of pure white light topped by a spark of intense blue.

Bhelliom rose from the depths, resting on the palm of Flute's incandescent little hand. Sparhawk gaped in astonishment as he realized that he could see through her, and that what had risen glowing from the darkness below was as insubstantial as mist. Flute's tiny face was calm and imperturbable as she held the sapphire rose over her head with one hand. She reached out with the other to Sephrenia. To Sparhawk's horror, his beloved tutor stepped off the ledge.

But she did not fall.

As if walking on solid earth, she calmly strolled out across the bottomless gulf of air to take Bhelliom from Flute's hand. Then she turned and spoke in a strangely archaic form. "Wrench open thy spear, Sir Sparhawk, and put the ring of thy Queen upon thy right hand, lest Bhelliom destroy thee when I deliver it up to thee." Beside her, Flute lifted her face in exultant song, a song that rang with the voices of multitudes.

Sephrenia reached out a hand to touch that insubstantial little face in a gesture of infinite love. Then she walked back across the emptiness with Bhelliom held lightly between her two palms. "Here endeth thy quest, Sir Sparhawk," she said gravely. "Reach forth thy hands to receive Bhelliom from me and from my Child-Goddess Aphrael."

And quite suddenly, everything became clear. Sparhawk fell to his knees with Kurik beside him, and the knight accepted the sapphire rose from Sephrenia's hands. She knelt between the two of them in adoration as they gazed at the glowing face of the one they had called Flute.

The eternal Child-Goddess Aphrael smiled at them, her voice still raised in choral song that filled all the cave with shimmering echoes. The light that filled her misty form grew brighter and brighter, and she speared upward faster than any arrow.

Then she vanished.

Here ends The Ruby Knight,
Book Two of David Eddings' splendid fantasy, The Elenium.
Watch for the surprising conclusion in
Book Three, The Sapphire Rose,
forthcoming from Del Rey Books.

ABOUT THE AUTHOR

DAVID EDDINGS was born in Spokane, Washington, in 1931 and was raised in the Puget Sound area north of Seattle. He received a Bachelor of Arts degree from Reed College in Portland, Oregon, in 1954 and a Master of Arts degree from the University of Washington in 1961. He has served in the United States Army, has worked as a buyer for the Boeing Company, has been a grocery clerk, and has taught English. He has lived in many parts of the United States.

His first novel, *High Hunt* (published by Putnam in 1973), was a contemporary adventure story. The field of fantasy has always been of interest to him, however, and he turned to *The Belgariad* in an effort to develop certain technical and philosophical ideas concerning that genre.

Eddings currently resides with his wife, Leigh, in the Southwest.